The Burning Bride

Manoj Kerai

Published by M.Kerai Publishing 2015

Copyright

Disclaimer

Prayer:

I call upon Lord Ganesh, Goddess Saraswati and Radha & Krishna with the hope that I achieve the objectives I set out to achieve through this novel.

Vakra-Tunndda Maha-Kaaya Suurya-Kotti Samaprabha
Nirvighnam Kuru Me Deva Sarva-Kaaryessu Sarvadaa

Translation:
O Lord Ganesha, of Curved Trunk, Large Body, and with the Brilliance of a Million Suns,
Please Make all my Works Free of Obstacles, Always.
(Ganesh Mantra)

Yaa Kundendu tushaara haara-dhavalaa, Yaa shubhra-vastra'avritaa
Yaa veena-vara-danda-manditakara, Yaa shweta padma'asana
Yaa brahma'achyuta shankara prabhritibhir, Devai-sadaa vandita
Saa Maam Paatu Saraswati Bhagavatee Nihshesha jaadya'apahaa.

Translation:
She who is as fair as the Jasmine flower, white as the moon, and adorned with a garland of flowers and white clothes.
She who plays the veena, and who sits on the pure white lotus;
She who is praised by Brahma, Vishnu, and Mahesh; and prayed to by the Devas
She is Saraswati, remove my mental dullness!
(Saraswati Prayer)

Hare Krishna, Hare Krishna, Krishna Krishna, Hare Hare,
Hare Rama, Hare Rama, Rama Rama, Hare Hare.
(Maha Mantra)

Part I: Shailputri
(The Daughter of the Himalayas)

Chapter 1: Avantika

The weather was unusually warm for a winter's day. A wedding hall located on the outskirts of Mandavi, a town in Kutch, was gradually emptying. Avantika walked around with a huge smile on her face as she greeted the guests and thanked them for their presence at her daughter's wedding. Despite showing laughter and expressing warmth and gratitude to the guests, Avantika secretly hid the inner turmoil raging within her. The past few weeks had been hell.

Avantika always knew that when her daughter, Uma, married it would be extremely stressful. The reality however, had been a lot worse than she ever imagined. Avantika and her husband, Vinod spent years budgeting for their two daughters' weddings. For the past six years Vinod walked to work instead of taking a shared car. The ten rupees he saved each day were put aside to pay for the weddings. Both Avantika and Vinod found a number of ways to reduce costs wherever possible so that they could make sure they gave their children the best they could afford. Avantika had also been inspired to save money as she possessed a covert desire to exceed the expectations her community had of her family. *If we give our beti, Uma, a grand send off, people will know we are something in this village.*

Avantika recalled the moment Uma revealed that she was in love with a boy called Vijay and expressed her desire to marry him. Initially she felt apprehensive about the fact that her daughter had chosen a boy without her consent. *What if he and his family cannot keep my beti happy?* All of her worries vanished when she met Vijay's wealthy family. Vijay owned his own business and Vijay's father had been an influential politician prior to his death. His family lived in a large mansion in Madhapar, the area where many rich people lived in Kutch. *By joining our family with the Rathods we would increase the prestige of our family. Our association with such influential people will open up so many doors for us. People in this community will know we are related to big people and they will shower us with the same respect that the Rathod family must be accustomed to. Above all, my Uma will never have to ask other people for money. They have enough money to keep my Uma happy for the rest of her life. She is going to live like a queen when she marries. What more could I ask for my beti?* Without further doubts Avantika agreed to her daughter's marriage.

As soon as the wedding was fixed, the atmosphere in Avantika's home became vibrant. Avantika recalled how she delivered the wedding invitations to her friends and relatives with a bounce in her footsteps. She had taken great pleasure in informing everyone that her daughter was marrying a man who owned a chain of hotels and was also the son of a politician. Avantika became engrossed in planning her daughter's and her own family's future. She always wanted her daughter to marry a wealthy man, but she had never imagined her daughter would marry into such a rich and influential family. Everything was going well. *The only time I will ever have a reason to cry from now will be when I give Uma away on her wedding day.*

Yet Avantika's happiness did not last until the giving away of her daughter. Her joy evaporated a few days after she finished giving out the wedding invites. This was when Madhu, Vijay's mother, started to make demands in order to allow the wedding to go ahead. Madhu stipulated the food that would be served at the wedding, which decorations would be used to bedeck the hall, what the bride and groom would wear. Madhu even made specific demands about which outfits Uma's relatives would wear. Avantika and Vinod had politely tried to explain to Madhu that her requirements were out of their budget. However, Madhu's response had shocked them.
"If you want your beti to marry into my family, you will have to maximise the budget," Madhu had said sweetly. "Vehvanji you should have kept our status in mind when organising the wedding. How will we face our friends if Vijay's wedding is down market?"
Avantika and Vinod found themselves in a difficult situation. They had told everyone they knew about Uma's wedding. *If the wedding is cancelled now, people will laugh at my family. No one will blame Vijay, he will simply find another girl, but Uma would be maligned forever. In our society, it does not matter who is at fault, people will always blame the*

girl if a marriage falls apart. That kutri knew this and deliberately waited till the invites were sent out. She knew we would not be able to say no. Vinod and Avantika saw no other option but to fulfil and agree with Madhu's demands. Avantika consoled herself by thinking about the benefits her daughter and her family would gain from associating their name with the Rathod family. One week before the wedding, Madhu requested an extra outfit for their maid Leela, who would also be attending the wedding.

Once Madhu's demands were accounted for, the cost of the wedding ended up being four times more than their initial budget. Avantika and Vinod worked tirelessly to gather all their resources to get the money together. Avantika had regularly thanked goddess Durga for her mercy. She felt it was because of her grace that her family was never short of money. *Hai Maa Durga it is because of your blessings that we managed to gather all the money to fulfil Madhuben's requests for Uma's wedding. Please continue to keep your hand on our heads and bless us with your grace.* They utilised their networks to get a number of favours and discounts which saved them a lot of money. Avantika used her exceptional haggling ability to reduce the overall cost of the wedding by twenty per cent. Finally, to fulfil the final demands they took money from the savings they had put aside for their son, Arjun, and younger daughter, Gauri. Uma had offered to help pay towards the wedding from the money she saved from working. However, both Vinod and Avantika refused to accept money from their daughter. It would be shameful for parents to accept money from their daughter.

As the wedding hall continued to empty, Avantika looked at the scrunched up and dirty serviettes on the floor. Some of the guests had not bothered to throw them into the bin. *These costs were so superficial. At least no one will say Vinod and I did not give our beti away with great pomp. People will talk about this wedding for many years to come.*

Another fifteen minutes later Avantika made up an excuse to get away from the wedding hall. She walked upstairs and entered the room which contained Uma's belongings. She scanned the possessions Uma was taking to her new home and spotted a family photo they had taken a few years ago. Avantika walked over and picked up the image. The photograph contained the whole family, but Avantika's gaze focused entirely on Uma. Now that she stood in the room alone, the only person she could think of was Uma. The memories of her daughter flashed through her mind. Avantika recalled the tears of joy she cried the first time she saw her little girl. Uma had still been covered in blood, but she was the most beautiful thing Avantika had seen. *I didn't just cry tears of joy at her birth. I've done nothing but cry tears of joy since Uma was born. The first time Uma called me Maa, the day she learnt to walk without holding my hand, the day she got a job as a nurse at the hospital.*

As time passed, Avantika recalled more moments that she had spent nurturing her beautiful girl over the past twenty three years. Uma loved the stories Avantika told her as she sat near her knees whilst Avantika massaged coconut oil into her hair. Uma frequently asked her mother to tell her stories of goddess Durga, which were her favourite. Today Avantika was going to cry again, but for the first time her daughter was going to leave her with tears of sadness. *Today is the day I cut away a piece of my own heart and give it to someone else. I never thought this moment will be as hard as it is.*

Avantika had spent the entire day smiling. She smiled at the camera, smiled for the guests, smiled when she welcomed the groom and his family. Yet all she wanted to do was cry, and her sorrow had nothing to do with Madhu or the groom's party. It was the fact that she was going to lose her daughter. Avantika recalled her own mother telling her about the pain of giving a daughter away. She never imagined the pain would be as intense as it was. Avantika herself had cried tears of sadness when she was separated from her family and had gone to Mandavi to live with her new family. *I was fortunate. I went into a home that gave me lots of love. What if Uma fails to adjust to her new home? What if they do not accept her?* Avantika's fears added to the sadness she felt, but she held back her tears as she sat alone in the room.

Avantika heard her son's voice from next door "The priest said you should be leaving soon. Shall I let him know you're ready?"
"Yes," Avantika heard her daughter say. "Tell him I will be ready to leave

in ten minutes."
Avantika put the photo aside and sighed as she got up. She picked up a red box from the dressing table and walked towards the room where her daughter sat. The time had come to say goodbye, but there were a few things she wanted to tell her daughter. *I taught my daughter to talk, I taught her the difference between right and wrong. It is time to give her some final teachings.*

Avantika opened the door of the room that her daughter was sat in. She saw that Uma was no longer wearing her bridal outfit. She had changed into the blue farewell sari which Madhu bought for her. *Madhuben does have high standards. The sari she gifted to Uma makes her look like a queen. Vah, vah, vah.* As Avantika looked at the elaborate embroidery of the sari and how beautiful her daughter looked, the feelings of resentment she had been nurturing towards Vijay's family vanished. *Uma is now Madhuben's beti as well. I am sure she wants the best for her in the same way I do. In fact I am sure they will take better care of Uma than we were able to. My beti now has money to buy anything she wants. She will never have to go without.* Avantika looked up and made eye contact with her daughter. The moment their eyes met, Avantika's vision began to blur. Her eyes began to well up with tears.
"Can I have a few minutes alone with Uma?" Avantika asked Uma's friends.
The girls in the room all murmured in agreement and shuffled out of the room. The moment the girls closed the door behind them, Uma ran into her arms. She felt a mixture of emotions; she felt some warmth at her daughter's touch but also pined for her. For a few moments both women just cried. Avantika finally controlled herself and pulled herself away from her daughter.

"I have something I want to give you." Avantika handed the red box that she was holding to Uma. As Uma opened the box, Avantika explained to her, "You love to listen to the stories of Durga I always told you. So I want to give you a statue of Shailputri, Durga's first form, to take to your new home." Avantika watched as her daughter admired the idol and began to cry more. Before Avantika became overwhelmed with emotions again she began to talk. "Shailputri is the daughter of the

Himalayas. You were the daughter of this house for twenty three years. You have known the norms and cultures of our home. The time has come to forget all these norms and to adopt those of your new family." Avantika paused and then continued, "You need to become the beti of a new family. Win over the love of all your family members. Find me inside Madhuben; she is your new maa." Avantika watched as Uma continued to cry. She used her fingers to wipe away her daughter's tears. "If any of your in-laws upset you or talks harshly towards you, accept what they say, learn from it and smile. Win them over with your love. I told you to forget the norms and cultures of this home, but never forget the values and morals I instilled in you. I do not want you to become their ideal daughter-in-law; I want you to become their daughter. Earn their love and respect."

Avantika saw a small diva burning in the corner of the room. The diva was a single flame in a clay pot with oil to keep it burning. She remembered her own wedding day. Her mother had used a diva to teach her the duty of a married woman. Avantika held Uma's hand and took her over to the diva.

"The flame of this diva is tiny, but still this single flame is so beautiful that when people look at it they feel a sense of happiness and warmth inside them. The single flame drives away the darkness and lights up an entire room. On my wedding day your nani told me to burn like a diva in my marital home. Give people happiness and warmth. In times of sadness drive away the darkness in their lives and spread as much happiness as you can. I'm now telling you the same thing. Uma beti, become like this diva." Avantika held onto the idol of Shailputri "I pray to mata Shailputri, and beseech that she helps you to become an ideal beti for Madhuben."

"Maa! I will miss everyone so much," Uma said as she held Shailputri. "What if..."

"Don't even think about what if," interrupted Avantika. "Families sometimes argue. There is bickering, but the love is still there. Look at us, we argue at times, but we still love each other. If your husband, mother-in-law or anyone speaks harshly towards you, accept that as their love."

Avantika smiled and continued, "Do you remember how I used to punish you every time you got anything below an A in class? You might have thought I was being tough, but it is my way of showing you love. I wanted to bring out the best in you. Your mother-in-law might criticise you at times, but think of her as me and try to adapt. It might be hard at first, but you'll learn their ways and become a part of their family in the same way I became a part of your bapuji's family." Avantika put her hand on Uma's cheek. "Make me proud Uma."

The two women had tears streaming down their faces and continued to hug until Uma's friends came back into the room.
"They're calling for her. The groom's family is ready to leave."
Avantika prepared herself. *The moment I have dreaded for a long time is finally here.* She touched some of the eye liner from her eye and used the residue on her fingers to make a small mark behind Uma's ear. This was something she did regularly to prevent evil spirits from harming Uma. Now she had done it for the last time. Avantika and Uma's friends held Uma and escorted her outside the wedding hall. Arjun hugged and said goodbye to his sister before the rest of their family. One by one all of Uma's relatives came to say goodbye, all with tears in their eyes. Avantika began to cry harder as she watched her daughter say goodbye to various family members.
Vijay's mother came over and stood next to Avantika. Madhu held onto Avantika's hand and said, "Vehvanji, we're only going to Madhapar. It's not far from here, come to our house whenever you want. Come and see how happy Uma is in her new home whenever you want."
"If my Uma makes any mistakes, please think of her as your own beti and..."
"Avantikaben, you are embarrassing me by saying such things. Uma will be like my own daughter. I will treat her like I treat Charu."
"Madhuben, thank you so much for everything," Avantika said as she sobbed harder, making it difficult for others to hear what she was actually saying. "I trust you will all make her happy. My daughter is fortunate to have found a family like yours."
"Remember, we are only in Madhapar." Madhu hugged Avantika, briefly and then pulled away. She put her hands together and said goodbye. "Jai Shri Krishna."

Avantika looked over at Uma and Vijay and saw Gauri and some of Uma's female cousins teasing the groom. The girls had successfully stolen the groom's shoes earlier in the day and were now haggling for money to return the shoes before he left. After a few minutes of bartering, Vijay gave each of the girls 500 rupees in exchange for his shoes. Uma and Vijay got into a white Mercedes decorated with flowers and ribbons. Vijay's uncle and his sister, Charu, joined them in the car. Uma's sister and cousins were still feeling mischievous and as per tradition had stood in front of the car to prevent it from leaving. *I hope they never move.*
Avantika heard Gauri saying "You're taking away our sister, we won't let you go unless you pay us more money."
Vijay's uncle eventually got out of the car with a smile and gave each of the girls another 500 rupees. Once the girls moved out of the way the car began to move.

Avantika stood on tip toes and watched the car until it vanished out of sight. Madhu was still stood next to Avantika when the car vanished out of sight.
Madhu turned to Avantika and said "Would you be able to send us 10,000 rupees?"
She looked at Madhu, confused. *We have fulfilled all of their requests, why do they want more?*
Before Avantika asked the question in her mind, Madhu gave her the answer. "Your girls took 3500 rupees from my brother Ravi, by blocking the car and by stealing Vijay's shoes. Ravi will also pay for the petrol from here to Madhapar. What will I say to Ravi when he tells me he lost all that money?"
Avantika looked at Madhu with a panicked look that reflected her feelings. *Where do I get the money from now?*
"I understand you cannot give it to me at this moment. You are very busy right now," Madhu said with a gentle voice. "I will pay Ravi with my own money when he asks. If you can return the money to me next time we see each other I would be very grateful." Madhu smiled at Avantika and put her hands together in greeting. "I need to get to our mansion before our children do. Jai Shri Krishna."
Avantika watched as Madhu got into her car whilst waving goodbye to

the rest of the guests. The anger she felt towards Madhu before she saw Uma's expensive sari had returned.

Chapter 2: Uma

Uma sat in the car with her new husband. Her vision was blurred from the tears in her eyes. She desperately wanted to look back and see her family one last time but was compelled to resist the urge. Before departing from the wedding hall, the priest forbade Uma and Vijay to look back as it is highly inauspicious to look back once you leave. Uma had to keep looking ahead until she reached her new home. Two minutes after leaving the wedding venue, Uma's car drove past the place she called home for twenty three years. She felt a minor shock inside her at the sight of her home which made her burst into tears again. Uma desperately wanted to have a proper look at her home, but she resisted the urge. She did not want any ill luck to darken her new life. Driving past her home had been the most testing moment for Uma. She felt similar jolts when she passed the school where she studied, the Durga temple she worshipped in and the hospital she worked at. Once she overcame the urge to look back at the place that she called home, the rest had been easier. To make it easier to resist the impulses to look back, Uma focused her attention onto the elaborate henna patterns on her hands.

Once the car left Mandavi, the journey became easier. Despite feeling robbed of everything she knew, she looked forward to the beginning of a new chapter in her life. *Hai Maa Durga, I accidentally broke my Jaya Parvati fast many times, but you have still bestowed a wonderful husband like Vijay to me.* Uma never personally knew anyone who was forced to marry against their will; but she had read stories of girls in Gujarat who were coerced into arranged marriages. *It is because of your blessing Mata Rani that I got to marry the man of my choice.*

As the car journeyed towards Madhapar, Uma began to reminisce about the first time that she and Vijay met. She was on duty at the hospital when a foreign tourist brought an injured man into hospital. The tourist informed the hospital that her rickshaw collided with the man's motorbike. The casualty was Vijay who slowly muttered that he was

alright and did not need to be checked over. The white tourist insisted that he was checked over and she even paid for the costs. Uma smiled as she recalled every little detail of their first meeting. There was a small cut on the left side of Vijay's head. The cut was slightly bleeding but nothing a small bandage would not heal. His muscular arms were grazed. His white t-shirt was slightly ripped and covered in dirt. His well fitted blue jeans were also dirty due to the fall. Uma also noticed that Vijay was not wearing a helmet. She had spoken her first words to him as she put dressing over his wounds.
"If you continue to ride a motorbike you should wear a helmet." Uma told him in a slightly stern tone.
"I will." Vijay had laughed.

After this exchange, Vijay left the hospital with the tourist who had brought him. Uma became mesmerised by Vijay's good looks, but she thought she would never see him again. Eleven days later, Uma saw him again. She was on her way home when she saw him sat on his motorbike with no helmet. Uma hated it when patients ignored her advice and walked over to him to complain.
"I haven't been on my bike since the accident. Today is the first time," Vijay responded to Uma's criticism. "I will buy a helmet today, but under one condition!"
"What is that?"
"If you agree to go for dinner with me," Vijay said cheekily. "I want to say thank you for the help you gave me at hospital last week."

Excited about the thought of a date with an attractive guy like Vijay, she went home with a huge smile on her face. She acted like a little school girl and her sister, Gauri, had immediately realised that Uma liked someone. This was where it all started. Within a few weeks Uma thought she knew everything about him. She was highly amused to discover his phobia of clowns. As Uma fell in love with him, she began to accept his flaws. Vijay was perfect in every way, apart from the fact that he ate non veg. Uma had always been adamant that she would never marry someone who was not a vegetarian. However, she had learnt from her favourite TV show, Kahaani Ghar Ghar Kii, that love meant making compromises and accepting the person for who they were. Eventually she accepted his eating meat and knew he was the man that she will marry. *It has been thirteen months since we met. It feels like we met just yesterday, but at the same time it feels as though I have known him for seven lives.* Uma turned around to her right and saw Vijay next to her. He was dressed in a white Sherwani and donned a red turban on his head. *Even with a turban on he looks so handsome.*

Uma felt Vijay's put his hand on top of hers. He comforted her by gently squeezing it.
"Am I that bad, that you won't stop crying because you have to spend the rest of your life with me?" Vijay joked.
Uma began to laugh. In the weeks leading up to the wedding, her fears about joining the Rathod family had intensified. She did not just have to live with Vijay, but also with his mother, brother and sister. *What if they do not like me and I fail to adjust to their way of life? What will happen if the rest of his family hate me?* Uma knew that this was probably something every Hindu bride worried about in the lead up to her wedding. However, Vijay's one joke drove out all of the worries from her mind. *I am sure Vijay will not let anything bad happen to me. We both love each other a lot. I am sure the rest of his family will give me the same respect that he gives to me.* Uma and Vijay talked all the way back to Madhapar.

As the car approached Vijay's home Uma's fears came crashing back. She saw the black gates open revealing the large court yard. The car stopped in front of the two large mahogany doors which led to Rathod Haveli, the large mansion where she would live. Vijay's Uncle, Ravi opened the car door and allowed both the bride and groom to step out. Uma saw the large mansion, decorated with white lights and marigold flowers. She had been to Rathod Haveli a few times but was still mesmerised by the grandeur. Uma stood in front of the house and her heart began to pound. She spotted Vijay's brother Jigar, and his sister, Charu, amongst their other relatives waiting at the threshold of the mansion to welcome them. Vijay's mother stood in front of everyone else.
"Leela," Madhu said in an authoritative voice. "Bring the aarti so that I can welcome my new beti into my home."

Uma saw the maid walk over to her mother-in-law and hand the aarti plate to her. There was a single lit diva, flowers and some rice on the golden plate. Madhu held the plate and began to venerate both Uma and Vijay. She made clockwise circular movements with the plate and then showered the bride and groom with rice and flowers. Leela took the aarti plate back and Charu brought forward a small copper pot filled with rice and put it on the floor at the threshold of the house.

"Uma beti, use the toe of your right foot to kick this kalash of rice," Madhu instructed Uma. "The rice signifies the luck, wealth and prosperity that you will bring into our home."
Uma did as she was told. After the tipping of the kalash, she stepped into a plate of kumkum water. Uma walked into the house leaving red footprints behind her. Her mother-in-law explained that this signified the entry of Lakshmi, the goddess of wealth and good fortune. After the entry rituals were over, Uma and Vijay sat on the floor opposite each other, surrounded by the groom's family.

"Madhuben, your new bahu is very beautiful," said a woman who Uma knew was a widow because of her plain clothing.
"Thank you Purbai! My beta has made an excellent choice."
Uma nervously smiled at the widow, Purbai, who smiled back.

Various ceremonies continued throughout the night, including koda kodi, a game which involved hiding a ring in opaque water. The bride and groom competed to find the ring. The champion would be the dominant person in the relationship. Vijay beat Uma by cheating. He waited for Uma to find the ring and then grabbed it out of her hand.

Finally once all of the ceremonies were over, Charu escorted Uma to her new bedroom.
"Vijay bhai told me that gerbera are your favourite flowers. Leela and I scattered those over your bed instead of roses."
Impressed by all the effort everyone had gone through to welcome her, Uma felt touched. *Their maid behaves like a family member. If they treat their maid with so much respect, they will give me more respect than her. I have nothing to worry about.*

Uma sat on the marital bed with her hands wrapped around her legs. She patiently waited for Vijay. When Uma heard their bedroom door open and close again, she looked up. Vijay locked the door and turned around to face her. He had a smile on his face that usually made her go weak at the knees. He no longer wore his turban. *His hair looks good even though he has been wearing a turban all day.*
"Did you leave me waiting here on my own, so that you could do your hair again?" Uma joked.
"I had to look sexy for you," Vijay confessed. "But that wasn't the only reason I took so long." He sat on the bed and put two pieces of paper into her hand. "My wedding present to you."
What is this? Uma examined the pieces of paper.
"We are going to London for our honeymoon tomorrow."
She looked at the tickets in disbelief, trying to confirm what Vijay was saying. *He must be joking.* Once she confirmed that he was not joking Uma screamed with delight.
"Vah, vah! I love London! I went once in the summer. I have always wanted to go during the winter to see snow. It's a beautiful city." Uma kissed her husband and thanked him. *This is our first kiss as husband and wife,* Uma thought excitedly. They kissed a few times, but Uma pulled back realising a flaw in his surprise plan.
"I don't have a visa! How can we..."
Vijay put his hand over her lips. "I sorted everything before. Your passport, visa, tickets, everything. Gauri helped me to pack your suitcase. We leave early tomorrow." He removed his hand and kissed her again.
Uma kissed him but pulled back again. She remembered something her friends had told her.
"I was told that I am not to fulfil your desires until you find your name hidden in my mehndi," she teased her new husband.
Uma smiled and put both her hands out. Vijay sat up on his knees and searched for his name. It took him more than five minutes to discover his name. It was covertly hidden amongst the swirls and curves of a flower on Uma's right hand. Once he found it, Uma lay on her back as he took control. After Vijay had finished making love to Uma he rolled over and fell asleep. Uma lay awake for a while admiring Vijay's efforts

to surprise her. She put her head onto Vijay's smooth chest as she stroked his muscular body. *From now my life will only get better.*

Chapter 3: Madhu

Without saying thank you to her maid, Madhu grabbed the cup of tea Leela had freshly made for her. She walked towards the living room, swerving around the workers who had come to take down the wedding decorations. She slowly shuffled over to the sofa to sit down as she was exhausted. Madhu sat cross legged on the sofa and massaged her feet. Both of her legs ached from dancing so much at her son's wedding. When she finished her cup of tea, she turned the TV on and lay down. *Hai Bhagwan, I am getting old. I did not feel this tired last time.* Madhu had drained herself out making preparations for her son's wedding. There had been a lot of work to do in the two weeks that led up to Vijay's wedding. Madhu hoped she would get some rest once the wedding was over but she had woken up at 4am to pray earlier that morning. Whenever Vijay left home for a night, even if it was to visit one of his hotels, Madhu would pray to God to keep her son safe. Once the puja ended she would apply holy tilak on his forehead to ensure his safe return. This morning was no different. Vijay and his wife were leaving India to go on their honeymoon and therefore she made sure the puja for her son's safety was complete before he left.

Despite her exhaustion this time round, Madhu loved every single moment of her son's wedding. With her eyes closed she recalled how she danced with delight when the wedding band announced the arrival of the groom's party. She had thrown money in the air wanting to share her joy with everyone. All of Vijay's favourite dishes were served at the wedding. Even the colours of the Uma's saris were Vijay's favourite colours. *It is not every day that I get to be the groom's mother. I need to enjoy myself when I get the honour. My Vijay deserves the best. I had to apply a bit of pressure onto those middle class people to make sure they were not kanjoos and actually spent some money. If they got their way they would have married my son in their courtyard. I knew they were capable of giving my beta a grand wedding. I just had to demand it from them.* Madhu expected more of a struggle from Avantika and the rest of the Desai family. She had been surprised at how easily they gave in to all of her demands. To gauge how much power she held over Uma's family, Madhu even demanded a sari for their maid, Leela. When they fulfilled that demand without any qualms, Madhu realised how much control she had over the Desai family. *If Vijay's wife tries to act too clever with me, at least I can always use my authority over her family to make sure she remains within her boundaries.*

Vijay was Madhu's pride. His birth gave her something she desperately wanted; a reason to continue living. The political environment she married into and the behaviour of her family caused her to distrust them all. Vijay was the first person whom she could totally trust. When Vijay decided he did not want to follow in his father and grandfather's footsteps, Madhu had been heartbroken. She felt her son would have been a much better politician than her father-in-law or husband. However, her desire to see her son succeed was still fulfilled. Vijay opened a five star hotel in Ahmedabad and then a second one in Delhi. Madhu was proud of her son. Not only did he make more money than his father and grandfather but the future generation of her family would not be tainted by political mindsets driven by votes.

There was one time when Madhu despaired for Vijay and her family. By this time Vijay owned a third hotel in Goa and her husband had retired from politics. Madhu discovered how her son expanded his business so quickly. He was making money by gambling. In the early days he had made a lot of money, but once his addiction got out of hand, the Rathod family came close to being declared bankrupt. Madhu supported her son and managed to save them from bankruptcy. She arranged for money through various sources and helped break her son's gambling habit. Now back on track again, he was going to open a fourth hotel in Mumbai.

Madhu bided her day by lounging on the sofa. She tuned in and out of the Bollywood movie on TV at various intervals. Madhu also spent part of the day making plans of how she would retain the power she had over her home. *I will not become like Purbai or other widows who lose their status in their own home.* Uma was a pretty girl. She appeared to be well cultured, caring and friendly. However, there was something about Uma that made Madhu feel slightly uncomfortable. *Vijay's wife is too educated for my liking. Educated women answer back to their husbands, and she studied further than Vijay did. What if she controls my son and poisons him against me?* The fact that Uma could discover more information than she needed to know also worried her. She had formulated a plan to ensure Vijay was not humiliated in public by some woman who thought she was better than him because she received a higher education. Madhu had already told people that Uma left school having only passed eleventh grade. Vijay had passed twelfth. Madhu also decided that when Uma came back from Honeymoon she would tell her that she will stop working as a nurse and will become a housewife. Uma would take care of her children, assist with the cooking and do anything else the servants did not have time for. *The best thing I did was to stop working and take control of running the house. It gave me the opportunity to be a mother to my three children. Uma will be grateful that I am not sending her to work.* The other advantage to coercing Uma into becoming a housewife was the fact that Madhu would find it easier to remain the matriarch of her family. *I can keep my eyes on her at all times and make sure she does not develop any haltu faltu thoughts against me or my family.*

Madhu spent most of the afternoon fantasising about how she would order her new daughter-in-law around. Her mirage was disrupted by their maid, Leela.
"Madhuji," Leela said with a South Indian accent. "I have finished my work."
Madhu opened her eyes and saw their dark skinned servant standing near the sofa where she lay. *I need to train Uma so she is like this Leela. If I make her into this mouse like girl, then she will not even squeak against me.* Madhu sat up and took out the wallet from her bosom. She handed the money that Leela was owed for the work she did over Vijay's wedding. Leela's smile faltered after she took the money.
"Madhuji," she said timidly. "You said if I work more for the wedding, you will pay four times more than normal. I worked on Mehndi night, the Mandavo Ropan, the wedding and today. I have also worked extra for two weeks."
"Forgive me Leela," *I thought the mouse would forget to ask, or be too*

scared. "I forgot. I need to go and get the money from the safe. I will get it now." Madhu saw that Leela began to smile again. She stood up and felt the pain in her sore legs. As she walked up the stairs she made a mental note to herself. *I must remember to get more money from the Desai family to cover Leela's cost too.*

Chapter 4: Uma

As the end credits of Bachna Ae Haseeno played on her screen, Uma looked outside the window. *The clouds look so beautiful from up here; it is almost as if they are all made of cotton wool.* A few minutes later, she returned to her screen and saw they had less than two hours before they reached Mumbai. *It is not enough time to watch another Bollywood film.* Uma browsed through the Hollywood movies available and began to watch Up. As the Pixar animation played, she relived the highlights from her honeymoon.

When they first landed in London, Uma shivered from the cold. She previously visited London in May, so it had been mildly warm. Initially Uma thought she had come in the middle of British summer as people were wearing such little clothing. A few days later she discovered that British people took their clothes off at the slightest sight of the sun. The skies were blue in May. The grey skies and the freezing cold temperatures of December made Uma wish they had waited a few months for their honeymoon. After a few days passed, she realised that London was just as beautiful in December as it was in May. The city was decorated with green Christmas trees of all sizes and sparkly ropes of various shiny colours. The Christmas lights came in so many different shapes, sizes and colours which even included umbrellas made from white lights on Oxford Street. The Christmas lights of London did not compare to Diwali in India, nevertheless, Uma was still impressed by the lights that looked like falling glitter from the night sky.

Some of Vijay's distant family members lived in Wembley and therefore, he had visited London a few times. Uma felt there would not be much to do in London during the winter. However, Vijay knew of many things to do. He took her to Winter Wonderland in Hyde Park. Uma became mesmerised by the Magical Ice Kingdom. The castle of ice had been magnificent and she especially adored the woodland creatures carved out of ice. The owls, foxes and rabbits in particular had caught her attention. *This is what Narnia must have looked like.* However, the moment Uma attributed the ice sculptures to the Ice Queen, she became slightly disturbed by them and moved on.

Vijay even convinced Uma to try ice skating. She was terrible and fell over a lot. Vijay, on the other hand, had evidently ice skated before. He persuaded her to skate around the Christmas tree at least once. Vijay held her hand and attempted to take her around, but she fell over too many times that he gave up. Uma sat on the side for a bit and watched him skate on his own. Uma felt slightly jealous of all the people skating because she hated not being good at something. Once Vijay got bored of skating alone, they went to a bar within Winter Wonderland. Vijay ordered some mulled wine and Uma a hot chocolate. Alcohol was banned in Gujarat; hence Uma had never tried it. Vijay kept on trying to persuade her to try some mulled wine. In the end she took a few sips to keep him happy. The taste of the mulled wine caused Uma to scrunch her face up with disgust and gag. *Why does anyone think such a bitter tasting drink is nice?*

They also visited various landmarks including Tower Bridge, Houses of Parliament and Trafalgar Square. *None of them looked as pretty in the winter as they did in the summer, but Vijay's company was all that I needed to make London a better place.* Vijay had taken Uma to Oxford Street, where she bought everyone in India presents. She was surprised but excited at the same time when she saw white men dressed in monks' attire chanting "Hare Krishna, Hare Krishna, Krishna Krishna, Hare Hare, Hare Rama, Hare Rama, Rama Rama, Hare Hare" on Oxford Street. *Foreigners chant the name of god as well and some of them even dress the way we dress at home.* Seeing the monks made Uma feel slightly homesick and miss home cooked food. The monks even convinced her to buy a book which she put aside intending to read it on the plane back home. *Oh no! I was meant to read that book on the way back home, but I packed it away in the suitcase. I will read it when I get to Madhapar.*

Uma had not missed home cooked food for too long. Vijay took her to visit their relatives in Wembley a few times. She really enjoyed their company even though his old aunt kept on calling her Siya. Vijay's cousins lived just off Ealing Road in Wembley. The sight of a mini India in London further fuelled her feelings of homesickness. There were many Indian sweet shops, sari shops and even a beautiful hand carved mandir. She even heard people shouting across the streets in Gujarati. Some of the old women even ran across the roads, in their sari and trainers, as they would in India. In three weeks, Uma visited them five times. She enjoyed every visit even the time she had to stay over at their house for three nights, without Vijay. One week into their honeymoon, he confessed to her that he had planned a business meeting before coming to London. As a result he needed to go to Manchester for three nights to meet with a business partner. He arranged for Uma to stay with his relatives so that she would not be lonely. Chanda and Shilpa, the wives of Vijay's cousins, were very welcoming, and therefore she had enjoyed the experience, despite her initial reluctance. When Vijay came to collect Uma, she had been angry at him for ditching her on their honeymoon. At first Uma refused to talk to him but that was the evening he took her to Winter Wonderland, causing her to forget her anger towards him.

They spent Christmas Day in Wembley. Their cousins had invited all of their relatives to their house for a Christmas Party. Uma was looking forward to seeing how British people celebrated this festival. First they all exchanged gifts. His uncle gifted Vijay a Rolex watch and a gold chain with an Om pendent for Uma. Once all of the gifts were exchanged they sat down to watch a message from their Queen. *Why is she all alone on this big day? She looks very lonely.* Before Uma could ask where the rest of her family were, Shilpa and Chanda announced that dinner was ready to be served.

The family had placed a tablecloth on the floor for all the guests to sit down and eat together. They laid the tablecloth with white plastic plates with six compartments. There was a shiny tube next to each plate. Uma did not know the name of these shiny tubes, but they were pulled with another person. The tube made a soft bang, nothing in comparison to the noise fireworks made at Diwali. Once it broke they had to wear the paper crowns that came out. She thought the hats were ridiculous and only put it on because everyone else was wearing one. Once the hats were on, Chanda and Shilpa served a traditional Christmas buffet which they normally ate every year. Uma thought the samosas, khaman dhokla, naan and paneer were delicious. She only tried the vegetarian items but the other dishes included chicken curry and kheema paratha. During the dinner, Shilpa's sister Maya, read out a joke that came from inside the shiny tube. Uma did not think the joke was very funny, but laughed out loud when Maya delivered the punch line. Uma refused to be the only one who did not laugh. However, half way through cackling, she realised that no one else around her had laughed and they were all staring at her. It seemed like no one else got the joke either.

Chanda and Shilpa served ras malai for dessert as they all sat down in front of the TV to watch a British Drama called EastEnders. Uma was not sure exactly what was happening. She understood English, but found it difficult to understand the way they talked on the show. Uma did notice that everyone on the show appeared to be rather upset even though they were celebrating their biggest festival of the year. An old man was even murdered with a Queen Victoria statue at the end of the episode. *The English serial was not as good as Kahaani Ghar Ghar Kii, as it lacked special effects but it was interesting. I will have to find somewhere in India to watch EastEnders, I need to know who killed Archie Mitchell.*

At the start of the honeymoon, Uma did complain about the cold weather, but she realised that there were advantages. There were more excuses to snuggle with Vijay and every night they slept with his arms around her. They made the most of their time alone. Once they returned to Madhapar they would not have as much privacy, living with the rest of Vijay's family. As the honeymoon went on, the love making got better. They made love everywhere that was not a public place (Uma had insisted they maintained some decorum). They made love on the sofa in their hotel room lounge, the bedroom and the shower. Uma giggled as she recalled the time that Vijay tried to get intimate on the elevators. This was one of the times that she had insisted they maintain some dignity and decorum as she had felt uncomfortable that someone could walk in and see them. She held him off, but the moment they got into their hotel room, Vijay kicked the door shut behind him. Uma remembered how he pushed her against the door and made love to her there and then.

Chapter 5: Madhu

"Leela?... Leela?" Madhu shouted. "Is she dead or something?" she muttered to herself as she walked around the house looking for her maid. She walked into the living room where her younger son, Jigar, was watching TV whilst having his breakfast.
"Are you looking for Leela?" Jigar enquired.
"Yes, Vijay and Uma are coming back from honeymoon today." Madhu huffed. "They will be back in three or four hours and there is a lot to do."
"Oh, I didn't know they were back today. Leela asked if she could come a bit later on because the woman she lives with is back from Chandigarh today. She had to clean their house and make their breakfast after their long train journey. I said she could come in the afternoon."
"You are telling me now? There is so much to do to welcome them back," snapped Madhu. She walked over to where her son was sat, grabbed the TV remote and turned it off. "Quickly finish eating and then you can help me."

As Madhu walked away she heard the television turn back on. She rolled her eyes when she realised Jigar wasn't going to help her. *He is stubborn, just like the rest of the children of this family. If you ask the men in this family to do any housework they are useless.* Madhu looked at the time. *Vijay and Uma phoned to say they have landed in Ahmedabad and are on the luxury coach to Bhuj. They will be home in a few hours. Hai Bhagwan how will I finish everything? I have to go shopping for fruit and vegetables. I need to make sure food is ready for Vijay and Uma when they come because they will be hungry. I need to tell Purbai that I want to make mango pickle tomorrow. I also promised Vijay I will have gajar no halwo ready for him when he got back. How am I going to get everything done without that Leela?* Madhu decided she would start with making the gajar no halwo before she did anything else.

Leela arrived just as Madhu finished making the halwo. Without saying hello, Madhu ordered her to clean Vijay and Uma's bedroom. When Charu returned from college, Madhu told her to help with the dinner. Madhu heard Jigar leave to pick Vijay and Uma up, which made her more worried. She ordered Charu to keep stirring the kadhi whilst she checked to make sure Leela had cleaned Vijay's bedroom properly. Madhu walked into the bedroom and looked everywhere carefully. Leela had left the room spotless. However, Madhu still walked around her son's bedroom and altered the position of a few objects. *Everything should be perfect for Vijay. He has been away for too long.*

Just as she was about to leave the bedroom, Madhu heard Vijay and Uma's voices coming from the living room. *My Vijay has returned.* Excited to see her son she ran down as fast as her aching legs would take her. She went forwards and hugged her son. After a few moments she pulled away and inspected Vijay.
"You have lost weight." she told her son.
"The food in London didn't compare to yours mumma," Vijay said. "I'm looking forward to dinner, I'm so hungry."
"Both of you go and freshen up. Dinner will be ready once you are both down again. Leave your bags I will arrange for our security guard to carry them up." Madhu began to walk away. She stopped and looked at Vijay with a smile on her face. "I have made something special for you. Freshen up quickly before it goes cold."
"Is it gajar no halwo?" Vijay asked sounding very pleased.
"Maybe!"
"Mumma! You are the best." Vijay said as he walked up the stairs with his new wife.

Seeing Vijay look excited gave her a warm glow inside. She sensed this every time she saw excitement or happiness on the faces of Jigar, Charu or Vijay. Madhu thought that she was addicted to the emotion she felt at her children's happiness. She always did everything in her power to attain that glow as often as she could.

The Rathod family completed their dinner ninety minutes after Uma and Vijay's return. Throughout dinner, Madhu pretended to be interested in

all the stories Uma and Vijay shared with the family about their time in London. Once dinner was over, Madhu cleared her throat to make a special announcement. She had intentionally been saving the announcement until dinner was over.
"Tomorrow Uma bahu will make dinner" Madhu looked directly towards Uma and smiled. She saw that Uma looked mildly surprised and slightly worried. She gained satisfaction at the fact that Uma was feeling uncomfortable. *I did not say anything before because I do not want you to get overly comfortable.* "Uma bahu, it is a Rathod family tradition that on her first full day with the family, their new daughter-in-law cooks a meal for the whole family" Madhu smiled. "Tomorrow will be your first full day with our family. This is your chance to show off your rasoi skills. I shall let you know what we all want to eat tomorrow morning. Is that ok with you?" *I doubt you have the audacity to say no even if you do have a problem.*
"Yes Maaji," said Uma, a bit too enthusiastically for Madhu's liking.

Madhu recalled the meal she made on her first full day as a Rathod. Her husband did not take her away on honeymoon and therefore she cooked the meal the day after her wedding. Madhu had been keen to impress her new family. She knew of her father-in-law, a politician, a long time before she married Harshad. She was extremely nervous due to her desire to excel and consequentially accidentally added too much salt into the food. Her mother-in-law had spat out the food the moment she tasted it. She then ordered their maid to feed the food to the dogs as it was not suitable to be consumed by human beings. This event was something Madhu's mother-in-law constantly reminded her of for the years that followed. For many years Madhu was controlled by her in-laws. Madhu reclaimed her independence a few years before her mother-in-law died. Madhu was pleased by her death, she felt liberated. However, Madhu had cried false tears to show the outside world how upset she was. *That devil was unworthy of my tears, but if I had not cried then the neighbours would have gossiped about me. The neighbours in Ahmedabad were just like Purbai; they loved to gossip.*

After years of being the head of the household, she had become accustomed to having things her way. Madhu knew that Uma was a threat to her power. *I decide what the family eat for dinner. I decide where the money is spent, what colour the walls are painted. This educated girl is a threat.*

The first few days will be important for me to make sure the power stays with me. Madhu bided the three weeks Uma and Vijay had been away by formulating a plan to ensure that she retained the power and the upper hand. Madhu knew if she established herself as the alpha female now then it would be harder for Uma to do anything about it later. *This family tradition is just an excuse for me to show Uma that I control this house.*

"Uma bahu, Leela had to leave early today. Can I ask you to do the washing up?" Madhu asked Uma politely.

"Yes maaji." Uma responded with a smile on her face.

She watched as Uma began to gather all the plates on the table. Uma put the cutlery together on the top plate and carried it to the kitchen. She made a few trips back and forth to pick up the rest of the pots and pans. Madhu watched Uma without raising a finger to help her. *Not even a squeak of resistance or a hint of complaint. You are going to be easy to control just like your parents.* For the second time that evening, Madhu felt the glow she felt inside her when she saw a smile on her children's face. This time, however, the glow was due to her first win over Uma.

Chapter 6: Charu

"Stop stop," Charu said to the rickshaw driver. "I need to buy something from the medical."
"OK but I will keep the meter running."
"I will not pay for waiting time. I will take a new rickshaw to go home," Charu took her purse out. "How much money do I owe you?"
"Oh, go and buy the medicine," the rickshaw driver said irritably. "I will wait here and will not charge waiting time."

I knew you wouldn't leave. Charu smiled at herself, feeling proud of the haggling skills that she had learnt at boarding school. As a student in Bangalore she was always overcharged because rickshaw drivers, and shop owners all knew that she was not a native of Bangalore. When she learnt the real cost of things she had to learn to haggle in order to avoid being ripped off.

Charu quickly walked to the chemist and bought some antiseptic for her sister-in-law. Earlier that morning Uma was helping Charu to prepare her packed lunch. Uma had accidentally cut her finger whilst slicing tomatoes for Charu's sandwich. Charu squirmed to see Uma in pain caused by the deep cut. Charu quickly found a bandage and covered Uma's finger. However, there was no antiseptic to clean the wound so Charu stopped by the medical supplies shop to buy some on her way home.

Once she bought the antiseptic she returned to the rickshaw. She saw hundreds of rickshaws, motorbikes, cars, bicycles and pedestrians coming from every single direction. She noticed her rickshaw driver was getting some food from a street stall and her mouth began to water. *I love pani puri I have not eaten any in such a long time. Uma bhabhi is making dinner tonight. She is cooking non-veg tonight, but she is a vegetarian. What if her food is not tasty?* Charu walked over to the pani puri stall and decided to whet her appetite just in case dinner was not edible.

As Charu waited for the stall attendant to prepare her portion of pani puri she recalled the events from that morning. She was getting ready for college, when her mother came into her room to ask what she wanted for dinner. She had forgotten that Uma would be cooking dinner and therefore immediately replied that she wanted kheema paratha. When she was leaving the house to go into Bhuj she overheard her mother telling Uma what she had to make for dinner.
"You will be making kheema paratha as well," Madhu told Uma. "It is what Charu wants to eat."
"Maaji I do not know how to cook chicken."
Charu laughed at Uma's response. Her mother, on the other hand was not amused. She hit her forehead with her hand and sighed loudly.
"This girl thinks that mutton is chicken. Did your mother not teach you anything before she sent you to our home?"
"We are all vegetarian maaji," Uma explained. Charu heard the worry in Uma's voice. "We don't know how to cook these... these things."
"You are now the daughter-in-law of the Rathod Family," Charu's mother snapped. "You are not a Desai anymore. The Rathod name means something to people. If you want to live with us, you have to learn our ways."

The stall attendant gave Charu her plate of pani puri. She poured brown tamarind chutney over the hollow and crispy puri which was stuffed with chickpeas and potatoes. As soon as the pani puri touched Charu's tongue her taste buds went wild as a result of the tangy and spicy tamarind chutney. She finished eating her food at the same time as the rickshaw driver, and quickly got back into the rickshaw.

As Charu got closer to home she felt some guilt that Uma had to make meat because of her. *I forgot that Uma bhabhi was making dinner when I requested mutton. I should have just told mumma that I changed my mind about what I wanted to eat. But I already left the house and I had a presentation at college today. It is inauspicious to turn back once you have left and there was a rickshaw waiting outside our gates. If I went back another rickshaw might not have come for ages.*

Once the rickshaw pulled up outside Rathod Haveli, Charu paid the driver and quickly walked into the house. She was the last person back home and the family were all waiting for her to have their dinner. The moment she walked in through the door, her mother began to shout and summoned the rest of the family for dinner. Her mother also ordered Uma to bring the dinner to the dining room. Charu washed her hands and headed straight for the dinner table. She looked at the various dishes which Uma had made. Despite having eaten some street food already, her mouth began to water when she saw that Uma had cooked her favourite dessert Ras Malai. Charu opened the other dishes and saw Uma also cooked samosas, khaman dhokla, kheema paratha, raita, daal, rice and two different chutneys. Uma served a bit of everything to everyone. Charu noticed that Uma took extra rice instead of the kheema paratha.

Once Uma finished serving the food, she sat down and everyone began to eat. Charu picked up a samosa and took a bite. *Hmmm, this is delicious. I am glad I did not fill up on pani puris. If everything tastes this good, there is so much to sample.* The spices in the filling were just right and the samosa was fried to perfection. After three bites Charu heard her mother splutter and choke. She looked towards her mother and saw that she had spat out the paratha.

"Get me some water," her mother screeched.

Uma quickly stood up to help. She filled a glass of water from the jug and handed it to her mother. *What is so bad about the paratha?* Charu picked up the paratha and dissected it with her knife. She picked up some of the filling to taste it. *The kheema is undercooked! It is almost raw.*

"Is this your revenge because of what I said earlier Uma bahu?" Charu's mother screamed at Uma. Charu saw that Uma's mouth was open to respond, but before she could reply her mother continued the verbal assault.

"Earlier today you burnt the kheema to cinders and I told you to start again from scratch. Because I told you off you got upset and tried to poison us by serving us undercooked meat!"

"No maaji I…" Uma began to explain.

"Are you stupid bahu?"

Uma averted her eyes and looked down. She did not respond.
"I asked you a question," her mother said firmly. "Are you stupid?"
"No," whimpered Uma so quietly that Charu just about heard it. Charu looked away feeling slightly uncomfortable by her mother's behaviour. *Uma bhabhi probably didn't try to poison us. She just cannot cook.*
"When someone makes a mistake for the first time, you accept the mistake. When someone makes the same mistake again, they are either stupid or they are doing it on purpose." Her mother said fiercely. "So are you stupid, or did you attempt to poison us as revenge?"
Charu shifted with discomfort. Despite looking away, she could still hear her mother shouting. She noticed that both of her brothers had also stopped eating and were watching Uma. Charu returned her gaze to Uma and saw that her eyes were filling with tears. Charu took a deep breath feeling unsettled and picked up a samosa and began to eat. *If I say anything mumma will just tell me off for interfering between elders. It is better I just stay silent.*

"You used to be a nurse," Charu's mother continued her tirade. "You must know about food poisoning!"
"Maa stop. She made a mistake." Vijay said quietly. "She will do a better job next time."
"LEELA!" Madhu yelled.
Their maid ran into the dining room in response to her mother's summon. Leela stood in front of Madhu waiting for a command.
"Throw all of this food away," Madhu pointed at the food on the table. "I do not want any of my children to become sick from bad food"
"Maaji everything else is fine. I tasted..."Uma began to say before she was interrupted.
"I do not want your incompetency to be the reason that everyone gets food poisoning Uma bahu. Leela throw all of this rubbish out into the bin. Order food from a restaurant, order kheema naan, mutton rolls and some chicken curry for everyone."
"What about Uma mumma?" Vijay asked.
"In my house people are always punished when they are insolent," Charu heard her mother reply curtly. "She has wasted food twice today and has insulted Annapurna mata. Her punishment for insulting the goddess of food is to stay hungry tonight."

Charu saw a glint of a smile on her mother's face. Her mother quickly walked away from the scene leaving Uma in tears at the dinner table.

Charu squirmed guiltily in her seat. *If I had not asked for kheema paratha then none of this would have happened. Everything else was delicious. Why did mumma throw that away too?* As Charu waited for the delivery of food, she became hungrier. She felt her stomach rumble and gradually became irate. The hungrier she got, the harder she found it to sympathise with Uma. *I was able to make kheema paratha perfectly at the age of twelve. Mumma and I made it together. She is twenty three. She should be able to cook.* By the time the food arrived, Charu was starving. She devoured the food along with her brothers and mother, without a second thought for Uma who already went to bed hungry.

Chapter 7: Uma

"UMA. IT IS 8.30 AND YOU ARE STILL SLEEPING. WAKE UP NOW YOU LAZY GIRL." Uma heard a loud voice shout through the door.
Aree yaar let me sleep. She closed her eyes and went back to sleep again. Her snooze did not last long.
"Uma, maa said if you don't get up now, you will not get any breakfast."
I was up late, and now I am being forced to wake up so early. Hai Mata Rani all I wanted to do is sleep for another quarter of an hour.

Uma opened her eyes and rubbed them. She sighed and got out of bed. She grabbed a towel and the clothes she was going to change into. Uma unlocked the bedroom door and began to make her way to the bathroom. When she reached the landing, she saw her mother put some clothes up to dry.
"So you are finally awake," her mother said without diverting her attention from the clothes. "Your in-laws must always complain about you waking up late."
Uma ignored her mother's comment and continued walking to the bathroom. Uma was used to her mother constantly worrying about how she was adjusting to life at her in-laws. She faced an inquisition almost every day about her life in Madhapar.

As Uma brushed her teeth, she thought about all the information she had withheld from her family. Her mother did not know about Madhu throwing out all of the food she cooked six weeks ago. The memory of the cooking disaster still caused Uma to burn with embarrassment. *Why did she throw out all of the food? The paratha may have been undercooked, but everything else was fine. Apart from the paratha, I tried everything myself and it tasted perfect.* Uma cried herself to sleep that night. No elder had ever spoken to her in such a harsh manner before. When she woke up the next morning, she remembered her mother's words. *If anyone in your in-laws upsets you or talks harshly towards you. Accept what they said, learn from it and smile. Win them over with your love.* Since then, Uma took greater care to avoid doing anything to anger Vijay's mother. She made every effort to find ways in which she could win over her mother-in-law. However, there were still moments when his mother directed snide remarks towards her. Whenever her mother-in-law made nasty comments, Uma closed her eyes, recalled her mother's teachings and ignored Vijay's mother. On some occasions, she had even apologised without any fault of hers.

As Uma rinsed her mouth out, she could hear her mother continuing to complain from the landing.
"When I got married, I never once woke up late. I did everything your dadi asked me to do."
Uma ignored her mother's complaining. She was used to it. Once she turned on the shower she drowned out her mother's voice and enjoyed some peace. Despite finding her mother's moaning slightly irritating, Uma was pleased to be back home. She missed the comfort of her own home. She missed the warmth of her family, even the way her mother constantly told her off. Most of all she missed being able to be herself, without worrying that her in-laws may not approve. When Vijay's mother told her off, it lacked the affection and warmth that her own mother's scolding had. Madhapar felt totally alien to Uma, the culture and norms of Vijay's family were completely different to theirs. The only place Uma felt comfortable in her new home, was in her bedroom. Her and Vijay's bedroom was somewhere that she could be who she was because no one other than Vijay came into that room. The rest of the mansion felt unfamiliar to Uma.

Four nights ago Vijay went to Mumbai to oversee some work on the new hotel he was going to open in Mumbai. Before leaving he dropped Uma to her parent's home to allow her to spend a few days with her family. *Staying with maa and bapuji has liberated me for the first time since I got married. I have not felt this free since the day before my wedding. What people say is right, there is nowhere else like home and Mandavi will always be my home.* This was Uma's final day with her parents. Later that evening Vijay was going to return and take her back to Madhapar. Whilst she dreaded her return to Rathod Haveli, Uma missed her husband a lot. She was looking forward to being reunited with him again. The four nights felt like an eternity.

When she came out of the shower her mother was setting up the table with her breakfast.
"I have made your favourite for your morning meal," her mother said. Uma saw the pauva in a steel pan and smiled. She sat down but before she started to eat she looked around to see if anyone else was around to share breakfast with. Everyone else appeared to be out of the house. Uma immediately felt some discomfort. *Hai Mata Rani, what will I tell her this time, if she asks me more questions about my married life?*
"I will leave you to eat, I need to go to work."
Uma felt relieved that her mother would not be around to grill her about life in Madhapar again.

On her second morning, Uma and her mother were alone. Her mother began to ask her a lot of questions about her new life and her new home. She had lied because she thought her mother would worry unnecessarily. She told her mother that Charu was like a sister to her and that Vijay's mother was like her own mother. Uma did make some effort to tell the truth.
"It does all feel slightly new. I..."
"It takes time to adjust to new customs and traditions," her mother interrupted. "I took more than a year to adjust. You are already doing very well if Charu and Madhuben are like family already. It takes time to make your place in people's hearts."
"I just miss this house sometimes that is all."
"Never let this be known to your mother-in-law. You do not want to upset them. They may think that they are not keeping you happy."
"Vijay's maa doesn't want me to work either. I..."
"Vijay's maa? Why are you calling her Vijay's maa? She is your maa too now."
"Fine, maaji doesn't want me to work. I have become a housewife to please Vijay's... my maaji."
"I am proud of you Uma. Keep your maaji happy like this and you will never have any difficulties in your new home."
"Once I win everyone over. I will go back to working in a hospital again."
"Not without Madhuben's permission. It takes years to build respect and make a place in someone's heart. It takes only moments to destroy it.

Make a request to Madhuben once you have been there for some time. I am sure she will agree for your happiness. But Uma beti, tell me why do you need to work? Your husband must have money trees everywhere. Tell me what the high society parties that you go to are like."

Uma had not fabricated Madhu's niceness to only her mother. She withheld Madhu's reality from the rest of her family. *I don't want anyone in my family to worry unnecessarily. Maa already worries over the smallest of things. I am adjusting; it is just taking me longer than I hoped. I am sure if I keep accepting everything maaji says to me I will win her over eventually. This is exactly what happens in many serials on television. The mother-in-law and family hate the new wife. She wins them over and they live happily ever after. I have already started to win people over. Charuben likes me. Leela and Purbai like me too. I just need to work on Vijay's maa and Jigar and then I too can be the ideal bahu like Parvati Agarwal.*

Uma's mother put some pauva into her plate.
"Tell me when to stop."
Avantika put three serving spoons of pauva into the plate before Uma told her to stop. Most people traditionally ate pauva with yogurt, and that was how she ate it in Madhapar. She did not dare to do anything weird that could potentially irritate her mother-in-law. Worried by the thought of how Madhu would react, Uma ate pauva the normal way. However, now that she was back home, Uma decided to eat it how she had eaten pauva since she was seven. When people saw Uma mix tamarind chutney with pauva, they always thought she was odd. Uma did not care, she loved the mixture of sour and spice with the texture of flattened rice and potato. Uma looked around and saw the little bowl of tamarind chutney her mother had prepared. Her mouth began to water at the thought of eating pauva with tamarind chutney after so long.
"Maa you have made tamarind chutney too."
"I am your maa Uma. I know you like this odd mix," Avantika said with a slight shudder.

Uma watched as her mother picked up the silver bowl and began to mix some of the chutney into her meal. Her mother put in the right amount

and stopped without having to be told.
"Why do you have to go to work maa?" Uma said. "You never used to work before."
"Uh," Avantika paused. "Arjun wants to do a Masters degree. We are going to have to save more money for him."
"You don't have to work; dadi will be left home alone. Vijay and I..."
"Not at all. We cannot accept anything from you," her mother said bluntly. "You are a daughter of our family. What will people say if they find out we are taking money off our beti? Some people do not even drink water from their daughter's home, and you want us to take money."
"People will not..."
"Holi is coming up," Her mother abruptly changed the topic. "What are you doing for Holi?"
Uma noticed the quick change of conversation and did not probe further. She knew how proud her parents were. They would never accept money from their daughter. So she began to tell her mother about the Holi party her family were hosting. By the time her mother left for work, she had finished eating and spent the rest of her day with her grandmother.

By 6pm that night, Uma had a heavy heart and started to feel restless. The few days she spent with her family were her happiest moments since she came back from her honeymoon. Some of her friends had visited a few times. She laughed so hard in their presence that she had tears in her eyes. The only person who could make her laugh in Madhapar was Vijay. *People in Madhapar appear to have no sense of humour. None of their jokes are as good as the jokes we have here in Mandavi.* She took a deep breath and recalled the emotions she felt when she bid farewell to her family on the day of her marriage. She did not feel as sad as she did on the day of her wedding, but she still dreaded the idea of returning to Madhapar. *Why couldn't Vijay stay in Mumbai for a few more days?* To make the parting for her parents less distressing, Uma mentally prepared a list of things she was looking forward to when she returned to Madhapar. *Vijay.* Uma struggled to think of anything. A few moments later she thought of a second thing to look forward to. *Holi. I love Holi and it is coming up.* The thought of spending her first Holi with Vijay caused Uma to delve into her own world and fantasise about how amazing the festival would be with the Rathod family. *Vijay will be very romantic during Holi. He is going to be the first person I throw colour on and I will be the first person he covers in colour.* Developing a fantasy about how amazing Holi would be in Madhapar gave Uma something to look forward to and reduced her apprehensions about going back home.

Vijay arrived a few minutes after sunset. After dinner with her family they were both ready to leave. Vijay's presence made it easier for Uma to leave her family once again. The ninety minutes she spent with him since he arrived, made her realise how much she had missed him. *I love him so much! Putting up with maaji is worth it because it means I get to be with him. I am willing to work harder to make maaji love me like she loves Charu. Once she realises how much we both love each other, and how obedient I am, she will accept me and love me too.*

Uma sat in her husband's new car and saw her family waiting outside. They all came to the door to say goodbye. As she waved to her family only one thought went through her mind. *I did not tell maa what Vijay's maa is truly like. Did I do the right thing by hiding the truth?*

Chapter 8: Avantika

Did I do the right thing by hiding the truth? I lied to her about why I am now working. Avantika watched her daughter climb into Vijay's car. *Uma is now a married woman. She has her own family. I do not want her to constantly be thinking about our problems at her in-law's home. The truth would just eclipse the happiness she has found in her new life.* Avantika waved as she watched Uma and Vijay drive off in their car. *What would she gain from knowing the truth? Our problems are no longer her problems.* Once the car was out of view, she spotted some of the neighbours whispering. Avantika smiled as she overheard the murmurs about the expensive car her son-in-law had driven to pick Uma up. The neighbour's admiration made Avantika's heart fill with pride. She walked back into the house delighted that the neighbours had noticed the expensive car parked outside her house. Uma's marriage resulted in a drastic change in people's attitude towards her family. Avantika's neighbours always greeted her in the past; however, the way they greeted her now was different. The Desai family were now minor celebrities in their community.

Once Avantika overcame her brief burst of joy, she remembered the worries she experienced before she saw her neighbours. *How do I tell Uma the real reason her dadi has to do the housework at this age? The guilt Uma would feel if she knew that I had to work for her happiness would impact on her new life. She might even resent Madhu. I do not want anything to come in the way of her happiness.* Avantika took a deep breath. *I did the right thing. At least she can continue adjusting to her new home if she does not know what is happening here.*

Avantika and Vinod did not have the funds to fulfil Madhu's demands for Uma's wedding. The final cost of the wedding, with the discounts included, was more than triple their initial budget.
"Where will we get the money from in such short time?" Avantika said panicked.
"We will have to use up all of our savings," Vinod said sombrely. "Go to

the bank tomorrow and take out all the money we have. We will see how much we can get with that."
"But we saved all that money for a time we're in desperate need for money. What will we do if you lose your job and we have no money to eat?"
"This is our daughter's reputation Avanti. We can rebuild our savings, but if Uma becomes maligned then people will spit on our names forever."

Helpless Avantika emptied out their bank accounts of all the money they put aside. Before going to the bank she had a dilemma of whether she should touch the money they put aside for Gauri's wedding, and for Arjun and Gauri's education. *What if we cannot rebuild our savings? Is it right for me to use money put aside for Gauri and Arjun?* In the end, she took the money they had put aside for Gauri's wedding, but did not touch the money put aside for her children's education.
"Gauri is still young," Avantika explained to Vinod. "We can save the money again. We might even save more. We will not have to save for Uma anymore. I did not touch the money we saved for Gauri and Arjun's education. Their education is more important than some of the other things we have."
"I am going to go to the bank tomorrow and find out if we can get a loan for the wedding. This will ease our situation for a while."

When Avantika discovered that Vinod had successfully taken out a loan from the bank she felt relieved. They finally managed to get together all the money they needed for Uma's wedding. After Uma's wedding Madhu made a further demand for 10,000 rupees to cover other costs. Avantika secretly took 5,000 rupees each from the savings for Arjun and Gauri's education. *I can easily replace 10,000 rupees before anyone even knows it is gone.* Avantika felt some relief. In the weeks leading up to Uma's wedding she had a few nightmares about the wedding being cancelled and her daughter being left in the mandap alone because Madhu was unhappy with something. Once the money was paid Avantika felt finally at ease. She believed that there were no further obstacles to overcome for her daughter's future.

After Uma's wedding, Avantika started to plan ways to further boost her family's prestige. *People will soon start asking for my Arjun's hand in marriage. My Uma has married into a big house, but she belongs to another family. At least Arjun's wife would live here and become a part of my family. With everyone revering my family, there will be a line of girls wanting to marry Arjun. I will get to pick the best from all the proposals he will get. I will accept nothing less than a doctor or lawyer for my daughter-in-law. My Uma will be surrounded by big influential people. Maybe she could find a nice, cultured and respectful girl from an elite family for her brother. Why just Arjun? She can find a prestigious family for my Gauri too. I will tell her to start looking for both of them.*

Her planning for Arjun and Gauri's wedding ended up being short lived. A week after the wedding Avantika received a letter from Madhu. She knew to expect a money request, but expected a request for 10,000 rupees. The request however, was for 300,000 rupees. Avantika was shocked at the amount Madhu requested. She looked at it again to make sure she had not misread the amount. Avantika read it a few times to make sure she was not confusing 30,000 rupees with 300,000. Once she saw there was no confusion she immediately picked up the phone to inform Madhu about the error. *How did 10,000 rupees turn to 3 lakhs?* Avantika heard the ringing tone. Her frustration increased with each ring. After a few rings Madhu had picked up the phone.
"Madhuben, Jai Shri Krishna" Avantika said.
"Oh Avantika? Jay Shri Krishna," Madhu responded. "How did you think of us today?"
"Madhuben, you told us you will let us know how much we owed for the petrol, your brother and other wedding costs."
"Ha, I did. Did you get the bill?"
"Ha. It says you are asking for... for 3 lakhs."
"Is there anything wrong with it?"
Wrong? Has this woman lost her senses? How can she just ask us for 3 lakh rupees from nowhere? We don't have trees to grow money.
"You said it would be 10,000 rupees Vehvanji. How did..."
"Oh Vehvanji the mistake is mine. I should have told you what the costs were for." Madhu began to monotonously recite the costs. "I had already told you that we needed to repay my brother and the petrol. That was

10,000 rupees. Our maid worked extra hours for the wedding, I promised to pay her more for the wedding. That is another 5,000 rupees. Your beti and my beta will go on honeymoon. We had agreed that your family would pay for all wedding costs. Honeymoon is part of the wedding. There are flights, hotels and spending money for the wedding. Adding everything together works out to just over 3 lakh rupees."

"3 lakhs?" Avantika said quietly. "Vehvanji, we don't have that kind of money."

"Not 3 lakh, it was slightly more. We thought we would round it down to make it easier for you."

Easy for us? My sandals! How is getting together 3 lakh easy for us? This evil witch planned this all along. She didn't ask us for a dowry, because she did not want to look bad. Instead she has taken just as much with these unreasonable demands around the marriage.

"We are not unreasonable Avantikaben. I know you might not have that money straight away. You can, pay us in small instalments."

"But..."

"Avantika... you want Uma to be happy don't you?"

"What? Of course I..."

"Then this is a small price to pay for your beti's happiness," Madhu said quietly. "Vehevanji I need to go. I have guests coming to my house. I need to get ready. Jai Shri Krishna."

Avantika heard Madhu put the phone down. She stood there holding the phone for a second shocked at the amount Madhu was requesting. *A small price to pay for my beti's happiness? Was she making a threat?* Unsure what to do next Avantika told her entire family about what had happened. She told them about the amount Madhu requested and what she felt had been a threat. Vinod immediately went to the bank to increase their loan. The bank accepted the loan request; but the monthly payments they had to make were very high. *Hai maa Durga, how will we make these monthly repayments? Vinod's salary will just about cover the repayments. How will we feed 5 people? We have bills to pay and have to start saving for Gauri's wedding.*

"In my day, girls weren't sent to school," Vinod's mother said. "We did not waste money on educating them. They are going to go into someone else's family. Why waste our money educating them when they will

not...”
“Baa we’re not going to stop educating Gauri. Times have changed,” Avantika told her mother-in-law.
“I can work for one year and...” Arjun began to say.
“Definitely not,” Vinod interjected. “You are not going to stop your education to...”
“Bapuji, I’m not ending my studies. Just until we have enough money to repay the loan. I am educated enough to get a well paid job in an office somewhere...”
If my son goes to work, what will happen about his studies? He can’t stop his studies to work, without a graduate degree how will he ever get anywhere? No, no, no. I will have to find a new source of income. I will have to get the job.

Avantika looked for work for a few weeks. She had refused to do any jobs that involved cleaning. *If the neighbours find out that Uma’s maa is cleaning for money all the respect we have will all turn to dust.* Fortunately she found a job as a receptionist at the hospital Uma used to work in. The only negative side of the role was she would be working full time. Avantika had hoped for a part time job. *How will I run this household if I am away all day? I cannot expect baa to do everything at this age. We cannot even afford a maid to help us out.* When Avantika told her family about the job she had been offered and the implications it would have on the household chores, Vinod’s mother had immediately agreed to help.
“Until I am alive, you don’t need to spend money on a maid Avantika. My hands and feet work as well as they did years ago.”
“Baa how can we ask you to clean?” Avantika asked her mother-in-law.
“Is this not my family? Do you consider me an outsider?”
“No baa, but you’re not as young as you used to be. You have arthritis...”
“Uma is my daughter too. I am part of this family too. I will do the housework you used to do. You earn money.”

Avantika started to work at the hospital. When she came home there was still more work to be done. Her mother-in-law was not as fit as she used to be. She could not do all of the housework with arthritis in her hands and right foot. Therefore when Avantika came home she took over. Avantika always felt drained out by the end of the day. The only thing that got her through each day was the notion that she was buying her children's happiness. *The money we give to Madhu will buy Uma respect from her mother-in-law. If we didn't pay, what honour would she have in her home? Without dignity and respect people are nothing and I do not want that for my Uma. I want her to become a beti to that family. If the only way I can achieve this is by working day and night then so be it.* Whenever she became too tired to do anything she motivated herself by thinking of Uma's happiness. Despite being really tired by the end of the day, she did not always fall straight asleep. Fears that more requests for money would come kept her awake. *What if they make more requests? How will we fulfil them?*

The nightmares Avantika used to have about Uma being left in the wedding mandap were now replaced by nightmares of the Rathod family returning Uma as a shamed woman.

Chapter 9: Purbai

Normally Purbai prayed at the Swaminarayan Temple in Madhapar but as it was the day of an important festival, Holi, she had gone to the main temple in Bhuj. Purbai looked at the beautiful murti of Lord Swaminarayan. She crouched down, put two hands together and moved both index fingers up and down to pray. Once she finished praying, she stood up and turned around. She looked at the devotees who were sitting down listening to the Swami's sermon. Purbai made eye contact with Dhanbai, another woman from Madhapar, who was also from her community. Dhanbai whispered Jai Swaminarayan to Purbai, who nodded and whispered it back. *I have to sit and listen to the katha now or Dhanbai will tell everyone that I come to mandir and leave straight away.* She went and sat down next to Dhanbai and took out her mala beads.

When she sat down to pray Purbai heard the priest narrating the story of Vishnu's Varah Avatar, when Vishnu took the form of a boar to kill the demon Hiranyaksh. After Hiranyaskh's death his brother Hiranakashyap wanted revenge.
Purbai saw Samu, who was her daughter-in-law's sister. *How brave of Samu to show her face at mandir after what happened with her beti.* Purbai's mind buzzed with excitement. *Whenever she comes to visit Kesar she always thought she was better than my family. She used to prevent me from coming to social gatherings because I am a widow, and she thought that widows are unlucky. Now her beti was caught blackening her face with another boy. Once this katha ends I will go and gloat. Since my husband's death she looked down on me and my family and now it is my turn. I'd rather be a widow than an impure whore.* Purbai's excitement to gloat in front of Samu meant she found it difficult to refocus on the story of Holi.

When she finally refocused, she heard the swami narrating how Hiranakashyap had pleased Brahma with his difficult penance and meditation. Pleased with Hiranakashyap, Brahma granted the demon one wish. The demon was allowed anything except immortality. The cunning demon thought he found a way to cheat Brahma to become immortal. The demon asked to die, but only under the following conditions:

1) He cannot be killed indoors or outdoors.
2) He cannot be killed by a man or a beast
3) He cannot be killed on the ground or in the sky
4) He cannot be killed in day or night
5) He cannot be killed with a weapon or an instrument.

Brahma granted the demon his wish. He could only be killed if all five of the circumstances occurred at the same time. Hiranakashyap began to believe he was immortal. He thought that he could not be killed in any way and believed himself to be the most powerful person in the universe.

At this point Purbai's mind wandered once again. She saw Pushpa sitting amongst the people listening to the story. *Pushpa's husband stole all of the money left in his bapuji's will. He did not share the money with any of his brothers and kept everything to himself. You would think he would buy his wife nicer saris after all of the money he has stolen. The sari she is wearing was in fashion when I was allowed to wear fancy saris.* As a widow, Purbai was no longer allowed to decorate her body with jewellery or wear beautiful saris. She was even forbidden from participating in Holi celebrations. Many people prevented Purbai from going to social events as they felt it would be unlucky for her to attend. However, the Rathod family invited Purbai to the Holi party they were hosting. *Madhuben came to invite me personally to her Holi party. She gives me so much respect. She gives me more respect than anyone else has given me since Harji died. Even my own son and his wife think I am a burden.*

Purbai once again refocused her mind back onto the story. The priest now narrated how the demon became inebriated with power. He misused his powers and terrorised innocent people of the universe. He even demanded they worship him as God. Anyone who refused was tortured and killed. Only one person had the courage to stand up to the demon; his seven year old son Prahlad. Prahlad worshipped Vishnu and refused to accept his father as God. After many futile attempts to coerce his son into worshipping him Hiranakashyap ordered his servants to murder Prahlad.

Purbai's mind wondered again when she noticed Samu sitting near her. She became excited at the prospect of gloating once the story ended. *She always told me my shadow would be unlucky at her daughter's wedding ceremonies and made me sit far. She always told me that my daughter was fat, and because of her weight she would not find a nice boy to marry her. Despite being a widow I instilled dignity and morals into my beti. She found someone to marry her, but after what your beti has done who would take her as their wife? I always knew Samu's beti was of loose character. Ever since Madhuben has moved to Madhapar her beti is always swarming around Jigar and Vijay.*

Purbai took a deep breath and once again brought her attention back to the story of Prahlad. The swami recited how Prahlad had survived several murder attempts as he was protected by Vishnu. When everything else failed, Hiranakashyap's sister Holika offered to kill the boy. The swami narrated how Holika planned to murder Prahlad by burning him. She would enter a fire with the boy and hold him down until he burnt. Holika knew that she was protected against fire because Brahma had granted her a blessing that fire would not burn her. Confident that her ruse to kill Prahlad would be successful she sat on a bonfire and ordered the demons to light the pyre. Once the fire was lit, Prahlad once again called out to Vishnu. Vishnu protected Prahlad from fire whilst Holika screamed in excruciating pain. Carried away with evil thoughts, she forgot that Brahma's wish had been granted to her for self protection. Her attempt to kill Prahlad had not been for self protection. She used her blessing to harm others and consequentially burnt to death herself. Following Holika's death, spring arrived. People celebrated the arrival of spring and the death of evil by throwing colour onto each other. The swami explained that people sometimes destroy themselves with evil, and went into a sermon.

The katha is almost over! Purbai began to fidget with excitement. *I am going to tell her that I am invited to the Rathod family's Holi celebration tonight. Then I will say how my friend Madhu's son is fortunate to have a wife like Uma because there were many shameless girls after him. I am sure she will understand what I mean. She will not be able to make a drama about it either. I could just say I was talking about someone else. I am going to enjoy gloating to her, for all the bukvaas she has said about me and my beti.*

Wanting revenge for his sister's death, Hiranakashyap decided he will fight Vishnu himself. He commanded his son to tell him where he could find Vishnu. Prahlad told his father that Vishnu is everywhere, even inside the pillars of his palace. Hiranakashyap picked up a mace to blow the pillar to smithereens. When he struck the pillar it crumbled. The momentary glee evaporated when the demon saw what the pillar contained. Vishnu came out of the pillar in his Narsingha avatar. Lord Narsingha was half man and half lion; hence neither man nor beast. Narsingha grabbed the demon by his hair and dragged him to the threshold of his palace. He sat down in the middle of the doorway; the demon was neither indoors nor outdoors. Narsingha lifted the demon onto his thighs; hence the demon was no longer in the sky or on the ground. The sun was about to set and it was dusk; so it was neither day nor night. The half man and half lion killed the demon and punished him with his claws; he used neither weapon nor instrument to kill the demon. The priest explained the importance of Holi and the significance of starting afresh with spring.

Purbai ignored his sermon on forgiveness. As soon as his preaching ended, Purbai stood up to talk to Samu. Her mouth was wide open as though she was about to swallow a juicy fly.

Chapter 10: Nilambari

Nilambari stood in a corner staring at the fire which blazed in the middle of the Rathod's courtyard. Red, purple, blue, green, yellow, pink and orange mounds of powder were laid on plates all over the garden. Paddling pools and buckets filled with coloured water were also strategically placed around the courtyard. Nilambari stood well away from the celebrations as she did not like Holi. She watched the children who ran around screaming and laughing as they threw paint over each other. The adults sounded just like the children, with the only difference being that the men's screams were deeper.

Nilambari noticed a group of men standing right next to her. She felt the back of her throat contract. She panicked and looked around to see where everyone else was. She found a group of women a few yards away. As she started to shuffle towards the group of women she realised that Jigar was amongst the group of men.

"Eh yaar. I saw a hot girl on the back of your bike yesterday. Who is she?" One of Jigar's friends asked him.

"She's a friend," Jigar winked and laughed with the rest of his friends. "You're all early. You better stay right to the end."

"We will party and rock all night long," another one of Jigar's friends said. "We only came early to make sure we didn't miss out on any good stuff."

"Good," Jigar lowered his voice. "We have alcohol and bhang..."

"That's why we all came early yaar. We wanted to enjoy ourselves before the alcohol ran out."

"Alcohol is illegal in our state." Rishi, one of Jigar's friends commented. The rest of Jigar's friendship group groaned at the guy who made the comment.

"Rishi do you always ruin our fun with stupid comments yaar?" Another friend snapped.

"I'm not complaining," Rishi defended himself. "I just want to know how you always get alcohol for your parties. And I also want to know why you never get caught. Everyone knows you're drinking."

"I am a police officer yaar," Jigar said smugly. "I make the law."
His friends all laughed and cheered boisterously. They were highly impressed by their friend.
"So that hot girl on your bike. Are you fucking her?"

Nilambari did not want to listen to anymore. She walked away repulsed by Jigar and his friends. She weaved in and out of groups of people, watching everyone else celebrate Holi, without participating herself. Nilambari was covered in colour, which had been thrown onto her by random people. *I used to love Holi, but now I hate this festival. I am only here because the Rathod family told me to come.*

Nilambari recalled the Holi from two years ago, which resulted in her fear of the festival. She had been playing Holi with her husband's family when she drank lassi spiked with cannabis. She could not recall much of what happened after. The events after drinking her spiked drink all seemed to be a blur. The only thing Nilambari could remember is being raped repeatedly by a few men. She could not even remember exactly how many men there were. Once the effects of the cannabis wore off, Nilambari woke up in a room she did not recognise. She realised she was naked and her body ached everywhere. That was when she had obscure flashbacks, reminding her of what happened to her before she regained consciousness. Nilambari let out a pained howl as the memories returned to her. Before the gang rape she had already been stripped of her dignity and identity, but now she nurtured a new wound. She felt the dignity she clenched onto had now been looted from her as well. After lamenting for a while she realised she had to get away before anyone came back. She quickly got dressed and walked away as quickly as she could. The excruciating pain meant she could not walk straight.

Worried about the agony she felt, she went to a doctor. The doctor phoned her husband who picked Nilambari up from the hospital. Nilambari did not think her situation would get worse. She had been wrong. Nilambari's in-laws branded her a slut and blamed her for the rape. They maligned her with accusations of walking around and talking to men all the time. They told her she dressed provocatively and had instigated the men into raping her. Nilambari was forced to flee the house she lived in. She did not collect any of her belongings, she had just enough time to escape without being thrashed by her in-laws. Nilambari hit rock bottom. She had no home, no family and no friends. Returning to her parent's home was not an option either. *I lost everything when amma and acha sold me.*

Nilambari grew up in Ernakulam, Kerala. She spent a lot of her childhood working for a Gujarati family, as her parents did not send her to school. Nilambari's childhood consisted of eating, sleeping, working and marriage proposals. Due to female genocide, Kerala was the only state in India where there were proportionately more girls than boys. As a result there were not enough women to marry in other states and brides were imported from states like Kerala. When she was fifteen, Nilambari's parents finally accepted a proposal and she was sold like an object. A rich merchant offered her parents a large sum of money in exchange for Nilambari's hand in marriage. The merchant brokered the son of a rich Gujarati family, who wanted to remarry. Her parents agreed to the match and accepted the large payment from the Gujarati family in exchange for Nilambari. The merchant took his share of the money and gave a small percentage to Nilambari's parents. Without her consent Nilambari was married off to a man twice her age. She saw her family for the last time on the day she married. The following day she moved to Gujarat, almost two thousand kilometres away from everything she knew.

When Nilambari arrived in Gujarat she was adorned with new clothes, new jewellery. Everything she owned was replaced. Her family felt the name Nilambari was not Gujarati enough and even gave her a new name, Deepali. Nilambari felt that the name Deepali symbolised that fact she now belonged to the Virani family. Every time she heard the name Deepali she felt it oozed with spite and disgust. Unfamiliar with the language, culture and even cuisine of Gujarat, Nilambari became withdrawn and isolated with no friends.

A year into the marriage Nilambari discovered the reason her husband remarried. The first wife had been thrown out due to her inability to have children. The only time she had any contact with people was when her husband came to impregnate her. Another year passed and Nilambari did not become pregnant. Despite being worried that she too could be kicked out, Nilambari secretly rejoiced. *How can one man have so many infertile wives? His bad karma must prevent him from finding a fertile wife. The fault is in his bad karma.* Before anyone had the opportunity to question her husband's infertility; Deepali was held responsible for her rape and kicked out. She had no way of returning to Ernakulam and became one of the many homeless in a city unknown to her.

With no one to turn to, she turned to the only ally she felt she had in this world; Lord Guruvayur. She found a temple of his in Bhuj and her prayers were answered immediately. When she left the temple, she saw a thief running away with a Sikh woman's purse. Nilambari saw the woman running after the thief shouting. With nothing left to lose, Nilambari stuck her foot out causing the thief to fall. In a panic the man dropped the bag and the contents of the bag onto the floor and continued to run. Nilambari picked up the stolen bag and returned it to the Sikh woman. The woman introduced herself as Amrita Oberoi and offered Nilambari some money as a reward. She declined the reward.
"Please," Amrita said. "It was not just money in here. You saved something for me. Something which belonged to my sister. Please take this money. I do not believe in owing a debt to people. I am indebted to you."
Nilambari looked at the money Amrita held in her hand. *This money will not last long. It will buy me food and shelter for a week. What good will it be next week? O Guruvayur Swamy what do I do?* This was when an idea occurred to her.
"If you want to help me, I need a job."
"Oh," Amrita looked confused. "I don't know how I can help you with that."
"Dayavai," Nilambari begged the stranger. Something about the stranger's manner invited Nilambari's confidence for the first time in Gujarat. She told the stranger everything right from her parents selling her at fifteen to getting kicked out of her in-laws at seventeen. "I have nowhere to go. No one to turn to."

Amrita's eyes were filled with tears. Nilambari's story had moved her. She gave Nilambari a room to live in. There was a small room in Amrita's courtyard where the old maid used to live. Amrita allowed her to live in the room for free. In return, Nilambari cleaned and did the family's washing. Amrita even helped Nilambari by finding her another job, which would help her to save more money. With a new home, Nilambari created a new identity for herself. She cast away the identity her parents had given her. *Nilambari was not allowed an education because she was a girl. Nilambari was sold by her parents. Nilambari was raped. I will start again.* She slowly learnt to speak a new language and became friends with Amrita and Amrita's husband. They were the first people who she had met who treated her like an equal.

Holi always depressed Nilambari; that day left her life in ruins and whenever she felt depressed she remembered her life as Nilambari. She walked around and watched the people enjoying themselves. *How many women will wake up tomorrow and find themselves in the same situation I found myself in two years ago? O Guruvayur Swamy give them all strength. May the men who do such things become impotent!*

Out of nowhere she felt arms grab her from behind. Nilambari kneeled down to make it difficult for whoever had grabbed her to drag her away. She was filled with terror. *Save me Guruvayur Swamy, not again.* She let out a piercing scream and waved her arms in the air in an attempt to fight the person behind her. The person who grabbed her loosened their grip and Nilambari broke free. She turned around to face the person and saw it was Uma.

"I'm so sorry if I scared you," Uma apologised. "I was trying to find you for a while to wish you happy Holi."

Nilambari's heart thumped. The adrenaline rushing through her had prepared her to fight. She was breathing rapidly and saw Uma with green powder in her hands. Uma rubbed the powder onto Nilambari's cheeks with a smile on her face. Still breathing heavily, Nilambari relaxed. She did not feel hostile towards Uma for wishing her, as she had felt towards the strangers who threw colour onto her. On the contrary, Nilambari smiled at Uma, as she felt happy that Uma wished her. *Most big people think they're better than me. The rest of your family have all walked past me a few times today and none of them have bothered to wish me. Even the Virani family ignored me on Holi. People think I am unworthy of their time and affection because I do not have the same status as them. But you are like Amritaji, you treat me like a person.*

“Are you enjoying the party Vijay has organised?” Uma asked.
“Yes,” Nilambari lied. *I will not burden her with my misery.* “How is your first Holi with your new family?”
“Excellent,” Uma began to tell Nilambari everything about the day. She explained how Vijay and her had both played Holi. Nilambari noticed that Uma quickly skimmed over playing Holi with the rest of Vijay’s family. “Everyone is so busy with our guests. I am sure we would have spent more time together if we weren’t busy with the party.”
Nilambari smiled and pretended to believe Uma. Every single day Nilambari witnessed the way Madhu and Jigar treated Uma with contempt. *They treat you like a dog, and you still attempt to save their honour by covering up how they really behave towards you. Why do you lie about the fact that you are hiding from Madhuji and Jigar sir? I hid everything from the outside world for two years. Nothing improved. Your situation will not go away if you ignore it.*

Uma continued to stand with Nilambari for a few moments. They watched people walking around the fire and throwing things inside the bonfire. That was when she spotted Amrita coming over.
“I was looking for you,” Amrita told her.
“I was just talking to Umaji,” Nilambari said to Amrita.
Nilambari realised that neither Amrita or Uma knew each other so she introduced them.
“Jai Shri Krishna,” Uma said with her hands together.
“Sat Sri Akal,” Amrita responded also putting her hands together. “So you’re the new wife of Vijay that Leela tells me about?”

Leela! Nilambari remembered her new identity. *Nilambari brings me nothing but misery. I always remember the injustices I have faced when I think of myself as Nilambari. I need to remember I am now Leela. Leela is a human being, not an object like Nilambari. Seeing everyone celebrate*

Holi made me forget myself for a while. Nilambari closed her eyes and took a deep breath. *Nilambari is dead. She died the day Amritaji marked me an equal. I am Leela.*

She opened her eyes and saw the Holi bonfire burning. She looked around and faced Uma. Leela saw the flames of the fire reflected in Uma's eyes. Uma's face glowed amber.

Chapter 11: Uma

Uma watched the fire burn. She had spent the past fortnight fantasising about how brilliant her first Holi with Vijay's family would be. Uma imagined that her mother-in-law would apply colour to her face, with the same affection her mother did each year. She had also pictured playing Holi with Charu and Jigar the same way she played with Arjun and Gauri. *Letting them win against me in a paint fight would make them like me more.* As Uma began to walk around the fire she felt disappointed with the reality of Holi in Madhapar. The rest of the Rathod family were too busy playing Holi with other people that they ignored her. *Even Vijay hasn't played Holi with me. Maybe I was hoping for too much, in such little time. I need to be realistic with my expectations.* Despite an imperfect Holi, Uma cherished the good things that had happened that day.

Early that morning, Leela and Purbai had both come to help with the preparations for the Holi party. Her mother-in-law gifted Uma a sari, in Purbai's presence. Uma had felt ecstatic. *Maaji gifted me a sari, before she even gave a gift to Charu. Hai maa Durga, it is because of your mercy that I have started to make a place in maaji's heart.* After Purbai left, no one spoke to Uma for the rest of the day. They were all busy preparing for the party. She noticed that her mother-in-law was gradually becoming more civil to her. Uma would not describe her behaviour as polite, but her words were no longer intolerable like an extremely spicy chilli.

As Uma walked around the fire, she began to pray. *Hai Holi mata let my relationship with my in-laws continue to improve. This time next year I hope to see my own maa in Vijay's maa, and Arjun and Gauri in Jigar and Charu.* Once she finished orbiting the Holi bonfire she put her hands together and bowed her head towards the flames. As she walked back home she saw people in her courtyard. They were covered in purple, yellow, pink, blue and green. The Bollywood music was drowned out by the screams of delight from various people having a paint fight.

People of all ages ran around and threw coloured water and powder over each other. Uma did not know any of them and she was unable to find her family members so went indoors.

Once she reached her bedroom, she saw a few plates of coloured powder on the floor and dressing table. *Who put this here?* She then saw the sari her mother-in-law had gifted was still on her bed and forgot about the colour. *It is a beautiful sari! Maaji would not spend so much money on me if she didn't care about me. I should put it away before it gets ruined.* Uma carefully folded the sari up and put it away in her wardrobe. When she shut her wardrobe, she felt she saw someone move in the room from the corner of her eye. She quickly turned around and screamed as someone jumped out at her. Vijay jumped out from their en-suite bathroom and threw green powder on her.

For a few moments she waited for her heart beat to return to normal as Vijay laughed. Once Uma recovered from the shock she grabbed the colour closest to her and threw it on Vijay. His white tank top and black jeans were now covered in yellow powder. They both laughed and threw more colours over each other.

Once they were both covered in lots of different colours, Vijay bolted his bedroom door shut. He grabbed the end of Uma's sari and began to unwrap her. They made love and played with colours at the same time. *Vijay was not ignoring me, he was waiting to surprise me. His surprise is so much better than my silly fantasy of playing Holi with him putting colours on my cheeks. Having him put colour over my breasts is much more satisfying. Hai Mata Rani, this is the best day I have had since I moved to Madhapar, with your blessing my life will continue to get better.*

Chapter 12: Madhu

Madhu sighed as she sat down on the sofa. She looked at the time. *Charu and Jigar should be home soon.* Madhu was tired and her legs were aching again. Once again she had danced too much and her feet were paying the price. She saw Leela wiping the floor in the living room from where she was sat.
"Leela," Madhu shouted out as soon as she sat down. "Get me a bucket of warm water and bring me some Tiger Balm. Do not forget to bring me my chai as well."
Leela got up and walked off to get the things Madhu had ordered. *Hai Bhagwan, my legs are telling me I am getting too old.* Madhu put her swollen feet up on the table and turned the TV on.

The repeat telecast of an Ekta Kapoor serial was on. The characters were all celebrating Holi. Madhu watched a scene of an evil daughter-in-law trying to ruin Holi. She remembered how she had put some colour on Uma at the start of the celebrations. It was now just over three months since Uma and Vijay's wedding. *Everything is going to plan. Uma fears me and that is exactly what I want. I refuse to be like Purbai in my own home.* Madhu was pleasantly surprised to how easily Uma had been subjugated by her. She recalled with pride her first attack against Uma. *I never thought simply making a drama over the food she cooked would give me complete victory.*

Three days after the cooking fiasco, Uma had told Madhu she was going to see whether there were any vacancies at Bhuj Hospital or any local doctors. Madhu venomously responded by saying "I thought I brought a bahu into my house who would help with the housework. If I wanted a doctor I would have phoned one." *One little comment and the coward changed her mind about going to work.* This was the moment Madhu realised she had already won. *I won without any effort. I defeated my phoosar of a bahu. She did not even make a fuss or utter a word against me. I owe Avantika for making Uma easy to tame. Avantika taught this girl respect for her elders, not to talk back to her elders. She will do exactly what I tell her to.* Even fifteen minutes ago, Madhu had told Uma to go and do the grocery shopping. *The girl left without a word of complaint. She is giving me everything I want; a life filled with peace. I will not allow her to work in a hospital and think she is better than me because she works and earns money.*

Madhu got bored of the soaps on Star plus and began to flick through different channels. She took her eyes off the TV when she heard Leela panting. She watched as Leela struggled to bring the bucket of water over. Once the bucket was in front of Madhu, she dipped her feet into the water and felt a soothing and warm sensation rush through her. Madhu began to sip the chai made by Leela, and finally found something she wanted to watch. She felt as though she had not been this comfortable in a long time. After a while she fell asleep in front of the TV.

Madhu woke up after a while feeling very refreshed. She saw that Leela was about to leave work and coughed. Leela looked around to see where the cough came from. She noticed Madhu was awake and walked towards her.
"Madhuji I have finished," Leela said quietly. "I did not want to disrupt your sleep so I was leaving quietly." For a few moments Madhu did not respond. The awkward silence was broken by Leela. "The house is clean ... the only room that is dirty is Vijay sir's room."
"And why is that?" Madhu asked with a flat tone. Madhu saw Leela shift uncomfortably. *She is scared of me too. I will train Uma to be like this nobody.*
"I changed the bed blanket because they were covered in colour. I wiped the colour off the floor. But I could not get the Holi colours off the walls. I tried my best but the paint won't come off."
"Colours from Holi on the bedroom walls?" Madhu repeated. "What are you saying?"
Madhu got up and pushed Leela aside as she began to walk up the stairs. The aches Madhu felt in her feet exacerbated her mood.

Madhu finally got to Vijay's bedroom and she opened the door. She stood in shock at the state of her son's bedroom. The beautifully painted

walls of the bedroom, had swirls of red circles and splodges of purple. She could see Leela's attempts to wash the colour off but the Holi colours were merging with the wall paint. *Which animal has done this to my house?* Madhu thought as anger bubbled inside her. She narrowed her eyes looking at the assorted paint all over the walls. *The décor of this room is totally ruined.*
"VIJAY! UMA!" Madhu screamed.

Neither Vijay nor Uma were home.

Chapter 13: Charu

Charu walked with a bounce in her step. She was on her way home after a picnic in the park with her boyfriend, Rajan. *I have found the boy I will marry! He is so perfect it is unreal. No one else makes me smile as much as him. I am always so happy when he is around.*

As Charu continued her journey home, she relived some of her memories with Rajan. She recalled the moment Rajan told her he loved her. Three weeks ago he had picked her up from college on his motorbike. He took her to Khatri Lake near Naranpar. They sat on the bank talking and watching the wildlife. They put sev mamra into the water and saw the water churn as the fish came to eat. The cranes seized this opportunity to swoop down and grab as many fish as they could. Rajan had held her hand and taken her closer to see the crocodiles. She was not brave enough to get too close and so they sat on the bench until just before the sun set. *That was when he told me he loved me. He is so romantic.* Charu walked home with butterflies in her stomach.

Charu was in the courtyard when she heard her mother shouting. *Who is mumma shouting at now?*

"Who do you think you are?" Charu's mother screeched. "You come into my house and defile it!"
She walked into the house and saw Uma with tears in her eyes. *Ah mumma is shouting at Uma Bhabhi again.*
"I have been nothing but generous to you and your downmarket family. I allowed a family beneath us to become our relatives, but you have given us nothing but difficulties," Charu heard her mother pause for air. She then continued her verbal assault. "For your wedding your parents gave us absolutely nothing. Sushilaben, who lives in the house next door to Purbai, got a car, fridge, money and clothes. You did not bring anything and you still think we have money trees. You waste our food. You go to the stupid temple and throw money away by making

donations, and now you have ruined the decoration of this house. Do you think money grows on trees?"
Uma stood in silence with nothing to say, giving Madhu ample opportunity to continue.
"Sushilaben even got a refurbishment for her whole house. Hai bhagvan, what bad karma did I do in a past life that you have given me this selfish and tight-fisted bahu? Kanjoos!" spat Charu's mother.
"Maaji," Uma squeaked. "Maa worked so hard to pay for the wedding. You got jewellery and clothes. They were expensive. How can you say you got nothing?"
Charu saw her mother walk over to Uma. She gasped and opened her eyes wide with shock as she witnessed her mother slap Uma. Uma stopped talking immediately. The slap had made a loud sound. Uma began to rub her cheek where she had been whacked.
"You dare talk back to me in my own house?" Uma was slapped again. "Do not ever think you can talk like that to me! All I got was jewellery to wear at the wedding. The jewellery was so light that a gust of wind could blow it away. It was cheap and probably something you downmarket people wear. It was not befitting of our status. The clothes your maa bought was for the wedding. You think your maa did something grand by paying for the wedding? A bride's family always pay for the wedding. Do not try to be great in front of me. Where is everything else that a girl should bring to her new family? You did not bring a bed, no furniture, no jewellery for yourself, nothing. Did your maa think you would be camping?"

Charu saw her mother walk away from Uma. Her mother sat down on the sofa and began to shake her head.
"I think the reason you are so careless with money is because you do not contribute anything towards running our home. Maybe if I made your parents pay for the damage you have done then you would appreciate the fact that money does not grow on trees and Vijay and Jigar work very hard."

Mumma is right. It is normal for a bride to bring furniture to her new home. Uma bhabhi did not bring anything. She did not even give a dowry. Her parents promised to fulfil every custom which they have not. It is traditional and customary in our religion to give a dowry. Mumma must feel deceived by Uma's parents. Mumma put so much money into raising Vijay bhai and now he has a wife, she just wants to become his wife for nothing. I just wish mumma had sorted this out before Uma came here. I do not think the poor girl deserves to be beaten, because it is her parent's fault that they went back on the agreed dowry. It is not Uma's fault.

Once Uma left the living room, her mother continued to mutter to herself.
"My son is loving, patient, polite, generous and that girl is a fool. She is a bad influence on my son! My son would never play Holi in his bedroom. They played Holi in the bedroom and now the colour will not come off the walls. The whole room needs to be redecorated."

If Uma played Holi in the bedroom, Vijay must have played as well. Mumma is blaming Uma because she thinks Uma bhabhi is a bad influence. Mumma could be right. Vijay has never played Holi in his room before. Uma must have suggested the idea. But Vijay bhai is old enough to know what is sensible. He should not have been influenced by her stupid ideas.

Chapter 14: Avantika

"Baa Chai," Avantika said as she walked into her mother-in-law's bedroom with a cup of tea. Her mother-in-law sat up and took the cup of tea from Avantika. She shook her head in approval and began to drink the tea. After waiting for her mother-in-law to take a few sips, Avantika took out some money from her wallet and gave it to her.
"Baa, this is some of the money I have left over from my salary this month. Add it to the money we've been saving for Uma."
"Do you still think this is necessary?"
"I don't want to risk anything Baa. Madhu is..."
"Madhuben," her mother-in-law corrected. "She is your vehvan, show some respect."
Respect is given to those who deserve it. "Madhuben has not asked for anything for over two months, but my heart still panics every time I watch the news and see a dowry case. I want to put this money aside in case she asks for anything. I don't trust that woman."

Avantika believed that once they fulfilled Madhu's request for three lakh rupees, everything would return to normal. She thought that she would begin to enjoy her new found status and it would make her very happy. However, Avantika was far from being content and happy. Two days after the Desai family had paid Madhu's three lakh rupees; the news report showed a story regarding a dowry death. The nineteen year old woman had been doused in petrol before being set on fire by her in-laws. After months of torturing her for more and more money, the girl's family ran out money. To punish her parents for refusing to fulfil their demands, the in-laws killed the woman. The news report showed the guilty family being arrested by the police. The women had draped their saris over their face, whilst the men tried to cover their faces using their hands. Avantika quickly made a connection between the girl's murder and Uma's situation. *That Madhu too seems to be asking for more and more each time what if she does the same to Uma?* Avantika was so overcome by fear and grief that she phoned work and told them she felt sick. Avantika confided in her mother-in-law and told her about her

fears and how terrified she was for her daughter's life after seeing that report. Her mother-in-law calmed Avantika down by phoning Uma and allowing Avantika speak to her.
"She is safe for now baa, but what if they ask for more money?"

Avantika lost count of how many dowry abuse related stories she had seen in the news. It seemed a dowry story made it onto the news every other day. Each time a dowry related story was shown, the reporter always announced that over 8,500 dowry related cases were lodged in India each year. This figure excluded the many cases which went unreported, listed as accidental deaths or suicide. Some women were murdered by being set on fire, others were poisoned. In some cases the relatives of the girl's family committed suicide as they were unable to fulfil their demands. The more stories Avantika saw on the news, the more her fear intensified. *What if my Uma becomes one of those girls who are set on fire? Vinod and I paid all the money for the wedding because we were worried they would cancel the wedding. If they stopped the wedding our Uma would have ended up as a spinster for the rest of her life. I would rather my Uma end up a spinster forever than go through the horrors some of these women go through. Why didn't I think before agreeing to Madhu's conditions? I immediately said yes, without a second thought.* With the exception of her mother-in-law, Avantika did not tell anyone else about her fears. *I have already lost my mental balance. What if my family are driven to suicide like some of the cases we've seen? I will not let this ruin their peace of mind. I can't sleep at night fearing for my Uma. I won't let them lose sleep over it too.* In the end Avantika's mother-in-law suggested to create a secret pot of money so they were prepared should another demand come. This provided some relief to Avantika's mind. Whenever she spotted loose coins on the floor, no matter the value of the change, Avantika would pick it up and add it to the pot of money. Similarly, any money left over from her weekly salary was also added.

After setting up the secret pot of money, Avantika initially refused to haggle over the price of items when buying them. *Haggling before I was associated with the Rathod family was ok, but now I have my reputation to think of. If people see me haggling over the prices of potatoes, what will they think of me? They will lose any respect they now have for my family.* However, after seeing a few more dowry related news stories, she forgot all about her prestige and began to haggle even if it meant saving two rupees. *Two more rupees to save for Uma.*

As the days passed, there were no further demands from Madhu for money. Each time she saw a dowry related story Avantika felt an increase in her tension. Nonetheless, as no request for money had come for over two months, she felt less worried. Avantika started to convince herself that the nightmares she was having would end. *It is traditional for a bride's family to pay for the wedding. Perhaps Madhuben just wanted a wedding for her son that suited their standards and that's why she made these demands. She just wanted the best for her son, like I want the best for my children. As for the honeymoon, maybe these big families consider the honeymoon as part of the wedding. High society girls don't want to associate with people who have middle class thoughts. I must accept their thoughts and traditions if I want a high status wife for Arjun.* Despite feeling a sense of calm, the only way Avantika's tension decreased when she saw a dowry news story, was by adding more money to the secret saving. Twenty four hours ago Avantika had seen another dowry related story in the newspaper, and as a result she stood in front of her mother-in-law to give her more money to save for Uma.

Avantika heard the phone ring. She gave a confused look to her mother-in-law and looked at the clock in the living room. *I have to leave for work in twenty minutes. Who is phoning at this time?* She walked over to the living room and picked up the phone.
"Hello?"
"Jai Shri Krishna Vehvanji."
Madhu! Why is she phoning now? Avantika's throat constricted. She became apprehensive.
"Jai Shri Krishna," Avantika said back.
Madhu and Avantika continued to talk for a few minutes. Avantika became slightly more confident as she listened to Madhu talking about their Holi. They discussed trivial matters for a few minutes before Madhu handed the phone over to Uma.
"Jai Shri Krishna Maa," Uma said.

Avantika felt a rush of affection for her daughter at the sound of her voice. She listened as Uma told her all about their family's Holi celebration. Uma told Avantika all about her life in Madhapar. As she listened to Uma tell her about her new life, Avantika gradually cleared her mind of the fears she nurtured over bride burnings. *Hai Mata Rani, my beti is happy. You blessed our family with enough wealth so that I could secure my daughter's happiness. Tara gana gana dhanyavaad Mata Rani.*

"After we played Holi together, my sasu gave me a brand new sari maa" Uma told Avantika.

My daughter has adjusted to her new family very quickly. Avantika became immensely proud of her daughter. *I have taught her well. The money we paid was worth every penny. Who say's people cannot buy happiness with money? My Uma is living like a Queen.*

"Uma I need to go to work soon, is there anything else or shall I put the phone down?"

"Maa," Uma paused. "Maa, my bedroom has become old. My sasu says she cannot have her son and bahu living in an ugly bedroom. She wants to refurbish my bedroom."

"Oh that sounds nice," said Avantika flatly. Her sense of foreboding began to rise again. The fears she had vacated her mind of, slowly began to stir again. *Hai Mata Rani they are about to ask for more money again. I know it.*

"They're paying for some of it," Uma said very quickly. "But they're a little bit short and wanted you to add the last bit so they could finish sooner."

Avantika took a deep breath. "How much do they want?"

"2 lakh rupees."

"HOW MUCH?" Avantika said loudly. "You could refurbish the entire house for that money"

"Maa..."

"Uma beti we don't..."

"Vevhanji," she heard Madhu say. Avantika immediately went silent and stopped half way through her sentence. Madhu had evidentially taken the phone off Uma. "Do you want your daughter to be happy?"

What kind of question is that? Do I want my beti to be happy.

"Ha vehvanji... our beti means a lot to us." Avantika ensured she kept

the anger out of her voice.
She is my beti's mother-in-law. She holds the reigns to my Uma's happiness. If I say anything to offend her she might take it out on Uma.
"We don't need to worry about Uma's happiness. We know your family will keep her happy."
"Vehvanji it is your responsibility, as much as it is ours to keep your beti happy. When Uma married you did not give any of the traditional gifts of beds or any furniture. We did not say anything," Madhu continued with a sweet voice. "Do not worry I will not ask you to go shopping and buy new furniture for us. Just give us the money. I understand it might be too much to arrange. We are reasonable people Avantika. Give us half now, and half later. Jai Shri Krishna."
Avantika attempted to reply to tell Madhu that she could not afford to give that much money. Before she could say anything, Avantika heard the dialling tone and realised that Madhu had put the phone down.

Avantika ran into her mother-in-law's room as fast as she could. Her mother-in-law was putting the money she had given to her into the savings pot. Avantika ran over to her mother-in-law and grabbed the pot out of her hand. She ignored her mother-in-law's questions and emptied the pot of money out onto her bed. She began to count the money. The total money was nowhere near the amount Madhu commanded. Avantika's heartbeat became faster. All of the fears that she had pushed to the back of her mind regenerated. *What if they hurt Uma because I don't have the money? Hai Mata Rani how am I going to arrange for this money? I don't even have a fourth of what Madhu wants.* She thought of a few options to try and secure some more money, unfortunately, each option seemed as unlikely each other. As her hopes of arranging the money began to diminish, her thoughts became more and more vivid. *What if I can't get the money together? 8,500 women every year! What if my Uma becomes one of them?* Avantika had a mental image in her mind. Uma was draped in a ripped red sari. Uma's body and hands were covered in burns and scars. She was unable to distinguish Uma's face as she had been so badly burnt. Her fears began to intensify and she sat on the floor breathing heavily.

Avantika did not realise that her mother-in-law had been calling her, trying to get her attention until her mother-in-law shook her. Avantika snapped out of her thoughts with a slight jump and looked at the hands that had grabbed her shoulders. She saw her mother-in-law's bare hands. *No bangles. I have a lot of jewellery and gold.* Without saying a word, Avantika stood up and ran into her own bedroom. She grabbed as much gold as she could. Without caring about her appearance or her attire she ran out of the house as quick as she could, in search of someone to buy her jewellery. Once Avantika sold the three jewellery sets and the gold chain she took with her, she went back home with the money she had made. *We're still a little short.* She went into her mother-in-law's room and fell to the floor crying.

"That Madhu knew what she was doing when she asked you for money after the wedding cards were distributed," Baa muttered.
"Baa we should have stopped Uma's wedding," Avantika said hysterically. "Vinod and I, we feared for Uma. If her wedding was cancelled people would have looked down on her. I couldn't bear the thought of ruining Uma's happiness over money. If we refused the demands, we would have been worried that no one will take Uma. Worrying about my beti remaining a spinster for life is better than worrying about how she is being treated. We should have stopped the wedding. Baa what if they kill..."
"Do not say inauspicious things Avantika," Baa interrupted angrily. "Do not even think about it."

Avantika heard Baa walk towards her wardrobe and watched as she rummaged through it. She returned a few minutes later and put something heavy on Avantika's lap. Avantika opened the package and saw a lot of jewellery on her lap. Avantika's mouth opened to see how beautiful the jewellery inside the package was. There were bangles, necklaces, rings and various other jewellery items. *This all belongs to Baa?*
"Baa?"
"Sell it! Sell it all."
Avantika looked at the jewellery in the package again. *Some of these pieces are so beautiful. They don't make them like this anymore. They must be really old. Some of these must have been gifts from Bapuji or*

even Baa's parents.
"Baa did Bapuji give these to you?"
"It does not matter. I have no need for any of them anymore. I'm a widow. Widows do not wear jewellery. I don't need these anymore. Sell them. Help Uma, she needs them more than I do," Baa paused for a while. "Forgive me for not giving these sooner. They were sentimental. Some of them were given by your father-in-law. Some were given by Vinod. Some belonged to my baa. I was going to give them to Gauri and Uma."
"We can't sell these Baa they..."
"If I do not sell these I might not have anyone to give them to. Take them."
Avantika took the jewellery with tears in her eyes. She could not find the words inside her to say thank you.
"Baa..."
"Don't make me a stranger by saying thank you. Uma is my beti too."
Avantika smiled at her mother-in-law. She was about to go and hug her when she jumped in shock. Someone pushed the door open and walked inside the bedroom. It was Arjun. He looked furious. *How long has he been standing there for? Has he heard everything?*
"Why are you crying maa?" Arjun asked.
"Oh," Avantika struggled to think of a lie. "I was cleaning. Dust allergy."
Dust allergy? You illiterate woman, since when did you have an allergy to cleaning you do it every day.
"Dust allergy, or Uma?"
Avantika looked at her son. She took a deep breath. *I don't want Arjun involved.* Avantika remembered another story she had seen on TV. A police man's family who extorted a girl for dowry put a false charge against the brother and put him in prison. They used his imprisonment as leverage to get money. *I can't have Arjun getting involved in this. I need to shield my family from people like them. Baa and I can sort everything. We have enough jewellery between us. Once Uma becomes pregnant they'll stop harassing us for their grandchild's happiness.*
"Maa don't try and think of another story. I've heard everything from outside. How much money do they want?" Arjun asked firmly.
He knows. Avantika felt a jolt to her heart. She began to cry again and told Arjun everything. Once she finished telling the story, Avantika saw

the look of anger on her son's face. Her sense of foreboding increased. *What if Arjun does something for revenge? It might get him into trouble or even worse, make matters deteriorate for Uma. If he gets involved he might go to prison and they may not have even planned to ruin Arjun's life.*

Arjun went over to his mother and took the package of jewellery out of her hand. He took it back to his grandmother.
"Dadi, put this away. You wanted to give these to Uma and Gauri. You won't sell them."
"But beta..." Baa began
"I'm going to sort it, dadi."
Sort it? What does he mean sort it? He might make things worse.
"Arjun what are you going to do?" Avantika asked worried.
"I'm going to take this money and give the money to Uma's in-laws tomorrow."
"Arjun it's not enough."
"I said I'll sort everything out tomorrow," Arjun said stiffly. "Trust me. I'll sort everything out."

Arjun took the money and left the bedroom. Avantika sat on her mother-in-law's bed for a while. *Arjun is hot headed, and sometimes he acts without thinking. I saw how angry he was when he took the money. What if he does something wrong? One wrong move and he could ruin Uma's life. If they send her back, then everything I've worked hard for the past few months will be ruined.* However, there was something else which worried Avantika just as much as Uma at this moment. *Uma's brother-in-law is a policeman. One wrong move and my son could end up in prison.*

That night Avantika tossed and turned, unable to sleep. Now she feared not just for Uma, but for Arjun as well.

Chapter 15: Uma

Uma lifted her hand to wave goodbye to her brother. However, he did not turn around and left without saying goodbye. Arjun came to give the money her mother-in-law asked for. Madhu's bullying finally compelled Uma to ask her family for money. She had not yet told her family or Vijay about the way Madhu behaved towards her. *She only uses harsh words against me. She was not violent towards me. I don't want to make a mountain out of an anthill. Vijay would laugh at me if I told him that his maa was calling me names. Sticks and stones...* Uma took a deep breath. *As for that slap, if I tell people about little things like slaps then I would just bring shame onto my family. My maa always slapped me when I was little. It didn't kill me; it taught me to be a better person. If I told maa about the slap she would just say to persevere and win her over with my love.*

Madhu's verbal tirade had hurt Uma more than the slap. Uma declined her demand for more money, which resulted in Madhu becoming more vicious. Firstly, Madhu had told Uma how her lower class parents were unworthy to be their relatives. Secondly, she told Uma that her nose was too big and was too ugly for her son. She even threatened Uma by telling her that if the money she wanted was not given she would find a new wife who was more suitable for Vijay. The impact of Madhu's word caused a lot of distress to Uma. She finally agreed to ask her parents for the money.

Uma recollected the phone conversation with her mother. Vijay's mother spent the entire time tapping and poking her. The few minutes she had to speak to her mother were overshadowed by Madhu's constant jabbering and coercion to ask for the money. She continued to whisper even when Uma began to ask for money. In the end, Madhu had snatched the phone from Uma's hand and asked herself. *I was not doing it right.* Uma thought bitterly. Instead of thanking Uma for her efforts and help to arrange for the money, her mother-in-law had simply glared at her. Her eyes were full of contempt. Once she finished staring at her,

Madhu simply walked off. After asking her mother for money, Uma expected the verbal abuse to stop. However, the past twenty four hours proved otherwise. Instead of criticising her looks and her class, Madhu was now criticising Uma's inability to do tasks properly.

Uma walked back into the house when Arjun vanished from sight. Just over an hour ago Arjun came over with the money to fulfil Madhu's request. He first entered the house and greeted Uma by hugging her. He then went over to Uma's mother-in-law and touched her feet. He got up and lifted the bag he was carrying and gave it to her mother-in-law.
"What is this beta?" Madhu asked, smiling sweetly at Arjun.
"The money you got my sister to ask for," Arjun replied without returning the smile.
He handed the bag of money to her. Madhu put her hand out to accept the money with a look of delight on her face. The moment Arjun let the bag go, her mother-in-law gasped in pain and dropped the bag onto the floor.
"My hand!" Madhu complained in agony.
"Sorry the bank didn't have enough money in notes," he lifted up the bag and handed it to her again. "This bag is full of 5 rupee coins. There is another bag with 5 rupee coins in the rickshaw outside and then one bag with notes. Come and get them. Let me know if there are any shortages."

"RAJA!" Madhu summoned the security guard of her home. "Take this bag to my room. Then bring the other bags from outside and take them to my room too."
Madhu smiled at Arjun.
"Would you like to have anything to eat or drink?"
"No, thank you." Arjun said in a polite tone.
"Oh you must beta. We cannot have you going back home without anything to eat or drink."
"I didn't bring any extra money," Arjun said curtly. "I won't be able to pay for eating or drinking anything."

Arjun's comment, wiped the smile off Madhu's face. He asked Uma to come and see him out. As they both walked to the rickshaw, the

conversation was one sided. He gave one word replies to all of Uma's questions. Once they reached Arjun's rickshaw he finally began to talk. He told Uma exactly what their mother and grandmother had gone through every time a demand for money came. Without mincing his words he told Uma about their mother and grandmother's fears. Uma was shocked to find out how much Vijay's mother was taking from her family. *Maa told me she was working for Arjun and Gauri's education. I thought Vijay paid for everything. Hai Mata Rani how much torture have my dadi and maa been through?*
"Your family needs to find other ways of financing their needs. They can't exploit maa and dadi anymore," was the final thing Arjun said to Uma before he got into his rickshaw.
Arjun told his driver to drive, and left without turning around to say bye.

Uma walked back into her house and walked to her bedroom, the only place she felt safe from her mother-in-law's abuse. *Hai Maa Durga, why did Maa and dadi hide everything they went through for me? Maa said they couldn't afford to pay for all of the wedding costs. I was the one who convinced Maa to pay for everything. When they said they could not afford it, I begged them to fulfil their demands. I didn't want anything to come in the way of my marriage to Vijay. I didn't even realise that I had taken away their peace of mind. I only thought about myself each time I convinced maa and bapuji. Hai Mata Rani please forgive me my sin.*

Uma walked around her bedroom lost in her thoughts. It was a while until she realised that night had fallen, and she was engulfed by darkness. She opened the window in her bedroom and saw the moon glowing in the sky. She smiled at herself when she remembered how her mother always told her the moon was her uncle. *Chanda Mama! Maa always said you'll watch over me.* Uma closed her eyes and took a deep breath. She remembered her mother's smile, each time she told her about Chanda Mama. The image, in her mind, of her mother's smile turned to an image of her mother crying. *There is only one way I can rectify the sin I have committed by bringing tears to maa's eyes. I need to stop them. I will never ask for more money again.* Uma remembered the savings she had from her job as a nurse. *I will use all of the money I have saved when I worked. By the time that money runs out I will have won them over and maaji will love me as her own beti. I have more to offer them than money. I will offer her my friendship, love and respect. Money is just material. Maaji would much rather have my friendship.*

As Uma planned how she would win over her mother-in-law, she heard a knock on the door which startled her. It was Charu. Uma invited Vijay's sister into her bedroom. Without saying anything else Charu got straight to the point.

"Mumma wanted me to tell you that Raja finished counting the money. There is 600 rupees less."

Part II: Brahmacharini (The Bearer of Hardships)

Chapter 16: Uma

It was mid-July and the monsoon season had started. Uma lay awake listening to the storm raging outside. The sound of raindrops falling on the roof and the roaring thunder kept her awake. She could see Vijay fast asleep next to her. Since her marriage, Uma had at least two sleepless nights a week. Uma's sleepless nights were normally due to Vijay working away from home to manage one of his hotels in Goa, Ahmedabad or Delhi. With a fourth hotel opening in Mumbai he was now spending more than two nights away, leaving Uma alone in Madhapar. Vijay's presence meant that Uma slept easier. This was not simply because he was a comfort to Uma, but also because she did not have to go to bed hungry.

Four months ago Uma decided that she would not ask her parents for any more money. That was the same day Arjun gave 600 rupees less than the amount her mother-in-law had requested. Without telling anybody else, Uma took money out of her own savings account and gave Madhu the missing money. Eight weeks ago, once more, Vijay's mother started to harass Uma for more. Uma stuck to the promise she had made to herself. She did not ask her parents for any more money. Her bank account was now almost empty but her mother-in-law's demands did not seem to be ceasing. The never ending demands for cash began to stress Uma out. To end the constant pestering, Uma lied to Vijay's mother and told her that she would ask her parents for money. Without actually speaking to her parents, Uma told Madhu that her parents were unable to fulfil the demands due to financial constraints. She also added that her parents would try to get the money together as soon as they could. That night Vijay's mother got their cook to make chicken curry. Uma opened all of the pots to find the vegetarian dish prepared for her. Once she had opened all of the pots, she heard Vijay's mother clear her throat. Uma looked towards her and saw a smile on her face. "I have a new house rule. It is too costly to make different food for different people. From today we will all eat the same meal, or not eat at all," Vijay's mother announced. "You will either eat what has been prepared, or you will go to bed hungry."

Uma knew the rule had been passed as punishment for not bringing the money that Madhu wanted. *Before I married, I used to fast all the time. I am used to remaining hungry. I can handle the hunger until maaji forgets about this new rule.* Three weeks after the announcement of the rule, her mother-in-law showed no signs of relenting. Meat dishes were being cooked more and more, especially with Vijay working away from home. Uma noticed that when Vijay was home, his mother would tell their chef to make a vegetarian side dish along with the meat dish. However, when he was away from home, there were many nights when there would be no vegetarian option for Uma. One night Vijay's mother only ordered meat for dinner.
"I wish we had more money," Madhu commented. "Then we could have more food variety." Madhu said directing the comment towards Uma by looking straight into her eyes when she spoke.

I know that comment was directed towards me. She was discreetly telling me that I won't eat properly until she gets the money she wants. Uma turned to the other side and continued to listen to the sound of the raindrops. As Vijay was currently in Madhapar she had eaten well that night. Nonetheless, she still lay awake, not because of the storm, but because of the bad news Vijay gave to her. Earlier that day, he told Uma that he would be working away from home for four months.
"There is so much work to be done with the new hotel I am opening in Mumbai. I need to be as close to the project as possible to make sure everything runs smoothly."
"Please take me with you Vijay," Uma had begged her husband in desperation. "Don't leave me here, take me with you."
Uma was worried about spending such a long time without Vijay. Not only would she have to contend with his mother's behaviour, but she would not see the man she loved for such a long time. *How will I cope with Vijay being away for four months? I already hate it when he is away from me for two or three days, but four whole months? I won't feel his strong arms around me, or the sensation of his lips on mine. I won't have the security I feel with him around. I will lose the only person who cares about me in Madhapar. Hai Mata Rani, please help me to convince him to*

take me with him.
Vijay had kissed Uma on her forehead and hugged her.
"My gulab, the Mumbai hotel is the biggest hotel I am making. There is a lot of work to be done. Every second of my time and energy will go towards constructing and setting everything up for the grand opening," He held her hand and kissed her on the forehead again. "You will get lonely there. You won't know anyone there or have anywhere to live. In four months time, once everything is ready, we will both move to Mumbai and live there. Our children will grow up in the city and receive the best possible education. Their future will be in the city of dreams. But we can only do that once the hotel is completed. I am sorry to do this to you, but I have to ask you to go through some difficulties for our and our children's futures."

Mumbai! That is the ray of light I am looking for in this darkness. Moving to Mumbai will resolve all of my problems. I will be free of maaji's rules and her bitter words. She won't be able to make constant demands when I am not living with her. Vijay and I will live our lives in the city of dreams far away from her. Our children will have everything they could ever dream of. With the incentive of becoming free from her mother-in-law in four months, Uma agreed to let Vijay go.

Uma got out of bed and walked over to the window and watched the rain. Seeing the monsoon rain always put her mind at ease. However, thinking about the third of a year she would spend without Vijay made her feel uncomfortable. Suddenly Uma remembered the story of Durga's second form; Brahmacharini. Her mother had told her that in her form of Brahmacharini, she underwent many hardships to attain her goal. She fasted on very little food, trekked through the harsh winds of the Himalayas and lived as an ascetic to win Shiva as her husband. Once she overcame the hardships and tribulations she attained her goal. Brahmacharini attained Shiva as her husband. Once her hardships ended, she lived in endless bliss. *Hai mata Brahmacharini, give me the strength to bear all of the hardships that will come my way over the next few months.*

Uma closed her eyes and saw a mirage of what her life would be like when they moved to Mumbai. The mansion in Mumbai was bigger and grander than Rathod Haveli. There was a little boy and girl dressed in expensive Indian clothing laughing with their father. Uma served her family a vegetarian meal that she had cooked with the help of their personal chef. *Once I prove I am able to overcome all of the hardships, I will get the happiness I deserve.*

Chapter 17: Madhu

"Please come with your whole family," Madhu said, as she gave Purbai an invitation card to Charu's engagement.
"Thank you," Purbai said. "We will all come, and please congratulate Charu."
"I will. Charu will be pleased to have you all there."
"I have just made some chai, come and have some," Purbai told Madhu.
"Not now Purbai, next time; I have many things to do before the engagement."
"It must be very tiring to have another wedding so soon, Madhuben!"
"If Harshad was still here today I would not be as worried about Charu's wedding. There is so much to do when a daughter gets married, and a beti's wedding is very expensive."
"But you have two sons who are both very successful. Jigar and Vijay will help you. You have nothing to worry about, Madhuben."
"So much of Vijay's money is invested in his business for now," Madhu began to boast. "He has opened a brand new 5 star hotel in Mumbai. It is for all of the rich people who visit Mumbai. My sons could pay for Charu's wedding like this," she clicked her fingers. "But a mother's heart still worries."
"At least this time you have Uma to help. You won't be burdened with all of the work women have to do for the wedding."
"Yes you're right. Jai Shree Swaminarayan Purbai, I am late." Madhu put her hands together.
"Jai Shree Swaminarayan," Purbai said as Madhu began to leave.

Madhu began to walk home. *Purbai thinks that ox will help reduce the burden. She has been married to my Vijay for eight months and she is still useless.* In less than two minutes Madhu walked into her living room. Tired from inviting the neighbours to her daughter's engagement ceremony, she sat down. She remembered what she said to Purbai about Harshad. She looked at the garlanded photograph of her dead husband. *When you were alive, you were always too busy making plans to lead India to pay any attention to me. When we first married I pined every day for you to give me some time. By the time you finally left politics I had built my own life which did not include giving you any importance. I had built my own life that revolved around our children. I never realised your importance in my life until after your death. The day you died, I was stripped of my bindi. I had to shatter my bangles and throw out my jewellery. My wardrobe was emptied of the beautiful saris I owned, replaced by plain pastel colours worn by widows.*

Madhu recalled how a few months after her husband's death she slowly started to refill her life with colours. Once more she began to wear jewellery and stunning saris which many widows were denied the right to wear. Some people in society had judged Madhu because a widow was supposed to wear plain saris and no jewellery. Madhu refused to allow society to dictate what she could and could not do as a widow. She had seen many widows wearing what they wanted to after their husband's deaths and she was going to be one of them.

I brought the colours back into my life. However, the day you died, I realised I lost the security that came with being a married woman. You left all the money and property in Jigar and Vijay's names. I was left without a single rupee to my name. The idea that she owned nothing had filled her with fear. Madhu realised that everything she once owned now belonged to her sons and their future wives. *If Vijay or Jigar's wives decide they do not want me around anymore they might kick me out or leave me at a widow's ashram. If I am lucky I might be given a corner in the house to sleep in, but would have to fight for my own rights with no wealth in my name.* Madhu had made a promise to herself that day. *I refuse to end up in a widow's ashram. I will make sure that I have the upper hand when Vijay and Jigar marry.*

As Madhu recollected the promise she made to herself, she momentarily looked away from her husband's photograph and contemplated how well she had done to ensure she held the power in her own home. *I made sure that I got the upper hand when Uma came into this house. If she had become more powerful than me, she might have thrown me out or made me a servant in my own home. I would have been left with nothing. No home, no money and no family. The fact that she did not bring a dowry gave me ammunition against her and now I have won. She is the one who is my servant and I will never allow her to overpower me.*

Madhu returned her gaze to her husband's picture again. *These last few days I have once again realised what your death has meant.*

Two months ago, Charu informed her family that she had fallen in love with a man named Rajan. She also expressed that they both wished to marry. Madhu had been delighted that her daughter was going to marry a man she loved. *I always wanted Charu to marry for love and not a business exchange like my marriage. Hai Bhagwan make sure Charu is happy forever and let no one's evil eye affect her happiness.* Madhu met with Rajan's family. They were happy with the alliance and both set a date for their children's engagement. Madhu spoke to both Jigar and Vijay to find out if they could help support the costs of Charu's wedding. Jigar agreed to help by contributing money towards all of the ceremonies. Vijay, on the other hand, could not supply any money. His finances were tied up with the construction and opening of his hotel. He had taken a large loan to fulfil the execution of the hotel and until he repaid the loan, he could not help fund the wedding. The news Vijay was unable to subsidise the wedding, came as a blow to Madhu. *What if I cannot fulfil Charu's dream wedding? She has been planning her wedding since the day I gave her the bride and groom doll set.*

What Madhu worried about more than Charu's wedding was the dowry. She knew that Jigar earned enough money to fulfil most of Charu's dream wedding. The thing that bothered her the most was the fact that the Mehta family declared that they did not want a dowry and would be happy to take Charu without one.

I waited for the right moment to make my demands at Vijay's marriage. Once Avantika sent out the wedding cards I knew there was no going back because of how people would react towards a girl whose marriage was cancelled. If Uma became a tarnished woman no one would accept her. I played my moves carefully and checkmated Uma's family into fulfilling my demands. Now that it was her own daughter getting married Madhu felt very uncomfortable. *What if the Mehta family play the same game I played? I do not have a single rupee to my name. Vijay and Jigar would not be able to fulfil any dowry demands.* Madhu took a deep breath. She could only think of one source of financial income to secure her daughter's future: *Uma's parents.*

Chapter 18: Charu

Charu looked out of her bedroom window and saw the large white marquee in their courtyard. *Today is the first step I will take to becoming a proper woman.* Charu's mother always told her that a woman is blessed the day she marries and the day she becomes a mother. She turned around and saw the two dolls which lay on her bed. The bride and groom dolls were given to Charu on her fourth birthday. She called the bride Charu and the groom Lado, the Gujarati word for groom. Four months ago she gave Lado a new name: Rajan. Charu put the dolls down and picked up a notebook which contained photo clippings of brides and weddings. The scrapbook even contained photos of handsome grooms on white horses. She started to make the scrapbook when she was old enough to buy her own magazines.

After getting dressed, Charu walked into the large tent in which she and Rajan were going to have their official engagement ceremony. *Wow this looks so beautiful.* Charu admired the marigold flowers and the fairy lights which were used to decorate the marquee. The purple lilies used as part of the centre piece for the tables matched the colour of Charu's heavily embroidered engagement dress. The engagement ceremony united two families by the exchange of auspicious gifts. *Rajan's sisters have good fashion sense. I cannot wait to see the sari and jewellery they have picked for me.*

Charu sat on one of the chairs, on the raised platform, at the front of the marquee. There was an empty chair next to hers, which Rajan would fill. She remembered Rajan's proposal as she waited for him to arrive. She lied to her mother by telling her she was revising with Suneeti, her college friend, and would have to stay the night. In reality both she and Rajan went to the White Desert of Kutch. They rented out a hotel room where they spent the night. Once the sun set, they both went out into the desert. It was a full moon night. The White Desert was not made from sand but salt. The grains of salt glimmered in the moonlight. As the Rann of Kutch sparkled around her, Rajan got onto one knee and proposed. Charu instantly said yes and now they were getting engaged the traditional Gujarati way.

Charu's heart leapt when she knew Rajan arrived. She did not see him enter because the welcome ceremony happened at the threshold of their home, but she heard the dhol players which indicated his arrival. A few minutes later he entered the marquee followed by his family. He walked over to Charu with a big grin on his face. Charu's heart fluttered at the smile on Rajan's face. He was followed by his family, some of them bearing gifts. Rajan's mother and father held the sari they selected for Charu and draped her with it. *It is a gorgeous sari. I knew his sisters have classy taste.* Once the gifts had been exchanged, the part of the ceremony that Charu dreaded most started. *Yuck! I hate warm milk! I don't even drink milk when mumma warms it up for me. I should have had milkshake instead.* She looked at the sweetened milk mixed with pistachio, turmeric and sugar. *I will make an exception today. Drinking this milk is auspicious and takes away bad luck. I do not want any bad luck casting a shadow on my life.* Charu and Rajan both held a glass of the warm milk in their hands. They both crossed their hands over and fed each other with milk. Charu expected the milk to taste horrible and was able to keep herself composed when she drank it. However, the milk ceremony was far from over. Two by two, the guests came to feed them both milk. Fortunately, Charu felt that she had already fulfilled tradition and ended the bad luck. As a result, she pretended to drink the milk each time someone came to feed her. Rajan introduced her to his family and she introduced him to everyone from her side.

Finally the time for family photos arrived. Rajan and Charu's families both stood together in the photo. Uma stood on Charu's left. It had been a while since she saw Uma properly. *She looks a lot thinner than she was when she married. I should be a fussy eater like her and lose weight before my wedding. I need to start dieting so I can look good for my wedding.* As soon as she thought of the diet she remembered the extravagant engagement party which followed the ceremony. The ceremony in the marquee was attended only by close family and friends but her family invited everyone they knew to the engagement party. This included Jigar and Vijay's friends and business partners. Her mother even invited Purbai and the other neighbours. *There will be such variety of delicious dishes tonight. I will start the diet tomorrow.*

Chapter 19: Alice

Alice stepped off the plane and stepped into Mumbai airport. She closed her eyes and inhaled. *If I was blind I'd still know I was in India. It still smells of mothballs.* It had been fourteen months since Alice last visited India. She fell in love with the country and was now back after leaving her old job in London. *I'm back to start a new life in a country where they worship women.*

Alice hoped things in India would be different. She hated working at the estate agent in London. She was one of two women employed by the company. Her sales figures were higher than most of her male colleagues but she still missed out on promotions. On two separate occasions, a male colleague with less experience was promoted over her. If she did not present herself in a certain way, with heels and a skirt, the manager reprimanded her for not dressing professionally enough. She hated the way the male estate agents described their sex lives and the sluts they fucked when they were out. She detested the sexist jokes they made, the worst of which were rape jokes. She had to tolerate lewd whispers about her appearance and body. Sometimes it was supposed to be banter between the customers and the other agents. At times it was laddish laughs between the agents. *I was supposed to be flattered. The fact that I felt self-conscious about my appearance every day because of it was apparently my problem. My manager's face when I quit was a picture. He looked as though his balls had been squeezed tight. With me gone, with my supposed lesser experience, I'd love to see him continue to sell as many properties.* The worst part of her job was showing potential buyers properties. When she showed some male customers the bedroom there was generally some vile comment about trying out the bed to make sure it worked. When Alice discussed her discomfort in these situations she was told to develop a thicker skin as it was part and parcel of her job.

Alice walked towards the immigration check desks. *I don't need to think about all of those dicks in England anymore. I don't have to tolerate their bullshit anymore. I now own a hotel. It is a new beginning for me and my boyfriend.*

Alice met her boyfriend in India eighteen months ago. They met when she had gone for a trip to the beach. Her rickshaw driver accidentally hit a motorbike and injured the biker. After helping him out at the hospital they became friends. He travelled with her to various places in India, and they slowly fell in love. In Mysore, Alice found out that he was married. The revelation left her devastated. In anger, she threw a tub of moisturiser at him and told him she never wanted to see him again. She packed her bags and sat on the street crying feeling severely betrayed. Fortunately, he found her on the street and begged for the chance to explain himself. Alice was reluctant to listen to him but he had been very persistent. To get rid of him, she gave him five minutes.

"I was forced into an arranged marriage," he told Alice.
She had immediately stopped crying and began to listen.
"I was given no choice in the matter. My parents just forced me into it. There are no feelings between me and my wife. We don't have sex, we just share a bedroom and a family. I don't even talk to her."
Her anger quickly evaporated and transformed into pity. *Imagine being forced into a relationship you don't want to be in? The poor girl was forced to marry a man she doesn't love and he has to live with a woman he probably hates. I could never do it. If my mum or dad suggested such a thing I'd leave home.*

"If I declined the marriage, or end it now, my family would disown me. I love you but they would never accept you because you're white."

As Vijay spoke to her, Alice remembered how her brother, Alex, had been disowned by their parents. *Alex told mum and dad he was gay and they kicked him out. He would have been left homeless if it was not for the welfare state. The weakness of the Indian welfare state is why my boyfriend is another woman's husband. He can't help it. If the Indian government supported people then he wouldn't be forced into a marriage he doesn't want to be in.* The sympathy she felt meant that her fury vanished. She let him into her life and once again they began to get closer to each other.

After leaving the airport, Alice got into a taxi to make her way to the hotel. She looked out of the taxi window. Despite having been to Mumbai before, the poverty and slums that existed in Mumbai still shocked her. Both slums and mansions surrounded the airport. There was a grand white mansion with a red slated roof, surrounded by palm trees and black and gold gates. Just outside the mansion there were six or seven tiny shacks. They were held up with rope, metal sheets and tarpaulin. Little children prepared their lunch a few centimetres away from the gutter which drained urine and excrement.

Alice's taxi finally got into the city centre where she would be working. The place became denser. It was still dirty but cleaner than the outskirts. Alice's taxi pulled up outside the hotel she would be working at. The construction of the hotel had only just been completed. She saw photos before she arrived, but seeing the finished project with her own eyes was mesmerising. *Oh my god! It looks amazing!* There were fountains on each side of the door entrance. A red carpet on top of marble steps led the guests to the reception desk where they could check in. On top of the double glass doors a black sign with gold letters read "Hotel Rathod."

Chapter 20: Uma

Uma dipped the ring finger of her right hand into the red kumkum paste. She made a dot on Vijay's forehead. *Hai Mata Rani, keep my husband safe from harm.* Since Vijay's announcement that he was going to Mumbai for four months, Uma had very little opportunity to spend time with her husband. The whole family were extremely busy in the lead up to Charu's engagement ceremony. After the ceremony, Uma hoped to make their final night together memorable. However, the sex was over very quickly, and Vijay rolled over and fell asleep. Feeling she did not have the opportunity to say goodbye properly, Uma stood in front of her husband as she prepared to send him off. She forced herself to stay strong, and withheld her tears. *I will see him again in four months. I shouldn't be too sentimental and cry in front of maaji.* Uma could feel her throat tighten from the tears she was holding back. She repeated the fact that she would see him again in four months again and again in her mind.

The entire family was going to drop Vijay off to Bhuj airport.
"We will leave in twenty minutes," Madhu announced. "Anyone who wishes to come should get ready. We will not wait for anyone."
Uma looked at the time and quickly ran upstairs to get ready to leave the house. When she went out in Mandavi, she could dress in simple clothes. As the daughter-in-law of the Rathod family, she was expected to dress appropriately. Uma rushed to ensure she looked reasonable in Madhu's eyes. *I don't want maaji to shout at me for being late. I need to start doing as she says now. If I give maaji no reason to complain then my four months without Vijay will be easy.*

Uma was ready within fifteen minutes and went downstairs to wait with Vijay. The house was silent. She could not hear anyone. Confused, she checked the time on her phone. *There are still five minutes left before maaji said they were leaving.* Uma heard the sound of a plate clatter in the dining room. She walked over to the dining room assuming they were all eating more of the food Uma cooked for Vijay's leaving lunch.

However, the noise was only Leela tidying up.
"Leela, where did everyone go?" Uma asked her friend.
"They left one minute ago. Madhuji..."
Without waiting for Leela to finish, Uma ran out of the dining room. *They must be waiting for me in the courtyard ready to leave. Maaji will definitely shout at me if I'm late.* Uma ran as fast as her feet would take her. *They won't have left without me.* When Uma went out into their courtyard she saw no car waiting for her. She began to walk as fast as she could towards the gates to their mansion. *They might be waiting outside, ready to leave as soon as I get in the car.* The closer she got to the gates, the less likely it seemed to her that they were waiting outside. Tears began to fall from her eyes. *You left me without saying goodbye Vijay.* Uma left the parameters of her house and realised the car was gone. She stood there for a few moments hoping she would hear a sound telling her where they were, but other than the children in the neighbourhood, Uma could hear nothing. Crestfallen, she walked back into the house.

Uma stood alone in the huge living room. *He left without saying goodbye! Why did he do that? He always tells me how much he loves me, and he couldn't even wait for me.* She took a deep breath and recalled his promises to take her to Mumbai to start a new life. *Perhaps he had to leave without saying bye because of some problem. Maybe they misread the ticket time and his flight was much earlier than he thought.*

Uma heard footsteps enter the living room. It was Leela.
"Uma didi, I was telling you that Madhuji said they were late," she told Uma. "Madhuji said there was not enough space for everyone in the car. Whoever was already downstairs when they left got to go and drop off Vijay sir."
"Did Vijay ask for me?"
"He said he should come and say bye to you."
He did ask for me! Uma felt relieved. *He didn't just go without thinking about me.*
"Madhuji said they were going to miss the plane and had to leave immediately."
I knew that woman would be behind it. She is the only one responsible

for all my problems since I came to Madhapar.

Uma smiled at Leela before she began to walk towards her bedroom. Her temporary relief had been replaced by feelings of resentfulness and bitterness. *I'm Vijay's wife. I had more right to go with him than any of the others.* She closed her eyes and concentrated on breathing to hold in her tears. *I don't want Leela to think I am crying over little issues. What will people think of me if I cry over small matters?* Uma wanted to be alone so that she could shed as many tears as she wanted in private.

"Uma didi, they were wrong," she heard the softness in Leela's voice. "You have every right to be upset. They should have taken you."
"You do not think I am overacting by being upset over little things?" Uma turned around to face Leela.
"Illa. They should have waited for you. If the others did not think about you, at least Vijay sir should have. If he loves you, he should say bye properly."

If? What does she mean if?
"Vijay does love me," Uma defended Vijay. "He always tells me how much he loves me. He treats me like a queen when his maa..." Uma paused.
Saying bad things about maaji would be a betrayal of my family. Uma silenced herself and turned away from Leela once again.
"My husband respects his maa, like every good beta should," Uma paused for a second. "When his new hotel is complete he is going to take me to Mumbai to live with him. She won't come with us and we will both be very happy."
"I hope Guruvayur Swamy completes your wish." Leela smiled and walked back into the kitchen.
Uma stood in the living room. *Maaji is the root of the problem. She poisons everyone against me and conspires against me. Maa always said when you marry you have to accept his family as part of the package. I have to accept her venom if I want to fulfil my duty of being a good wife to Vijay. Hai Mata Rani please let Vijay's hotel get finished quickly. I will have the strength to tolerate her when she is in Madhapar and we are both in Mumbai.*

Chapter 21: Leela

I am just a maid! What right do I have to question Uma about Vijay and his actions? Leela finished the washing up in the kitchen. She saw many parallels between her parents' relationship and Uma's marriage. *Uma didi tries to justify everything Vijay does. She makes excuses for his incompetency. She magnifies his small acts as a sign that he must love her. I spent many years watching amma do the same thing when acha treated her badly.* Leela began to clean the kitchen surfaces. *I know they will ruin her life. Vijay and his family see Uma didi as an ATM machine. My parents too saw me as an item to bring them lots of money. Then my in-laws thought I was a baby machine.* She scrubbed the kitchen surfaces really hard, venting her frustration onto Madhu's kitchen counters. *O Guruvayur Swamy please give her the strength to keep smiling. Make her strong too so she can deal with the pain they will give to her.*

I have never been in love, or been loved, but I do know if he loved Uma he would defend her. Leela had observed Vikram and Amrita Oberoi's relationship. *They love each other! They laugh together; they enjoy spending time with each other. They could not bear to be apart for four months. Vikramji even defends Amritaji when someone is unfair to her. He moved to Gujarat to protect Amritaji. I have seen Madhu treat Uma didi badly in front of Vijay. He sits and does nothing. He is like acha; when amma was upset he would console her, and for a few weeks amma would remain pleased and ignore his rubbish. Vijay is devilish like his amma. He gives Uma enough to delude her into thinking that loves her. Uma didi is blinded by her love for a man who is using her for his own benefit. I always knew I was being used by the people who bought me because I wasn't blindfolded by love. I always knew my position.*

Leela had a lot of faith in Guruvayur Swamy. She believed he had disguised himself as a robber so that her path and Amrita's paths could merge. *He vanished as soon as we both met each other. O Guruvayur Swamy, you saved my life when I had no one else. Help Uma didi see the*

light. If the gossip is true then Vijay had another... Leela stopped mid thought. She could hear voices in the house. She felt adrenaline rush through her, worried about who was in the house. When she listened closely she heard Madhu's voice. Leela gave a sigh of relief. She then heard the voices of Jigar and Charu. Charu was telling her mother about her extravagant wedding plans. Leela rolled her eyes and stopped working for a few seconds to listen to the conversation. *Why do rich people waste so much panam on one day? The panam could be saved and put towards something that will benefit both of them.*
"I want this sari mumma," Charu pointed to photograph in a magazine.
"Charu beti, 35,000 rupees?" Madhu said sounding worried. "And an elephant? Charu beti, you know that your brother's money is all tied up in his hotels. We have to be sensible. We can have a grand wedding that no one in Kutch has ever seen before, but do you need an elephant and a white horse?"
Pointless waste of money.
"Mumma, it is my dream wedding. I have planned it for years. I've been planning it ever since you gave me the bride and groom dolls. If you want the dreams I have nurtured for years to be ruined then ok."
What a manipulative girl. She knows her amma will do anything for her. My amma did not even fight to stop my acha selling me. I could not manipulate her even if I wanted. We were both helpless.
"I think we can find a way to make sure you get everything."
"Thanks mumma, you're the best mumma in the world," Charu ran up to her mother and hugged her. Madhu had a big grin on her face.
That woman has spoilt her children.
"Uma Bahu," Leela heard Madhu shout.
Ende Ammo! She is going to ask Uma for more panam to fulfil Charu's demands.
"We will need help from your parents for Charu's wedding."

Leela stopped listening and returned to scrubbing the work surfaces. She already knew how the conversation would end. Madhu would coerce Uma, who would eventually agree. *Now that Vijay has gone, Uma will do everything that witch tells her to do. This is why she didn't spin her words like she normally does. With Vijay gone, Madhu can do things her way.*

Chapter 22: Alice

Within an hour of reaching Hotel Rathod, Alice finished unpacking and showered. She then sat in her brand new office attempting to do some work. *I can't believe I have gone from being an employee at a shitty estate agent to being the co-owner of a five star hotel.*

Alice looked through the spreadsheet with the room bookings and saw that many of the rooms were already filled. *We've only been open a week and already we're doing much better than we had expected. If I continue playing my cards right then I'll be richer than those bellends that I used to work for.* She looked up from the computer screen and saw their receptionist, Fatima, hand the keys over to the new guests checking in. Seeing the newly married couple all over each other made her feel sexually frustrated. *Oh god, I've not had any since he visited me in London for three nights and that was six months ago.* Alice made the most of their time together before he returned to India to be with his family. *I need to distract myself for a few hours more.* She turned her attention to the email inbox. *I'll get what I want when he gets here in a couple of hours. I've waited six months, I can wait a bit longer.*

The telephone rang. Alice saw that Fatima was still speaking to the guests so she answered the call.
"Hotel Rathod, Mumbai. Alice speaking, how may I help?"
The caller enquired about costs of the hotel rooms.
"A double bedroom is 10,500 rupees per night, this includes a continental breakfast. It's 10,000 rupees without the breakfast. If you book a week in advance it's 8,500 rupees and breakfast is free."
Alice became flustered when the caller said he would like to make a booking. She only just started and did not know how to use the system. She passed the phone over to Fatima, and watched her book the reservation for three nights. *That's almost five hundred quid and in India it'll go really far!*
Delighted the business was going well, Alice left Fatima on the reception desk and went to sit in the office.

"Fatima, I'm going to go back and finish responding to emails."

Alice put the blinds down from the window in their door. She had no intention of checking emails. She felt exhausted from the journey from England to India. She watched some trending videos on YouTube to distract herself and keep sex out of her mind. She saw a Bollywood music video of a couple dancing on Goa beach. The video stirred memories of Alice's first time with her boyfriend; they were in Goa when they first had sex together.

After recovering from being knocked off his bike, Alice phoned him to make sure he was OK. They started talking and she revealed that her next stop was Goa. He told her about his hotel in Goa and invited her to stay for free. When she arrived at the hotel, he was waiting there to surprise her. They spent a lot of time together and he even showed her around. They had sex on their third night in Goa and that was where everything started. For the remainder of her four months in India, they travelled to some places together. Sometimes he would leave to sort out his business but after a few days he usually returned to her. She was in Mysore when she found out about his wife. It was in the peaceful surroundings of Hampi she realised she loved him. *We confessed that we loved each other in Hampi and then I had the most mind blowing fuck that I've ever had.* Despite her efforts to stop thinking about sex, Alice could not help herself as she remembered all of the times she had spent with her boyfriend.

An hour or so later, Alice heard the door open. She saw her boyfriend stood in the doorway. *Damn! He looks so fucking hot in a suit.* She jumped up and went to hug him. She felt his arms around her. *He's been working out since I last saw him.* The moment her hands were around his neck, he kissed her. Feeling his soft lips on hers gave Alice a warm sensation. He closed the door behind him as he walked into the office. Alice grabbed his tie and led him over to the desk behind her. As it was their first day in the office there was not much on the desk. However, Alice dashed whatever was on the desk onto the floor. He lifted her onto her desk and undid his flies. They had hot passionate sex on the desk in their office. *It was definitely worth the wait. He's so good.*

When she climaxed she could not help but scream out his name.

“Oh Vijay.”

Chapter 23: Charu

If you live in a house made of glass then you do not throw stones. Who does she think she is? Who is she to question the wedding outfit I have chosen? Charu was furious with Uma who had come to her bedroom a few minutes ago. Uma told her that the wedding outfit she wanted was too expensive. Uma also said how they could buy ten or eleven beautiful outfits for the amount Charu wanted to spend on one. Charu snapped back at Uma to remind her about her own extravagant wedding before storming out of the room to speak to her mother. She stood in the dining room complaining about Uma to her mother, who was the only person listening.

"Her parents conned us. They sent her to our home empty handed, without anything in dowry. Just because you didn't ask for anything does not mean they send her with nothing. Now she thinks she can question my expenses. Who is she? Where did Vijay find her?"

Once she finished complaining, Charu sat down and began to open the dishes to see the food being served for dinner. *Oh, everything is vegetarian. I hoped for non-veg today. Maybe starving her would shut her up.*

"Mumma why is there no meat today?"

"Uma bahu is bringing 40,000 rupees today," her mother replied dully. "This is her reward."

"Oh, is that the money for my wedding?" Charu asked enthused. "My friend Tanvi's brother paid for her entire wedding and Uma is being stingy about having to pay for part of it."

"Charu beti, the Ox came here empty handed, so I have told her that she will contribute to your wedding. She will bring the money today. Do not worry."

When Charu saw Uma coming down the stairs, she tutted and rolled her eyes. Once Uma sat down Charu looked at her mother. *Ask her for my money then.*

"Leela! Dinner." Leela came in and followed Madhu's order.

Uma took a bit of everything onto her plate. *Why is mumma not asking?* Charu looked at her mother who watched Uma as though she was captivated by an interesting television programme. *What's so interesting about her?* She looked at Uma and saw her tear some roti with her right hand. She dipped it into her curry and began to bring her hand closer to her mouth. As Uma opened her mouth to eat the food, Charu heard her mother's voice.
"Uma bahu, did you get the money that Charu needs for the wedding?"
"I did ask," Uma said quietly. "But they do not have any money to spare at the moment."

Charu gave an irritated sigh. Unable to contain herself she burst out "Siya's parents would have arranged the money immediately."
The moment she mentioned Siya, Charu saw the look of fury on her mother's face. *Oh shit, mumma said I should never talk about Siya again.* Uma opened her mouth with a confused look, perhaps to ask who Siya was. Before Uma could say anything Charu's mother spoke.
"They did not have the money?"
"No but they will try and arrange for it as soon as they can," Uma responded. "They are in debt right now and cannot promise anything."
"Debt? Cannot promise anything?" Charu heard her mother repeat dangerously.
Uma broke eye contact from Madhu and looked to the ground. *She is lying. What a rubbish excuse.* Charu pushed her plate away too agitated to eat her own dinner. However, she jumped up in fright when she heard the sound of a crash and scream. The scream belonged to Uma. She looked around and saw that her mother had thrown Uma's dinner onto the floor.
"Jigar explain to this Ox who Monty is."
"Err..." Jigar looked confused. "Monty was our pet dog. He died two years ago."

Charu saw her mother stand up and walk to Uma. Her mother grabbed Uma by the hair and Charu recoiled at the sight of Uma's hair being grabbed. Charu ran her fingers through her own hair, as if to protect her hair from being pulled. *What is mumma doing? She will rip out Uma's hair if she's not careful.* Uma stood up to avoid her hair being pulled more. Her eyes were squinting with pain. Her mother then pushed Uma to the ground, who screamed again. Charu winced as Uma hit the floor. She felt uncomfortable by Uma's pain and looked away. "Our dog Monty did not pay anything towards the running of this house. He lived off everything we gave to him out of our generosity. You came here empty handed, like a dog." Her mother said to Uma scathingly. Her mother bent down to Uma's level. "If you are going to behave like a dog then you can live like one as well. Monty ate his dinner off the floor. Go on then... eat your dinner."

Uma did not move for a moment, her eyes were filled with tears.
"EAT IT THEN!" Madhu shouted at Uma.
Uma jumped with shock and picked up some chapatti and dipped it into the daal scattered over the floor and ate the morsel of food. Charu was still annoyed at Uma's audacity for questioning her choice. *At least mumma is allowing her to eat. Mumma could have sent her to bed hungry.*

After watching Uma's helplessness for a few moments, Charu's anger vanished slightly. She began to feel some sympathy for Uma. Watching Uma eat caused her to feel nauseous. *How can mumma stand there and watch this?* Charu, unable to continue watching Uma being forced to eat her dinner off the floor, grabbed her plate and walked to the kitchen. She stood in the kitchen and completed her meal there. *She deserves to be punished for her selfish attitude, but mumma is being too strict. She does not deserve to be treated like a dog.*

Chapter 24: Uma

Hai Mata Rani, if this is how bad things are now, how much worse will they get before Vijay returns? Uma recalled how two nights ago Madhu had forced her to eat her dinner off the floor. Since then only meat had been cooked. As a result of Madhu's house rules, there was no food for Uma. *Even if I wanted to eat the meat, I wouldn't be able to. They only cook enough food for three.* Uma closed her eyes and thought of goddess Brahmacharini. *Hai Mata Rani, only you know how many more days that woman will starve me for. Please give me strength to keep going until Vijay comes back for me. You tolerated snowstorms, the wrath of your mother, obstacles from demons and more to attain Lord Shiva as your husband. Give me the strength to follow in your footsteps.* Uma ran her fingers through her hair and sighed as she sat in her bed, conserving her energy. The only thing that distracted her from the hunger pangs was the woman Charu compared her to. *Who is this Siya? I tried to ask when Charuben mentioned her but Maaji's chilli infused tongue didn't give me the chance to ask anything.*

Uma was distracted when she heard a sound and turned to see the bedroom door open. Leela walked in without being invited to do so. She was carrying a large bag. She put the bag down and bolted the door shut behind her. Uma was not sure if Leela knew that she was sitting in the dark. *Why has this Leela secretly come into my room? Has she come to steal?* Leela turned the light on. She bent down and took out a stack of silver food containers from the bag. *A tiffin box? What is in there?* Leela began to open the boxes. A heavenly smell of spices and curry filled the room. Uma noticed the tiffin boxes contained rice, dal, potato and cauliflower curry and chapatti. Uma's mouth watered at the sight of food before her.

"Uma didi," Leela whispered. "Hurry up and eat. I told Madhuji that I was going to tidy your room before I went home."
"Where did you get all of this?" Uma asked in disbelief.
"I saw they were cooking meat today. I brought leftover bakshanam from

Amritaji's house."

Leela's act overwhelmed Uma. *How could I have thought you came to my room to steal? You are the only person in Madhapar that I trust other than Vijay.*
"Leela," Uma said overcome with emotion. She put her hands together. "I have no way of thanking you. I hope Maa Durga blesses you with..."
"Eat quickly Uma didi," Leela interrupted. "Madhuji will get suspicious if I spend too long here."
Uma quickly stood up and sat down on the floor to eat. The moment she ate her first morsel of food her taste buds exploded releasing more saliva in her mouth. *This food is delicious! It is better than anything else I have eaten in Madhapar.* Uma devoured the food in front of her, as though she had never seen food before.

Uma did not distract herself from her meal but from hearing sounds she deduced that Leela sat on her bed for a while before opening the window in her bedroom. Then Leela began to sweep the room around Uma.
"Uma didi, why don't you go back to Mandavi until Vijay sir comes back?" she questioned Uma. "Your amma and acha will enjoy your company."
Uma stopped eating for a moment and looked to Leela who continued to sweep the floor.
"When..." Uma paused to swallow the food in her mouth. "When I married, maa told me that my husband's home is my home, and his family is my family."
"Vijay sir is not here. You should spend time with your amma and wait there until Vijay sir calls you to Mumbai?"

I miss maa, and want to go home, but what if maa is disappointed if I come back? She might think I failed to make Vijay's family my own. Uma remembered the words her mother said to her on her wedding day. *"Win them over with your love. I told you to forget the norms and cultures of this home, but never forget the values and morals I instilled in you. I do not want you to become the ideal daughter-in-law, I want you to become their beti and earn their love and respect. This single diva brings warmth and happiness into people's lives, and in times of darkness brings light."*

If I go back maa might find out that I failed to become the diva. None of Vijay's family have accepted me. Though if I continue to tell maa, everything is going well, she will never know about my failure. She took a few more bites of the food and mulled over what Leela said. *Leela is right. If I go and stay in Mandavi until Vijay returns at least I won't have to look at his maa's face. I can wait there until Vijay comes back to take me to Mumbai. I just need to make sure maa isn't disappointed in me and doesn't think I failed.*

With a full stomach and the prospect of going to Mandavi, Uma felt happier than she had done in a very long time. Uma was about to stand up after the meal when she heard a vibrating noise. Leela's phone was ringing.

"Hello? I am leaving work now. I will be home in twenty minutes." Without saying bye, Leela hung up and obliterated the room of any evidence that Uma had eaten. Uma helped by packing up the tiffin and went to wash her hands in the en-suite bathroom. Uma thanked Leela for the food, before she left.

Once Uma was alone again she paced around her room thinking. *How do I convince maaji to let me go back to Mandavi?*

Chapter 25: Purbai

Purbai and Madhu both laughed. Madhu had been complaining about her daughter-in-law and Purbai was telling her about Sharla's daughter; who had run away with an untouchable and now expected an untouchable baby. Purbai picked up the cup of chai Leela had brought. She began to blow on the hot chai to cool it down. Purbai enjoyed spending time with her neighbour Madhuben. Madhu inspired her because of the way she retained control of her own life even after her husband's death. *If I took control of my life when Harji died, then I would not be in this state. I should have been strong like Madhuben.*

Three years ago Purbai felt her life had ended when her husband, Harji, died. Purbai was forced to shatter her glass bangles, stripped of all of her jewellery and beautiful saris. Purbai's daughter-in-law, Kesar, kept any jewellery she liked and sold the rest. She also kept the saris she wanted and donated the rest to charity. Purbai made the decision not to argue with Kesar. She knew she had no use for accessories that made her beautiful anymore. With her husband dead, she was forbidden from wearing even a bindi. Whenever Purbai saw Kesar wearing some of her jewellery, she felt a pang of sadness. *I worked hard work to save money for that jewellery, but I cannot wear any of it. Hai Swaminarayan Bhagwan, why did you call Harji to you before you called me?* She was now restricted to wearing pale, plain saris with no patterns.

As time progressed, Purbai had seen other widows wearing nicer saris to weddings. She gathered up the courage to wear a less plain sari to a family wedding. However, she spent the entire wedding feeling extremely uncomfortable. Purbai attracted many glares from other people who felt it was inappropriate for a widow to dress so glamorously. Since that wedding she never deviated from wearing plain saris. Purbai did not merely lose her fashionable clothing. She also lost the security that came with a living husband. For many years Purbai worked with her husband on their farm but she never owned anything. Everything was in her husband's name. When Harji died, everything transferred to her son, Khimji; their mansion, their land, their wealth. Purbai, who had spent her entire life working hard, was left with nothing. In the early days it made no difference to her. As time passed Khimji's wife, Kesar, became more controlling. Kesar moved Purbai out of the master bedroom saying the room was too big for one person. Purbai shifted into one of the smaller rooms in the mansion. Gradually Purbai's importance in her own home diminished. *When Harji was alive they would ask my opinion on the smallest of matters, now they don't even ask me when they make important decisions.*

As Madhu and Purbai both sipped their tea, Uma entered the living room carrying a small suitcase. Uma put the suitcase down and spoke to Madhu.
"Maaji, Vijay has gone to Mumbai," she said quietly. "I want to go and stay with maa in Mandavi for a few days."
Madhu smiled and walked over to Uma.
"Bahu my home will feel empty without you and Vijay," Madhu said sweetly to Uma. "But I know that spending time with your parents will make you very happy."
Madhu pushed back the hair on Uma's face and touched her face. Purbai noticed Uma flinch at Madhu's touch. *All daughter-in-laws are the same. We treat them like our own beti but they do not treat us like their maa.*
"Do not forget about Charu's wedding sari," Madhu said. "She will be upset with you, if you forget about it when you return here."
"Ha OK. I won't forget." Uma bent down and touched Madhu's feet before leaving.
Kesar has not touched my feet since Harji died. Even my own son does not respect me anymore. At least Uma has some respect for Madhuben.

Madhu sat back down and drank her tea in silence until Uma left. Purbai and Madhu both ignored the maid, the only other person in the room.
"Uma seems very different to how you described her," Purbai commented. "She seems very cultured and respectful."
"It is because she has to be respectful," Madhu said. "She came with no dowry. She has not paid for her right to do as she pleases in my house."

"In our Kanbi community we do not give or take dowries," Purbai claimed superiorly. "It is illegal according to Indian law."
"Oh Purbai!" Madhu scoffed. "Alcohol is illegal in Gujarat but everybody secretly drinks. It is a victimless crime. If I remember correctly, your Khimji was drinking alcohol at our Holi Party."
My beta was led astray by your Jigar, otherwise he would never lay a finger on the stuff. Eager not to disrespect Madhu, she smiled and agreed with her.
"You are right. If the police spent time on silly crimes like alcohol and dowries then who will solve murders and robberies? The police do not have enough eyes to stop everything that happens in this big country," Purbai laughed.
"I was too generous. Uma's family are middle class and not to our standards but Vijay fell in love with her. What could I do?" Madhu took a sip from her tea. "Nowadays all these new laws try to get rid of our old traditions. I always vote BJP in the elections. They are right, we need to return to what our scriptures tell us. This country will be great again if we were governed by our traditional laws." Madhu took another sip of her tea. "I did not ask for anything in dowry from Uma's family. I am now asking Uma to simply help with Charu's wedding. I do not want anything else. This way we will abide by what our religion tells us is right, and it will be a burden off my shoulders."
"You are right Madhuben. Fulfilling religious obligations is very important."

Purbai sipped her tea and began to grin. Listening to Madhu justify dowry with religion reminded her of a story that her mother-in-law told her. When she was alive, Purbai's mother-in-law did not eat onion or garlic for religious purposes. When Purbai asked the reason for her abstinence from eating onion or garlic; her mother-in-law narrated a story to her. She claimed that Lord Swaminarayan sat down to eat his dinner one day and the onion rolled away. The Lord picked up the onion, put it back and resumed his meal. The onion once again rolled away; after retrieving it a few times the onion kept rolling away. Lord Swaminarayan cursed the onion and said his true devotees would never eat it. This was a story many people talked about as justification for not eating onion and garlic. However, Purbai had researched everything and found out the true reason behind why people do not eat onions. Onions and garlic came under a category of foods that were believed to be evokers of tamasic behaviours and anger. *Madhuben used religion to justify dowries. I have never read in any religious texts that a dowry should be given. Madhuben and my mother-in-law are both the same. They make up religious stories that they think are true and then tell people about it if it justifies their actions. But if Madhuben thinks it is a religious requirement, and still she didn't demand one, then she is very generous. She could have demanded one but instead she is merely asking Uma to help towards Charu's wedding. Helping to pay for Charu's wedding will not turn Uma's family into beggars. It will be very little in comparison to what some people ask for in dowry.* Purbai's respect for Madhu increased. Not only was Madhu a widow who kept control of her rights, but she was also very generous. She did not have to be that generous towards Uma.

Chapter 26: Avantika

Avantika walked into her courtyard and shut the door behind her. She dragged the bed from one side of the court yard and placed it under the sapodilla tree. Before she sat down, she picked a few ripe sapodillas and began to eat one. It was a warm and beautiful day there were no clouds in the sky. As she sat under the tree, a gentle breeze created the perfect atmosphere. She would have been at complete peace if she was not feeling frustrated. *My beam of moonlight has refilled this house with happiness since she's been here. But the people in this village can't bear to see others happy. They have nothing better to do than to gossip about others. People like Nirmala find it difficult to digest their food if they don't gossip for a day.*

A few minutes ago Avantika bumped into one of their neighbours, Nirmala. Without asking how she was, Nirmala immediately asked about Uma's wellbeing. Avantika thought Nirmala's question was odd but responded and told her that Uma was fine.

"Avantikaben," Nirmala had asked. "Please do not take offence at what I am asking, but Uma's been back for a whole month. Is everything ok with Uma's married life? She has not been sent back from her in-laws has she?"

Avantika became extremely irritated by Nirmala but responded to her politely. "She has come to stay with her parents, until her husband returns. Who has been saying such nonsense?"

"Avantikaben please don't be offended by my question," Nirmala said.

If you ask me rude questions, what do you want me to do? Get incense and venerate you?

"Some people were talking about how Uma had been in Mandavi for a long time. You know, married women belong with their husband's family and people here take any opportunity to gossip," she continued with a smug smile.

Yes, people like you. I don't think anyone said such things until you started it.

Avantika had politely ended the conversation and walked home.

However, Nirmala's question still prickled her.

One month ago Uma came to Mandavi to live with them until Vijay returned from Mumbai. She had turned up unannounced and Avantika panicked when she saw her. *Why has she come back suddenly? Have they kicked her out?* Uma put her mind at ease when she told her she would only be staying until Vijay returned from Mumbai. Relieved Uma was simply visiting, Avantika wasted no time in pampering her daughter. One of the first things she noticed was that Uma had lost a lot of weight since she got married.
"Oh... Maa, my family are health conscious. They don't eat food with lots of ghee. They have a person who cooks only healthy food for us," Uma dismissed Avantika's concerns.
Vah vah vah a cook, these big people and their dieting, bieting. Seeing how quickly Uma was adjusting to her new life impressed her. *She's even started eating better food. Haai haai, I hope she's not eating non veg.* Avantika felt Uma did not look good as thin as she had become. As a result she became accustomed to standing behind Uma during meals and making sure Uma ate seconds and thirds of everything she made.

There were times when Avantika had been worried that Uma was going to ask for more money. Every time Uma mentioned Charu's expensive tastes and her wedding Avantika gulped and mentally prepared herself for the worst. However, Uma made no requests. In fact Uma told Avantika how successful Vijay's hotels were and that he would be paying for everything. She had also used every opportunity to probe Uma about her life at home. She was delighted whenever Uma told her about her grand life in Madhapar.
"My mother-in-law knows how much I love masala dosa," Uma had told Avantika. "Our maid is lovely. She always makes food for me. Her masala dosas are the best I've ever tasted."

Pleased about everything her daughter said about her in-laws, Avantika lit a small diva at the shrine in their home. *Hai Mata Rani, it is because of your blessings that they have accepted Uma. I spent weeks worrying that I have given my beti to money grabbers who will ruin my Uma's life but they are keeping my beti happy. The stress, the payments, the sleepless nights; it was all worth it. Without your blessings we wouldn't have had the strength to go through everything those first few months. Hai Mata Rani I pray to you that you continue to protect Uma and keep her happy.*

The only news that upset Avantika was when Uma revealed that she would be moving to Mumbai in a few months. *She lives sixty kilometres away at the moment and I already see so little of her. How often will I see her when she's thousands of kilometres away?* However, after the initial disappointment Avantika became pleased. *Mumbai is the city of dreams, people go there and make their lives and become millionaires. Vijay is going to buy my beti a palace in Mumbai. My Uma will be further away from me, but she'll be happy. That is all I care about, my children's happiness.*

With the exception of her initial shock about Uma's moving to Mumbai, she had loved every minute of having Uma with her in Mandavi. The only thing that bothered Avantika was the gossip about Uma. *I don't care what people have to say. They're jealous that my Uma married into such a prestigious family. Their jealousy makes them gossip. I won't let their gossip affect me.* Avantika attempted to ignore the gossip, but she knew the impact people's gossip would have on their family reputation. *People talking bakvaas about Uma will destroy our family honour. Arjun is of an age where families will start taking an interest in making him their son-in-law. If the gossip spreads and people believe the rubbish then parents will think twice about sending their beti to our home. If idle gossip damages our family honour, nobody would want to send their beti to us. A maligned family would only get a daughter-in-law who has something wrong with her. I wouldn't send my Gauri into a disgraced family, so why would someone else send their beti to my home if gossip taints our honour?* Avantika looked at the sapodilla seeds on the floor that she had spat out. *I don't want to send my beti back, I love having her here, but I cannot put my own desires before my family's happiness. If I let Uma stay here it will just add ghee to the fire.*

She thought about the situation for a while. *The sooner Uma goes back to her in-laws the sooner the gossip will stop. That is the only way. Uma is happy in Madhapar, she can go back to living like a queen, and people like Nirmala can find something new to gossip about.* Avantika stood up and walked into the house. As she walked towards the house she recalled all the happy moments from the last month. *I've become so used to having her here. It's going to be like giving her away all over again.* She took a deep breath. *I will tell her tonight that she has to go back to Madhapar.*

Chapter 27: Uma

Uma sealed the suitcase shut. Her luggage was packed and she would soon be escorted to the bus stand. Whilst helping her to pack, Uma's mother reminded her about a wife's duties.
"A wife's primary duty is towards her husband and his family. If you neglect those duties by staying here people will talk badly."
"People will find new things to talk about maa."
"Your mother-in-law needs you," Avantika said desperately. "You are her eldest bahu. Her son is away and she is a widow with no one to look after her. You have to support her."
That woman doesn't need my support. I am the one who needs support against her.
"Uma beti it is your duty to go back and care for her," Uma's mother told her.

Uma did not argue. She knew exactly why her mother was sending her back. *Maa is worried what people will say if I stay for too long. People are already gossiping about me. I would stay in Mandavi just to wind people up. I don't care about what people think of me. But the rumours about me would damage my family's reputation.* She felt like a lark that had lost her freedom. Uma felt liberated and free in the month she spent with her family. Now she was going to return to the birdcage-like mansion where she would live like a prisoner. *It wasn't until this month that I realised how much I hate Madhapar. I have not been this happy since my honeymoon.*

At 3pm the time came for Uma to return to Madhapar. Her mother had tears in her eyes. Uma could feel tears forming in her eyes, but she held back the urge to sob in her mother's arms. *If maa finds out how upset I really am to be going back, she might get suspicious and worry unnecessarily.* She plastered a forced smile onto her face as her vision blurred from tears.
"I am looking forward to eating Leela's food again," she told her mother quietly.

Uma felt her mother's arms around her. She felt the same way she had done on the day she married and left her paternal home behind. This time Uma's apprehension was worse. This time she departed with the knowledge that there is no place for her in Vijay's family. She had no hopes to win them over anymore.

Both Arjun and Gauri came to drop Uma to the bus stand. They waited until the bus came. Uma waited for the bus in total silence. She just listened to Arjun and Gauri joking with each other. Uma fought back her tears and only let her grief out once Arjun and Gauri left. Her tears stopped a few minutes later when she realised that she was going back to Madhapar with no money for Charu's wedding. *Hai Mata Rani, what will maaji say when I come back without a single rupee? I didn't think I would ever go back without Vijay, I never thought of trying to gather money for her.* Uma was flooded with fear.

As the bus progressed towards Bhuj, Uma's thoughts fluctuated between her memories of the past month in Mandavi and her worries about what will happen when she returns to Madhapar. *I ate as much pauva and tamarind chutney as I wanted. So many of my childhood friends came to visit and I walked around my home without fearing anyone. Everything I go through in Madhapar I do for you Vijay. I wouldn't go through that for anyone else. The next few months will be like penance. I need to go through the hardships to attain what I want. Maa was so proud of me when I told her how much Vijay's mother and I get on. What would she say if she knew I lied?* Uma had kept mentioning family members to a minimum. Talking about Leela usually made her mother happy.
"My daughter has a servant who waits on her hand and foot. She lives like a queen," Uma heard her mother tell some of the neighbours. Since then Uma always spoke about Leela to prevent her mother from discovering her lies.

Uma fondly remembered how her mother cared for her in Mandavi. *She made sure I ate enough, she put coconut oil in my hair and she made sure all of my needs were met. I miss being cared for in the same way maa cares for me. People always said when you go to your husband's house your maaji becomes your new maa. I have not got a new maa, I have been given a witch instead. She is a churel.* Uma instantly felt guilty for thinking badly of her mother-in-law. *Hai Mata Rani, forgive me for thinking badly of maaji. One should not think such bad things of their in-laws.*

As the bus came into Bhuj, her fears about going home heightened. *Maaji will be angry that I have come back empty handed. I had no way of asking maa and bapuji for more money even if I wanted to.* Whilst in Mandavi, Uma discovered the true extent of the debt her parents were in. Gauri told Uma everything, including how Arjun had taken a year out of his studies in order to pay for his tuition fees. Uma felt unable to ask her parents for more money. She felt too cowardly to confront her parents about their debt and feared they would discover what was happening to her. Not wanting to add to her parents' burden, she remained silent. Uma took a deep breath. *I will explain to Vijay's maa why I can't get money from my parents. She will have to listen to me. I will make her understand the troubles that she has inflicted onto my parents.* She inhaled again. *I won't let maaji shout over me this time. She will listen to me. Give me strength Mata Rani.*

Chapter 28: Madhu

The ox has been home for two hours and still has not said anything about the money I wanted from her parents. I am certain she has come back empty handed. Madhu sat at the dinner table having dinner with Charu, Jigar and Uma. She did not eat much food herself, but simply watched Uma eat her meal. *Eat, eat. If you came back empty handed, like I know you have, this will be the last thing you eat for some time.* Once everyone finished their meal, Leela began to clean up. Madhu saw Uma get up.
"Bahu, how was home?" Madhu asked Uma.
"Very nice Maaji. I'm very tired though so I will go to sleep early tonight," Uma replied.
"Do you not want to watch Saathiya today?" Madhu said with a sweet voice. "I know it is your favourite serial. I thought we would all watch it today. With that excuse we could all sit together and gupshup for once. You have been gone for so long."
Madhu pretended to affectionately stroke Uma's hair. She was delighted to see that Uma flinched at her touch. *By the end of Saathiya Leela will be gone, and then you will know the real reason I wanted to watch this rubbish.*

Madhu ensured that her whole family watched the serial together. There were moments which highly amused Madhu. She chuckled loudly when the protagonist of the soap opera said "The truth is like a flowing river. If you try to block it, it will find another route." *So much rubbish about good winning over evil, in real life this would never happen.* Five minutes before the end of the show, Madhu noted that Leela had left. *She has gone. I cannot take any more of this rubbish.* Madhu bolted the door shut, and then walked over to Uma. Madhu was about to go and sit back down when she had another thought. *If I stand the ox will be more frightened of me.* She walked over and stood in front of Uma, blocking her view of the TV. Uma attempted to shift her head so that she could see the TV. When she realised Madhu was standing in front of her, she looked up to her face looking slightly scared.

“Uma bahu, have you brought the money we needed for Charu’s wedding?”
“No Maaji,” Uma began to explain. “Maa and Bapuji they don’t… they couldn’t afford to give anything. Things aren’t financially good at home so I…”
“Jigar give me your belt,” Madhu said flatly.
“What?” Jigar said looking confused.
“Maaji…” Uma attempted to explain herself. Uma began to ramble which Madhu chose to ignore. *I have no time to listen to your bukvaas. You failed to obey my orders now you have to pay.*
“Undo your belt,” Madhu said loudly over Uma’s rambling.

Jigar stood up slowly and undid the buckle of his belt. Jigar stood there with the buckle hanging from one side. Madhu walked over and pulled the belt out from her son’s jeans. She walked over to Uma who was still sat down on the sofa.
“Maaji, please listen to me. Maa and bapuji have no…”Uma tried to say in a desperate attempt to get Madhu to listen to her.

Without any warning Madhu whacked Uma with Jigar’s thick belt. She heard Uma jump up from her seat with a squeal. Madhu whipped Uma again. She felt satisfied to see that this time Uma’s scream was accompanied with tears brimming in her eyes.

“Did I not warn you about coming back empty handed?” Madhu questioned Uma with anger in her eyes.
“Please maaji,” Uma begged. “Please, I tried. Maa and bapuji are in so much debt. How could I ask them for more money? Their financial situation is so bad that…”
“What about our situation? You can see the problems of your own family, but what about OUR problems? Do we mean nothing to you?” At the end of each question, she whipped Uma. “I explained to you very lovingly the day you left. I was nothing but nice. It seems to me that this is the only language you understand. I think this is the only way that I can get the message through to your brain.”
Madhu saw Uma’s skin, which was covered with pink rashes where the belt had made contact with her skin. She beat Uma with the belt a few

more times until her hand became tired. She turned to her son once again.
"Jigar, take her mobile and sell it. The money you get from it can be the ox's first contribution to Charu's wedding."

Jigar did as his mother bade him to. He walked over to Uma who began to protest again.
"Jigar, please don't take my phone. I use it to keep in touch with your brother. It's also my only way of keeping in touch with my parents, Arjun and Gauri, my friends," Uma begged Jigar with tears running down her eyes. "How will I speak to your brother? How will he get in touch with me?"
Uma tried her best to not give up the phone, but Jigar seized the phone out of Uma's grip. Jigar then pushed Uma to the ground and kicked her to release his frustration. He had not appreciated having to wrestle for the phone.

Jigar handed Madhu the phone as Uma lay on the floor weeping.
"Silence," Madhu ordered.
Once again she beat Uma after each sentence.
"I run this house. What I say is final. If you have a problem, you are free to leave my son and go back to your parent's home."

Madhu walked away leaving the ox snivelling on the floor. Madhu felt adrenaline rush through her. *Another victory over the ox! She was already scared of me but now I have isolated her from the outside world. Anything she wants to say to anyone outside these four walls she has to say in front of me. She will not be able to tell anyone anything about me. I have total control over her life.* Madhu recalled the line from Saathiya that made her laugh earlier. *The truth is like a flowing river. If you try to block it, it will find another route.* Madhu snorted again at the stupidity of these idealistic serials. *I am an expert at preventing people from finding out the truth. I am cleverer than the idiots on these stupid serials. My intelligence is the reason no one knows what happened to Vijay's first wife. Now that Uma has no contact to the outside world, no one will ever know what is happening to her.*

Chapter 29: Charu

Charu walked to college, lost in her own thoughts. *Mumma beat Uma last night... hard.* She felt weird about the entire situation. She did not feel guilty or pity towards Uma. Her emotions were much more complicated than that. When Charu saw her mother whip Uma the first few times, she felt nothing but happiness. *I was delighted. Uma's parents deceived our family by not giving us the dowry they promised. Because of their lies I cannot have my dream wedding. The anger I feel towards Uma evaporated with each beating. If I got caught lying at school, the teacher would always hit me with a ruler. Uma only got what she deserved.* However, the joy she experienced did not last long. Later that night, Charu heard Uma vomiting in the bathroom. This stirred an emotion in her which she could not explain. It was a mixture of guilt and vindication. *Maybe mumma was too strict on her. She should have whipped her two or four times and then just left it. I am sure she would have realised by then that her family's lies are ruining our lives.*

Charu walked past a pharmacy shop. She remembered the time she had gone to buy bandages for Uma, unable to see her in pain. *What has changed these past few months? Am I becoming stone hearted?* Charu continued strolling around Bhuj, lost in her own thoughts. *I am not stone hearted. Months ago I did not know how Uma's family deceived my family. It isn't just her family's fault, she is involved as well. Her family does not want to pay us the money they owe us, and that is why I have to make compromises for my wedding. Selfish people never prosper. They get what they deserve.*

Mentally Charu contrasted Siya, Vijay's first wife, to Uma. *Siya bhabhi always did so much for our family. I didn't get to spend as much time with her because I was at boarding school for most of the time she was married to my brother. Yet she always did so much for me. Whenever I came to Ahmedabad for holidays she came to pick me up, she bought me presents all the time. She even helped Vijay set to up his hotels with her own money. Siya bhabhi even said she will give me an extravagant send off for my wedding. On the other hand, I have lived with Uma for longer because I don't live in Bangalore anymore. She won't even talk to me properly let alone buy me a sari for my wedding. She is a waste of space.*

Charu had been at school when she heard the news that Siya was missing. Devastated by the news, she fasted sixteen Mondays in the name of Shiva, hoping Siya would return. Charu's prayers were answered inadvertently when Vijay married another woman who she thought was like Siya. She felt both women were calm, polite and caring. However, as time went on Charu felt that Siya and Uma were very different. *Siya went to any lengths to make me happy. She constantly asked me if I was OK when I visited. I am sure she would have done anything to make sure I got my dream wedding. The waste of space on the other hand cares only about herself. Why am I wasting my time feeling guilty for someone who only cares about herself? I shouldn't waste my energy thinking about her.*

Chapter 30: Uma

Uma sat on her bed, with her arms wrapped around her knees. She looked at the marks all over her arms. Some of the marks were red cuts where Jigar's belt cut through her skin. The other marks were bruises from when she fell to the floor. *These marks are nothing. They will heal. They are already healing.* Twenty hours ago, Uma's arms were covered in angry red rashes where the belt had made contact with her skin. Uma heard her bedroom door open. She continued looking at her scars, unbothered by whoever had entered the room. She thought about goddess Brahmacharini and how she tolerated worse hardships than her. She heard the sound of sweeping and realised it was Leela. Relieved that her solitude would soon be broken by a friend, Uma looked up and watched Leela tidy up. Leela did not appear to be interested in Uma. She simply continued to brush the floor without making any eye contact or acknowledging her.

Uma was bewildered by Leela's silence. *She has not seen me in over a month and now she is saying nothing to me. She didn't even say hello.* Uma began to play with her fingers unsure whether she should distract Leela or not. *Has she joined Vijay's family against me as well? Is she going to ignore me as well? Hai Mata Rani, I do not think I could get through the remaining three months without Leela.* Uma watched as Leela continued to sweep the floor. There were a few moments when Uma thought she should speak to her, but she restrained herself. *If she doesn't want to speak to me why should I speak to her?* She continued to listen to the sound of Leela cleaning as neither woman spoke to the other. After what seemed like ages to her, Leela finally broke the silence. "Why did you come back?" she asked quietly.

Uma looked towards Leela to face her. However, Leela continued to clean with her back towards Uma.
"Maa and bapuji sent me back," Uma replied.
There was another uncomfortable silence. For a few moments Leela continued tidying Uma's bedroom.

"Did you tell your amma and acha what was happening here?" Leela said, breaking the quietness again.
"What do you mean? Nothing is happening here!" Uma retorted defensively.
Leela stood up and finally faced Uma. She put the broom down and walked towards Uma and held her arm. Uma gasped in pain as Leela grabbed her arm and lifted it.
"This! Uma didi look at your hands."
Leela pointed to the cuts and bruises on Uma's arms. She then let go of Uma's arms who exclaimed in pain again as her arms fell. Leela picked up the broom and began to sweep again. Uma rewrapped her arm around her legs. This time she also put her head down and rolled up like a ball. She wanted to shield her face and thoughts from Leela. *What do I tell her? My parents sent me back because they thought I was bringing shame onto the family?* Uma listened to Leela's footsteps around the room. Without lifting her head, she knew Leela was near her.
"Uma didi, why don't you tell your parents?"
"Tell them what? It's nothing. They are small bruises. I can deal with them. I do not want them to worry over little cuts. I used to get these all the time when I was a little girl," Uma said everything very quickly.
"I'm sure your amma would want to know."

What would I achieve by telling maa? They can't do anything to help me. They are in so much debt already that if I add this burden onto them their troubles will increase. If I told them everything they would increase their debt, or I will end up here because the other option is me living in Mandavi as a shamed woman and tolerating gossiping. Maa would kill herself out of shame if I was sent back home. I lose both ways. I don't need to tell maa anything. I don't want to raise baa's blood pressure, or add tension to maa and bapuji's lives. It will be detrimental to their health. Uma sighed and thought about her other options. She looked up at the calendar on her wall. Vijay will be back in eleven weeks. *I only have to tolerate this hell for eleven weeks. In just under three months I will be moving to Mumbai. There is no need for them to increase their loan. I can handle everything like mata Brahmacharini.*

“Maa wouldn’t want to know that I have failed my duty of being a good wife,” Uma finally responded to Leela.

Chapter 31: Amrita

Amrita's mouth watered as she scooped some of the phirni she freshly made into a bowl. Amrita craved something sweet since the morning and so she decided to make something she ate a lot of when she lived in Amritsar. Amrita heard the gate in her courtyard open. She paced to the window and saw Leela was back from work. She walked back to the kitchen and filled another bowl with phirni. She walked over to Leela who sat down in front of the door that led to her bedroom. Amrita gave one bowl to Leela and sat down next to her.

"I ran out of saffron," Amrita told Leela. "I added cinnamon instead but it's still very suadi."
Amrita watched like a hawk as Leela put a spoonful of the dessert into her mouth. She hoped to see signs of approval or disapproval from Leela's face, but her facial expression gave nothing away. Leela ate her dessert in silence and Amrita felt agitated with no feedback. *Haai Rubba, what's wrong with her? She's not this quiet with me.* Confused, Amrita ate from her own bowl. She felt the rich creamy texture in her mouth and she felt as though she was in heaven. The hint of cinnamon gave the phirni a very different taste but Amrita thought it worked well. *It will never be as good as beeji's phirni but almost as good.* For a few moments she became lost in her own world, remembering her life in Amritsar with her mother, siblings and father. Amrita's reminiscence was interrupted by the sound of Leela finishing her phirni. Leela put the steel bowl down, which made a clattering noise. Amrita's attention was redirected to the fact that Leela was quieter than usual.

"Why are you so quiet today Leela?" Amrita asked Leela.
Leela looked at Amrita but did not say anything.
"Did you not like the cinnamon?" Amrita persisted.
She remained quiet.
Haai Rabba, something is wrong with her. Amrita put her bowl of phirni down and looked directly at Leela.
"Tell me Leela. Kya hua?"

"Why do parents think their reputation is more important than their child's happiness?" Leela asked.
Amrita was slightly taken aback by her question. *She has not seen or spoken to her beeji or papaji since they sold her. Why is she talking about them?*
"Has something happened with your family?" Amrita questioned.
"I was just talking to someone today. Her parents married her into a rich family thinking they will buy their daughter's happiness. She is living in a mansion now but she is very sad. The people she lives with scorn her. It just reminded me of my own marriage. When I moved to Gujarat my life transformed. It was like a beggar becoming a queen but none of the riches made me happy. My in-laws wanted a baby machine. That was my sole purpose. I did not have any dignity or respect. Everything was about me getting a baby. I was just thinking about how many parents in this country think wealth will buy their children happiness? So many parents claim they are doing it for their child's happiness when they do it for their own greed. Acha told me he had set me up with a boy which meant I was going to live like a queen. He made out how happy I would be. But really he sold me for money. He would have sold me to a beggar if his bid was highest. He didn't do it for me."

Amrita saw that Leela's eyes were filled with tears. The happy memories evoked by the phirni were shattered and Leela's story brought Amrita back to the reality of her own life. Amrita began to fill up with emotion.

Reluctant to show Leela her vulnerability she stood up and went to her bedroom. She bolted her bedroom door shut. Amrita inhaled and exhaled a few times before she walked over to her wardrobe. She rummaged through her wardrobe and found the small package wrapped in a red cloth. She picked up the package and put it on her bed. Amrita pulled up the sleeve from her dress and saw the N carved into her own skin. She opened up the red package and rummaged through the items in the bundle. Eventually she found what she was looking for. Amrita picked up the small razor blade inside it and held it to her hand. She then used the sharp edge of the razor to reopen the wound along one of the lines where the N had been carved into her skin. The pain caused by the cut made Amrita gasp. Once she absorbed the shock of the pain she sat for a few moments to recollect her thoughts. *I need to continue punishing myself. I promised myself I will not let this wound heal until I got justice.* Leela's rant stirred painful memories for Amrita. *My papaji made the same mistake. He too had been enchanted by wealth.*

Chapter 32: Uma

Uma lay in bed rubbing her sore stomach. Since her return to Madhapar, a week ago, she had vomited frequently. *Who knew feeling homesick could really make you sick?* Despite her obvious illness, Madhu still expected Uma to contribute with the housework. She recalled Madhu's taunts on the third day of her return.
"Do you want me to get Leela to shower flowers onto the floor maharani?" she asked standing in her bedroom.
Uma thought it wise to not retaliate, and thus did not bother to clarify her confusion.
"Since you have come back from your maa's house you have been behaving like a queen. I thought you wanted us to treat you like one." Madhu's smiled vanished from her face and her tone became stiff. "It is time to stop feigning illness and help with the housework."
"I am sick maaji, I..."
"Your natak will not work on me. I used to go to drama classes when I was a little girl. I know when someone is overacting. Nautanki!"
I bet Vijay's bapuji could tell when you were overacting. Uma took a deep breath and shook off the thought without laughing. She knew that Madhu would starve her for a month if she vocalised her thought.
"I am sick of your drama. Get up and go help Leela with the housework."
I am really sick but there is no point in arguing with this woman. Anything I say or do she will use against me. Without making complaints, Uma got up and began to help with the work Madhu wanted her to do. She helped Purbai and Madhu make mango pickles. Uma noticed that Kesar, Purbai's daughter-in-law, did not help at all. She helped Madhu spread chilli and papad on the roof of their house to sun-dry them. Despite feeling nauseous at various intervals throughout the day, Uma continued to help with any work that her mother-in-law wanted her to do.

Madhu was not the only one who thought Uma was pretending to be sick. Two nights ago Charu also accused her of exaggerating.

"Initially I felt bad that you were sick but now I'm bored of your drama!" *Both maa and beti are the same. How can they think I am pretending to be sick? Maybe they don't realise because it's them making me sick.*

Uma pulled the blanket over her face to shield herself from the outside world. *With Mata Rani's blessing when I wake up tomorrow I will feel better.* Despite the vegetarian menu earlier that night, Uma was still hungry.

The day Uma returned with no money, Madhu had created a new rule; Uma will only eat once everyone else has finished eating. After everyone completed their meal earlier, the rotli was finished and there was hardly any food left over. Uma ate all of the meagre rice and daal but an hour later Uma vomited it all out. Once again Charu complained about the noise and smell, making Uma feel uncomfortable. *At least tonight I did not vomit on an empty stomach.* Uma shuddered as she remembered vomiting the night before on an empty stomach. This resulted in Uma bringing up only stomach acid which caused a severe stinging sensation in her throat and oesophagus. It left her mouth and teeth feeling sore. *How can I vomit so much when I hardly eat anything? What is wrong with me? When I was sick, Maa would take care of my every need. She would give me milk mixed with turmeric, she would check on me every half an hour. All this woman does is insult me. She is not worthy of my respect. If she won't behave like maa, I refuse to treat her like one.*

They are pretending to think I am acting because it gives them another reason to torture me. Uma took another breath. *Ten more weeks and then Vijay will be back.* Thinking of her husband caused Uma to pine for him again. *In Mandavi I got to speak to you at least once a week. You were very busy so our conversations were short, but I still had something to look forward to. I was able to SMS you whenever I thought of you.* Uma thought about all of the text messages which Vijay must have been sending to her since her phone was seized by Jigar. *You must be worried about why I am not replying to any of your SMS messages. I hope you do not think I do not care about you. I care about you more than anyone else in this world.*

Uma stood up and walked to the window. She saw the crescent shaped moon. *You are the only thing we can both see at this very moment. Hai Chanda Mama, you can see us both. Tell Vijay that my thoughts are with him. Tell him I think of him every day. Tell him to call the house phone so that I can speak to him.*

Chapter 33: Alice

Alice sat at her desk completing a letter to a bank company who wanted to book the Hotel Rathod conference rooms and all of their bedrooms for three days. A conference was taking place in Mumbai and their whole company was attending. *This conference will make me more money than what I made in six months with that damn estate agent.* Alice heard the phone ring, as she attached the invoice in an email to the bank. She was about to press send when she heard a knock at the door.
"Come in."
"Alice maam, do you know where Vijay sir is?" Fatima asked. "There is a phone call for him."
"He's just popped up to our room. Who is it? I might be able to help?"
"Erm," Fatima hesitated. "She said she's his wife."
"Oh," Alice said feeling slightly put out. *What does she want?* "Erm... put her through to me I'll take a message."

Alice felt a mixture of emotions as she anticipated the phone call. She had known about the woman for nineteen months. In those months she saw a photograph of her and knew her name. Vijay never spoke about her, and she had no desire to ask questions about her. Alice imagined her to be a spiderlike woman who spun a web around her man. This spider trapped her boyfriend into a web and imprisoned him. Alice heard her phone ring. *What will she be like?* Apprehensively she picked up the phone.
"How can I help?"
"Hello I'm calling from Madhapar."
Her voice is calm and soothing. She's more softly spoken than I thought she would be. Alice, lost for words, shifted uncomfortably.
"Can I speak to my husband Vijay?"
She felt an uncomfortable jolt in her stomach. *Her husband Vijay! She's calling my Vijay hers.* Alice began to dig her nails into the desk. She had never heard another woman call Vijay hers. She could not explain why but for the first time she felt intimidated by this woman. Until now she was a mere photo and name, a spiderlike thing. Now that Alice spoke to

her, she did not want her rival talking to her boyfriend.
"Vijay isn't in. Would you like to leave a message?"
Alice did not bother to pick up a pen as she listened to the message. She did not intend to pass the message on. Just as she was about to hang up, Vijay walked in.
"Is the call for me?" he asked.

Alice saw Fatima in the background. *She must have told him.* Unwillingly she handed the phone over to him. She had no desire to listen to him talking to his wife. She began to leave but she could not find the energy to move. A part of Alice wanted to suss out the enemy and find out what she was like. *If I listen at least I'll know more about his relationship with her. If I listen to him talk to her at least I can know for sure he prefers me.* Alice played around with papers on her desk and typed on the computer pretending to work. She had no idea what she was doing because she concentrated entirely on Vijay's conversation with his wife. Rooted to her chair she listened to him converse with her. *He's polite to her. Is he being nice to the poor cow because he pities her or does he actually like her?* Alice remembered the photo he showed to her in Hampi. *She is a beautiful woman, and men always think with their dicks.*

Alice continued her charade of working. She listened to Vijay speak to the woman in Gujarati. *I have no clue what he's saying to her, but I don't like it one bit.* She could see the big grin plastered on his face and began to feel jealous. *Why does he have that fucking grin on his face when he's chatting to her? Does he smile as much when he's talking to me? Or am I just his bit on the side?* Alice regularly wondered whether she was just his mistress in London. However, this was the first time she felt uneasy since she had been in India. Having Vijay with her at all times gave her a sense of security. Seeing him speak to this woman robbed her of the security she felt.

Now and then, Alice heard a random English word thrown into the conversation. She gathered he was talking about the hotel. From the word busy Alice deduced Vijay must have said something about being busy and overworked so he could not go home. *More like he's busy*

shagging me; she thought spitefully. Once Vijay put the phone down, he bent over and kissed Alice on the head.
"You looked like you were having fun," she commented coldly.
"Darling don't get upset. I was being polite, Vijay said softly. "She is my wife."
"How can I forget?"
"Listen," Vijay held Alice's hand. "I don't love Uma. I love you. Uma means nothing to me."
"Uma?" Alice asked confused. "I thought her name is Siya?"
"Ah... yes," Vijay mumbled. "It is Siya. Uma's her nickname."
"You have a nickname for her?" Alice said outraged.
"That's what my whole family call her," he said lamely. "It stuck."
"Oh how sweet." Once again Alice pretended to work on the computer. "I'm going to send this invoice off and then go to bed. I'm tired. See you later."

Alice randomly pressed a few buttons and then walked out. She ignored Vijay's attempts to speak to her. Speaking to Vijay's wife caused Alice to crash back down to reality. Alice was not only feeling jealous. Her feelings of jealousy were mixed with guilt. *That woman's voice sounded as though she loves Vijay. Have I stolen another woman's man?* She answered her own question: *Yes. I have stolen another woman's man.*

That night Alice tossed and turned, unable to sleep. Two questions plagued her mind, causing insomnia. *Does this woman love Vijay the same way I love him? What are his feelings towards her?*

Chapter 34: Madhu

"Are you vomiting again?" Madhu shouted as she banged on the locked door. She could hear Uma vomiting in the bathroom again. "If you keep vomiting out everything I give you to eat, perhaps I should stop giving you anything to eat. It will save more money."
Madhu banged on the door one last time before she walked away. *This is the fourth time this week. How many more times will this ox vomit? Every time she vomits I have to make Leela clean and disinfect the place. Three days ago she didn't even make it to the bathroom and vomited all over the floor.* Madhu recollected how she had been revolted at the sight of the clear, liquid vomit. The putrid smell was even worse. Madhu picked up a sandal and whacked Uma a couple of times to punish her. *I thought the slipper would stop her amateur dramatics but she seems to be persevering with her theatrics. I need to do something to stop her overacting.*

Feeling slightly frustrated, Madhu stormed down the stairs and turned the TV on. She began to flick through the channels with her mind still focused on Uma. *The ox is a nuisance, a nuisance who isn't even bringing any money in to make up for her burden.* She continued to flick through the channels but saw nothing which interested her. Madhu did not actually care what was on TV. She channel hopped and attempted to concoct a plan so that she could maximise Uma's usefulness. *I disposed of Siya six months before Vijay married this ox. They will never find any evidence against me. Vijay, Jigar and I are the only ones who know what happened to her. Even Siya had no idea what happened to her. I can't get rid of Uma so soon after Siya, otherwise my careful planning will all go to waste. I am going to have to use every bit of my intelligence to find a way to make that ox useful. Otherwise the ox will treat this place like a free hotel for at least another six years.*

Madhu spent the entire afternoon thinking about nothing but Uma. At 4pm Leela brought her a cup of tea. As she sipped the tea, she finally relaxed her mind a little and paid attention to the programme on the TV.

Madhu watched a typical Indian soap that she hated so much. The mother-in-law was being nasty to the daughter-in-law. The ideal, Sati Savitri type, daughter-in-law attempted to win her mother-in-law's affection with her love. *What if Charu's mother-in-law is nasty to her? What if she has to go through these difficulties after marriage? The only way I can make sure I protect her from all this is by making sure I have enough money to pay a dowry. If I pay them a dowry even if they don't ask for one, they will respect Charu because of the goods she will bring to their house. That ox will have to buy her position in this house. I can use that money to buy Charu's position in her home. I will make Charu indispensable but the first problem is trying to get the money out of her. How will I make sure the ox brings the money in? She is scared of me, she has no way of doing anything without my say so. If she leaves these four walls she leaves with me. She is under my control and yet I am getting nothing out of her. Harsh words and punishment seem to be having no affect on her.* Madhu ran through the various options at her disposal but she had either already tried them and failed or she knew they would not work with Uma. *I could find Vijay a new wife, who would be more useful. But I cannot arrange for another disappearance and a divorce would be costly and time consuming. The other danger with a divorce is that the ox might take half of what Vijay owns.* Madhu closed her eyes and focused on her breathing for a while. She opened her eyes and thought of a final resort. *I have already killed for my children before. Would I do it again for Charu?*

Chapter 35: Uma

Uma lay on her back looking at the sky. The moon was partially covered by clouds and the moonlight illuminated the courtyard. *Chanda Mama you look beautiful tonight. Only you can see both me and Vijay right now. Send him my love and keep us both safe from the evils of the night.* Uma felt a gentle breeze against her skin. As she watched the stars and moon, Uma felt serene. A few minutes later, from the corner of her eyes, she saw a light turn on inside Rathod Haveli. She turned her head and saw the light came from Madhu's bedroom. Her tranquillity vanished at the sight of Madhu's shadow. *It is because of you that I am trapped here like a bird in a cage. Because of you I am a prisoner in my own home.* Uma had no money to pay for a bus or rickshaw to take her back home, or even speak to any of her family. *I am stuck in this birdcage until Vijay comes to rescue me.* She flipped to her side, turning her back on the light from Madhu's room. *Forty nine days to go. In forty nine days his four months will end. In forty nine days we will shift to Mumbai and leave this hell.* Uma turned again to look at the sky. *Until Vijay returns, Chanda Mama you have to keep me safe.* She shut her eyes. *Start with helping me get through this night.*

With her eyes closed, Uma remembered how she used to sleep outdoors with Gauri when they were both little girls. When the weather was very hot the fans were useless so Gauri and Uma would both sleep under the stars on their balcony. Living near the seaside meant that there was always a welcome breeze outside. As a child Uma loved sleeping on the balcony. However, this particular evening she was sleeping outdoors because she had been forced to by Madhu.

A few hours before, Uma felt slightly nauseous after dinner.
"I'm feeling sick again," Uma informed Vijay's family.
"Oh, go and sit outside," Charu snapped. "Have fresh air, it will be good for you. And if you vomit again at least the whole house won't stink."
"I think Charu is right," Madhu announced. "Uma should sit outside and get as much fresh air as she needs to feel better."

"I will be fine maaji," Uma began to say.
"Jigar take her outside," Madhu interrupted. "Perhaps a full night of fresh air is exactly what she needs. Monty always felt good when we left him outside. You and him are so similar so I think it might help you too." Madhu turned the TV on and pretended to be deaf to Uma's protests. "Jigar beta."
Jigar grabbed Uma's arm and began to drag her outside. Initially Uma attempted to resist but after a few seconds she gave up. *He is too strong for me. I will end up outside even if I struggle. At least if I go willingly, I will end up with fewer bruises.* Once Jigar took her to the threshold of their mansion he pushed her out, and Uma fell into the courtyard. Fortunately she did not injure herself in any way. She spent some time on the floor and thought about her next steps. *In around half an hour, she will calm down and I will go back inside. I will go straight to my bedroom and not show any of them my face. That way they won't have a reason to torment me more.* Uma got up and sat in the corner of the courtyard.

Before she could go inside, Madhu came over and bolted the door shut. When she realised Madhu had locked the door, Uma jumped up and began to bang on the door.
"Maaji," she shouted. "Maaji let me in."
"Charuben," Uma shouted.
She is my final hope. Maybe she will take pity on me and let me in.
Charu was the nicest person to Uma in Rathod Haveli. Whilst Uma could not call her an ally or a friend, Uma felt that Charu did not treat her as badly as Jigar or Madhu.
She continued banging on the door pleading for some time but no one let her in. Twenty minutes after being thrown out, a power cut resulted in all the lights turning off. Uma was plunged into darkness. Slightly scared of the dark, and not wanting to draw unnecessary attention to herself she gave up and sat down in the corner again.

Why did I think Charu would help me? Because you are foolish Uma! She is becoming just like her maa. Uma recalled how Charu could not bear to see her pain when she first moved to Madhapar. She gave Uma plasters for the smallest of cuts and went to the chemist to buy some if they were finished at home. *Now she sits there and watches her maa and brother beat me. She didn't intervene the night her mother beat me with the belt; she didn't even bring any plasters for my wounds. It is as though Madhu is controlling Charu.*

Charu had even stopped calling Uma bhabhi, and now called her a waste of space. *The day after I came back Charu tried to stop me from eating the leftover food in the kitchen. What has happened to that sweet girl? I have done nothing to her.*

"Mumma said you are not allowed food until you bring money," Charu told Uma before she threw the leftover food into the bin. "Mumma is right about you. She said since you married Vijaybhai there have been endless problems in our house. Mumma said you do not care about our problems and only care about yourself. I thought she was being unfair at first, but now I know she's right. I am getting married and you are so selfish. You don't want to give a single rupee towards my wedding. Siya would have given me everything. That is the difference between you and her."

Once again Uma heard the name Siya. However, all of her attempts to find out Siya's identity were futile. Even Leela had no idea who she was.

Perhaps Charuben is angry at me because I have done something to hurt her? Maa always said that people get angry at people they love. Perhaps I am not living up to Charuben's expectations? If I had the money I would pay for everything at her wedding. I would even make it grander than her dreams, but how do I explain to Charuben that I have no money? I spent all of my savings in fulfilling Madhu's demands. Charuben is understanding, I will explain to her about the difficult circumstances my family is in. I am sure she will understand. I might have failed with Vijay's mother and brother, but I will win his sister back.

Once she overcame the distress of being locked outdoors, Uma saw the moon and stars and remembered how much fun she had with Gauri sleeping under the sky. She closed her eyes and pretended she was with Gauri again. With her eyes closed, Uma failed to see the clouds that gathered and covered up the moon. It was the monsoon season, and it rained on and off. When the clouds burst, the rain came down very heavily and very quickly. As a child she danced in the rain and thought that rain was a blessing from god. However, now she needed to get away from the rain. By the time Uma got under the sheltered part of the courtyard she was drenched. She sat down cold and wet and realised she would not sleep all night. With the moon now covered by clouds, Uma had nothing to admire. She knew that the night ahead was going to be long.

Chapter 36: Purbai

Purbai had just finished washing the clothes in the bathtub. She took the bucket of wet clothes over to her balcony to dry the clothes in the rising sun. As the sun was shining, Purbai decided to dry the clothes before the monsoon rain started again. She wrung the clothes out and then shook them to remove creases in the clothes. As she hung up the clothes, her eyes wandered to Madhu's courtyard. That was when she saw Uma asleep on the floor in the courtyard. *Swaminarayan, Swaminarayan, why is that girl sleeping on the floor?* Purbai absentmindedly continued to hang up more clothes but her eyes were fixed on Uma. She recollected hearing Uma screaming during the night. *She was screaming to be allowed back into the house. She was begging Madhuben and banging on the door.* Purbai's eyes widened. *Has Madhuben thrown her out of the house? Uma must have done something shameful.*

Purbai continued watching Uma with her hawk like eyes. She realised that the girl was not asleep but lying on the floor, wet from the rain. *They made her sleep outside last night! Swaminarayan, Swaminarayan. Madhuben cannot have done something like that. Uma must have done something for Madhuben to kick her out of the house. That woman is an inspiration to other women like me. She would not commit atrocities onto her daughter-in-law.* Once Purbai finished hanging the clothes up, she watched Uma for a few minutes. *Should I ask her why she is outside?* Eager to satisfy her thirst for gossip, she was about to shout at Uma from her balcony when she saw the Rathod family's maid enter the courtyard. Purbai quickly hid behind the clothes to avoid the maid spotting her. She might think I am nosy. Still curious, Purbai continued to listen to the conversation between Leela and Uma.
"Uma didi," she heard the maid say quietly. "They made you sleep outside all night?"
"It's nothing," Uma told the maid dismissively.
"How can you say it's nothing? You're shaking from the cold," the maid said to Uma.

There was silence for a few seconds. Purbai peeked through the clothes to see what was happening. She could not see much, but she heard Leela speak again.
“This is why you should have stayed with your amma. There is nothing but abuse here for you.”
“Maa told me to come back.”
Leela began to whisper. Purbai strained her ears to hear better.
“If you tell your amma that Madhuji doesn’t let you eat, and she tortures you...”
“Leela I don’t want maa to know all this. You will be late for work. Go inside before maaji shouts at you.”

Purbai sat hidden behind the drying clothes, gobsmacked by what she heard. *Madhuben does not let Uma eat? She tortures her? What is that maid saying?* She could not believe the woman she idolised was guilty of such crimes against her daughter-in-law. *Madhuben cannot be that greedy for dowry that she tortures her bahu. But when it comes to money people always change their colours. It is true when everyone says that people are like elephant’s teeth. The teeth they show outside and the teeth they eat with are very different. I never thought that Jasu Khetani would steal from her brothers. Swaminarayan Swaminarayan.*

When she became sure that no one would spot her, Purbai got up and made her way down the stairs. She went back into her house and paced around, reeling from what she heard. *What do I do now? There is a woman next door who is being tortured. It is my responsibility to do something about it. I should tell the police about it.* Purbai stopped pacing for a moment. *I don’t actually know that much to tell the police. That maid knows more about it than I do. I don’t actually know anything about it. I’ve only heard little bits of conversation. If I say anything to anyone they will ask me for proof. I don’t have proof. If I tell anyone without knowing the full facts then people will spit on me and call me a gossip. If anyone wants to help it should be the maid’s responsibility to do something. She knows more about it than I do. She has seen it all with her own eyes. Anyway I should not interfere it is none of my business. It does not affect me or my family, so why should I put my foot in it and interfere? It is none of my business.*

Purbai's internal conflict was disrupted when she heard her daughter-in-law, Kesar walk into the living room.
"Eh Kesar," she said excitedly. "You'll never guess what..."

Chapter 37: Charu

Charu added raisins to the milk, as instructed by her mother, before boiling it. Once the milk was ready she poured it into a cup. She took the boiled milk into the living room where Jigar and her mother were sat.
"Mumma Charu's brought the milk," Jigar announced to his mother.
"Oooh," Madhu exclaimed with pain, as she sat up. "My back and stomach hurt so much. Hopefully this milk and raisins will make me feel better."
"What's wrong mumma?" Charu asked.
"I have not been able to go to the toilet for a few days. I am having trouble passing stool. Purbai told me to mix raisins with milk, boil it and then drink it. She said it will help."
"This woman always has a remedy for any illness. She should work for cancer research," Jigar joked.
"I am surprised that this remedy did not include turmeric," Charu laughed.
"Oh my god," Jigar said. "This is why they don't have a cure for cancer. They are not using turmeric to cure people."
Both Charu and Jigar were overcome by a fit of hysterics. Charu laughed so much that her stomach hurt.
When Madhu groaned again Charu stopped laughing and felt worried about her mother.
"Why did you not tell me you were constipated mumma? We have laxatives. They will work better than this home remedy."
"Oh get me that too then," Madhu said as she drank the milk. "Anything to make my stomach better."

Unable to see her mother in pain, Charu quickly walked over to the kitchen to find the laxatives. She saw that Uma was in the kitchen. At the sight of Uma, the good mood, which Jigar's jokes put her in, vanished. She caught Uma's eye, who gave her a weak smile. Charu chose to ignore the waste of space's smile. She started rummaging through the cupboard to find the laxative. *Why is she so happy? She spent all of last night outdoors and she's still smiling. She is stubborn, this one.* She heard Uma's fast footsteps. Charu looked back and saw Uma running out of the kitchen with her hand over her mouth. She rolled her eyes and turned her attention back to the cupboard with the medical supplies. *Not more of her theatrics! How much longer will she pretend to be sick?*

Charu heard someone enter the kitchen. It was Jigar.
"Did you find them?" he asked.
"Not yet," Charu picked the bottles up one by one and looked at the label on each one. "Here! I found it."
She grabbed the bottle of laxatives and held it up to show Jigar. Charu saw a smile on his face. She put the bottle down and smirked at him. From the look on his face she knew he had some mischief in mind.
"What?" Charu asked.
"Is that Uma's chai?"Jigar asked as he pointed to the saucepan that Uma was making tea in.
"Yes," she replied shrewdly.
Jigar looked back and began to smile. He grabbed the laxative bottle out of Charu's hand.
"Shall we put this into her tea?"
Jigar and Charu looked at each other and began to giggle.
"Imagine if she had to keep on going to the toilet. She would be jumping up and down all day long."
Jigar did an impersonation of Uma jumping up and down. It looked like some sort of geeky dance which made them both laugh even harder.
"The toilet in her room is broken. If we lock Uma into her room, she will shit herself like a baby. Mumma will tell her off."
Charu looked at the bottle of laxative in Jigar's hand and the unattended saucepan of tea. *The more desperate she gets the more she will bounce.* She pictured Uma doing the geeky desperate for the toilet dance Jigar had done and both brother and sister laughed again. *The more desperate she gets, the more she will bounce.* Charu realised something and stopped laughing.

"Let's not lock her in her room," Charu whispered to Jigar "I do not want the house stinking of her poo as well."

He looked somewhat disappointed.
“She can fight Mumma for the toilet. We both know who will win. We will just sit back and watch as she runs back and forth. This way we both get to see her bounce.”
“Good call,” Jigar said as his face lit up again.

Charu grabbed the bottle of laxative out of Jigar’s hand. She glanced around to make sure no one was coming. She opened the bottle of laxative and poured it into the tea. She quickly closed the bottle and ran away from the saucepan, worried she might get caught. She picked up a tablespoon and walked back into the living room to give what remained of the laxative to her mother.

Once Charu administered the laxative she closed the bottle. She saw Jigar walk into the living room with a look of glee on his face. He put both of his thumbs up and winked. *She is drinking the tea. Now we just sit back and watch the fun. Maybe this will teach her to stop being so selfish.*

Chapter 38: Leela

Leela picked up the food tiffin which contained food leftover from the night before. She was on her way to work when she heard Amrita shouting.
"Leela! Did you remember to pick up the leftovers for..." Amrita stopped. Leela lifted her arm to show the silver food containers she was holding. Amrita smiled and walked back into the house.
"See you when you get back from work," she shouted to Leela.

Amrita always had food leftover from the night before, and every day she would tell Leela to distribute the leftover food to the hungry. Leela occasionally used the food to secretly feed Uma. She looked at the time and saw there was still some time before night fall. She started to take the shortcut that she usually took during daytime to the Rathod family's house. She approached the Harsiani family's farm which she walked through as part of her route. When she approached the gates of the farm, she was surprised to see a familiar car parked near it. *Why is Jigar's car parked here?* Leela walked through the farm and looked around to see if she could spot Jigar anywhere. As she continued to walk she froze. She heard the sounds of a girl moaning. *O Guruvayur Swamy what is that noise?* The moans made the hairs on the back of Leela's neck stand on end. She quietly stepped forwards to see where the noise was coming from. Leela saw the hands of the moaning girl. The hands belonged to Aarti, the farm owner's daughter. Her hands were wrapped around Jigar's head and Jigar's trousers were around his ankles. Leela saw Jigar's bare bum thrusting. *Ende Ammo! Oh my god.* Leela quickly looked away embarrassed and ashamed by what she saw. *Both brothers are shameless! They do filthy things with anyone just because they think they are good looking.* Not wanting to witness anymore Leela began to walk away. After a few steps she heard Jigar groaning. They were finished and she heard his voice.
"I'm going to let you go today Aartiji," he paused to catch his breath. "If you break the law again, you might not be able to work off your crime again." Leela heard Jigar pause as he shut the zip on his trousers. "Next

time I might have to arrest you.”

Ende Ammo that girl is filthy! She sold her chastity to buy her way out of jail! As Leela continued walking towards Rathod Haveli her initial disgust towards Aarti turned to sympathy. *Jigar is the one to blame. He abuses his position because he can.* In the past Leela had seen Jigar serving alcohol he has confiscated as a policeman, at his own parties. She even heard him boasting to Vijay how he took bribes off people to turn a blind eye to their crimes. *I thought drinking the seized alcohol himself was bad, but I never thought he'd sink lower to let people off crimes. Accepting sex as a bribe! Disgusting.*

By the time Leela reached Rathod Haveli, night had fallen. She looked at the house and noticed the light in Uma's bedroom was off. *She is normally in her bedroom at this time. Where else can she be?* She began to panic a little. *If Uma didi is not in her room, Madhu might notice me bringing food in for Uma. She might kick me out of my job.* Leela paused for a moment. *I will take the food up to her room and leave it there. That is the best way to do it. Madhuji never goes into the room.* When Leela walked into Rathod Haveli she saw Madhu sat downstairs. She quickly walked up the stairs and headed for Uma's room. No one ever questioned where Leela went into the house as long as she got the work done. She opened Uma's door and turned the light on to find somewhere to hide the tiffin. Before she found a place to hide the tiffin Leela saw something that made her insides go cold. She saw Uma lying on the floor unconscious.

Chapter 39: Avantika

"What has happened to my beti?" Avantika asked as she ran up to the doctor extremely distressed.

Two hours ago, Avantika had been preparing dinner when she received a phone call telling her Uma was in hospital. She dropped everything and desperately sought Vinod, Gauri or Arjun so one of them could take her to Bhuj Hospital. *Something has happened to Uma. They've done something to her. I know it. I need to see her immediately.* She ran around like a thirsty woman in desperate need of water. *Hai Mata Rani, what happened to her?* The images of Uma that often haunted her nightmares flashed through her mind. Avantika tried her best to suppress the horrific images, but they finally got the better of her. She slowly convinced herself that something untoward had happened to Uma.

By the time Gauri came home, she had dug her fingers so deep into her skin that her hands were bleeding. She failed to realise that her hands were bleeding until Gauri asked her what happened. Avantika looked at her hands and ignored Gauri's question. She did not care about her hands; she could only think of getting to Uma as quickly as possible. Avantika persuaded Gauri into taking her to Bhuj. The journey to Bhuj was torturous for her. Her sense of foreboding increased with each kilometre. When Gauri finally made it to Bhuj hospital, Avantika ran into the hospital as fast as she could. She quickly discovered the ward in which Uma was being treated in and ran towards the room with haste. When Avantika looked into Uma's room through the window, she saw her daughter lying unconscious on the bed. An icy chill went through her to see Uma in such a state, connected to machines and drips. *Is she in a coma? What has Madhu done to her?* She saw the doctor inside Uma's room and she immediately rushed in.

"Doctor Sahib, what is wrong with Uma? What has happened to my beti?" Avantika asked.

“We’re not sure yet but your daughter will be fine,” the doctor replied. “She fainted at home. We’re just waiting on a few tests to come back so we can find out what happened.”
Avantika stopped talking; she felt warmth spreading through her again. *My beti will be fine. Hai Mata Rani tara gana gana abhar.*
“Please maam can you wait outside with the rest of the family,” one of the nurses said as she showed Avantika to the waiting room.
The temporary relief which Avantika felt when she saw that her Uma was not a burnt corpse vanished. *What is wrong with my Uma?* She remembered that not all dowry murders were carried out by burning the bride. Sometimes they poisoned the bride, or even drove her to suicide. *What if they’ve chosen to poison Uma?* Not knowing what was wrong with Uma drove Avantika mad. She began to pace around the waiting area hoping the doctor would bring her news immediately.

Avantika heard footsteps that were not her own. She hoped they were the doctor’s who was bringing her more news about Uma. She felt slightly disappointed when she saw Gauri coming to the waiting area with Madhu, the maid and Jigar. She walked as quickly as she could to Madhu to find out what happened.
“Madhuben, what happened?” She asked desperately. “What happened to my beti?”
“Vehvanji do not worry. Everything will be fine,” Madhu said with the calm voice that irritated Avantika so much. “Leela found her unconscious in her bedroom. We brought her over as soon as we found out.”
“Why did she faint? What happened to her to make her faint?”
“I am sure the doctor will be able to tell us soon,” Madhu lowered her voice. “But I think it could have been avoided if you did what you were told.”
Initially Avantika was slightly confused. However, she immediately realised what Madhu meant. *We didn’t give her the full amount for her refurbishment.* Her eyes widened in shock and she looked directly at Madhu. *She did all this for 600 rupees? What an evil money hungry bitch.*
“Vehvanji, because of our lack of money, we don’t have enough food to go around. Your beti did not have a Bollywood body and still she ate

more than everyone else. Perhaps she feels the strain more than everyone else? Anyway God is gracious, your beti won't be fat anymore."

Madhu's words finally confirmed Avantika's worries. *My beti is being mistreated.* Her months of frustrations and fears surfaced. Anger erupted inside Avantika like a volcano. She seethed with fury towards Madhu.
"YOU..." Avantika shrieked.
"Ssssh," Madhu said calmly. "Vehvanji, this is a hospital. Don't forget where you are." Madhu moved closer to Avantika and whispered "It would help if you remembered your status too. Your position in society is so low that you can't raise your head and look me in the eye when you speak to me. What makes you think you have the status to raise your voice at me? It will also do you good to remember that your beti lives with me. Never forget that."
Madhu's final words doused the fire inside Avantika as quickly as it engulfed her. She took a step back from Madhu and saw the grin on her face. Avantika averted her eyes and looked to the floor. *She's right. My beti lives with them. If I do anything wrong I could destroy her life forever. Hai Mata Rani what do I do now? If I leave Uma with these people, they will destroy her. I need to take her back to Mandavi to save her, but what will people say if I take back a married girl? They will malign Uma's character.* The embers of the fire Madhu's words doused were still glowing inside her. She took a deep breath. *I'll find a way to take her away from these demons. If anyone in Mandavi has anything to say they can say it. I'll cut off any finger that dares to point fingers at Uma.*

"Uma Rathod's Family?"
Avantika turned around to see the doctor. She hastily walked towards him to find out what was wrong. However, Madhu beat her to the doctor.
"What's happened to my bahu doctor? She is like a daughter to me," Madhu asked with tears in her eyes.
Avantika saw a single tear fall from Madhu's left eye. *This woman is a bloody good actress look at her feigning fear, and calling my Uma her beti.* Madhu's pretence made Avantika hate her even more.
"Congratulations," the doctor said with a smile on his face. "You're going

to be a grandmother."

All of Avantika's anger evaporated. She went from one extreme to another. Adrenaline rushed through her body. Tears filled her eyes, but they were tears of joy. *I'm going to be a nani.* Avantika was excited. *Vinod and Baa and everyone at home will be so happy.* She became lost in her own world and thought about her grandchild. Her fantasy ended when she felt someone hug her. She was surprised to see the arms around her, belonged to Madhu. Madhu hugged Avantika to express her happiness. Once again her mood fluctuated from one extreme to another. Her happiness vanished again and she was filled with fear once more. *Uma is going to be a maa. I can never take her away from these people. How many tongues and fingers can I control? The shame of being a single mother will ruin her life and the life of my other children.*

Chapter 40: Uma

Uma looked at the drip she was attached to. The doctor had told her that she fainted due to malnourishment, which was not good for her baby. *I am going to be a maa!* Uma thought with delight. She looked down at her stomach, which still looked rather flat, and she began to stroke it with her right hand. She felt as though she could feel a pulse in her stomach which covered her hand in goose bumps. *It won't just be me and Vijay in Mumbai! We will have a little gift from the gods with us too.* Uma imagined a mansion, larger than the one in Madhapar, and grander. Uma's fantasy looked like a promotional advert for a new soap opera on Star Plus. A beautiful, fair skinned boy, played with his toys on the floor. Vijay walked into the huge living room in a suit. Uma already had all of his favourites dishes laid on the dinner table, ready for him to eat. Before dinner Vijay went over and kissed their son, before kissing her on the forehead. *The three of us will be so happy once we go to Mumbai.* She looked down to her stomach and stroked it again. *Your grandmother will never bother us there.*

Uma continued to rub her stomach for some time. She mentally communicated with the child growing inside her. *As you continue to grow, the love between your father and I will grow. Perhaps your father will return from Mumbai quicker now, or call me to Mumbai sooner when he hears about you. He will want to be closer to the symbol of our love growing inside me.* Uma had a moment of panic. *Oh no I need to teach him the Durga mantra. That is the first thing I should have taught him.* Uma closed her eyes and recited the Durga mantra. *Om Jayanti Mangala Kali Bhadra Kali Kapalini Durga Kshama Shivaa Dhaatri Swaha Swadha Namo Stute. Hai Mata Jagdamba, keep us all safe.*

Uma continued to communicate with her child non-verbally until she heard the door to her room open. She saw Madhu walk in. Uma inhaled and held her breath. *I doubt she has come to congratulate me or be nice to me. Whatever she's come for can't be good news.* Madhu walked over to the table and picked up a knife. Uma gasped and panicked at the sight of a knife in Madhu's hands. She desperately looked around to see if anyone else was around. *Hai Mata Rani is there anyone I can call for help?* As she panicked she failed to notice that Madhu had sliced an apple and put it on a plate. Uma only noticed the plate of cut fruit when Madhu put it right under her nose. Uma looked at the apples suspiciously. She looked at Madhu worried and confused at the same time.

"Uma beti," Madhu said with a smile on her face. "You have not eaten anything today. You need to eat."

Snow White got poisoned by an apple! Has she poisoned it because she doesn't want me to have her son's child?

"Eat, eat," Madhu picked up an apple and held it near Uma's mouth. Uma saw no way of not eating the apple. She took a bite out of the apple and looked up to see Madhu smiling. For the first time Uma felt that Madhu's smile was sincere. *Perhaps now that I am pregnant she will finally consider me as part of her family.* Uma took another apple slice from Madhu's hand and continued to eat it herself. Madhu put down the plate on top of the bedside table next to Uma's bed. She pulled up a chair and sat down.

"I have a few important things that I must discuss with you Uma bah... beti."

Part III: Skandmata (The Mother of Skanda)

Chapter 41: Uma

Uma was now six months pregnant. It did not matter to her whether she had a boy or girl. Nonetheless, she harboured a hope that she would have a boy due to her lack of trust in Madhu. Uma knew that many people in India saw girls as a burden. A girl was nurtured and raised for someone else's family and the dowry they had to pay for someone else's belongings made them an expensive burden. She knew of stories in which women were forced into aborting female pregnancies. Even worse were the stories that Uma heard about people returning their daughters to the gods by drowning them in milk.

Uma noticed a change in the way her mother-in-law behaved towards her. Two months ago when Madhu found out Uma was pregnant; she came into her hospital room. Expecting her mother-in-law to be nasty, Uma was surprised when Madhu simply told her to take better care of herself.
"You must take plenty of rest. If you want anything to eat, tell Leela. She will make anything you want to eat. If Leela is not here, tell me or Charu."

Uma had been stunned by her mother-in-law's pleasantries. However, they did not last long. *I no longer go to sleep hungry, but she still has a chilli infused tongue. Her anger and hatred for me appears to have subdued since she found out I was pregnant but her comments are still hurtful. Perhaps she does not realise her comments are hurting me? I think once my child is born, she will become even nicer to me. She will have more reason to love me. I have already started to make my place in her family. Once my child is born I will definitely be a part of her family.*
Whilst Vijay's mother was better behaved towards Uma; his siblings were more hostile. Charu had even started to physically harm Uma. She remembered being pinched by Charu a few times. She was not sure whether Charu's pinches were getting harder or whether she was becoming more sensitive to them. However, she did know that Charu was causing her more pain.

Despite Vijay being in Mumbai, Uma no longer felt alone in Madhapar. She began to fantasise and build dreams about her new family life. She even began to pick potential names for her son. *Hai Maa Durga, please let my son's rashi be a K. If that is the auspicious letter given to him by the astrologer I want to name him Kartikeya.* She chose the name Kartikeya based on a story her mother told her about the fifth form of Durga; Skandmata.

A demon called Tarkasur gained a wish from Brahma that he could only be killed by the son of Shiva. The demon thought he had outsmarted Brahma into giving him a boon of immortality. Shiva had adopted the life of an ascetic after the death of his wife Sati. He thought Shiva would never remarry, and even if he desired to get married again, no woman would tolerate his ugliness. The demon began to spread terror and evil in the world. He became flabbergasted when he heard Shiva's marriage was fixed to Parvati. His desperate attempts to end their relationship were futile.

After the wedding, the consummation of Shiva and Parvati's marriage was interrupted. This resulted in Shiva's semen falling onto the Himalayas instead of impregnating Parvati. Shiva's semen was so powerful that only Durga or one of her manifestations could handle it. The semen solidified and began to burn the Himalayas. The people of the universe began to worry about the impact this fire would have on the world. Agni, the god of fire absorbed the fire and essence of Shiva for the welfare of the world. After a few moments he began to scream from the excruciating pain. Ganga, the river goddess, told Agni to save himself and deposit the semen into her waters. Her waters flowed from the feet of Lord Vishnu and would be able to calm the fire. Ganga let Shiva's essence flow down her river, which gradually cooled. Ganga controlled the flow of her waters and led the essence of Shiva into a lake in the Shravan Forest. Six Kritika sisters were bathing in this lake. The essence, which had finally cooled down turned into a baby. The Kritika sisters heard the sound of a child cry and immediately went over to him. They named him Kartikeya after themselves and nurtured him and raised him as their own child until he turned seven. He was then returned to Parvati, who renamed him Skanda. At the age of seven, people begged him to destroy the evil demon Tarkasur. Parvati, overcome by love for her son refused to allow him to go to war. People called out to Skandamata, the mother of Skanda, with cries filled with agony. Moved by their pleas she finally agreed to allow Kartikeya to fight the demon. Kartikeya killed Tarkasur and liberated the universe from his atrocities.

Skandmata's Kartikeya liberated the universe from Tarkasur's atrocities. My Kartikeya will liberate me from Maaji's atrocities.

Vijay was currently in Madhapar. He came home to celebrate Diwali. Uma attempted to discuss baby names with her husband but he appeared uninterested which left her feeling slightly dejected. She became further distressed when he quashed her dreams of giving birth in Mumbai. *When Vijay initially went to Mumbai he promised he would come back for me in four months. It has now been six months and he still has no date when I can move to Mumbai with him.* Vijay told Uma all about his workers going on strike which stalled the building works. The strikes set the scheduled project back by a few months and as a result she would have to deliver the baby at Bhuj Hospital.
"The place I am working is no place for pregnant women. I want you to stay here. Mumma will take care of you," Vijay ordered his wife.
Hai Mata Rani, I have to live with his family for longer than I hoped. What did I do in my past life to deserve this? She took a deep breath. *Vijay is right, I will need plenty of care. I am pregnant and he will be busy. We can go to Mumbai once our child arrives. Then I can take care of our child, and I will not be alone in Mumbai.*

Uma listened to the sounds of fireworks. She looked out of her window and saw glittering fountains the children a few doors down had lit. Having Vijay back for Diwali made Uma really happy. But, as Diwali came to an end she felt a lump at the back of the throat. *He is going to leave me here again.* Uma inhaled and exhaled. *I cannot allow this to distress me. He is only working so hard so he can build a better life for me and our children. Everything he does, he does with our best interests in his mind. My husband is very brave. I could never stay away from home for as long as he does. It is because he loves us all so much that he tolerates months of loneliness in Mumbai.*

Uma saw Vijay enter their bedroom with a smile on his face. She felt a warm glow inside her seeing the man she loved smiling again. When he arrived five days ago, two days before Dhan Teras, he appeared subdued. Uma realised he was depressed because of something in Mumbai and she desperately wanted to help him. She begged him to tell her. This was when he told her about the worker's strike which left his project incomplete. Only three rooms in his hotel were complete. To generate more money the three rooms were already being let out, but the strike had left him almost bankrupt. If he did not finish the project soon he would be forced to close down the hotel. The bankruptcy could also result in the loss of their house and his other hotels. Uma became upset by Vijay's depression. She was determined to see her husband succeed. To fulfil her husband's dream, Uma did something she promised she would never do. She asked her parents for money again.

She phoned her mother to ask for money the day before Dhan Teras. She assured her mother that the money was a loan and that Vijay would repay them as soon as he made the money back. Uma was very grateful when her mother agreed. When she put the phone down she became overwhelmed by guilt. *Maa and Bapuji have just started to sort their financial situation out again. Paying for all of maaji's demands left them with almost nothing.* She battled with her conscience but she felt justified. Vijay's request for money was different to Madhu's request. *Vijay is like maa and bapuji's son too. They want to see him succeed because it means I succeed. They don't want us to fail. At least Vijay will pay them back soon; this is just a loan and not a disguised dowry.* In her mind, Uma began to picture the hotel Vijay was building. *So much money has gone into this hotel. It must look like a palace. If this hotel does very well he might even build a palace for me and our children to live in.*

Uma believed that her first Diwali with the Rathod family was exceptional. She spent hours decorating the mansion with rangoli patterns. She used the different coloured powders to make designs all over the courtyard. Uma glowed with pride at the compliments Leela and the neighbours paid to her rangoli. Her best rangoli was the large one in which she depicted Rama and Sita. Uma also covered the house with divas. There were so many that even with the lights off you could still see everything clearly. As she lit each diva she remembered her mother's words. *Become a diva and bring light and warmth into the lives of the people around you. Maa was right. Whenever I look at the divas lit around this house they fill me with peace.* Uma knew that lighting so many divas and creating such beautiful rangolis would mean that goddess Lakshmi will visit their home and bless their family with good fortune and wealth for the year.

Uma had a lot of fun at Vijay's Diwali party. The fireworks they bought lit the streets and sky. The gifts were also beautiful. Vijay gifted her a stunning gold necklace, intricately designed and studded with red and green gems. Her mother-in-law had gifted Uma a small gold statue of goddess Lakshmi. She opened the box of the Lakshmi murti and smiled. *This is a token of maaji's affection towards me. If she hated me why would she spend so much money on a beautiful gold murti? Maybe I am the one who does not understand maaji. Perhaps the way she expresses her love is different. Some people gift loved ones roses. Others gift them thorns for their own benefit. Maybe maaji shouts at me for my own benefit. It is her way of expressing her love towards me. Maa used to hit me with a ruler if I did badly in class. It was her way of bringing out the best in me.*

Uma turned away from the window. She was excited about the final day of Diwali. The final day of Diwali was Bhai Beej. Traditionally a sister hosted a meal and party for her brothers. Before she married, Uma always went to two; one hosted by her mother, and one hosted by her father's sister. *In two days I will host my own for the first time. I cannot wait to see everyone here.* There was another reason Uma looked forward to her family's visit. Her mother promised to bring the money for Vijay on Bhai Beej. *I can give Vijay the money and alleviate all of his worries.*

Chapter 42: Madhu

Madhu plastered a smile on her face and put her hands together to greet Uma's family into her home.
"Jai Shri Krishna," Madhu said with a smile. "Padharo Padharo. Come in."
I hope this is over quickly. I do not know how long I can pretend to like them. Madhu watched as Uma's family entered her home. Avantika and Vinod went straight over to Uma and Vijay to greet them both. Uma's grandmother, brother and sister waited at the entrance in front of Madhu. *The entire collection of freeloaders are here tonight. I hope mother ox makes this worth my time. I do not want to sit here smiling all evening for nothing.* Uma's younger sister eventually stepped forward and came over to hug Madhu.
"Nutan Varsh na Abhinandan," Gauri and Madhu said to each other as they hugged. Madhu and Gauri's cheeks momentarily touched as they hugged. Madhu pulled away from the girl quickly and then examined Gauri's figure. *Look at this fat girl. Who is going to marry this hathi? The ox is obviously pretending that her parents have no money so they do not have to give me anything. If they really had no money they wouldn't be able to fatten up this ladoo. I will increase the amount I am asking for. That will be their punishment for lying to me.*

Madhu greeted Arjun and Vinod in the same way she greeted Gauri. Finally Avantika was the only person left to greet. Madhu looked straight into her eyes. Avantika shifted uncomfortably and looked around avoiding further eye contact. She walked over and hugged her. First they touched their left cheeks together and then they touched their right cheeks together. Avantika's hug lacked enthusiasm. Madhu knew that Avantika was thinking about the phone call she made to her a week before. *Excellent! Her lack of enthusiasm means she understood exactly what I meant when I phoned her last week. Hopefully I knocked some sense into her and she has finally brought me all the money she owes our family.*

Madhu had been reluctant to have Uma's family come over for dinner. On the fifth day of Diwali it was customary for the sister to host a meal or party for her brothers. Madhu allowed Uma to host one as she did not want to stress out her pregnant daughter-in-law. She meticulously planned her Diwali invite to Avantika. Prior to inviting them, Madhu engaged in chit chat with her. Under the guise of polite gossip, Madhu told Avantika about one of their neighbour's pregnant daughter who got kicked out of her marital home and was forced to return to her mother's home. She then expressed pity towards the girl because everyone in their community shunned the poor woman, who would soon be a single mother. Madhu fabricated this story to subtly threaten Avantika again. Based on Avantika's reaction earlier, Madhu was certain that mother ox understood the threat.
"Nutan Varsh na Abhinandan Avantika," Madhu said. Madhu always called Avantika by her name to shift the power balance into her own favour.

The Desai and Rathod family sat down together to have dinner. Madhu saw Uma talk animatedly to her siblings. She was surprised to hear Uma's laugh. Madhu doubted she had heard the girl laugh so much before. *Hai Bhagwan, the ox laughs like a donkey. Now that I have heard her laugh, I am pleased I do not have to listen to it. I am glad she has no reason to laugh when she is here.* Madhu also noticed that Avantika's plate was almost empty despite having not eaten much. *That fat girl has eaten enough for two so it is fine. I will not encourage her to eat more.* Madhu's attention from observing Uma and her family was disrupted by Vinod and his mother who were adamant on having a conversation with Madhu. *Hai Bhagwan, why did I have to sit next to these bores? The sooner this evening ends the sooner I can stop talking to this buddhi and her dull son. I should have sat next to the fat girl. She would have been too busy putting food into her mouth to talk to me.*

Once dinner was over they all sat down to watch television together. To avoid talking to Uma's grandmother, Madhu even paid close attention to the soaps she hated so much.
"Madhu beti," Uma's grandmother said.
Madhu sighed deeply at the sound of Uma's grandmother talking to her

again.
"Why did you not invite your brother tonight? It would have been fun to join your Bhai Beej and Uma's Bhai Beej together."
The food I served to my brothers yesterday is too good for you. You are only fit to eat their leftovers. "Ravi could not come from Ahmedabad today. They work very hard but I will go and visit them next week."
If buddhi ox kept up her pech pech when my brother was here then how would I have enjoyed his company?

The night dragged for Madhu. She had hosted her Bhai Beej a day earlier which included singing, games, dancing and loads of fun. However, Madhu felt the Desai family were unworthy of having any money spent on them and thus kept the event simple. *These freeloaders are not financially lucrative. If I invest any money in entertaining them I will just end up making a loss for myself. If I arranged entertainment for them, this buddhi would have kept on talking and the fatty would have wanted more food.* Madhu continued to focus her glare onto the show coming on Star Plus. *When will this old lady stop talking? When will they leave? The sooner they go the sooner I get my money.* When the advert break came on, Madhu closed her eyes. She thought this would be a cue for Uma's grandmother to start talking to her again but the old woman had fallen asleep on the sofa with her mouth open. *The freeloader thinks this is her bedroom. Well at least this one isn't talking to me.* She sat up with excitement. *This is my chance to get rid of them all.*

"Vinodji, your mother has fallen asleep," Madhu pretended to laugh. "She must be so tired, what time does she usually go to sleep?"
She saw Vinod look at his mother. He looked slightly embarrassed and began to wake her up. Once the old woman was awake, Vinod announced it was time to go home. He began to stand, but Madhu's delight was short lived.
"Wait bapuji," Arjun said.
Hai Bhagwan now what? Will these freeloaders ever leave?
"I have to give my sisters their gift."
Gift? Madhu began to get excited. *If mother ox understood the message I gave, she will have the money. If she is as stupid as the ox she gave birth to then she will have come empty handed.* She watched as Arjun gave

two packages to Uma and Gauri. The packages were packed in pink shiny wrapping paper. *That does not look like my money! And why is he giving the fatty her present here? She will now make a mess opening it up.* Madhu watched as the girls unwrapped their presents. Gauri was gifted a green and blue bandhani sari. *Green? I think she needs a black sari, green will make her look fatter.* Uma opened a sari of the same design, except her sari was pink and orange.
"Very nice," Vinod said to his son. He handed his son a bag. "Gauri and Arjun take your grandmother to the car. We'll be out in a minute."
Madhu watched as Gauri waddled to the car and Arjun walked out with his grandmother. Once they left Vinod took out a cotton bag and walked over to Vijay.
"Vijay beta, I have something for you too. Here's the money you asked for your hotel." Vinod handed the money to him.
Money? Where has this money suddenly come from? For so long they had nothing, and now they're bringing in bundles of notes.
"Thanks papa," Vijay said. "I did not think you would sort it out so soon. Thank you so much." He bent over and touched Vinod's feet.
"No thank you beta. It is for your and Uma's future. May Bhagwan keep you both happy."
"How much money is it?" Madhu asked unable to contain herself.
"Vijay needed some money for his hotel. I am just helping him out. He is my beta too. It is nothing Vehvanji."
"You misunderstand me Vinodji," Madhu said trying to keep a polite tone. "I was not saying do not give him money. I was just shocked you have so much money. You still have to complete the other requests we made but you give Vijay so much money."

Vinod put his hands together and stuttered as he attempted to explain his money situation.
"Vinodji please don't put your hands together," Madhu said sweetly. "Paying me respects will not pay my bills or for Charu's wedding. Respects are nothing in the face of debt. Feeding an extra mouth in our home is costly. If I do not get the money you owe me how will I manage to feed Uma AND pay for Charu's wedding? I will have to stop one thing so I can afford the other."
"Vehvanji," Vinod stuttered. "We… we… we'll get… the money soon."

"Soon? When is soon?"
Vinod stood in front of Madhu in silence, his hands still together.
Madhu looked towards Avantika who immediately looked away from her and walked away. *No wonder she's mother Ox. She's as stupid as her daughter.* Madhu was surprised to see Avantika coming back with a silver box in her hands.
"I have something too Vehvanji," Avantika said.
Madhu looked at the box "What is this?"
"I made magdariya ladoo for everyone," Avantika looked at Madhu.
"Uma loves them. I thought everyone here will like them so I made them."
Avantika handed the silver metal food box to Madhu who looked directly into her eyes. *Where is the money? If you can read my thoughts you know how much your daughter will pay for your stupidity!* She continued looking directly into Avantika's eyes. For a few moments she shifted her eyes and looked at Uma and then directly back at Avantika. She hoped mother ox would understand the threat behind her gesture. Madhu saw Avantika's eyes widen. *I would think you understood what I just meant, but subtlety is wasted on fools like you.*
"Thank you," she said stiffly. "Avantika... I'm sure your daughter will love to eat... ladoos."

Madhu put the box on the table and waved Uma's family out. The moment Uma's family drove out of their drive way, Madhu closed the door and locked it behind her. She walked over to Uma furious. *That family has eaten my brain so much today with their pech pech. I am going to teach this ox a lesson she'll never forget.*

"Why are your family all annoying?" Madhu asked quietly.
Uma looked confused and did not respond. The stupid gormless look on Uma's face angered Madhu more.
"Why are all of your family foolish and stupid as well?" Madhu asked, her voice full of venom.
Once again Uma remained silence. Since Madhu discovered that was pregnant she had controlled her behaviour towards Uma. Her silence caused Madhu's built up frustration to explode. She slapped Uma.
"When I ask a question, I expect an answer." She picked up the metal

container with the ladoos. “I told her to bring me money and she brings me ladoos?” Madhu paused for a second. “THIS IS WHAT I THINK OF YOUR MAA’S LADOOS,” Madhu threw the box and aimed it at Uma. The box made contact with Uma’s face, who yelled in pain. The container fell onto the floor and opened up. Madhu opened her mouth in shock at the contents of the food container. There were no ladoos, but lots of rupee notes inside. *Oh mother ox did get my message after all.*

Madhu was too busy looking at the money to notice that Uma’s nose started to bleed.

Chapter 43: Amrita

"Do you need help with the saphai?" Amrita asked Leela who was cleaning the house, post Diwali celebrations.
"No, no I am fine. There is not much to clean. It will be all clean in one hour," Leela replied.
"If you need any help shout for me. I will be inside."
Amrita looked at the large heap of exploded fireworks in the corner of their courtyard. The rangoli on the floor was no longer immaculate. The powders had started to merge. The fresh flowers she used to decorate the house were beginning to wither. Amrita walked back into her house with a smile on her face. This had been the first Diwali in many years that she spent with the extended Oberoi family. They all came over from Chandigarh to celebrate with them. After years of shunning Amrita's family they finally relented and reaccepted them into the family. Amrita fondly recalled taking blessings from her mother-in-law and father-in-law. She remembered the smiles on her children's face as they lit fireworks with their cousins for the first time. Amrita still felt a warm glow in her as she recollected the squeals of delight her children made to have so many presents.

Amrita walked over to her bedroom and bolted the door shut. She saw the gifts Vikram bought for her this Diwali and picked one of them up. *Vah vah, this necklace is beautiful. Vikram knows me very well.* She took out the necklace and placed it around her neck as she looked at herself in the mirror. *This necklace will match the anklets Vikram gave to me when we married.* Amrita had been twenty one years old when her father told her that he accepted the Oberoi family's request for her hand in marriage. *Papaji believed he was setting up my life permanently by getting me married into a wealthy family. He thought that amir families would buy mine and Nirmal's happiness. Waheguru was happy with me the day he blessed me with a loving husband like Vikram. His beeji gave me so much love that she filled the empty space my beeji's death had left in my life.* Amrita smiled as she reminisced about the awkwardness of her and Vikram's wedding night. They had only spoken a few times before their marriage. They were practically strangers. The thing that worried Amrita the most about her wedding was the consummation of the marriage. She did not want to have sex with a man she hardly knew. She sat in her marital bed, decked with flowers and covered in rose petals twitching regularly feeling very uncomfortable. When Vikram entered the room he bolted the door shut, she inhaled deeply, and worried the moment had come when they consummate their marriage. They were alone together for the first time and Vikram made some awkward attempts at conversation. Throughout their first night, Vikram did not once attempt to sleep with her. They just stayed up all night talking.

In the early days Amrita felt Vikram was a snob and often found some of his habits irritating. As the days went on, they both got to know each other more. She began to adjust to his family and his habits. He even adjusted to Amrita's habits and their relationship turned into friendship, and eventually they fell in love with each other. The more they got to know each other, the more their love for each other intensified. Vikram's parents treated Amrita like their own daughter. *I never felt like a stranger in their house. Even the extended Oberoi family were really caring and loving. Diwali and Vaisakhi were the best times of the year. Celebrating it with the entire Oberoi family was so much fun. It was just as fun as it had been to celebrate the festivals with my own family twelve years before my marriage.*

Amrita put Vikram's necklace back into its box and remembered the Diwali gift she cherished more than any other gift. She walked over to her wardrobe. She opened it and took out the package in which she kept important things. She opened up the bundle and found a pale yellow envelope with the Ik Onkar symbol on it. Her name was written in Punjabi on the envelope. The envelope contained a hundred and one rupees. Amrita held the envelope close to her chest and closed her eyes as she attempted to recall the way her mother smelt. She opened her eyes and looked at the money envelope again. Amrita was nine years old when her mother gave her this envelope of money. A few weeks after Diwali her mother lost her fight against breast cancer. For a few moments Amrita held onto her mother's final gift. Whenever she missed her mother she normally picked up the envelope to look at her mother's handwriting. *Diwali in those days was completely different to what it is like now. Beeji and papaji spoiled all three of us. They did so much to put a smile on our faces. Even when beeji was sick during her final Diwali she still went through so much effort for us all.*

Everything changed after her mother's death. Amrita's childhood ended the day her mother died. Her siblings were both four years old when she stepped into her mother's shoes and worked relentlessly to make sure her sister, Nirmal, and her brother, Gurpreet, never missed their mother. She did her best to ensure she gave them both the same love their mother gave to them. She used the money her father gave to her on Diwali to buy presents for Gurpreet and Nirmal. Thinking of her mother and her siblings reminded Amrita of Nirmal, reawakening painful memories. Amrita became overwhelmed with guilt once more driving out every bit of happiness she felt during Diwali. *I forgot all about Nirmal, I had no right to enjoy myself so much when I still have unfinished business.*

Amrita put the envelope back into the package. She rummaged through the package and after a few seconds she found what she was looking for. She looked at the razor blade which she used to remind herself of Nirmal whenever she forgot about her. The Diwali and Vaisakhi festivals she had been remembering were all before Amrita's life crumbled around her. For many years after, she lit many divas hoping to bring happiness into the vacuum she felt. This Diwali had been the first one Amrita enjoyed in a very long time. Now that her children were growing up the magic of Diwali was reignited in Amrita's life.

After being forced into leaving Punjab, Amrita became secluded from her friends and family. She was lonely when Leela entered her life. Amrita found someone who reminded her very much of her sister Nirmal: shy, loyal, friendly and reliable. Now that the rest of the Oberoi family were on speaking terms with her family again, everything was beginning to look up again. However, each time Amrita became too engrossed in her own life she became compelled to remind herself of the injustices done to her family because of her father's belief that rich families will buy his daughters' happiness. She rolled up the sleeve on her left hand and looked at the N she had been carving into her hands for the past six years. *I promised myself I will not allow this wound to heal until I have punished the people who ruined my family's lives.* Amrita placed the edge of the razor blade onto the scarred N on her arm and cut herself. She gasped as the sharp pain caused her anguish. The stinging caused by the cut released Amrita of her guilt and reminded her once again of everything that Diwali made her forget.

Chapter 44: Uma

Uma was once again confined within the four walls of her bedroom. Vijay had left for Mumbai earlier that day. This time she accompanied Vijay to the airport, but Uma was under no more delusions. *Madhu will never accept me. All she wants is money. If she doesn't get it she will never treat me like her son's wife. Hai Mata Rani, the sooner Skanda comes, the sooner I can move to Mumbai. At least then I will escape this prison.*

Uma paced around her room, still worried. She looked at the time again. *It is 10 o'clock and Vijay still hasn't called to tell me that he reached Mumbai safely.* She continued to walk around her bedroom, her anxiety increasing with every minute. *He hasn't told anyone that he's safely reached Mumbai.* Uma had an overactive imagination when it came to loved ones being late. She remembered as a little girl, if either of her parents were not home before dark, she would begin to cry. She thought her parents had been kidnapped by monsters. She usually prayed to goddess Durga, which always resulted in the safe return of her parents. Whilst Uma grew out of believing in monsters, she never grew out of driving herself crazy from worry. *What if his plane has crashed? Or his car in Mumbai? Hai Mata Rani protect my husband! Keep him safe.* Uma continued to shuffle around her bedroom. She walked outside of her bedroom and saw the light in the living room was still on. With no desire to spend time with the Rathod family she returned to her room. However, she still felt restless about the lack of news. *If there is no news in thirty minutes I will use the house phone to speak to him.* Uma spent the next thirty minutes watching the clock and counting down the minutes.

Exactly thirty minutes later she walked to the living room. Charu was still sat down watching television.
"Has your brother phoned yet?" Uma asked Charu.
She ignored Uma. Unperturbed by Charu, Uma picked up the phone and began to dial the number to his incomplete hotel. She heard the

phone ringing, which stopped after two rings. A female receptionist answered the phone.
"Hotel Rathod, Alice speaking how may I help?"
"Hello," Uma said quietly. "Can I speak to Vijay Rathod?"
"He's just popped out. Can..."
"Oh he is in Mumbai?" she interrupted. "I was worried. He did not phone to tell me he reached Mumbai safely." Uma heard a beeping noise on the phone. *The phone line must have got cut again.* She redialled the number.
"Hello?"
"Is there anything else I can do for you?"
"Yes! Tell him his wife called."
"Anything else?"
"No that is all," Uma was about to put the phone down when she remembered something else. "Oh wait. Tell him that our baby misses him very much. He's been kicking me all day today."

Chapter 45: Alice

"Baby? What Baby?" Alice asked. *He told me they don't have sex. How the hell is she pregnant?*

Her heart pounded. When she answered the phone, Alice felt the same mixture of jealousy, guilt, irritation and moodiness. Like all previous times the woman called, she had not bothered to write down the message because she would not have passed it anyway. She even lied about Vijay being out, he was sat in the room next door to her. The moment his wife mentioned a baby, Alice became alert. The muscles inside her stomach contracted. *Whatever her answer is, I'm not going to like it.* A small part of Alice hoped she had misheard the woman. *She'll clarify my misunderstanding and tell me someone else's baby misses him.*

"Our baby," Vijay's wife said. "I am six months pregnant. We are going to be parents in three months."
Fuck! There is no mistake. Alice felt her stomach drop. *He's been shagging her! That fucking liar.* Angrily she slammed the phone down. She sat behind her desk in disbelief. She put her hands together over her nose, her fingers near her tear ducts. Alice was breathing heavily, trying to calm down her anger. She knew she had seconds before the phone would ring again. Vijay's wife always phoned back within a minute whenever she hung up on her. *What will I gain by talking to her? In the past I had a weird perversion where I wanted to talk to her. I wanted to suss her out, find out what my rival is like. Now I don't want to think about her let alone speak to her.*

Alice sat in silence stewing in the mixture of emotions she felt. Anger because Vijay deceived her. Shock over the revelation that not only was he unfaithful, but he was going to be a father. Sadness because she felt betrayed. *I can't believe I am upset that he was unfaithful to me. I'm the one who got involved with a married man. I deserve this.* She fluctuated between two thoughts. At times she blamed herself. At other times she blamed Vijay. *He's a lying dickhead. He's been cheating on me since... he's not been cheating on me. I'm the other woman.* At this realisation, Alice began to feel pity as well. Her eyes stung but she held back the tears. *I didn't know he was a married man when we first started seeing each other. I'm not wrong. He is! But I found out very early on that he was married. I should have left him there and then, but I kept making excuses for him. He was gorgeous, treated me like I was the only woman in the world when he was with me. I chose to ignore the small part of my brain telling me that he won't remain loyal to me. I allowed myself to be convinced by him because I was in love.*

Alice waited for the phone to ring she knew what she had to do. *What goes around comes around! Indian people talk about Karma so much. I still set out to make another woman's man my own. I allowed myself to be fooled by his words because I wanted to be fooled. If I bothered to find out more, I'd have known he's a lying dick. I just didn't want to stop having sex with the best guy I've been with.*

The phone began to ring. *It's her!* The feelings of anger resurfaced. She wiped her eyes. Alice did not even know when she started to cry. She took a deep breath and picked up the phone.
"Hello this is Vijay's wife. I think the phone got cut off again."

This was when the anger, pity, sadness and jealousy inside her erupted. "Do you know who I am?" Alice shrieked down the phone. "I'm Vijay's girlfriend. He's been sleeping with me for two years now."
Once she had started, she was unable to stop. Alice told Vijay's wife everything; every little detail.

Chapter 46: Charu

"The phone is not free you know," Charu told Uma, who jumped back in shock.

Charu saw that Uma seemed severely upset. *I need to find out who has upset you so much. If I make friends with them, then I can learn how to train you to stop being selfish.*

"Why are you always crying? Seriously yaar, always so melodramatic," Charu jibed.

Uma turned around without an answer and started to walk away.

"Mumma is right," Charu shouted behind her. "You have no integrity, no morals, no backbone. Did your downmarket family teach you no manners? When someone is talking to you, you do not turn your back to them."

She got angrier as Uma walked away, without reacting to her.

"You know it is your fault that my wedding got postponed." Charu shouted. "You do not want me to be happy which is why you will not give any money for my wedding. Even if you brought the money your parents promised us that would be a start, but no your parents deceived my family."

Uma carried on walking. *She ignores everything I say. She does not even have the etiquette to explain herself to me. If anyone called me those things I would defend myself. She ignores me because she knows I am right and she does not have anything to say.* Charu saw an apple on the table. *I will give you something to respond to.* She grabbed the apple and threw it at Uma. The apple hit Uma in the arm and she moaned in pain. *The arrow hit the target!* Charu's delight was short lived. She became agitated again as Uma just walked off without turning back. *My wedding has been postponed because we cannot afford the dowry Rajan's family want. If that bitch wanted to give money she could, but instead she just claims she has no money. Her parents managed to get some money when Vijay needed it. They managed to buy presents for Diwali, where did that money come from? Siya bhabhi would have paid for my wedding if she did not get lost. In fact she would have known it is her duty as the brother's wife to pay for my wedding.*

Charu walked to her bedroom and changed into her night clothes. She continued her rant against Uma in her mind. *When I marry I will be the first person to offer Rajan's sisters support for their wedding, because I understand what family means. I will care about the rest of my family members. Mumma was right about this waste of space. She only cares about herself. She wastes our electricity, food, water and does not bring in a single rupee.*

Today Charu threw an apple at Uma, but on other occasions she had her own ways of getting revenge on the waste of space. A few days ago she put itching powder into Uma's newly laundered clothes. Watching Uma scratch herself gave Charu lots of satisfaction. However, today she still felt annoyed by Uma's careless attitude. *Mumma was generous enough to allow the wedding to go ahead without a dowry. She said they could pay the dowry at a later date but they are making more and more excuses to avoid giving the money. She is not as innocent as she claims to be. She is a liar just like her parents. She sheds crocodile tears to make us sympathise with her. She is a sly bitch who has money to give when it benefits her. She claimed she had no money to give for my wedding, but when Vijay needed money for the hotel she had plenty to give to him.*

Mid rant, Charu eventually fell asleep, but she did not sleep through the night. In the middle of the night she was woken up by sounds of someone retching in the bathroom next to her. *Hai Bhagwan morning sickness at this time?* Charu looked at the time and saw it was 2am. She sat up for a few moments and listened to Uma vomit very loudly. *She does not have morning sickness in the middle of the night. She is doing her theatrics to irritate me because I threw an apple at her. Mumma is right, she is as stupid as an ox. It is called morning sickness, it happens in the morning, she should know this if she is putting on a drama for us.*

Charu gradually became angrier. She stood up and quickly walked to the bathroom. She saw Uma flushing the toilet and wiping her eyes. The months of anger she attempted to suppress churned inside her.
"SHUT UP!" Charu said as she slapped Uma.

Uma took a few steps backwards in surprise. She rubbed her cheek where Charu had slapped her.
She felt vindicated for having slapped Uma. She felt a soothing sensation course through her after she hit her. It was as though all of the resentment she felt towards Uma left her body in one blow. *You deserve the slap for your overacting. Maybe now you will realise that no one is falling for your nautanki.*

Chapter 47: Avantika

Avantika sat down on her bed with her face in her palms. She was surrounded by darkness, reeling from the shocking news Uma gave.

Just over an hour ago, Uma turned up at the house with a small suitcase. Uma dropped the suitcase in the courtyard and sobbed uncontrollably rooted to the spot where she stood. The sight of her daughter in evident pain was heart breaking for Avantika to see. She quickly paced over to her daughter and held Uma in her arms in an attempt to comfort her. Avantika felt Uma grab her tightly and felt her warm tears dampen the blouse of her sari. She spotted the suitcase Uma had dropped on the floor. *That witch must have kicked my daughter out of her house! I did everything I could to fulfil all of her petty demands and now she's just kicked her out like an unwanted object. My Uma has rights! She cannot just kick her out. She is pregnant.* Avantika made a few attempts to ask Uma what was wrong, but failed. After a few minutes she let go of Uma and slowly guided her into the house. Avantika sat her daughter down in the living room and asked Gauri to bring a glass of water for Uma. She eventually managed to calm Uma down. Uma then revealed she was not kicked out by her in-laws but left at her own free will. Through Uma's uncontrollable sobs, Avantika deciphered that Vijay was having an affair and that his family were mistreating her daughter. Uma also informed Avantika that she had returned to Mandavi permanently.

Avantika sat on her bed crying due to what Uma had just told her. *Every time I thought of Uma being in Madhapar alone, I always thought at least Vijay was there. Whenever Madhu gave me reason to worry, I thought of Vijay and thought he loves my daughter very much and wouldn't let anything bad happen to her. He was the only thing that stopped me going completely crazy every time I saw news related to dowry. He turned out to be just as deceptive as the rest of his family. I got what I asked for. I thought if my daughter married into a prestigious family with a lot of money she will live like a queen. But these people turned out to be grand externally but empty and hollow on the inside. They took away my peace and comfort. I was fine by that. I thought at least Uma is happy, but these rascals didn't even spare her happiness. Even a lowborn untouchable family would have kept my Uma happier than these demons. Hai Mata Rani, how on earth did I think the Rathod's money would buy my daughter's happiness? I've fantasised that Arjun and Gauri will also find big families to marry into. Now I only pray that the person they find keeps them happy. That's all I ask from you Mata Rani. I don't want the jewels, mansions or wealth for my other children. I just want them to be happy.* Avantika remembered Uma's intention to never return to the Rathod family. *Hai Mata Rani, I prayed to you to find a solution to my problem. I didn't think this was the solution you'd find. My sleepless nights worrying about Uma's safety will now be replaced by sleepless nights worrying about her future.*

Avantika heard the bedroom door open, she looked up to see who had entered. She heard the person turn the light on. As her eyes adjusted to the sudden brightness she squinted trying to make out who had entered the room. Once her eyes adjusted she saw it was Vinod. He walked over and came and sat down next to her. She turned her face away from him and saw her face in the mirror. Her eyes were bloodshot red from crying.

"I cried the day Uma was born," Avantika told Vinod. "Tears of joy at the beautiful gift god gave to us. That was the same day you stopped taking a rickshaw to work. You started taking a shared car to save money for her wedding." Avantika felt Vinod place his palm over hers. He gently squeezed her hand to provide Avantika some comfort. Avantika was sure they both shared the same ambition: to provide the very best they could for all their children. "Twenty three years we saved for Uma's wedding. I was worried about the fact that she had found someone herself. What if he or his family weren't suitable for Uma? When I found out how wealthy they were all of my worries vanished. Their display of wealth blinded me and led me to believe their money would keep Uma happy. I immediately accepted their proposal and didn't even bother to find out more about them. If I hadn't been so awestruck by the fact such a big family had asked for our beti's hand in marriage, maybe I would have picked up on the signs and rejected the proposal."

"It's not your fault Avanti," Vinod said. "Could you really have said no when Uma told us she loved this man? If you said no, one day you would have accepted him for Uma's happiness."
"When a daughter marries, parents are upset that their beti is leaving their home behind. I was the same. I was worried about everything. Will my Uma adjust to this new environment? For some people it would be a comfort that it was a love marriage and their daughter would be happy. Instead my mind was occupied with the new lifestyle Uma would have and how much happiness this new lifestyle will bring to her. I thanked god she won't have to face the same problems my maa or siblings faced as children. We had nearly everything as children. A loving family, a home, good health... the only thing we didn't have was money. Maa worked very hard to save every single rupee she could but Bapuji drank away the money. He died young because of alcohol. After his death, we didn't become rich overnight, but the money maa saved meant we never went to sleep hungry again. We still struggled to afford luxuries. I was jealous of what my other friends had, but overall I was still happy. When I was little, I used to ask god for enough money to feed myself and my family. Once that was fulfilled, I asked for enough money to live in a comfortable home. When that was fulfilled I desired for a bit more. I became trapped in a web of desire and my ambitions grew and grew. I became comfortable and yet I wanted more," she took a short breath and sat in silence for a while. "We have a saying that a man's mind is filled with dreams and ambitions. The world we live in now was created by these dreams and ambitions. Without dreams and ambitions we have nothing. But those who have no control over their desires attempt to seize everything they can get their hands on, without thinking of the consequences. This is what happened to me. I saw my desire for Uma to marry into a prestigious family being fulfilled and I grabbed it without thinking of the consequences. My blind ambition has ruined Uma's life. Those demons have..."
"The family you're insulting is Uma's family," Vinod said calmly. "We cannot speak badly of them."
"They were Uma's family," Avantika corrected her husband. "Uma's left behind that family who are empty of all emotions."
"Vijay is Uma's husband. She has to go back to him."
She was gripped by anger once more and stood up fuming. "What? You

want to send our beti back?"
"We have no other option Avanti. We have to send her back."
"We don't have to send her back. She's our beti! We can..."
"We must send her back," Vinod said firmly. "It's for her own good and for the wellbeing of the child she's nurturing in her womb."

How can you want to send our daughter back to that hell? No one there has any respect for her. They're deceitful, evil, cunning. She opened her mouth to argue with her husband, but was interrupted by him.
"I am Uma's bapuji. Do you think I will think ill for her? I have Uma's best interests too. If I could keep her here I would, but that isn't how things work in our society."
"Uma deserves better than those," Avantika was too angry to finish her sentence. "Even an untouchable family would have been better than them."
"Uma will be better off in Madhapar than she will here. We'd be destroying her life by letting her stay here. You know the saying from our society: The home in which a bride's palanquin enters, is the home she will leave on a funeral bier. Jee ghar ma beti ni palki jai, eej ghar ma thi eni aarthi oothe."
"That was a long time ago. Women have rights now. They can get divorced."
"What rights does a woman have? Yes she can divorce, but a divorced woman in our community is looked down on. People think she's damaged goods, unchaste and dirty. People might even shun her from society. People don't care whose fault it is."
"Many women get divorced now. Some even remarry and live happier lives than in their first marriage."
"This is what happens in films and the stupid soaps you watch on Star Plus Avanti. Real life isn't like Kahaani Ghar Ghar Kii."
"If we tell people the truth, they will know Uma isn't wrong."
"Like I said before, people won't care whose fault it is. All they will see is Uma is divorced. Look at my friend Hiten who lives two streets away from us, his beti Mansi got divorced. She left her in-laws because they were abusive. She won the divorce case against them, her in-laws were forced to pay Mansi a lot of money and spend time in prison. When Mansi's ex-husband came out of prison he remarried. Mansi is still

single, no one wanted her because they think she's damaged goods."
"Uma is beautiful. Much more beautiful than Mansi, she will find someone suitable."
"Uma is pregnant. Which man will take her and another man's child? Uma is less likely to get remarried than Mansi was. At least Mansi never had a child. If Uma comes back, what will she do as a single mother? People will forever look down on her and her child will be considered illegitimate."
"Uma doesn't need to remarry. We can take care of our beti," Avantika argued desperately. "I will take care of her and her child and I will cut off any finger that points accusations towards her."
"How many of our children will you keep?" Vinod questioned his wife. "Do you think people will want to marry Arjun or Gauri if Uma's divorce ruins our family reputation? Mansi's failed marriage ruined their family's reputation and had an impact on Hiten's younger daughter's marriage. The only proposals she got were from boys with something wrong with them. She ended up marrying a disabled man because no one else wanted him or her."

Avantika was stunned to silence. *I have no response to Vinod. He is right. Arjun and Gauri's lives are tied to this too.*
"Who do you think would give their beti to our family, or take Gauri to be their bahu if we've had mud splattered all over our reputation?"
"We can tell everyone the truth of what happened. Uma isn't unchaste. Vijay is impure," Avantika said at a final attempt to convince herself and her husband that their daughter should be allowed to stay in Mandavi. Deep down Avantika knew she was fighting a losing battle.
"If you want what's best for all of our children, we have to send Uma back. Uma will learn to forgive her husband's infidelity if she gives him a chance, but the society will never forgive a single mother. I love Uma. I love our children as much as you do. I want the best for all of them and this is why we need to send Uma back."

Avantika sat back down on her bed for a few minutes. She took a deep breath and wiped away her tears. *Vinod is right.* She looked towards the door of her bedroom. She inhaled and stood up. *I have to tell Uma to go back to Madhapar. Hai Mata Rani, give me strength to do this.*

Chapter 48: Alice

It was 3.18am. Alice tossed and turned in bed, unable to sleep.

After finding out about Vijay's lies she had lamented and cried for a few hours. She stopped crying when Fatima knocked on the door to the room Alice and Vijay lived in. At the end of her shift, Fatima came to make sure Alice was alright as she had seen her leave the office in tears. With a lack of close friends in Mumbai, Alice unloaded her sorrows onto Fatima and told her of Vijay's betrayal. Alice noted that Fatima did not look too shocked at the news.
"Am I the only one who didn't know this?" Alice asked Fatima, who remained silent. She saw the look on Fatima's face. She knew that Fatima was hiding something. "Tell me everything you know."
"Alice Maam," Fatima began to get up. "It is very late. I need to go home, Ammee will be wondering where I am."
"SIT!" Alice commanded Fatima, who froze. She stood up and held onto Fatima. "Tell me everything you know. Everything."
After some persuasion, Fatima told Alice everything.
"We all thought that you knew Vijay sir was married."
Fatima also told Alice that Vijay had been with a few other women in her absence. Fatima did not know who the other women were.
"I didn't say anything because it was not my place."
Finding out that everyone else knew all along caused Alice's initial distress to turn into fury.
I refuse to shed anymore tears over that bellend. I'm not like Indian women, who will sit back and tolerate everything their man does. I never grew up aspiring to be Sita or Savitri or all those other women Indian women are told they should be like. I learnt to get even. Alice wiped her eyes and planned to punish him. She spent the following day thinking and planning her revenge on him. Once she had a concrete plan she asked Fatima to buy some items for her, so that she could put it into action.

Thirty hours had passed since she found out about Vijay's lies. Unable to sleep, she turned to her side and watched him sleeping. Her desire for revenge pumped her body with adrenaline which prevented her from sleeping. Despite being wide awake all night, she was not tired; she was excited. *I can't wait to see the look on your face tomorrow. You've made me look the fool in front of your staff. Tomorrow you're going to look the fool not just in front of our staff, but our customers too.* Alice looked over at the clock again. It was 4.02am. She lay back again and could not wait for morning. Imagining the look on Vijay's face when she was done with him, gave her a lot of satisfaction. Before she knew it, it was 5.30am and Vijay's alarm went off. The moment Alice heard the buzzing noise she closed her eyes and feigned sleep. *One more hour to go.* She listened as Vijay walked around the room. She heard him showering; the moment he turned the shower off she sat up waiting for Vijay to come out of the shower. She was ready to get her revenge.

Vijay stepped out of the shower with a towel around his waist, he was surprised to see Alice awake.
"How come you're up so early darling?"
"Couldn't sleep," she got up and walked into the bathroom and locked the door behind her. "I was feeling horny and couldn't sleep."
"Well unlock the door, I'll come in and sort you out."

That's the last thing I want. Alice pretended to laugh.
"Not right now babe. I'll come down and find you in the office once I'm done here." She put toothpaste onto her toothbrush. "There's a lock on our office door for a reason." Alice said working hard to modulate her voice.
She then proceeded to brush her teeth. *That arsehole won't know what's hit him.* Alice deliberately took long in the shower to make sure Vijay had gone to work when she stepped out. She opened her wardrobe and picked out a dress she felt made her look stunning. *Time to make myself look so good that he won't be able to resist me.*

It was a few minutes after 7am, when Alice finally got to the reception desk. Fatima was already there working. Alice walked over to her and smiled.
"Did you get them?" Alice whispered.

"Alice maam, are you sure you want to do this?" Fatima asked quietly. "You might make him angry. He might badly..."
"I can handle him," Alice interrupted "I've handled bigger fish than him before." She took the blue bag from Fatima. "Thanks for this."

Alice smiled at Fatima and walked into the office behind the reception desk. She closed the door behind and pulled the blinds down to cover all the windows in the room. She walked over to Vijay who was sat on the chair behind the desk. She stood behind him, bent over and stroked his penis through his suit trousers.
"You look so sexy in this grey suit." *What a shame for you that no one will see you in it.*
Vijay turned his chair around and stood up. He began to kiss Alice who kissed him back. He winked at Alice, which usually meant he wanted to have sex. Vijay removed his tie and suit jacket. Alice undid his shirt buttons and opened his belt. When Vijay was completely naked Alice decided it was time to shame him, just as he had embarrassed her.
"Let's make this more exciting," she said to him. Alice pushed him onto his office chair and got onto her knees. "Close your eyes" she said to Vijay.
Vijay let out a sigh, tilted his head back and shut his eyes. She could tell he was expecting a blowjob, but the moment he closed his eyes, Alice grabbed the blue bag and took out two cable ties. She saw his hands were both resting on the arms of the chair. She loosely tied the two cable ties around his wrist and the chair making little noise as possible. She put three on each arm just to be sure.
"Can I open my eyes yet?" Vijay asked attempting to peep.
"Not yet," Alice said
"Can I open my eyes now?" he asked again.
"No and if you peep you won't get your surprise," she told him.
Alice pulled two cable ties together very tightly on both arms. At the tightness around his arms, Vijay opened his eyes.
"Oh Kinky! What is this?" Vijay asked confused.

Alice looked at Vijay who was looking at his arms. She tightened the remaining four cable ties. Without saying a word she stood up and walked over to the mirror in their office. She readjusted her makeup

before redressing herself. Once she looked perfect again, she turned around to face Vijay who was tied to his office chair, completely naked. Alice unlocked the office door and opened the blinds. She came back and stood behind his chair.
"What are you doing?" Vijay asked uncertainly.
"Fatima," Alice called. "Can you please open our office door?"
"What the fuck?" he said panic stricken. "No, No. What are you doing?" he shouted.
Vijay writhed like a fish out of water in an attempt to free himself. Fatima came and opened the door. Fatima looked directly towards Vijay and Alice. Out of embarrassment she quickly looked away and held the door open.
"What is it maam?" Fatima asked deliberately looking anywhere but towards Vijay.
Without a word Alice pushed Vijay's chair out of the office. He made futile attempts to cover up. In the end he had to cross his legs to stop his penis being on show. However, his attempts were ineffective as it could still be seen. Alice saw that Fatima was looking very uncomfortable with the situation, but she did not care. *This is why men walk all over women here. They're too embarrassed and shy to stand up to them.* She gazed at the scarf Fatima wore to cover her hair. *You won't even tell men that you don't want to wear that hijab, there's no hope for you love. You're just going to be a man's play thing.*

Once Alice finished pushing Vijay's chair into the reception area, she got out another cable tie and tied the leg of the chair to a bar at the bottom of the reception desk. Alice watched as Vijay continued to struggle.
"Unless you want your hands to bleed, I wouldn't try to get out," She told him scathingly.
"What the fuck are you doing?" Vijay screamed.
"I spoke to your wife yesterday. The pregnant one you never have sex with." Alice saw Vijay stopped struggling. "Was it immaculate conception like Jesus?"
"She's..."
"Not lying... I'm not a fool. If you thought you could get one over me, you picked the wrong girl."
Vijay took a deep breath.

"I'm sorry..."
"I don't want you to be sorry," she snapped. "I want you to sit here in front of our guests coming in and out. When someone eventually lets you out of here, you'll find your stuff outside our room. You insisted we live in one of our rooms just until we had enough money to buy a house. I thought that was fine hoping we'd be out of here soon but I don't want that anymore. I'm going to look for my own place away from here. Until then you can't stay in the same room as me. Feel free to move into another room but bear in mind if you take up another room we will lose even more money. Oh yeah, and most of the rooms are already booked."

Without listening to anything else Vijay had to say, Alice walked away feeling elated. *The look on that bastard's face was worth this*. As she walked away she could hear Vijay shouting apologies, and curses.

Chapter 49: Uma

Uma sat in silence watching TV as her mother cleaned the house. Uma could tell that her mother kept glancing towards her every few minutes, hoping to get a reaction out of her. Nonetheless, since her mother told her that she would have to return to her in-law's house, Uma maintained a stubborn silence and coldness towards her family. *When I was little, maa always gave in when I was silent and sulked in the corner. She will relent and let me stay if she realises how upset I am.* Therefore Uma ignored her mother's attempts and continued to fix her gaze at the TV.

Uma recalled how she came to Mandavi with no intention of returning to Madhapar again. However, two nights ago her mother told her she must return to her in-laws home. Uma felt the ground slip from beneath her feet. She was a hundred percent certain that her parents would support her and that she had escaped Madhu's clutches. Uma cried and desperately pleaded with her parents to allow her to stay in Mandavi. At one point she even felt that she had convinced her parents to let her remain with them, but her father interrupted and revealed his final decision.

"A girl leaves her parent's home in a wedding palanquin. She can only leave her in-laws home on a funeral bier," her father told her.

He then continued to inform her about family honour and how a divorce would shatter their family's reputation. Her father carried on regurgitating things he had heard from other people: A single mother would never fare well in Indian society. A married woman's place is with her husband and his family.

Uma was distraught that her parents prioritised their family honour over her happiness. The following day her father even tried to explain that his actions were for Uma's own good. Uma maintained a stubborn silence and did not say a single word to him.

Today I will have to leave this house. I will not leave with a smile on my face. Let them worry about me. I do not care anymore. Next time maaji wants more money I will not think twice before I ask. I am going to prioritise my own happiness now. Every now and then Uma heard her mother quoting something which justified her reasons for sending Uma back, or something Uma should consider changing about herself when she returned home. Uma ignored everything that was being said and simply focused on the episode of Shri Krishna playing on the TV, a drama based on the life of the Hindu God Krishna.

This particular episode dramatised the story of the Raas Lila. Radha and all of the other milkmaids of Vrindavan fasted and prayed to Durga's sixth form Katyayini. Pleased with their fast the goddess appeared before Radha and the other milkmaids. She told them to close their eyes and think of the man they love. She promised them that in exactly three months they will get the man of their dreams as their husband. Every single milkmaid desired Krishna as their husband. Three months later, on the night of the full moon, the milkmaids of Vrindavan heard Krishna's flute. They knew the time of their union with Krishna had come. They left everything and immediately ran towards the River Yamuna, following the sound of Krishna's flute. When they reached the river, Krishna was still playing his flute. None of the milkmaids approached him they just stood and waited. Radha walked over and began to dance with Krishna. The supreme beings of the Universe united. Krishna, the source of creation and Radha, the strength behind creation had both come to Vrindavan in human form. The unity of Radha and Krishna was a beautiful sight to behold. The other milkmaids formed a circle around them and watched sadly as Radha and Krishna united. Their sorrow vanished as goddess Katyayini's blessing materialised. Krishna multiplied himself into many separate forms. Each milkmaid got her own Krishna. The souls of the milkmaids merged with Krishna and became one with him. The milkmaids of Vrindavan began the tradition of praying to Katyayini every year. *I did Jaya Parvati Vrat every year. These milkmaids got their own husband, despite having the same man. I couldn't even get my own husband, because he is playing Laila Majnu with another woman. I bet that white girl does not even know about Jaya Parvati Vrat, then why do I have to share my husband? Did you give me such a deceptive husband because I broke my fast a few times?* Uma turned around and looked at the idol of Durga in her parent's shrine. *People say you are the mother of all beings. Mothers forgive their children for their mistakes but you punished me for such a small mistake. Is this why you gave me that demonic family? Girls do this fast so they can get an ideal husband but instead of forgiving me you punished me for breaking your fast. You wanted to torment me with an unfaithful husband.*

When the time came for Uma to leave, she picked up her bag and began to walk out of the house.
"Uma my beti," her mother said. "Are you going to leave without saying bye?"
Uma turned around for a second and saw her mother. They both had tears in their eyes. Her mother stood with open arms indicating Uma to hug her. Uma refused to drop her suitcase. She took a deep breath and turned around and continued walking. *I do not want her to think that I am happy to be going back. If I hug her she will think she is doing it for my happiness. This way she will know I am not happy.* Uma heard her mother call her name a few times but she restrained herself from looking back. With every step she took, the part of her which believed the frosty attitude would make her mother change her mind diminished.

Uma still felt a small flicker of hope. She still thought her mother would send Arjun to pick her up from the station. Once the bus pulled out of Mandavi bus station, the final bit of hope she had left shattered. She began to recall the journey she took to Vijay's house on the day she got married. Uma cried and worried about her life in Madhapar, as she had done on her wedding day. However, this time she was alone. She harboured no more dreams about a happy ever after with Vijay. *Vijay's affair has given me more pain than what his family gave to me. I never understood women who cried over their husband's lies. I always said I would never cry over a man who did not deserve my tears, but now I am the deceived person I cannot stop the tears flowing. All I can think about day and night is of Vijay's betrayal.* Uma could not decide whether she was more hurt by Vijay's actions or her own parents' decision. *I always thought maa and bapuji would support me with everything. Never once did I think their fear of society was greater than their love for me.*

As Uma got closer to Madhapar it dawned on her that there was no life waiting for her in Mumbai. *I will spend the rest of my life living in that birdcage, remaining silent in case any predator pounces on me.* She looked outside the window of her bus, tears still streaming down her eyes. With less than two kilometres left to Bhuj, Uma felt her baby kick. *Skanda!* Uma put her hand on her stomach and began to stroke it. *My reason to continue fighting!* Uma found a new ray of hope. A tiny light glowed at the end of a dark tunnel. *Skanda had been the ray of hope and light for the universe when the evil demon Tarkasur spread his terror. Skanda destroyed the demon and re-established peace and righteousness in the world. My Skanda will re-establish my peace. He is my ray of light. If my family love my child they will have to accept me. I have seen this happen all the time. The moment a woman gives her in-laws a son they treat her like a goddess.*

Chapter 50: Amrita

Amrita finished packing the tiffin box with food for poor people and sealed it shut. She placed it at the door leading to her house.
"Leela," Amrita called. "I have put the leftover food at the door."
"OK, I will leave for work in a few minutes." Amrita heard Leela shout from her room.

Amrita walked back into the kitchen so she could begin cooking dinner for the evening. She added some salt and oil to the flour before mixing it around. She finally added boiling water to the mixture and began to knead the dough to make chapattis. Amrita intentionally prepared extra food, but always told others the food was leftover from the night before. She cooked the excess food for the poor so she could donate the food in memory of her father, mother and sister. She hoped the meals she distributed to the needy would accumulate good karma for their souls, which would lead them to a better life in the future. *Waheguru, I cook extra khana everyday with the hope you will not put them through the same pain they went through in this life. Give peace to their souls.* Amrita felt a stab of pain in her left arm which made her wrinkle up her face as a reaction to the stinging. She persevered and continued to knead the dough.

After beeji died from breast cancer I cared for Gurpreet and Nirmal as if they were both my own children, until I married. After a number of proposals, Amrita's father selected the Oberoi family and she moved to Chandigarh, two hundred kilometres away from her family. Amrita established a new life in Chandigarh but often thought about her family in Amritsar and visited whenever possible. Four years after her own wedding, Amrita was informed about Nirmal's marriage.

Amrita met Nirmal's in-laws for the first time on the day of Nirmal's Roka, the Sikh engagement ceremony. After the Roka ceremony her father told Amrita that due to the shortage of girls in Punjab, Nirmal received six marriage proposals. Her father picked the family that would

best keep Nirmal happy from the proposals he received. Amrita had no reason to question her father's choice. He had picked the perfect man for her and was confident he also picked the right family for Nirmal. It was after the Roka that Amrita realised her father's mistake. The Chadda family demanded a dowry for the wedding to go ahead.
"Papaji why did you not find out their dahej demands before the Roka?" Amrita had questioned her father.
"Mainu nahi pata. I thought they won't ask for anything, because they came to us for Nirmal's hand. I could not afford to let this relationship slip out of my hands. I agreed straight away. They own so much property and land. Nirmal would never lack any comfort. I wanted my Nirmal to be happy just like you..."
"It is not the money that makes me happy papaji," Amrita snapped. "Yes I have money which has improved my life, but without the respect and love my family give to me the money would be nothing."
"Respect and love will not fill your empty stomach if you had no money. The Chadda family will turn my dhi into a queen, just like the Oberoi family did with you."
"My family never asked for a dowry."
"Amrita puttar, I have trust in Waheguru. Waheguru will make sure Nirmal is happy like he made you happy."
Amrita realised that arguing would achieve nothing. The relationship was already finalised. Despite disliking Nirmal's in-laws, Amrita saw no other option but to let the wedding go ahead. Vikram and his family kindly offered to help Amrita's father with the dowry amount. Amrita's father declined the offer. He insisted that it was a matter of great shame for a father to take money off his daughter and took out a loan to fulfil their demands. Fortunately for Nirmal, after the wedding she remained in Amritsar as that was where her in-laws lived. Amrita spoke to Nirmal on a regular basis and even visited her a few times. Amrita was pleased to see how happy Nirmal was in her marital home. However, everything changed two years after Nirmal's marriage.

Out of the blue Amrita received the news her father had died. Amrita was astounded by the news of her father's death. *Hai Rubba he was well when I spoke to him a few days ago. What happened to him?* Distraught she made her way to Amritsar as quickly as she could. When they arrived at her father's house, Vikram and Amrita were confused to find her father's home padlocked. Perplexed she called her brother to find out where everyone had gone. *Surely the funeral would be held in papaji's own home?* Gurpreet informed Amrita to come to their aunt's house as that was where the funeral was being held. Without asking anymore questions she made her way to her aunt's house.

At the sight of her father's lifeless body Amrita fell to her knees. She began to cry, slowly remembering the man who gave her the love of both a father and a mother. She kissed her father's forehead and made way for other mourners to see his body. She found her brother and went over to hug him.
"Veerji what happened?" Amrita asked her brother. Gurpreet averted his eyes from her. Amrita stopped crying. *He is hiding something from me.*
"What happened to papaji?" she repeated herself more firmly.
"Not now bhenji," Gurpreet whispered. "I will tell you everything later. There are too many people."
"Where is Nirmal?" Amrita asked her brother as she looked around trying to find her sister. Amrita was certain that her sister would be devastated too and would need comforting. At that very moment people said it was time to take the body to be cremated and her brother walked away to carry the body. Amrita walked around for a while looking for Nirmal but realised she was nowhere to be seen. *Why would she not come to her own papaji's funeral?* Amrita began to grow worried but she knew she could do nothing about it until her brother returned to answer her questions.

Once the funeral was over, Amrita demanded answers from her Gurpreet. Her brother told her everything they had hidden from her since Nirmal's wedding. He told Amrita that Nirmal's in-laws regularly made demands for money, and always threatened to kill her if their demands were not met. Gurpreet described the ridiculous amount of demands they made which grew on a monthly basis. First they wanted a new fridge, then a new car, then a flat. Amrita's sense of foreboding increased due to Nirmal's absence. Worried about where the story was leading to, Amrita kept on rushing her brother to tell the story quickly. Gurpreet told Amrita how her father sold everything he owned,

including their home to fulfil the demands Nirmal's in-laws kept on making.
"Why did no one tell me?"
"Papaji said he did not want you to know. He was worried this would upset you and..."
"UPSET ME?" Amrita shouted. "I COULD HAVE HELPED!"
"Papaji would never have accepted your help. He refused to take a single rupee off you because you are his daughter."
"We would have forced him to take the money. Nirmal's safety is more important than his ego of not taking money from his dhi," Vikram said.
"Why did no one tell the police about their threats?" Amrita asked her brother.
"They said they will kill her if we got the police involved," Gurpreet responded. "The Chadda family is too friendly with the police. They bribe them."
Gurpreet continued to tell Amrita how the stress of being unable to fulfil any further demands drove their father to suicide.
"Things became so bad for papaji and still no one thought to tell me anything?" Amrita said seething with fury towards her brother. "Am I not a part of this family?" After everything I did for everyone in this family, you have all proved that you consider me an outsider."
"Amrita, I..." Gurpreet began to say.
"Don't you dare try and say papaji did not want you to say anything," Amrita snapped. "You are an adult veerji. You could have told me if you wanted."
Amrita stormed off without saying another word to her brother. She was so angry she left with the intention of never speaking to him again.

Once she and Vikram reached Chandigarh, Amrita felt calmer. She spoke to Vikram about helping her sister, and he immediately agreed to help. Vikram planned to give them some money and under the pretext of Nirmal coming to visit Amrita in Chandigarh they would rescue her. Two days later, the promise she made to never speak to her brother again was broken. He phoned her to inform her of Nirmal's death. Amrita felt like the air had been knocked out of her at the news of her sister's death. She had howled like a wounded beast. Vikram took Amrita to Nirmal's home with Gurpreet. By the time they reached Nirmal's home the body had already been cremated. The death certificate cited food poisoning as the cause of death. However, Amrita, Gurpreet and Vikram all knew that Nirmal was murdered and lodged a complaint with the police. With no body and a lack of evidence the case was dropped. In a fit of rage Gurpreet decided to punish Nirmal's in-laws. He threw a corrosive acid, which is used to clean toilets, over Nirmal's sister-in-law. Amrita lost her final family member. Gurpreet was arrested and sentenced to five years in prison for assault.

After her brother's prison sentence, the Oberoi family asked Amrita to leave their house because the actions of her family tainted the Oberoi family's reputation. Vikram stood by Amrita and left with her. The bank Vikram worked at allowed him to transfer to a branch in Bhuj. They both moved to the state of Gujarat with their children to start a new life. The day they arrived in Gujarat, just over three years ago, was the day Amrita carved an N into her hand. Amrita felt the cut she made prevented the anger inside her from annihilating her body. She felt the anger release from inside her when she felt her hot blood against her skin. *One day I will destroy their lives the same way they destroyed my bhenji's life and my family's happiness. Until then I will let this wound be a reminder that I have unfinished business with those pehnchods.*

Amrita redirected her attention to the meal she was making. She scrubbed the flour off her fingers against the edges of the bowl in which she mixed the chapatti dough. She poked her finger into the dough to make sure it was ready.

Chapter 51: Leela

Leela re-wrapped a shawl around her as she walked to work. *Winter is coming.* She was outside Rathod Haveli when she spotted Uma dragging a suitcase behind her. *Ende ammo, why is she back? And why is she carrying that suitcase on her own?* Leela went over to Uma and greeted her. Uma smiled at her and continued towards the mansion.
"Uma didi, give that to me," Leela took the suitcase from Uma. "Why are you carrying this on your own?"
Uma did not respond and carried on walking. Leela went after her. *In her condition she should not be dragging that suitcase.* Uma was at the gates of Rathod Haveli when Leela asked her again.
"Uma didi, why are you back? Why are you on your own?"
"Jee ghar ma beti ni palki jai, eej ghar ma thi eni arthhi oothe" Uma whispered.
Leela looked confused. She heard the saying before but was not sure why Uma was just mumbling it to her. Leela grabbed Uma's hand to prevent her from walking inside. Uma stopped. Leela immediately let go of her hand as she remembered her position in society. For a brief moment she forgot she was just a maid.
"Sorry Uma didi," Leela said. "What are you talking about?"
"Maa and Bapuji told me that my wedding palanquin entered that house," Uma pointed at Rathod Haveli. "I CAN ONLY LEAVE AS A CORPSE," she stormed.
Leela gasped at Uma's reaction. This was the first time Leela heard Uma raise her voice.
"I THOUGHT REFUSING THEIR HELP TO COME BACK HERE, REFUSING TO TALK TO THEM AND BEING ANGRY WOULD MAKE THEM CHANGE THEIR MIND. I THOUGHT THEY WOULD LET ME STAY," Uma's voice began to crack. "Their reputation is more important to them than me. They do not care that my husband deceived me or that his family haven't accepted me. They gave me away. Their responsibility towards me is over." Uma had an odd look on her face. As though she was holding back a lot of things. "I've seen this on TV a lot, but thought my parents were different." Uma began to laugh

hysterically.

For a moment Leela stood there unsure what to do. *Am I allowed to hug her?* Uma's laughter changed to sobbing. Leela dropped Uma's suitcase and walked over to her. Leela noticed Purbai standing on the balcony of her house. The moment Leela saw Purbai was watching, Purbai vanished out of sight. Leela was still unsure whether she should hug Uma. She settled with comforting Uma by holding her hand.
"Why are you standing outside my house and making a drama?"
Leela jumped in surprise to see Madhu standing at the front door. Madhu's voice was quiet yet harsh. "Get into the house before everyone in this village starts to talk. NOW."
Uma wiped her eyes and looked at Leela before she walked into the house.

Before people start talking? Is that all Indian parents ever think about? Leela recalled the words her mother-in-law spoke to her after she was raped. *"What will people say when they find out our daughter-in-law has been tainted?"* Leela's anger began to simmer. *What other people will think, was a weapon used against me. When will people put their own happiness before what other people think? I might have grown up poor and be uneducated but I am pleased that I never worried about what people think of me. If I worried about what people thought of me I would never have opened up to Amritaji about my past and I would probably have died on the streets of Bhuj. Even goddesses were not free of slander by society. When Devi Lakshmi came to earth in the human form of Sita, she too was maligned by the citizens of Ayodhya.* Leela picked up the suitcase and began to drag it into the house. As she took the suitcase she recalled the story of the humiliation Sita was forced to tolerate. Ravan kidnapped Sita and she was forced to spend ten months in his city. Rama rescued and her reinstated Sita with the status of his wife. He made her his equal again and both Rama and Sita became king and queen of Ayodhya. But after the coronation, the citizens of Ayodhya began to question the chastity of a woman who spent ten months in the home of another man. Unrest grew in the city because the citizens thought their queen may be impure. Compelled by the nation and as a King, Rama was forced to banish a pregnant Sita into the forest. After banishing Sita, Rama renounced all luxuries as a king. He had marked Sita as his equal and thus slept on the floor, and ate whatever he knew Sita could eat in the forest. *Humpf! If he had told the people of his city that he trusted his wife and her purity he would not have to live like a pauper despite being a king. People are brainwashed by keeping up a reputation.* Many years later Sita returned with Rama's twin sons. The citizens once again asked her to prove her chastity before they allow her to become queen again. Unwilling to give any more tests of chastity Sita called upon mother earth. She asked mother earth to open up and swallow her at that moment if she was chaste and pure. The ground opened up and swallowed Sita. The citizens of Ayodhya realised their mistake and felt guilt. Never again would they question the honour of a woman. *Yet today people still feel their image is important and point fingers to taint a woman's honour. If people like Sita were not free of gossip what chance do we normal women have?*

Leela got closer towards the house. *On one hand people in this country do grand pooja for women goddesses. Saraswati, Lakshmi, Parvati, Durga and all the other goddesses are worshipped. On the other hand fear of society or their own greed makes people thrust misery into their daughters' or wives' lives. They worship Saraswati, the goddess of knowledge and wisdom, yet they denied me an education. Where is the sense in that? They worship Lakshmi for wealth and good luck, yet lament the day a girl is born. My parents sold me for money but they would never part with the idol they had of Bhagya Lakshmi. They worship Parvati for strength and power, yet believe women to be weak and commit crimes against them. I was raped and I did not do anything about it. Perhaps I am weak.* Leela reached the threshold of Rathod Haveli and stood there for a moment. Her eyes began to sting. *Amma taught me that my life will be fulfilled when I become a wife and a mother. Being a wife brought me nothing but misery. People think I am unmarried and have no children; they pity me. I am much happier now than I have ever been before. If more people in this country were like Amritaji and Vikramji then this world would be a better place. Vikramji treats his wife as his equal. Neither of them care whether I am married or not.*

Leela finished the silent rant in her mind and wiped her eyes. She never vocalised her thoughts. *No one would listen to the rants of an uneducated lower caste girl.* When she stepped into the house she noticed that Vijay was back and he was holding Uma's hand. He was dragging Uma up the stairs. *Why does Uma didi look so worried about being taken up by Vijay? What happened in here whilst I was bringing the suitcase in?*

Chapter 52: Uma

Uma walked into the house and saw Vijay stood in the living room. Her heart leapt at the sight of her husband. Before either of them could say a word to each other, Vijay walked over towards her and grabbed her hand. His tight grip caused Uma pain. Without saying a word he began to forcefully drag her up to their bedroom. Uma had no idea why he was taking her upstairs. She tried asking a few times but her questions were met with silence. *His aggression is making me worry. He has never bent a hair on my head before. I have nothing to worry about.* A small part of Uma hoped; *perhaps he is going to apologise for his infidelity.* However, Uma knew that she was being optimistic to the point of foolishness, and thus suppressed her thoughts.

Outside their bedroom, Vijay let go of Uma's hand. She felt the blood rushing back into her palms. He opened the door and silently commanded her to enter the bedroom using his threatening eyes. Obediently, Uma entered the room. She turned around to see Vijay locking the bedroom door behind him. *Vijay only locks the door if he doesn't want to be interrupted when we are making love.* Uma stood up with a strong posture. *He has been romancing other women, and now he wants to come back to me. Does he think I am in the mood to be romanced?* Vijay walked over to Uma, and grabbed her arms. She could feel his nails digging into her skin. Uma gasped with pain and looked into his eyes. The look on his face frightened her. His eyes were full of anger.
"Who told you to phone my work and tell them about the baby?" he asked coldly.
This is not an apology. Uma pulled her face back and looked away.
"I... I..." Uma stuttered.
Uma felt Vijay grab her face and forced it to look directly at him. Her mouth was forced open by the way Vijay was crushing her jaw.
"Who told you to phone my work and tell them about the baby?" he repeated dangerously.
Vijay's face was so close to Uma's. She could feel his breath on her face

with every word he spoke. She struggled slightly and wriggled her mouth free. The places where Vijay had grabbed her face felt hot.
"I just wanted to speak to you. That lady asked me to leave a message. I told you the truth. The baby..."
Uma was interrupted by a slap from Vijay. She was stunned to silence. *Hai Mata Rani he hit me. Vijay raised his hand against me. No, no, no. How could this be happening? The Vijay I love would never raise his hand against a woman?*
"Do you know how much shame I've been subjected to, because of you?"
Uma was unsure as to whether she should reply or not. *What if he hits me if I say anything?* Unsure where to look she stared at the wall behind Vijay. Uma felt another slap on her face, which was harder than the previous slap.
"Look at me when I'm talking to you. Do you know how much shame I've gone through because of you?" Vijay roared.
Uma's eyes began to fill with tears. Having spent almost a year with his family she finally saw their traits in him. She knew he expected an answer from her. She gathered her courage and took a deep breath before she responded.
"I don't know what happened but believe me I had no intention of shaming you. I only wanted to speak to you. I did not do anything wrong," Uma said. As she spoke, some of the anger she felt towards his family came out. "I am the one who should be angry. You are the one romancing another woman when you have a pregnant wife at home."
Uma screamed in pain as Vijay grabbed her hair.
"Do you know who you're talking to, you fucking bitch?" Vijay shoved Uma to the ground. "I am your husband. Your whole purpose in life is to serve and obey me and my family. Women of your status shouldn't open their mouths to shout at their husband. You open your mouth only to suck my dick. And that's only if I allow you to suck it." Vijay spat on Uma, who still lay on the floor. He then bent down on his knees. "You've not just shamed me in front of so many people, but because of you the woman I love hates me."
Uma felt the air knocked out of her. She felt her heart pound against her chest as if it was about to burst. *Love? He loves that dhoiri? Hai Mata Rani, how can this be? All those things he said to me when we married, when he came home for Diwali...*

"You love me! You took me as your wife and went around the holy fire with me."
"Did you bring the dowry we wanted?"
Uma did not answer; slowly, he was showing how he was just like the rest of his family.
"What happened? Has a witch eaten your tongue? Let me tell you. A wedding is incomplete without a dowry. Your family gave us peanuts, which is as good as not giving a dowry. If you wanted the status of my wife you should have given us a dowry worthy of our status. Your peanuts make you fit enough to just lick the soles of my shoes."
"A dowry isn't part of the wedding ceremony," Uma shouted out. Much of the anger she had held in her was beginning to seep out of her. Seeing Vijay's real avatar she did not care. "Dowry was created by greedy people. Our religion doesn't say anywhere that a dowry is part of the ceremony."
This time Vijay punched Uma in her face.
Hai Mata Rani why is he doing this? I have never seen him angry. Even when Madhu used to speak badly to me, he was never angry towards his own maa. Is my husband inebriated?

Uma decided not to get back up. She felt she was safer on the floor. Uma looked up and saw him standing over her. She listened as Vijay narrated the story of how his white girlfriend humiliated him. He kicked Uma every time he paused. She winced and screamed unable to do anything to protect herself. Vijay delivered a kick really close to her bump.
"STOP!" Uma screamed when she realised her child's life was in danger. She knew she had to stop him at any cost. "Our baby... our baby," Uma said out of breath.
Vijay stopped when he realised what Uma was telling him. He turned around, unlocked the bedroom door and left.

Uma continued to lie on the floor. Vijay's brutality and true colours left her speechless, shattering every single dream she had seen. She put her hand on her stomach and felt Skanda. She struggled to get up from the floor and felt a sharp pain in her ankle where Vijay had kicked her.

Eventually, she managed to get up and closed her eyes. *I haven't lost everything yet. I still have Skanda, my reason to live.*

Chapter 53: Charu

"I'm running the Mumbai Marathon to raise money for charity," Suneeti said to Charu.
She was impressed that one of her best friends was running a full marathon.
"I would never be able to run forty-two kilometres," Charu said in awe.
"Do you want to sponsor me?"
Suneeti produced a sponsorship form and handed it to Charu.
"Which charity are you running for?" she asked.
"I am running to raise money for an orphaned girl," Suneeti explained.
"Well she's not really orphaned; she just lives in an orphanage."
Charu turned around looking sceptical to her friend. *What kind of child lives in an orphanage if she's not an orphan?*
"She was abandoned at birth by her parents who wanted a boy. She was found in the middle of the forest when she was one day old. She was being eaten alive by ants and they had already eaten her nose when she was found. She was lucky to have been found when she was; otherwise the ants would have eaten her completely."
Charu shuddered with repulsion, sickened by the fact people could be so cruel. *I hope those cruel people get eaten by ants. Actually, I hope they get a fate worse than that.*

"She has grown up with a missing nose. She is now old enough for reconstruction surgery. The orphanage cannot pay for the operation. I am raising money for her."
Charu was lost for words. *I cannot believe things like this still happen in so called Modern India.*
Disturbed by Suneeti's story, Charu finally spoke. "Years ago mumma told me that people used to pour boiling milk down a girl baby's throat or drown her in milk because they wanted a boy. I thought people stopped this stupidity."
"Not at all! Lakshmi isn't the only girl in this situation. Every week thousands of girls are aborted, killed or given away just because they are girls."

"I thought only poor people in villages did this?" Charu said. "Because they could not afford to keep girls?"
"Don't be silly," Suneeti said. "Richer people and middle class people are just able to disguise it better. But you are right about the fact that people think girls are expensive. Girls are seen as someone else's wealth. People don't want to invest money in bringing up a girl, educating her and then giving her away to another family's son. They also don't want to pay a dowry for her wedding, so they think it's easier to get rid of her before investing in her. For every thousand boys that are born, only 914 girls are born or survive."
Charu shuddered at the fact that humans could be so vile. *This must mean...* Charu attempted to figure out how many girls were killed every year. Confused by the maths she settled with thousands. *We live in a country where people call girls Lakshmi and they still kill them because they see girls as a burden! This is what happens in the Kaliyug. We are in the age of evil; people in this world are nasty.*

Charu opened her wallet. She saw the 10,000 rupees her mother gave her earlier that day. Charu was going to buy some new outfits but she no longer wanted new dresses. *That girl needs the money more than I do. My new clothes can wait.*
"Here have this," Charu said handing nine thousand rupees to Suneeti. "If you need any help to raise more money for this girl let me know."

Charu spent the rest of her day thinking about the shocking stories and statistics Suneeti had told her. When she got home she sat in her bedroom lost in her own thoughts. Charu did not hear her mother knock on the door so, when she walked into her room, she stood up surprised.
"Mumma! You scared me. I thought I was alone."
"What do you want for dinner?"
"I don't mind! Whatever you want."
Her mother sat down on the bed and smiled at Charu.
"So where is it then?" her mother asked.
"Where is what?"
"I gave you money so you could go shopping. What did you buy?"
"Nothing," she paused. "I gave the money to charity." Charu explained to

her mother what she had donated the money to. She expected her mother to get angry, because they were already short of money. However, her mother just took a deep breath and smiled.
"It is a great cause." Her mother had tears in her eyes and began to walk away.
"What's wrong mumma?"
"Oh I'm just very proud of my Charu putting other people before herself. When we lived in Ahmedabad one of our neighbours had her daughters killed in front of her eyes."

Before Charu could ask any more questions, Madhu left the bedroom. Her mother's response chilled Charu to the bones. She understood how important it was to do something for girl's rights. She felt inspired by Suneeti. *I want to do something to support survivors of this heinous crime. I will start my own orphanage one day but I need more money for that. For now I could give my time or help raise awareness or something.*

Charu walked down the stairs as she wrote a text message to Suneeti. She was informing Suneeti that she was coming to her house. Not looking where she was going, Charu almost bumped into Uma. Haai *haai! Why did this waste of space choose this moment to go up the stairs? I was about to go out to do something good and now her inauspicious presence has tainted everything.* Charu continued to walk down the stairs and did not question the bruises Uma had on her face.

Chapter 54: Uma

"Water," Uma said, holding a glass of water in front of Vijay. He had ordered her to go and get him some filtered water from the fridge.

Vijay lay on the bed reading a newspaper. He took the glass of water and drank it. He sighed with satisfaction once he finished his beverage and began to look admiringly at Uma. Uncomfortable by the way he was looking at her, she began to walk away.
"Come back here and stand in front of me," Uma heard him command.

Hai Mata Rani, what now? Uma's heartbeat began to speed up. She paused for a second. She saw her reflection in the mirror and saw some of the bruises on her face from the beating he gave to her last night. She looked at the bedroom door and saw it was unlocked. Relieved she walked over to where Vijay sat and did as she was told. Vijay put his newspaper down and sat up. He began to look her up and down with a smug look on his face.
"Even though you're covered in bruises and you're fat, you're still very sexy."
Uma screamed as Vijay slapped her bum hard. Vijay laughed and relaxed, laying back again. Vijay began to rub his groin area, she could see the outline of his penis through the black jeans he was wearing.
"Look at what you have just done to me," Vijay whispered as he continued to rub his penis. Uma began to feel uncomfortable and looked away. Vijay stopped laughing. Concerned by his silence she looked back at him and saw he was still smiling.
"Take it out," he ordered.
"What?" Uma began to walk towards the unlocked bedroom door. *I do not want him to touch me. I should leave this room then he can't do anything.* However, before she made it to the door she felt Vijay grab her hand.
"You don't want my dick inside you?" Vijay turned her around and pinned her against the wall with his left hand to her throat. He used his right hand to bolt their bedroom door shut. At the sound of the locked

room, Uma became terrified. "You always said that you love it when I fuck you. Go on take my dick out."
Desperate to get away, Uma used the first excuse she could think of. "Please Vijay. I need to go to the mandir. I am fasting."
"Why do you want to go to the mandir?" Vijay snapped. "Your god is standing in front of you. Pati Parmeshwar Namo Namah. Isn't that what Indian women believe? Your husband is god. Well I am here in front of you, so why go to the mandir? I will accept your worship Uma, but like any good devotee you need to get onto your knees to worship me."

Vijay forced Uma's hand to rub the outline of his penis. She tried to get her hand away but he was too strong. He eventually stopped and gave her some space. Uma began to breathe to refill her lungs with oxygen. *He let me go.* Relieved, she started to leave the bedroom, but he grabbed her hair dragged Uma to their bed.
"I told you yesterday that women like you can suck my dick but only when I let them," he said menacingly. "I also meant to say, when I want it sucked. You fucking suck it." Vijay slapped Uma and pushed her onto the bed.
"Vijay let go of me," Uma begged desperately. "I need to pray at the mandir."
Vijay pinned Uma down to the bed. He ripped open her blouse and pulled off her sari.
Uma heard Vijay undo the zip of his flies. She struggled like a fish out of water. The moment she felt Vijay enter her she screamed in pain with tears rolling down her eyes. She had made love to her husband in the past, but this time it was not making love. He was asserting his authority over her. The act which gave her pleasure in the past felt like torture.
Vijay held her throat and Uma felt the air squeezed out of her. Uma felt she was going to suffocate to death. Once Vijay was finished he let go of her throat. Uma once again felt the oxygen rushing back into her lungs. Vijay unlocked the bedroom door and left Uma on the bed.

She lay on her bed for a long time, her mind vacant of any thoughts.

Chapter 55: Avantika

Avantika waited as the automatic gates opened to let her into the Rathod's home. She carried a silver tiffin containing handmade sweets for Uma. *When Uma sees the mohanthal I have made for her she will be so pleased. These are her favourite. Everything will be forgiven.* She entered through the gates. With a smile, she walked towards the mansion. Once she reached the threshold of Rathod Haveli, she saw the front door was already open. The noise of many women crying echoed from inside the house. Avantika became worried. *Why are so many women crying? Something must have happened.* She walked into the house and found out what the source of lament was. In the living room, there were hundreds of women dressed in white crying. Madhu was beating her chest and howling. Avantika noted there were no tears in Madhu's eyes. As she looked around the living room she spotted a mound on the floor covered in a gold and red sari. Avantika immediately realised that the mound was a body. *Hai Mata Rani what is this? What's happened here?* Her sense of foreboding increased and her heartbeat began to rise. Avantika saw a photograph of Uma in front of the body. The photograph had a garland of fresh flowers around it. The jolt she felt at the sight caused her to drop the silver container with mohanthal in it. The crash on the floor opened up the container and the mohanthal crumbled all over the floor. Tears began to fill her eyes and she stumbled backwards in shock. Avantika felt a heavy breeze inside the living room. The heavy gust of wind blew away the red sari that covered Uma's body revealing what was underneath it. Avantika gasped at Uma's remains. She stood rooted to the ground unable to move. The skin on the body had been burnt off leaving pink, purple, red and black flesh which was exposed or burnt. There was no mouth covering the teeth as it had been burnt away, the white teeth still in place stood out against the burnt flesh. The body looked as though it was still screaming in pain. Uma was burnt beyond recognition, and her body was still seeping with pus.

"UMA!" Avantika shrieked as she opened her eyes.
Avantika found herself drenched in sweat and felt her heart beating rapidly against her ribs. She felt confused for a few seconds. She turned to her right and saw Vinod asleep next to her. The initial confusion vanished. She exhaled feeling a mixture of relief and horror. *It was just a bad dream. A bad dream.* She took a few deep breaths and lay on her bed for a while to allow her heart beat to return to normal again. Avantika's sleep had once again been interrupted by nightmares of Uma. Her frequent nightmares about Uma were becoming more and more vivid as time went on. She took a few minutes to recollect her thoughts before she realised it was dawn. *Haai haai, what is this inauspicious sign? It is twilight! The dream happened during twilight. If people have a dream during dusk it means the dream will come true.* Avantika began to panic and went to the only person she felt could prevent her dreams becoming a reality; goddess Durga. She stood in front of the shrine at a distance because she had not yet showered. Without lighting a diva, Avantika put her hands together and closed her eyes. *Hai Mata Rani only you can protect her now. Please do something to stop my dream from becoming a reality. I don't have anyone else to turn to. You're the only person who can help me.*

Avantika stopped praying and froze. The telephone was ringing. Her eyes widened with fear. *Who could be calling this early? People only call this early if it's an emergency or something bad has happened. Something has happened to my Uma! The inauspicious dream I saw during twilight has come true.* Avantika slowly walked towards the ringing phone dreading what the person was going to say to her. Just as she touched the telephone to pick it up, it stopped ringing. *Hai Mata Rani, whoever was calling has put the phone down. Now I don't even know who was calling. What if Uma was calling me because she was in danger? What if she needed my help but I didn't pick up the phone on time and now there is no one to help her?* Avantika heard Gauri's mobile phone ringing. She heard the ring tone stop.
"Hello?" Gauri answered the phone groggily.
She was fully alert once more. The hairs on the back of her neck stood on end as she waited with bated breath trying to deduce who was calling this early.

"What?" Gauri asked shocked. "What's happened to Umaben?"
I knew it's something to do with Uma. I should have known the moment I saw the dream. She walked over to Gauri as quickly as she could.
Avantika barged into Gauri's bedroom without knocking. Gauri had not expected anyone to be up this early and jumped with fright at Avantika's sudden entry.
"What's wrong with Uma? Phone aap." Avantika snatched the phone out of her daughter's hand without waiting for her to hand over the phone to her. "Hello? What's happened to Uma?"
"Hello," Avantika realised the voice belonged to Charu. "Uma is in hospital. Her labour pains have started. The baby is coming."
Relief swept through Avantika's body. *My Uma is fine.* The relief was replaced with excitement. *I'm going to be a nani. My Uma is going to be a maa. Wait till everyone else finds out.* The excitement was quickly replaced with worry. *Uma isn't due for another six weeks. Why is she having labour pains so soon?*
"Charu, why is the baby early?" Avantika asked.
"I don't know. I'll ask the baby when it's born, shall I?" Charu responded sarcastically.
Akal vagar ni chokri. That Madhu hasn't taught her girl any manners. She doesn't even know how to talk to elders. Rich with money, but poor in morals.
"I'm coming now," Avantika said as she hung up on Charu. "I need to go to hospital. Uma's labour pains have started, the baby is coming," she told Gauri very quickly.

Chapter 56: Madhu

Madhu sat in the hospital playing with her fingers. Every time the door opened she looked up eagerly to see if there was any news. Madhu felt deflated and disappointed every time she saw that it was not Uma's midwife or doctor and returned to twiddling her fingers. The only time she stopped fidgeting was when Vinod bought them all food.
"Vehvanji, I got some nashta," Vinod told Madhu. "Would you like dabeli?"
Madhu looked at the dabeli in Vinod's hand. It was wrapped in newspaper. *Do these people think that I eat street food?* She turned away from Vinod without responding.
He waited in front of her for a few minutes before returning to sit on the other side of the waiting room where his wife and daughter were. *Stupid middle class people! They are acting as though they are on holiday.* Madhu looked at Gauri. *In their defence, the fat girl might have fainted if they did not give her food. She has not eaten anything since she came here.* After this distraction Madhu continued to play with her fingers for another three hours.

Madhu finally spotted Uma's doctor coming towards her. The moment she saw him she stood up ran towards him.
She noticed Avantika speeding towards the doctor as well. However, Madhu got to the doctor first.
"How is she?" Madhu asked.
By the time Avantika reached the doctor she was gasping for air.
"Congratulations Madhuji. You're a dadi to a beautiful baby girl," the doctor announced. Madhu gave a jubilant cheer and screamed with delight. She heard the Desai family also join her with the celebrations. She saw the three members of the Desai family hugging each other with joy as she watched them standing beside them.
"Both mother and daughter are healthy," the doctor informed them.
"When can I see them?" Madhu inquired.
"You can see them now, but only one at a time. Uma is on the second floor. When you get out of the lift she's in the third room to the right"

"I will go first," Madhu said. "She is a Rathod and my granddaughter." Madhu gave a smug smile to Avantika who looked slightly disappointed. *A poti!* Madhu thought excitedly as she walked towards the hospital room. *I am a dadi at last. Hai Bhagwan tara gana gana dhanyavaad.* She walked as quickly as she could, desperate to see the face of her new granddaughter. She found the room which the doctor had told her Uma was in. Madhu pushed the door back and walked straight in. She saw that Uma was asleep. Without giving Uma a second thought, she walked straight over to the cot beside her. Madhu became overwhelmed as she watched the pink skinned baby's chest slowly rise and drop. The baby's little fingers were rolled up into two tiny fists. One of her fists was at the side of her head and the other on top of her stomach. For a while Madhu watched her beautiful granddaughter breathe in and out with a huge smile on her face. She bent down with the intention of kissing her granddaughter's forehead but froze when she was inches away from the baby. The scent of the newborn baby stirred something in Madhu's memory and tears formed in her eyes. She pulled back instantly and left the hospital room as fast as she could. Madhu saw the Desai family were approaching Uma's room. Madhu turned the other way desperately seeking a bathroom. *I will not allow these middle class peasants to see me with tears in my eyes. They will think that Madhu Rathod is weak. The months of hard work I have done to instil fear in them will be ruined.*

Madhu found a bathroom and walked in. She looked at her red eyes in the mirror and turned the taps on in the basin. She splashed some water onto her face and began to wash her eyes. Once Madhu turned the taps off, she looked at her face again. Her face had been replaced by the look of gloom. She knew exactly why her tears of joy turned into tears of agony. *I did not think she would look so much like my beautiful Indira.* Madhu took a deep breath as she recalled the little girl she gave birth to after a painful twenty seven hours in labour. The love she felt for the girl was so intense that Madhu felt she could not love someone as much as she loved that baby girl. Madhu spent every minute she was awake with her daughter. She held Indira, pulled the string to her cradle, fed her or simply watched her sleep. For five days her life revolved around Indira. On the fifth day Indira was taken away from Madhu. The pain she felt at her daughter's death was worse than the labour pains she tolerated for twenty seven hours. Madhu had fallen to her knees and beat her chest at her daughter's death. The pain of her daughter's death never left Madhu. Even now when she saw her new granddaughter she remembered how little time she had with Indira and how quickly she was taken away from her.

This girl is the carbon copy of Indira! My Indira has returned to us with new body. However, the idea of Indira coming back haunted Madhu more. *What if she leaves me again in a few days again? Na, na I will not let that happen. Hai Bhagwan, please help me protect my beti this time. Last time you took her away after five days, you did not even let her see her chatthi day. I pray you do not let history repeat itself again!*

Madhu looked at her face again and wiped it one last time, attempting to wipe away any evidence of weaknesses from her face. She returned to the room where Uma was with the little girl. Madhu had to wait outside as Avantika was with Uma. Through the window she could see the little girl asleep in her cot. She made her granddaughter the same promise she made to all of her children. *I will fill your life with all the happiness in this world even if it means sacrificing my own happiness.*

Chapter 57: Uma

Uma lay in bed as she pulled the string to the cradle in which her baby slept. Her daughter was now sixteen days old and was going to be given a name. Uma wanted to hold her daughter. She got up and groaned in pain. The stitches from the caesarean had been removed a week ago but sitting up and sitting down still caused Uma severe pain. The moment she saw her little girl, she forgot about the pain. *You are the most beautiful baby in this world. I went through so much pain for you, but it was all worth it because you are the only person in this world who I can call my own.*

Uma closed her eyes and remembered holding her daughter for the first time. At the time she had not mentally recovered from the ordeal Vijay inflicted on her and she was physically weakened by the caesarean. Still feeling the side effects from the anaesthesia, she wanted to be left alone to recover when her mother insisted she held her daughter. Uma felt no connection to her girl, she felt the process of holding her was a formality forced upon her. Uma held the girl and attempted to breast feed her as the nurse had directed her. The unpleasant sensation of breast feeding distressed Uma more. Once she finished breast feeding she immediately put the girl down into her cot and fell asleep to recuperate.

For a few days, Uma recovered from the after effects of the c-section and internally battled to convince herself that Vijay was guilty of raping her. On the fifth day after the girl's birth, Uma's daughter lay on her chest. She was not holding onto her as the nurse was not around to forcefully hand the baby to Uma. She heard the baby sneeze. Uma looked around and realised it came from the girl on top of her. Uma felt a rush of affection towards her baby. It was one of the cutest things she had ever heard. She touched the hand of her daughter and the girl gripped Uma's little finger. Her grip was so tight that Uma struggled to open her daughter's fist. She became overwhelmed with emotion and love for her daughter. The connection Uma felt with her daughter drove out all of the inner anguish in her mind. She was holding the most beautiful thing in the entire universe and nothing else mattered to Uma. Over the next eleven days Uma became more and more attached to the beautiful flower Goddess Durga bestowed upon her. Just after her daughter's birth, Uma felt there was nothing for her to live for and thought her life would be easier if she died and moved onto a new life. However, Uma's daughter refilled her life with happiness. She gave Uma a reason to live.

Uma picked up her daughter, who was still asleep. She hugged her and kissed her on the cheek before putting her back into the cradle. She never felt an attachment this strong for anyone else. Uma spent eleven days picking a name for her daughter. A number of lucky letters were given by the astrologer. Determined she was going to give her daughter a beautiful name, she chose the name Sharda; another name for Saraswati, the goddess of knowledge and wisdom. Two days ago, she told Madhu and Vijay about the name she picked for her daughter.
"You will not be choosing her name," Madhu said flatly. "It is traditional that the child's fai chooses their name. Charu will pick a name, and then name her."
Uma felt dejected when her name had been rejected. All of the stressful events she blocked out since the birth of her daughter returned to consciousness. Feeling drained once again, she did not have enough strength to argue.

Once she got over the initial shock that she was not going to pick her daughter's name, Uma began to feel sidelined in her daughter's life. She listened to Madhu and Vijay plan her daughter's future without any input from her. It had been just over twenty-four hours since Uma was discharged from hospital; both she and her daughter arrived to Rathod Haveli. Since then the only time Uma spent with her daughter was when she was feeding her or if she was sleeping. Uma felt slightly worried that the Rathod family were attempting to reduce her importance in her own daughter's life.

Uma heard the door open. Charu entered the bedroom and walked towards the cradle. Without acknowledging Uma, she picked up the baby and walked out of the room. Uma knew Charu was taking her daughter down for the naming ceremony, but felt angry that she took

her without permission.
"Charuben," Uma said politely. "I can bring her down. Let me just put on the new dress my maa bought for her naming ceremony."
"Mumma hated the dress Avantika Aunty bought," Charu retorted back. "She bought a new dress. A dress that actually shows people that she belongs to our family. Your mumma's dress was too down market for us. Mumma told me to bring her down so she can change into the dress WE chose for the naming ceremony."

Charu walked out holding Uma's daughter. Uma felt another pang inside her as her daughter was taken away. She inhaled deeply to recollect her thoughts. *They cannot take my girl away from me. She is part of me. A mother and daughter's relationship cannot be broken by anyone. I am being over protective. They love my beti as well. Stop over reacting Uma. They won't eat her.*

Chapter 58: Madhu

"Sheela Vijay Rathod," Madhu said with a mock baby voice to her granddaughter. "Your Charu fai chose the perfect name for you."
Madhu lifted Sheela and kissed her before placing the child on her right knee. She began to bounce her leg up and down as she held onto Sheela. Madhu was so engrossed in playing with her granddaughter that she did not notice Vijay enter the room. Vijay sat down and groaned in frustration, alerting Madhu to his presence. As her heartbeat returned to normal she saw that her son looked distressed.

"Beta what is wrong?" Madhu asked her son worried. She picked up Sheela and walked over to her son. "Here hold your beti," she said attempting to cheer Vijay up.
"Not right now," Vijay mumbled. "Put her in the bouncer."
Hai Bhagwan, what's wrong with him? Madhu put Sheela into her bouncer and carefully covered her up with a blanket. She turned to her son.
"What is wrong? Su Thayu?"
"Nothing,"
"Do not lie to your mumma," Madhu said. "You think I cannot tell when you lie to me."
Vijay paused and took a deep breath. "I need money," he said. "Urgently."
Madhu froze as her apprehension increased. *Is he... Hai Bhagwan not again.*
"Your hotels are successful. You told me a few weeks ago. What happened to the money from there?"
"I took out a loan for the hotel, with the bank repayments and living costs of Mumbai I'm struggling. I failed to make the bank payment last month. If I fail again they might take the hotel away to recover their costs."
"So the hotel is not making enough money to pay the loan off?" Madhu asked her son. She saw Vijay avert his eyes from her. He turned his back on her and that was when Madhu panicked more. *Haai Ram he is*

gambling again. What am I going to do? Last time he almost left us all homeless! Where will I go with Sheela?
"I..."Vijay paused. "I played cards and I lost the money I had."
Vijay's revelation caused Madhu's blood to boil. She walked over to her son and slapped him.
"How could you be so foolish?" she screamed at her son. "You almost lost everything last time you gambled. If Siya's parents had not bailed us out with money we would have ended up on the streets. You promised me you will never gamble again. You foolish boy." Madhu slapped her son again. She paused to take a breath before continuing her verbal tirade against her son. "You have more responsibilities now. If you do not care about leaving your mother, sister or brother homeless then think about Sheela. Look at her." Madhu pointed at Sheela. "She is less than a month old. Where will she go if she has no roof over her head? There is no one to save us this time!" *No one to save us this time?* Madhu's anger turned to fear. *What will happen to all of us if he ends up bankrupt again?*
"Is this why you never had any money to help contribute towards Charu's wedding? Because you were too busy gambling again?"
"Mumma it wasn't like that," Vijay said. "I was saving money to open a fifth hotel in Bangalore. I thought if I won it, I had an easy way to have enough money for one. But..."
"But you lost. You thought about what the benefits of winning would be but did not give a second thought to the consequences if you lost," She bellowed at her son.
"I was doing it to make more money for our family."
Madhu stopped shouting and sat down on the sofa with her face buried inside her hands. *Shouting at Vijay won't achieve anything. Hai Bhagwan how did I not realise what he was doing sooner? What will I do if he does end up bankrupt again?*

Madhu recalled how Vijay's gambling addiction almost left them bankrupt last time. However, Madhu used the money she extracted from Siya's family to clear his debts. The money saved her home and her son's business. Siya's family continued to fulfil Madhu's demands, who continued to secure her family's future. To prevent another situation arising like this again, Madhu continued to extort more money from

Siya's family. They fulfilled all of Madhu's demands until they could afford to give no more. *Last time I saved my family from being destroyed by using the money we got from Siya, but the ox's family is not even giving me half of what I want.*
"Help me mumma," Vijay said falling to his knees. "Get me some money to save my businesses..."
"I have no money. All the money I have is going towards Charu's wedding."
"What about Uma's parents?"
"Nothing. They have nothing. You picked the wrong girl to replace Siya. They are poor and have no money or class."
"Get rid of her then," Vijay said quickly. "Just get rid of her."
Madhu felt shocked at what her son was asking her to do. She felt a jolt run through her.
"I can't lose everything I have worked so hard to rebuild," He beseeched Madhu.
"Get rid of her?" Madhu said really quickly. "How will I do that?"
"Like you did with Siya."
"It is very easy for you to just say get rid of her. You are not the one who has to do everything."
Madhu sighed heavily. "If I get rid of Uma so soon, people will get suspicious. It is not as easy as you think."
"There must be a way. You found a solution for Siya. Think of something before I lose everything." Vijay begged his mother with desperation.

Madhu took a step back and then turned away from her son as she remembered what she did to Siya. A few years after Vijay and Siya's marriage; Siya's parents sold their home and almost all of their possessions for their daughter's happiness. The money helped Vijay to stop the closure of his hotels. However, with nothing left for her parents to give; Vijay came to her bedroom to inform her he wished to marry someone else.
"She's reached the end of her use by date," Vijay told his mother. "She hasn't even given me a son."
"Does it have to be a son?"
"Mumma she hasn't even given me a daughter, let alone a son. With no

use what's the point of keeping her? She is just a burden on us. We need to get rid of her."

Madhu tried very hard to make her son forget thinking about getting rid of Siya. Now that everything was settled there was no need for her to bring in more money. However, Vijay told Madhu that he was in love with someone else and threatened to commit suicide if she did not get rid of Siya. Madhu knew her son always did what he said. Fearing her son would actually commit suicide she felt compelled to get rid of her and agreed. *If Vijay gets caught it might ruin his entire life. I need to make a foolproof plan to make sure none of us get caught.*

In the end Madhu took advantage of the 2010 Kumbh Mela in Haridwar. She remembered a documentary she watched about elderly people who were abandoned at the Mela by relatives who did not wish to care for them anymore. It was easy for people to get lost amongst 80 million devotees who came to bathe in the River Ganga. The documentary highlighted how many of the people who got lost were illiterate, did not know where they lived or how to use the transport system. The documentary gave Madhu the idea of arranging Siya's disappearance in Haridwar. *Only Siya's brother went to school. The girl speaks only Gujarati because her parents sent none of her sisters to school. She is uneducated! If I told people she got lost in Haridwar, no one would question it.*

Madhu explained her thoughts to Vijay and Jigar who both approved. The only flaw they saw in their plan was the fact that Ahmedabad was a well known city. If Siya found a policeman or a charity that helped to reunite missing people, it would be simple for her to find her way back. Jigar took over from that point, and said he had an idea that meant Siya would never find her way home. He told Madhu that all she had to do was separate from Siya at the Kumbh Mela.

When the time came for the Kumbh Mela, Madhu took Siya to Haridwar on a day when millions of devotees were expected on the banks of the Ganga. Before going to bathe in the river, Madhu told her to leave behind all of her valuables to prevent people stealing it in the crowds.

She stripped Siya of all the money she had, her gold jewellery and her mobile phone. With no valuables to sell to make money, or a mobile phone to call for help, Madhu sealed off any chance of Siya making her way back home. Madhu walked with her daughter-in-law hand in hand. She told her to go and bathe in the river first. As Siya walked over to the river and dipped inside it. Madhu turned around and walked away as quickly as she could.

For a few moments Madhu thought she could hear Siya calling for her, but she realised that she would not be able to hear her voice over the voices of the ten million devotees on the ghats of the Ganges. That was the last time Madhu saw Siya. She spent eleven days feigning distress at Siya's disappearance. She pretended to search for her through the charity and police before returning to Ahmedabad. She told her sons that she successfully lost Siya and Jigar informed them that his friend Rafique had prevented her from returning. Madhu was curious to know how Jigar prevented Siya from returning. When she asked her son he was very vague but promised Madhu that Siya was alive and well. Madhu did not want innocent blood on her hands and was relieved to know that she was not dead. Madhu then put on an act of depression at the loss of her daughter-in-law. Two months later the Rathod family sold their house in Ahmedabad and moved to Madhapar. This was to avoid gossip about Vijay remarrying so quickly and to be closer to the paternal home of the woman who would be Vijay's new wife. Belonging to such an influential family meant they were not completely free of slander, but the shift to Madhapar minimised the gossip.

"I cannot arrange for Uma to vanish just like Siya," Madhu tried explaining to her son. "People would get suspicious if another one went missing so soon after your first wife. We could get caught and it would ruin everything!" Madhu took a few deep breaths thinking about how she could pacify her son for now. *When he was little and he wanted to play with the moon I would show him the moon's reflection in the water and satisfy his desires. Now his desires are so big that I struggle to fulfil all of his dreams, but I have to think of some way to make sure my son remains happy.* Madhu spent a few minutes thinking about how she could help with Vijay's dilemma. She did not have to think for too long as she already fantasised about what she would like to do to Uma. "We cannot arrange for Uma to vanish but I think I have another idea."

Madhu saw a smile spread across Vijay's face. Seeing her son happy again reassured Madhu. She felt the warm glow she felt inside her every time she saw a smile on her children's face. *I will not allow your stupid mistake to ruin all of my children's lives again. I have to do something, but how will I execute my plan effectively?*

Chapter 59: Alice

It was one of the few days Alice got off from work. She had not made many friends in India as she spent most of her time at the hotel. Six weeks ago Fatima helped Alice to humiliate Vijay. Consequentially Alice made more of an effort to understand Fatima, who used to be an enigma. One of the first things Alice wanted to know was why Fatima worked seven days a week from 7am-11pm, with no days off. Fatima informed Alice that she put in the hard work to get money together to pay for her sister's wedding. She told Alice that she would need more money for her sister's wedding because of how her own marriage ended. Fatima told Alice how she was her husband's second wife. On their wedding night, when they consummated their marriage, Fatima did not bleed. The lack of blood on the bed enraged her husband who kicked her out of the house for not being a virgin. Alice fumed about the double standards. *Her husband was far from being a virgin, yet he wanted a virgin wife.* Alice felt angrier when Fatima told her that she was indeed a virgin. *Not all women bleed when they first have sex. Are these idiots ignorant of everything? There's so many other ways her hymen could have broken.* When Alice questioned Fatima about fighting for justice, Fatima rapidly changed topic and started talking about other things. Alice took this as a sign that Fatima did not wish to discuss life after her marriage.

That day Fatima took her first day off since the opening of the hotel to do some shopping for her sister's wedding. Alice, eager to see more of Mumbai, joined her. As they walked around the streets of Mumbai, Alice saw that Fatima was still wearing a scarf to cover her head. The streets were slightly chilly as Indian winter had started. Alice would have felt some envy about the scarf Fatima wore, if it was not a sign of her subordination to men. She had been desperate to ask her about the hijab for weeks. *Today is the best opportunity I've had to question her about it.*
"It must be nice to wear your hijab on a cold day like this," Alice commented.

“I enjoy wearing it no matter what the weather is like,” Fatima smiled.
“Why do you wear it?” Alice said abruptly. “You know some people in England want to ban it.”
“Why would they want to do that?”
“Some people think forcing women to cover up is wrong. Men and women are equal, why should women be forced to cover up?”
“If I choose to wear it, what is people’s problem? Why deny me my right to choose to wear this?”
“Why would someone choose to wear it?”
“Alice maam do not mind me saying this, but when you first came to work, I saw you wearing a short skirt and big shoes with heels. Not only did you expose your body to everyone but I heard you complain about the heeled shoes hurting your back. Why do you wear the heeled shoes if they hurt your back so much?”
Fatima’s response stunned Alice into silence. *It’s what I was expected to wear to work.*
“My hijab doesn’t hurt my back. It doesn’t show off my body to sexual predators. I don’t need to keep up with fashion trends which people judge if I wear out of fashion clothing. I feel more liberated wearing this than when I do not wear it.”
“Is it not a way of keeping women oppressed?”
“For some people it is. I choose to wear it. It helps me to cover…” Fatima paused. “Cover up things that make me insecure. It helps me to avoid unwanted attention.”

I hated working in an office where I had to be so fashion conscious. When I felt judged on a daily basis for my appearance and the whispers about looking rough made me feel rubbish. At least Fatima doesn’t have to deal with that bullshit. Alice’s thought process was distracted by children waving at her saying hello. Alice smiled and waved back to all the children who greeted her. She loved looking around the market Fatima took her to. The colours were vibrant, the sounds of people haggling and the smell of incense and flowers were pleasant to the nose. Her appreciation for the market quickly evaporated when a flamboyant journalism student accosted her.

“Maam Maam,” the journalist said gasping for breath. “My name is

Madhusudan, I am a journalism student. We are making a documentary on this market. Can we film you looking at it, and can you say a few words to the camera?"
"I'm sorry but I'd rather not," Alice declined politely.
"Maam Maam, you would help us so much by taking part."
Alice made a number of attempts to decline politely but the pushy Madhusudan did not seem to understand what 'no' meant. She had never succeeded in dissuading journalists in India. They all thought their reports would have more credibility if a foreigner was included. As Madhusudan talked at her, Alice felt her phone vibrate. She opened the text message she had received.
"How long are you going to remain angry at me? I want to make things up. I love you so much. Vijay."
Once she read the message she locked her phone and put it away. *Dickhead.* Vijay sent her so many apologetic texts since she confronted him about his pregnant wife. The day she tied him to the chair naked, he had grabbed his belongings and returned home. She had not seen him since, but heard his wife delivered a baby girl a few days after he went home. *He's busy playing happy families with his wife and kid. I don't care where he is, as long as it's far away from me as possible.*
Alice put her phone away still seething. She saw the persistent reporter was still begging her to partake in his documentary.
"Fine let's do this. Quickly!"
"Thanks maam. Thank you," Madhusudan said gratefully. "SURDAS CAMERA LE KAR IDHAR AAV."

Chapter 60: Uma

Uma held Sheela close to her as she breastfed her daughter. In the early days Uma felt uncomfortable with breastfeeding. She felt a constant pinching sensation that made her wince each time her daughter wrapped her mouth around the nipple. Uma overcame the discomfort as they both got used to each other. She felt closest to Sheela when she was breastfeeding, as it provided an opportunity for the two of them to bond. Now that she was back in Madhapar, on some days, feeding her daughter was the only time she got to spend with her. Madhu and the rest of Vijay's family were busy showing off Sheela to their friends and family whenever they came to visit. Sheela was dressed in the clothes Madhu or Charu chose. Slowly Uma felt she was losing her daughter. *What will happen to me when I am not needed to feed my Sheela anymore? I will only ever have her with me when she is sleeping. They will give my beti their morals and bring her up to be like them.* Uma looked down at her daughter who had her tiny hand on her breast. *I will not let you become like your papa's family. You are my beti. I will never let you become a demon. I will have to assert my right over you.* Uma flinched as her daughter sucked harder on her nipple. For the first time in a while, Uma was finding breastfeeding uncomfortable.

After Sheela's birth, Uma had a month's respite from what Vijay described as "fulfilling the duty of a wife." Once the month was over, Vijay started to have sex with her whenever he wanted. Last night, Uma tried to spurn his advances. As a result he pinched her nipples with severe force and twisted them making Uma wail with pain. She reluctantly lay down on the bed and allowed Vijay to finish.

Two months ago, I used to pray for the news that Vijay was coming back so I would not be left alone with his family. In those days at least I had this room as a sanctuary against his family. Now I don't even have this. I now pray that he goes to one of his hotels and stays there forever. How fate has changed what I want so quickly. She closed her eyes to ask for her wish to be fulfilled. The moment she closed her eyes she had a flashback of Vijay's face as he forced her to have sex with him. *It is his right to have sex with me whenever he wants. What is wrong with me? Why do I no longer enjoy it? I now feel violated, like a toy he plays with when he wants me and then throws me aside as soon as he is finished.*

Uma began to feel desperate for the toilet and put her daughter back into the cradle. The toilet in their en-suite bathroom was still blocked and thus Uma went to use the communal one near Charu's bedroom. She took her shoes off as she did not want to draw any attention to herself through her footsteps. She started to quickly walk to the bathroom. She walked past Jigar's bedroom and through the corner of her eye saw Jigar talking to someone. Her natural instinct was to satisfy her curiosity and so she realised that Jigar was talking to Vijay. Out of interest she stopped to listen to what they were talking about.
"Rafique is coming in two weeks," Jigar whispered quietly to Vijay. "He has many whores who work for him."
"He runs a house for whores. How will that benefit me?"
"Bhai the girls he has working for him are just..." Jigar clicked his tongue and winked at his brother. Both brothers laughed. "Sometimes I visit with the other policemen. The girls there are some of the best in our great country."
"You pay for it?" Vijay joked with his brother. "I don't need to pay for it, girls still want me left, right and centre."
"Who says I pay for anything? I actually get 10% of the money Rafique makes. Me and my colleagues turn a blind eye to what they do in exchange for some benefits. The best perk though is the fun they let us have with some of the hot stuff. Those girls are experts at sucking dick. You're my brother you can fuck any bitch you want for free."
"Just get to the point," Vijay said irritably. "You said Rafique will help me. How exactly will a pimp help me?"
"He wants to make more money. You want to make more money. So you both want more money. He has the hot sluts, you have rich customers at your hotels. He wants men who will pay more to enjoy his girls. You want to provide something more to your rich customers to keep them coming back."
"Whores at my hotels? Are you foolish? We will get caught. It will damage our reputation."

"Bhai, the girls would never say anything. They're too scared. If they open their mouth I'm a policeman I know how to shut them up. Think about it. You will get hot girls working in your hotel and you will provide your customers something new. How many men go abroad and fuck prostitutes? You would be giving them some pussy which is of a higher calibre so they'll stay with you each time. If you want you could have a go with these hotties whenever you want as well, and bhai these girls are too good."

Hai Mata Rani, what a neech Jigar is. At least Vijay knows his brother is stupid and has the decency to rebuke him. Chi chi chi.

Disgusted by Jigar's plans for Hotel Rathod, Uma was about to go when she heard her name. She stopped to listen.

"How does Uma fit into all of this?" Vijay asked her brother. "You told me you had an idea to make Uma more useful."

"Rafique came to Charu's engagement. He liked the look of your wife. Let him spend one night..."

"Are you out of your mind?" Vijay fumed. "She is a Rathod. Mumma will never allow it. If this got out..."

"If this got out I will silence everything, and we won't shout out about everything. Mumma doesn't need to know. Hell even Uma doesn't need to know. I can bring some bhang and she won't remember anything that happened."

"Why Uma? Can we not give him another girl?"

"I already told you. He liked the look of Uma at Charu's engagement. Give Uma to him, he will dance to your tune. Once you have his attention, you and your customers could be fucking the hottest girls. You'd be doing them for free, and benefitting from them."

Uma stood there rooted to the spot with her mouth open. She forgot she needed to go to the toilet. *Vijay will never allow his wife to be sold like that.*

"The risks..."

"You keep talking about the risks. I keep telling you there aren't any. I can handle everything."

Vijay thought about it for a few moments.

"It sounds like a good idea." Vijay said.

Hai Mata Rani Vijay is just as disgusting as his brother. He wants to sell me to make more money for himself? Uma felt as though she was

starting to suffocate. *I need to get away from here. I need to save myself from this disgrace.*
Without a second thought Uma ran as fast as she could. She took nothing with her. Struck with intense fear and the determination to get away, she forgot to take Sheela.

Chapter 61: Purbai

"Kesar is pregnant again Madhuben," Purbai told Madhu with delight.
"Oh where is the mithai to sweeten my mouth?" she replied enthusiastically.
"I will bring some barfi next time I come."
Madhu smiled, "Would you like a boy or girl?"
"I want a boy. I already have two granddaughters. A grandson would be nice."
Purbai cleared her throat which felt dry.
"Where is that Leela, with the chai? LEELA! Where is the Chai I asked you for?"
"I'm bringing it now Madhuji," the maid shouted from the kitchen.

Purbai watched Leela bring a tray out with two cups of chai. Leela put the tray on the table and handed them both a tea each. Madhu sipped her drink whilst Purbai blew on the tea to cool it down. Suddenly her eyes opened wide. *I forgot to tell Madhuben about Kokila.*
"Madhuben, did you hear about Kokila, who lives on the other side to me?"
"Is she pregnant?"
"No, she is barren."
"Has her husband decided to leave her and remarry?"
"Yes, he is already going around with other women. He is hoping to get one of them pregnant so he can marry her instead."
"This is why I did not invite Kokila to Uma's godhbharai ceremony. It would have been inauspicious for a barren woman to attend. Her evil jealous eye might affect my grandchild."
"After Uma's godhbharai, I heard Kokila's sasu shout at her more. She is always calling her names and..."
Purbai stopped midsentence. She saw Uma running down the stairs. *Is that Uma?* She could not believe her eyes when she saw Uma. Uma's hair was messy, her makeup smudged everywhere. Her sari was badly draped. It was as though she had just wrapped it around without making any effort. *She isn't even wearing her chandlo, she is a married*

woman. Uma's eyes were wide open. Her eyes were etched with fear. Purbai noticed Uma's arms and saw two large bruises on them. She felt her stomach drop. Purbai quickly averted her eyes and stopped looking at Uma. *I have not seen anything. She may have got those bruises from bumping into something. If anyone has seen anything, it is that maid. It is her duty to tell the police. I do not know all the facts. I cannot go to the police with half a story.*

"Uma Bahu!" Madhu said with an authoritative voice. "What are you wearing? Stop where you are."
From the side of her eye Purbai saw that Uma stopped at the bottom of the stairs. She focused her gaze on the brown milky tea. *I have not seen anything Swaminarayan Bhagwan. I do not know anything. Madhuben is not a wicked person. She cannot have done this. She could have got those bruises in so many different ways. How can I believe just hearsay?*

"Why do you look like a jungali?"
Uma stood in silence for a moment before walking towards the exit of the house. Madhu put down her cup of tea and walked over to Uma. She grabbed Uma's arm.
"Where are you going?"
Uma let out a cry. Purbai felt a chill run through her. The cry sounded like that of an injured dog. Purbai shifted uncomfortably in her seat.
"I'M LEAVING THIS PRISON," Uma shouted at Madhu. "I LEFT YESTERDAY BUT I CAME BACK FOR SHEELA."
Purbai opened her mouth in shock. Madhu looked around to see Purbai who quickly dropped her gaze and acted uninterested in what was happening in front of her. Purbai quickly sipped her tea to show Madhu she had not heard anything. She noticed Madhu's maid had come out of the kitchen and was sweeping the floor.
"Uma Bahu, what have you done to yourself?" Madhu said with an overly sweet voice. Purbai knew it was sugar coated. "Let's go to the kitchen and tidy you up."
Uma began to object, but Madhu grabbed her hand tightly. There were white marks around the bit where Madhu was holding Uma. Purbai watched as Uma was led to the kitchen by her mother-in-law.

Purbai looked at the maid who continued to wipe the floor. She looked around anxiously. *If I get closer can I hear what Madhuben is saying to Uma?* She paused. *What if I find out more than I need to know? I do not want to get involved with a police case or any other rubbish. If I find out more than the maid it would become my responsibility to do something.*

Purbai did not need to get closer, from years of straining her ears to listen into other people's conversations she was able to hear what Madhu was saying.
"You were going to shame our family by going out like this?" Madhu whispered venomously to Uma.
Purbai heard a slap. *Swaminarayan Swaminarayan.* Purbai took a deep breath. She was still trying to convince herself that she should not interfere in a family matter. *It is a family matter. I am not a Rathod and so I should not interfere. Especially as I didn't see anything, I would not count as a witness.*
"Have you set out to cut off our noses in public? What is the meaning of this?" Purbai heard Madhu tell Uma.
She gulped. Deep down she knew that she was running out of excuses to ignore what was happening in front of her. She knew that the right thing to do was to say something.
Purbai could not see what was happening but she imagined that Madhu was probing Uma's head and shoving her.
"I wanted to pray at the Amba temple," Uma told Madhu.
"Liar," Madhu whispered. "We have a shrine at home. Why go all the way to Mandir. You wanted attention. You wanted to bring shame on us."
"I WANT TO ESCAPE THIS HELL," Uma shouted. Purbai once again gasped. "YOU AND YOUR FAMILY ARE GREEDY, DOWRY GRABBING DEMONS. THE WOMAN WHO IS SUPPOSED TO BE A MOTHER TO ME BEATS ME. THE HUSBAND WHO IS MEANT TO PROTECT ME RAPES ME WHENEVER HE WANTS. I DON'T WANT TO LIVE..."
Purbai heard another slap. This time it was louder than the last time. She took a deep breath. She could no longer deny that the woman she admired was abusing her daughter-in-law. The pedestal Purbai had put Madhu on crumbled. *Hai Swaminarayan Bhagwan what do I do now?* She watched as the maid continued sweeping. *She still knows more than*

I know. It is her responsibility, more than mine. If she isn't saying anything there must be a reason. I should find out that reason before I get involved in a family matter.

"Shut your mouth now," Madhu retorted to Uma dangerously. "I can hear Sheela crying. I will see to you once Purbai and Leela are gone." *What is Madhuben going to do to her now? I have no more excuses. I cannot make excuses for Madhuben anymore. Hai Bhagwan!* Purbai began to get up to go home. *I will tell Kesar all of the new developments. She will know what to do.*

Chapter 62: Madhu

"I threatened her and said if she continues to talk she will never see Sheela again," Madhu told Vijay as he emptied his car of the shopping. Vijay attempted to give Madhu some of the shopping bags but she was infuriated by Uma's outburst earlier that day and was too busy telling her son about it.
"She was shouting at the top of her voice maligning our family name. Purbai was here but fortunately I managed to handle the situation."
"What did you say?"
"I told her that Uma was on anti-depressants because of postnatal depression." Madhu saw Vijay raise his eyebrows at the lie she told. Madhu became frustrated. "I could not think of anything else at the time. You are right Vijay. She has become too much of a risk. Something needs to be done to silence her, quickly."
"I told you to get rid of her a long time ago," Vijay said dully. "You were the one who wanted to keep the burden."
"I did not want to keep her," Madhu retaliated. "I just said we could not get rid of her. People will get suspicious."
"You promised me you'll get rid of her. You told me..."
"I said I will think of how I can get rid of her without drawing attention."
"You're a clever woman mumma. Just do anything just get rid of her. Wait two weeks before you do anything though," Vijay held all the shopping bags in his hand. "Can you shut the boot for me?"
"Why two weeks?" Madhu asked her son as she was about to shut the car boot.
Madhu's eyes fell onto a red plastic can in the back of Vijay's car. She forgot the question she asked Vijay and narrowed her eyes. *That is the can Vijay keeps filled up with petrol for emergencies or when the petrol is cheap.* Madhu bent over and leaned into the car to pick up the can.
"Mumma, what are you doing now?" Vijay asked slightly agitated.
"I just want that petrol can."
She got hold of the can and shook it to see if there was anything inside.
"There is nothing in it right now. It's empty," Vijay told her.
Madhu did not care that the petrol can was empty. She finally found the

solution she sought for so long.

“I know how to silence Uma,” Madhu said quietly. “Tell Jigar and Charu to come to my room immediately.”

Chapter 63: Nilambari

Nilambari lit a diva and put some flowers at the idol of Radha and Krishna. She sat beside the idols on her bedside table to calm the storm brewing in her mind. Nilambari could still hear Uma's piercing voice when she had screamed to Madhu about her rape. She looked up at the idol of Krishna. *O Guruvayur Swamy, she is going through the same pain I went through, and I have no way to help her.* Nilambari recalled everything she went through after her sexual assault during Holi. *People blamed me. They said I was drunk and dancing with the same men who raped me. No one wanted to listen to me. No one cared that those beasts mixed something into my drink. I was maligned with dishonour and was outcast by the community.* She recalled the struggles she went through after being thrown out by her family. Determined to clear her name, Nilambari went to the police to file a complaint. After waiting for seventeen hours the police attendant arranged a meeting with her. She was asked degrading questions by the police. They asked her to lift up her sari and show them where the men touched her. They even asked her to demonstrate exactly how they touched her. After going through the shame again, they asked her if she could provide any medical proof. Nilambari had not been medically tested, the doctors at the hospital told her the tests could leave her infertile and therefore, she decided against them. The police silenced her case and nothing was done. Homeless and rupee less, Nilambari thought she had been sent a saviour when a man in the village said she could live for free in his house and work at the same time. As time went on Nilambari realised the widower gave her a place to stay because he felt that she was a slut, and would open her legs for him. Before anything happened, Nilambari fled his house leaving everything behind. She was frightened to go back and collect anything and jumped onto the first bus she found. That was how she ended up in Bhuj.

Nilambari heard footsteps outside her room. She sat up alert. She heard a knock on the door and she quickly attempted to wipe her tears. Nilambari was not quick enough and Amrita saw her crying.

"What's wrong Leela? Kya Hua?"
Leela! I am Leela! Why does Nilambari still haunt me? I need to cut her away from me. She brings me nothing but pain.
"Leela?" Amrita repeated.
"Enikku sukhamaanu. I have dust in my eyes," Nilambari lied.

Amrita closed the door behind her and sat down.
"Leela," she said warmly. "Mainu pata hai, something is wrong. You can tell me. I have never seen you cry because of dust in your eyes."
Nilambari stood up in an attempt to distract Amrita. She started to make her bed to find something to do.
"Tidying your bed won't make your problem go away. If you talk about it, maybe I might be able to help."
Nilambari took a deep breath. *Amritaji already knows my story. Telling her my story the day we met is the whole reason she let me live with her. I can trust her. She wouldn't blame Uma.*
"You remember that..." Nilambari paused. "That... thing that happened to me at Holi... before I came here?"
Amrita nodded.
"I was just thinking about it."
Amrita said nothing. Nilambari took that as a sign to continue. *Perhaps Amritaji is right. Perhaps she might be able to help me decide the right thing.*
"When I was..." Nilambari paused, unable to say the word rape. "People blamed me. People pointed at me and said "There's the girl who said she was raped. There is the unchaste woman. " I was degraded by society, the police, everyone. Going through the ordeal was bad enough, but the way I was treated meant I relived the terror every single day."
Nilambari looked at the statue of Radha and Krishna and admired him for a second. She felt a moment of inner peace at the sight of her saviour, Lord Krishna.
"I was not murdered that day but I may as well have been killed that day. Those bastards killed a part of me. They destroyed my ability to trust people, my ability to be happy or ever live a normal life again. They took everything away from me, even the things my husband's parents could not strip me of. They stripped me of my dignity. This was not the worst part of the crime though. No matter how hard I tried to rebuild my

life, the community would not let me. No matter how hard I tried to forget, the community would not let me. I was reminded again and again that I was raped. Each time the wound reopened again. I lived in fear in Rajkot. When will I next be insulted because of the crime?"
Nilambari paused and looked at Amrita. Amrita's eyes filled with tears. "I then realised that I was not the only one. I saw it everywhere even in Ernakulam. People blamed the woman. Politicians tell us not to drink. Do not go out alone late at night. I did not do any of those things. My only fault was that I danced at Holi. Very few cases will result in the man going to jail. If the woman is lucky the person who wronged her will be imprisoned. But he will eventually get out despite committing the abominable crime. Society will forgive him, they will think he has been punished and accept him again. The victim on the other hand will be left with a life sentence. She is forced to live with what happened for the rest of her life. This is probably the only crime in which the victim is punished and the perpetrator is forgiven."
Nilambari stared at the wall ahead of her. She felt Amrita stroke her hair. Nilambari winced at Amrita's touch. When Nilambari realised it was just a friend who touched her she relaxed.
"Sometimes a husband thinks he owns the woman and she has to do what she wants." Nilambari's voice began to get high pitched as she attempted to hold her emotions in. "Many husbands get away with raping their wives. Where will a married woman go for help? No policeman or anyone would believe it if a married woman said she was raped. Who can she turn to for help? "
"There are laws," Amrita said. "To punish a husband who rapes his wife."
Nilambari looked confused. *When were these laws created? If what Amritaji says is true than Vijay had broken the law.* For a while Nilambari remained silent.

The silence was broken by Amrita.
"Has something happened, Leela?" Amrita asked softly.

Ende ammo what do I tell her? If I tell her what happened to Uma then people might insult her like they insulted me. I might ruin her life instead of improving it. Do I try and prevent people from pointing fingers at Uma, or do I attempt to punish the hands that beat her every day and ruin her life? If I tell anyone about this then I will increase Uma's suffering. People will taunt her wherever she goes. But if I don't tell someone then the wounds that have become part of Uma's life will never heal. What do I do Guruvayur Swami? Helping Uma is like throwing a rock at a house of glass. The broken shards of glass will wound Uma and shatter her world, but if I do not break the glass house then she will remain trapped in it forever. If I tell no one, Uma's life can go on as it is. If I tell someone, I could be destroying the happiness she has left. Whichever path I take will ruin Uma's life forever. Nilambari looked at the statue of Krishna. *O Guruvayur Swamy what do I do? Which path do I take?*

"Leela?" Amrita asked again. "What's happened?"
Leela! I am Leela, I stopped being Nilambari a long time ago. Nilambari would have remained silent; But what would Leela do? What will I do? Leela turned around to face Amrita. She opened her mouth to respond to the question Amrita asked. She knew which path Leela would take.

Chapter 64: Uma

Hai Mata Rani, what could I have done differently? What have I done to compel my husband to force himself on me again and again? Why does he want to sell me to other men? There must be something about me that is making him do what he is doing. Uma was on her knees sobbing. She looked at the empty cradle and thought of Sheela. *I even left my beti in this hell when I tried to escape. What would have happened to her if I left her here? Hai Mata Rani, forgive me for my selfishness.*

Uma wiped her tears. She got up and paced around the room. *I need to escape this place. Both Sheela and I have to go but how will I get Sheela out now they know I want to leave?* As Uma walked around the room she caught a glimpse of herself in the mirror. She recalled something she heard Jigar say before.
"If a woman did not want to get raped, she wouldn't go out with makeup or in tight sexy clothes. She is obviously looking to get some with her seductive looks."
Uma began to strip herself of everything she thought made her look beautiful. She dishevelled her hair. *If I do not look beautiful to him or those men they will not want me.* She smudged her eye makeup and lipstick and began to make circular movements to make sure all of her makeup was everywhere. *If I look ugly, Vijay will stop forcing me to fulfil my obligations. He will not be able to give me to that man if I look like this.* She looked at her face in the mirror again. Underneath the untidy hair and smeared make up she barely recognised herself. *He can't do anything anymore. Rafique and Vijay will both know that I don't want anything; maybe they will feel pity and let me go.*

Uma shuffled towards her wardrobe. *I need to destroy anything that makes me look sexy. None of my beautiful saris can remain.* She grabbed the saris she wore for special occasions and threw them onto her bed. She stopped when she heard footsteps coming up the stairs. There were a few people, maybe five or six. She fell to the ground. *Hai Mata Rani, protect my honour, protect my chastity, protect my dignity, protect my dignity.* Uma stood up suddenly as an idea occurred to her. *I can pretend I am asleep. I will not need to talk to see them. I can act like I am in deep sleep then they will turn back and-.* Before Uma got the chance to feign sleep she heard her bedroom door open. Charu, Jigar, Vijay and Madhu were stood at her door. The sight of the four of them looking at her like a toad gazing at a juicy fly drove out all thoughts from her mind. Fear was all that remained.

Uma saw Madhu's mouth move. "Do exactly as I taught you."

Chapter 65: Madhu

"What are you all doing here?" Uma whispered.
Madhu could see fear was etched all over Uma's face.
"Look mumma! She looks like a joker," Charu laughed.
Madhu examined the smudged lipstick and laughed at Charu's comment. *The ox actually does look like a joker.*
Uma began to step back but Madhu stopped laughing.
"What are you all waiting for? We will have lots of time for jokes in the future. Do as I said earlier."

Madhu saw Charu take off the red dupatta from her dress. Jigar, Vijay and Charu all walked towards Uma. Unsure by what was happening, Uma stepped away from them. Unable to see where she was going, she stumbled on the bed. After she fell, Madhu's three children surrounded Uma. She attempted to scream but Charu wrapped her red scarf around Uma's mouth and gagged her. The ox tried to kick her feet in the air and flapped her hands but her sons were too strong for her. Uma was tamed by her sons' strength and lay still on the bed as her hands and feet were also tied up. Madhu could hear Uma's incoherent words and stifled screams. *Scream as loud as you want but no one will hear you.*

Madhu continued to give her children instructions and supervised them as they carried out her orders. Uma writhed like a fish out of water as Jigar and Vijay picked her up. Jigar carried Uma holding the top of her body and Vijay held her feet. Jigar carelessly stubbed his foot into Uma's dressing table causing the mirror to fall and shatter.
"Jigar be careful." Madhu said to her son.
"The shattering of a mirror is unlucky mumma," Charu said wearily. "Seven years bad luck."

Madhu felt unease at Charu's words. She usually dismissed Charu's superstitious beliefs, but she too believed that broken mirrors were inauspicious. Madhu watched as her sons carried Uma out of the bedroom. She then looked at the broken mirror pieces on the floor. Each shard reflected the light bulb from above. Her anxiety around the broken mirror increased. A few moments later she heard Jigar calling her. *Broken mirrors are inauspicious but it will be unlucky for the ox. Tonight I am going to shatter her arrogance into a thousand pieces like this mirror. And like this mirror she will never be able to fix herself again.*

Chapter 66: Uma

Uma squealed in pain every time a part of her body made contact with the bannisters or floor. Whilst taking her down the stairs, Jigar got tired and needed a rest. For a while, Uma lay on the stairs in a weird slant, unable to speak. She could feel the edges of three steps digging into her back. That was when she heard Sheela cry. Uma felt her heart drop to her stomach. From the corner of her eyes she saw Madhu walk past her, up the stairs. The hairs on Uma's arms stood on end. *My beti! What is she going to do to her? Hai Mata Rani, do not let them do anything to my daughter.* A few moments later Uma heard Sheela's cries diminish. Uma began to panic for her daughter's safety. *These people are demons! They probably didn't want a girl. If anything happens to her I will kill myself. If they do anything to her, the only reason I have left to live will be over. Mata Rani, protect her. Protect us both, do not let any harm befall us.*

When Jigar was ready, he and his brother picked Uma up again and took her further away from Sheela. Uma's fears for Sheela began to intensify. Uma forgot about Sheela when she felt excruciating pain after Jigar and Vijay dropped her onto the ground at the bottom of the stairs. The drop took the wind out of Uma as there had been no warning. She lay on the floor with goose pimples on her arms. The Rathod family retreated, like a pack of hyenas leaving their prey maimed. They all sat down on the sofa. *What are they doing?* Uma became confused. She saw Madhu pick up the TV remote and turn the television on. *Did these people tie me up so that they could watch TV?*

"It is not working," Madhu said angrily as she pressed a few buttons on the remote.
"Mumma, you and technology do not mix," Jigar laughed. "It is so easy to use but Indian women always struggle to use modern technology."
"Excuse me," Charu said indignantly. "I have never asked you to help me with the DVD player."
"You asked me for help because you thought your hair straighter was broken. All it needed was a fuse to be replaced," Jigar jested.

"Enough," Madhu said. "Turn the film on."

Uma lay on the floor breathing slowly, unsure what was happening. She saw Jigar turn the DVD player on. The disc began to load and the film started. The opening credits of an old Bollywood movie began to play. *Why are they showing me this film?* Uma watched the story of a girl who was unable to provide a dowry at her wedding. Uma saw how the in-laws grew tired of her and eventually murdered her by setting her on fire. The police began to investigate the death but the in-law's convinced the police the woman had committed suicide. Uma opened her eyes wide in fear. She knew why she was being shown this movie. *They want to burn me! Hai Mata Rani they want to burn me! You are the only one who can save me now. You cannot allow your devotee to be burnt like this!* She began to struggle in an attempt to free herself from her bondage. *Maybe Mata Rani's blessing will help me break free.*

As Uma struggled to break free, she saw the Rathod family pause the film. The charges against the murdered woman's family were dropped. The four Rathods stood up and made a circle around her. She did not dare to lift her head; all she could see was their shoes.

Chapter 67: Amrita

Amrita sat down on Leela's bed lost for words as Leela finished telling her about Uma's abuse at the hands of her family. Leela told Amrita everything. How the initial verbal abuse turned to violence. How Uma attempted to return home but was sent back by her parents. To Amrita's disgust, Leela even spoke about her suspicions that Uma had been raped in the past few days. Amrita had tears in her eyes at the thought of what Uma was going through. *Waheguru this woman has gone through the same thing my Nirmal went through. The abuse that they have inflicted onto her is probably the same thing those bastards did to Nirmal.* Amrita's sympathy for Uma quickly turned to anger towards the people responsible for Uma's plight.

Amrita stood up and walked towards Leela to ask a question that had bugged her whilst she had narrated Uma's story. Amrita bent down and looked at Leela's face.
"Why did you not say anything about this before?" Amrita asked firmly. "Why did you take so long?"
"I did not want to gossip about my friend," Leela replied.
"If you told me sooner we could have saved her from the ordeal that you think she went through at the hands of her husband."
"I did not want people to judge her. I thought by keeping everything a secret I was protecting her honour and her dignity. People..."
"That is not an excuse to keep quiet," Amrita said angrily. "You should have prioritised another woman's need for help over the bukvaas people would say."
For a while Leela remained silent. Amrita stood up and began to pace around the room. *Haai Rubba how can I save Uma from those kutas? I need to do something before I am too late like I was with Nirmal. Waheguru help find me a solution.*
"Uma's neighbour comes every day," Leela told Amrita. "She ignores everything. Today Uma screamed that she had been raped in front of her, she just carried on drinking her chai and said nothing. Jigar is a policeman and everything that happens to Uma happens under his

nose. Who do I tell? They are big people, with high prestige. Who would listen to a woman of my status?" Leela paused. "I did my best for her. I told her to go back to Mandavi, I told her to leave them behind, but her parents kept on sending her back. They told her that once a daughter's palanquin enters a home, she leaves that home only on a funeral bier."
Amrita was lost for words. *Haai Rubba they must have thought keeping their married daughter will bring shame on their family. They thought it is better to send their daughter into a hell than to ruin their own reputation.*
"I did my best for her without telling people her business. I failed each time, and I told you everything because I do not know what else I can do for her."

"I do not want to hear any more excuses. You should have known that I would never judge her." Amrita snapped at Leela.
she looked ashamed and looked away from her. For a while Amrita looked at the back of Leela's head. Amrita felt some guilt over the way she spoke to Leela. *My words must have stung her... I am being too harsh on the poor girl. How was she to know she should have done something to help her? All she has ever known is women being mistreated. All she has ever seen when it comes to crimes against women is double edged justice. The perpetrators are punished but so is the woman. Leela is uneducated. She does not know the law. I know the law. I know how I can save Uma and get her justice.* Amrita clenched her fists. *I failed to save Nirmal, but Waheguru, I swear by you that I will save Uma and I will see to it that those animals are punished.*

Amrita walked over to Leela and turned her around so that they were both facing each other.
"Leela," Amrita said urgently. "We need to act fast. We need to save Uma."

Amrita spent five years thinking *"what if I had done this?"* or *"what if I had done that to save Nirmal."* As a result a plan on how she would rescue Uma was fully formulated in her mind.

Chapter 68: Charu

"Take her to the kitchen," Charu heard her mother say.
Charu watched her brothers pick Uma up again. Vijay took the waste of space by the arms and Jigar by the feet. The waste of space attempted to scream through the gag but was unable to make much noise. Charu followed her mother and brothers to the kitchen where they all stood around the fat lump. Charu felt gratification as she saw the waste of space wriggling around the floor like a fish out of water. *After today I will never have to argue with this thing because Mumma is going to end her disgusting attitude.*

"Uma bahu," Charu heard her mother's gentle voice. "We have tried again and again with you, but we are not getting anywhere with you. We tried to explain to you with love. I tried being harsher, I even gave you the same love and respect I give to Charu. Nothing seems to work on you. I just think you middle class people are not worthy to marry into my family. You are just too stubborn."

Charu saw her mother pick up a red jerry can from the kitchen worktop. Charu recognised it as the extra can they kept in the car to fill up with petrol for emergencies.
"I have no other option left but this," her mother began to unscrew the plastic lid on the petrol can.

Chapter 69: Uma

"Charu beti, untie the dupatta from her mouth," Madhu ordered. "I want to hear her scream."
Charu bent down in front of Uma's face and untied the gag. *Charu's face is so close to mine that I could smash my head against hers and break her nose.* Uma took a deep breath and held her anger in. *If I do that, I am guaranteed to lose my life and leave Sheela without a mother. Once this kutri removes the dupatta I will beseech Vijay to save me. He loves... loved me once. I am the mother of his child.* Once the gag was removed and Charu moved back, the anger Uma suppressed momentarily returned. She was gripped by the fight to survive. *I am going to do whatever I need to do to survive, and if I have to die, I will break something of their body so that they cannot say it was an accident.*

Uma rolled her fingers into fists, ready to fight. Uma felt a shudder as she felt a cold liquid splatter over her. The resolve to fight was weakened when she involuntary uncurled her fingers as a reaction to the liquid. She looked up and saw the source of the liquid. Madhu was pouring a fluid from a petrol can onto Uma. *Hai Mata Rani, I am still calling out to you. Do not let me go through this pain. Save me, Save me!*

Uma wanted to get up but struggled as she could not use her hands which were still tied up. She rolled around and got onto her knees and crawled towards her husband.
"Vijay... Vijay what is this? What have I done to deserve this?" Uma saw Vijay looked bored. "Remember how much fun we had in London? Surely it all meant something to you?" He turned his back onto Uma. Her desperation increased. "VIJAY SHEELA NEEDS ME! OUR BETI NEEDS HER MAA!"
"I warned you so many times but you did not listen," Madhu whispered. "We asked again and again and again but your parents did not listen to me. If you want to blame anyone for this, blame yourself and your pagal maa."
"It's money you want Maaji," Uma implored. "I can get it for you.

Everything you want. But if you kill me you won't get anything. You can only get the money if you let me live."
"We have asked too many times. We have given you too many chances. We still have nothing."
"One more chance," Uma begged. "One more chance and I will get everything you want."

Chapter 70: Charu

Charu was highly amused to see the waste of space snivelling at her mother's feet. *Not only does she look like a joker but she is acting like one too!* After begging for a few more seconds, the waste of space realised that her pleas were falling on deaf ears. Uma let go of Charu's mother's sari and crawled over to where Charu was stood. Uma grabbed the hem of Charu's dress.
"Charuben! Please save me," the waste of space squealed. "Please do not let them do this to me. I will get you the money you need. I will get you even more than you need. I will ask maa to pay for your honeymoon, you need to..."

I am in no mood for more of her drama. Charu looked at her mother. *Hurry up and end this now mumma.* Charu got bored of listening to the snivelling. She bent down to release her dress from Uma's clasp. As Charu pulled the dress out of the waste of space's hand, she looked at her face. This was the first time in a while that Charu saw Uma's face properly. For months Charu ignored her, avoided looking at her, even if she had to speak to her. Now that Charu looked at Uma's face properly she could not stop looking. Her face had fear etched all over it. Her eyes showed nothing but desperation. The look of terror that she saw on Uma's face stirred more emotions inside Charu. It was not hatred or spite. It was sympathy that she felt for the woman at her feet. Charu's amusement at the situation in front of her quickly evaporated.

Chapter 71: Uma

One by one Uma begged each member of her so called family. With her and Sheela's survival in mind, Uma thought of nothing else. She was not aware of the fact that she merely repeated herself over and over again. The only thing she did know was with each rejection, her desperation grew. She felt like an animal trapped in a hunter's snare waiting for death. *No one is helping me. No one. Hai Mata Rani where are you? Why haven't you come to rescue me?*
"HAI MAA DURGA," Uma screamed. "HELP ME... HEL"
Uma felt a hand around her mouth. She struggled but could not free herself.
"Do it now mumma," the man gagging her said. Uma realised the voice belonged to Vijay.

Uma heard the sound of a matchstick rub against the rough side of the matchbox. She turned to face Madhu who held the match. The pink coating of the match lit up. Her nostrils filled with the smell of sulphur. Uma's heart stopped.

Chapter 72: Madhu

Madhu saw the matchstick catch fire. She sniffed and could smell the sulphur caused by the burning matchstick. Madhu held the matchstick and looked over at Uma who was on her knees. Uma had her arms clasped together in a fist looking up praying to god. *It is said that if you die with the name of god on your lips or in your mind you break free from the cycle of birth and death and attain moksha. Unfortunately for the ox I am not kind enough to give her moksha that easily.*

Madhu saw the matchstick was half burnt. She threw the matchstick at Uma. The moment Uma saw the matchstick coming towards her she let out a shriek of terror. Madhu saw the match fall onto one of the wet patches on the floor near Uma. The moment the flame touched the liquid on the floor it went out.

Chapter 73: Uma

The lit match was dropped. Uma saw the matchstick fall in slow motion. With her hands tied together, Uma's natural instinct to shield her face from the blaze was impossible. She shut her eyes preparing her body for the excruciating pain. A few moments later, she felt nothing. *They say when you burn your pain receptors burn first. Perhaps this is it?* Uma heard laughter around her. *If I was dead I wouldn't hear them laughing. Perhaps maa Durga has saved me from the pain?* Without opening her eyes she remained where she was. She felt each heartbeat as her heart pounded against her ribs. Uma was short of breath, she had never felt her heart drum as quickly as it was. She opened her eyes minimally to peep at what was happening. There were no flames.

Uma opened her eyes to look more carefully at the scene. She became confused when she saw a burnt matchstick in a puddle of what appeared to be water. Uma felt more adrenaline rush through her. *It is a miracle! Mata Durga has turned the petrol into water.* Uma sniffed her surroundings. She could not smell any petrol. *It is a miracle!* Uma closed her eyes. *Hai Mata Rani, tara gana gana oopkar.*
"Do not thank God for saving your life."
Even with her eyes closed, Uma knew who the voice belonged to.
"Thank me."

Chapter 74: Madhu

The ox thinks that God saved her life. Madhu saw Uma open her eyes but the girl did not dare to raise her eyes and look at her. Uma looked confused by her announcement.
"I saved your life so thank me. Fall to my feet and thank me because I am your saviour," Madhu told Uma.
For a few moments Uma remained where she was and did not fall to Madhu's feet as she had commanded. Vijay then pushed Uma down forcing her head to touch Madhu's feet. She wailed with pain but did not struggle.

Madhu bent down slightly and grabbed Uma's hair. Pulling her by the hair she lifted her up, forcing Uma to stand.
"Being set on fire! Is that the way you want to die?" Madhu asked
"Na... no," Uma sniffed. "No maaji"
Madhu let go of Uma's hair and pushed her back. The girl kept her gaze to the ground unable to look into Madhu's eyes. Madhu took a step towards Uma and she touched her face. The moment she touched Uma with her fingers she gasped and jumped back.
"Don't worry beti," Madhu said softly. "You are safe... for now" she added. She let go of Uma. "We both agree that we do not want what we just did to become a reality. From your begging and screaming I also believe that you are willing to do anything to survive? Am I right?"
Madhu saw Uma nod as she continued to cry.
"Sorry I did not hear you."
"Yes maaji," Uma said quietly.
"Su kidhu? I still did not hear!"
"YES!" Uma said loudly. "Yes... I will do everything you say. I will ask my maa and bapuji to give me the money. I will find a way to bring money in."
"And if you don't?"
Uma did not respond. Madhu could tell she was trying to think of an answer, but she failed.
"Do not over exert your brain." Madhu smiled and began to walk in

circles around Uma. "I am a reasonable woman. I did not kill you tonight because I wanted to give you a chance. I thought maybe, just maybe the fact you are not bringing money in is not your fault. Maybe it is your worthless parents who are to blame. So I thought we will give you one more chance to prove your worth. You will live here like a queen, as long as you do what I tell you to. Do you understand?"
Uma nodded.
"Once again I did not hear you."
"Yes Maaji."
"If Charu wants money for her wedding, you bring it. If Vijay wants money for his hotel, you bring it. If I want a haircut… I'm sure you understand my simple rules?"
"Yes Maaji," Uma said robotically.
Madhu took a deep breath. "I'm not an unreasonable woman. If your parents cannot provide the money, there is nothing you can do about it. In those circumstances you will still have two options to save your life." Madhu lifted up two fingers to demonstrate to Uma her two options. She put one of the fingers down showing Uma her index finger. "Your first option is to leave my house. You sign divorce papers. You leave Sheela behind. You renounce your rights as Vijay's wife and Sheela's mother and never let your inauspicious shadow fall into our home again."
Uma did not react. She stood in front of Madhu and continued to look at the ground.
"Your second option," Madhu lifted her second finger up "is that you become a working woman who can bring money into this family. Vijay and Jigar have many friends who you could work with. You will not even have to leave your bedroom to go to work, if you understand what I mean? Vijay and Jigar's friends will pay you very well. That could be the way you fulfil your duty and support this family." Madhu saw that Uma merely continued to face the ground and did not respond to her questions. "Jigar, get the petrol."
Uma jumped in shock. "I understand. Yes I understand Maaji," she squealed.
"Good. There are also terms and conditions to this," Madhu stopped in front of Uma and once again looked into her face. She lifted her face to make eye contact with her to make sure she understood everything. "You better listen carefully. If anyone, and I mean anyone, finds out

what happened here the deal is over. We bring you back to the kitchen and this time it will be real petrol. I am sure it is something you never want to experience. So you abide by my rules and we will both live happily ever after. You understand?"

Uma shook her head and mumbled yes maaji again. Madhu was confident that she had forced Uma into a checkmate. Tears dripped from Uma's eyes, which were accompanied by a vacant facial expression. This was enough to tell Madhu she had nothing to fear anymore. *The ox will do everything I tell her to do. The drama I orchestrated tonight has instilled so much fear into her that she will never squeak against me. She will not even dare to tell another soul. She loves her daughter too much. Vah Madhu vah you are hosiyar. Although some credit must go to Vijay as he is the person who suggested the final threat of pimping her. I know she will never choose that option and I would never allow her to do such filthy things. My family honour is too important. But Vijay is right; she does not need to know it is an empty threat. The fear of being used for sex alone will make her do everything I tell her to.*

Chapter 75: Charu

Whenever Charu saw the sunrise she felt tranquil. When she felt stressed out over exams or was worried about anything, she stood on the balcony. The beauty of the birds flocking in front of the glowing red sun, surrounded by purple, pink and yellow sky mesmerised her. After a sleepless night she stood on the balcony to find some calm, but she found no peace. She was haunted by the same thoughts that prevented her from sleeping. *When did I become such a heartless person?*

Whilst Uma lay at her feet the night before, Charu had seen something in Uma's eyes. Charu could not pin point what she felt towards Uma but she felt deeply ashamed of herself. *How did I get to this stage where I'm torturing Uma? And I was doing all this just for money! I had forgotten that Uma had feelings and our actions were causing her severe pain.* Charu attempted to pacify her conscience.

I was led astray by mumma, Vijay and Jigar. I simply joined in with them, I never instigated anything myself. I was just trying to punish her for all the deception. She tricked my brother into marrying her so she could have a higher status for herself in society. Once she got the higher status she never kept to her word. She did not give us the dowry money she owed us. Both mumma and Vijay told me how Uma and her family lied to them about not having money and were not fulfilling their obligations. It was not our fault.

I knew mumma was not going to kill her! Mumma told me she just wanted to clip off the wings that the ant had sprouted. I would never have been involved in anything if they were going to kill her. I still have a conscience in me. However, no matter how much Charu protested her innocence, her conscience was not satisfied. She told herself; *you called her names to start with, then you started torturing her by playing evil pranks on her, then you started beating her. You were becoming more vicious and eventually you would have crossed the line.* Charu closed her eyes and put her face in her hands. The look of desperation in Uma's eyes flashed through her mind again and Charu quickly opened her eyes. She knew it would be a while before she could forget the look of pain in Uma's eyes.

Chapter 76: Uma

Uma struggled to swallow the dry chapatti but continued to eat. She had not eaten anything for twenty-five hours. Since the shocking events the night before, Uma had sat silently in her bedroom. She was like an empty shell whose soul had left the body but the body continued to breathe. The only time she showed signs of life was when she heard Sheela cry and Uma fed her daughter. When Uma smelt the scent of the food, her mouth watered; she walked downstairs to see what was for dinner. She saw that Leela served only meat that night. However, her hunger was intolerable so she sat down and ate chapatti without any other condiments.

Physically her body was amongst her family members, having dinner. Mentally she was still reliving the psychological torture inflicted onto her by her family the night before. One by one she looked at the faces of the demons she lived with. Madhu was scoffing down the chicken curry with a victorious glint in her eye. Vijay, Charu and Jigar were also eating dinner and none of them paid any attention to the fact that there was a fifth person sat amongst them. This suited Uma fine. She had nothing to say to the people she once attempted to make her family. She realised the night before that the Rathods were not her family. They were her owners and she was their possession. *Now I understand why women call their husband pati. Pati means master, owner, lord. These people own me, and my future will be determined by their decisions. Why was I so foolish to think my "pati" would be any different? The signs were in front of me all this time.* She continued to swallow the dry chapatti when she heard Sheela cry. *My beti must be hungry. She too has not had much food today.* Uma stopped thinking about her future and stood up to attend to her daughter.

Uma heard Madhu clear her throat. She looked towards Madhu who had one hand up, gesturing Uma to stop where she is.
"Leela," Madhu shouted, clearing her throat. "Get some milk for Sheela."
Milk? How can they get milk for Sheela? The milk for my beti comes from

me. How... Uma's confusion was cleared when she saw Leela bringing a milk bottle.
"Formula milk?"
"Do you have a problem with formula milk?" Madhu asked threateningly.
Uma stopped mid protest. She looked at Madhu's face whose eyes were threateningly wide. Uma relived the memory of Madhu pouring what she believed to be petrol over her.
"No, no problem at all," Uma said. She watched as Madhu tested the milk onto her skin. *Breast milk is better for my child than this artificial rubbish.* "Maaji, breast milk is better for a young child," Uma spat out.
"Uma bahu. Who knows what will happen tomorrow?" Madhu paused. She then began to speak very slowly and clearly. "If you are not here to feed her, we will have to take the responsibility over. We thought we should practise now." Madhu took a bite from her meal. "We do not know what will happen tomorrow. You might have to... go somewhere... soon."
Uma stopped speaking. She knew what Madhu was insinuating. *If my life is going to be like prisoner and servant, perhaps it is better that I am dead.* Uma saw Charu take the milk bottle from Madhu. Charu picked up Sheela and began to feed her niece. As Uma watched Charu feeding Sheela, she saw a vision of her daughter growing up and turning into her. Uma felt disgusted at the thought that her daughter might grow up to be a spoilt brat. *I cannot die. If I die now, my beti will become like these demons. I need to save her. I need to live for her.*
"Charu, most of your meal is still on your plate. You have not eaten," Madhu said to her daughter.
Uma saw that Charu's plate was still full. Uma's heart leapt at the thought that Charu will go and have her dinner. *I can feed Sheela myself.*
"I'm not hungry mumma."
"If you do not eat you will become sick," Madhu picked up Charu's plate and put half of Charu's meal into her own plate. "This much. Eat this much," Madhu said as she smiled at her daughter. "For me."
Uma looked at Charu becoming more excited, getting ready to step in to feed Sheela the moment Charu went to eat her meal.
"OK mumma," Charu said. "Let me finish feeding Sheela and I will eat."

Uma's heart dropped. She watched helplessly as Charu fulfilled what should have been her own responsibility. *They've already give me very little time with my diamond but now I don't even get to spend the time that I used to have with her. I thought there was one thing they could not take away from me, and that was Sheela. She's the only person in this world who I have to call my own and now they are taking that away from me too.* Unable to see her daughter being fed in the arms of another, she got up and walked away to her bedroom where she could vent her distress.

Uma walked towards the empty cradle and looked at it. Her eyes welled up with tears again. *I am being punished for committing the sin of wanting to die. Suicide is a terrible sin and I wished it upon myself. Mata Rani is now punishing me by separating me from my beti because I did not value human life.* Uma wiped her eyes. She began to rock the empty cradle. She looked at the friction burns on her wrist. Uma had not realised how much she struggled to free herself from her bondage until she saw the marks on her hands. She had sustained a number of injuries in the past that did not hurt until she saw the wound. However, this time, despite seeing the burns on her hand, Uma did not feel much pain. The pain of her family's reality and her daughter's separation was more painful than the wounds. Uma continued to rock the empty cradle and began to talk to the blanket inside it. *The only way I have of making sure that you remain mine is by doing... doing the... the... things... they want me to do. That is the only way I can make sure I can stop you becoming them. I will die every single day, doing what they want me to do, but I will tolerate it because it won't be worse than the pain of being separated from you. By doing what they want me to do, at least my body will keep breathing. That way I can make sure I do right by you. I cannot leave you in this hell; if a stepmother comes into your life what sort of torture will she inflict onto you? At least this way I can keep you safe. It is my only option to make sure you do not have a stepmother who ruins your life. My only option is to do as they say or... or take you with me.* Uma paused and breathed using her diaphragm. She stopped rocking the cradle and stood up. *Take her with me! If I leave this world and take her with me, I would not be leaving her here. Those demons will never give her a decent upbringing anyway. My beti and I will be happy in heaven.* Uma ran her fingers through her hair and pulled her own hair. *What are you thinking you foolish woman? How can you kill an innocent girl? You will be guilty of two murders in the eyes of god.* Uma began to rock the cradle again. *I have to stay here and do what I need to do for my daughter. I have nowhere else to take you.* She closed her eyes. *Hai Mata Rani, last night I prayed to you, with the hope you will save my life. Now I just want your help to help me escape this hell with Sheela, but not by taking both of our lives. Help me Mata Rani help me!*

Uma was unaware of how long she rocked the empty cradle for, but her fixation on the empty cradle was broken when she heard her bedroom door creak. A man she had never seen before walked into her room. Uma stood up terrified and began to wrap her sari around herself. "Who are you?" Uma asked her voice faltering. "What do you want?"

Uma's stomach began to churn. She thought she knew exactly why the man stood in her room. *I've been sold to him.* Uma began to shake as the man got closer to her. She looked around trying to find an escape route.
"My name is Vikram. Vikram Oberoi," The stranger said to Uma.

Chapter 77: Leela

“Please,” Leela heard Uma beg. “If you leave I won’t tell Vijay or anyone else that you left. Just don’t do anything.”
Leela looked around to make sure no one was around. She saw the four Rathods sleeping in the living room. She walked up to Uma’s bedroom and saw her cowering in the corner of her bedroom. Vikram was stood with his hands up looking around desperately, unsure what to do.
“Leela!” Uma screamed and ran towards her. “Leela save me from this man.”
Leela looked confused. She looked at Vikram who had his eyes wide open.
“Uma didi... this man is not here to hurt you,” Leela told Uma.
“My husband has sold me to him,” Uma screamed hysterically. “He is here to do stuff with me. You have to save me. I thought I could do anything for my beti but I would rather die than allow myself to be violated like this. Help me Leela,” Uma pointed at Vikram. “He has paid for me. He is here to tarnish me.”
“Uma didi...”Leela struggled to calm Uma down. She felt Uma’s nails dig into her skin. “Uma didi, he is here to help me. We are both here to help you.”
Leela repeated herself a few times before Uma understood what Leela was saying. Leela saw a look of confusion on Uma’s face. Uma looked back and forth from Vikram’s face to Leela’s. After a few glances she took a deep breath.
“Maa Durga sent you?” She asked.
“I think the goddess must have inspired me to come,” Leela told Uma. “Amritaji sent me.”
“I am Amrita’s pati,” Vikram said calmly. “Leela has told us everything. My patani sent us here to rescue you and your daughter. She’s waiting outside in the car.”
Leela saw the confusion on Uma’s face. She could see a flicker of hope in her eyes, however, it seemed she was still suspicious. *Uma didi does not trust Vikramji.* Leela took a deep breath.
“Uma didi do you trust me?”

Uma looked directly into Leela's eyes. She could tell Uma was weighing up her options internally. *She knows she can trust me, but after everything she's been through she doesn't know who else she can trust.*
"Uma didi, if you sit down I will explain everything to you."
Leela saw that Uma had a look of desperation in her eyes. A look that hoped this was not a joke.
"We need to get away from here as quickly as possible," Leela said. "Is it OK if I pack your belongings and Vikramji tells you?"
"Sheela... she..."
"Vikram already took Sheela. She is in the car with Amritaji. I will pack her things as well."
Leela saw that Uma nodded in agreement. She saw Uma listen to Vikram without looking at him. Leela turned around and opened the wardrobe. She could hear Vikram telling Uma how Leela finally told Amrita everything. How Amrita became distressed after she heard about the violence against Uma and how she refused to allow Uma to stay with the Rathods any longer. Vikram informed Uma how Leela mixed sleep inducing drugs into the Rathod's dinner and how she deliberately put meat in everything to prevent Uma from eating anything. He told Uma how he waited for Leela's text to tell him they were asleep and how he then bribed the watchman to let them into the house. Finally he told Uma that Amrita waited outside to give a signal should anything go wrong.
"Leela. You take over from here," Vikram said.

Leela put the packed suitcase down.
"Uma didi you do not have to come with us. The decision is yours but we will save you from this hell if you come with us."
"This is not a trick?"
"I swear on Guruvayur Swami that this is not a trick."
"Where will Sheela and I go if we get away from here? We have no..."
"Amritaji has said you can live with me. You and Sheela can both live with us."
Leela saw a look of relief and glee spread over Uma's face. Leela knew Uma now believed what they said.
"Leela! May Mata Rani protect you and bring you all happiness..."
"There's no time for that," Leela said urgently. "I didn't think Charu

would fall asleep. She didn't eat much. I need you to leave with Vikram now."
Uma looked uncomfortable at the prospect of leaving with just Vikram.
"Uma didi, I will follow you. I will finish cleaning. I made double of everything I cooked today. I need to throw away the food mixed with sleeping drugs and replace it with the food without them. I will then wait until Charu wakes up. I will act as if I know nothing. We do not want them to know where you are. You need to go quickly. I'll be with you soon."

Together Leela walked down the stairs with Vikram and Uma. Leela saw Charu stirring and she felt panic rush through her. Ende ammo, *if we get caught we could end up in prison. I drugged a policeman's family.*
"Quickly," Leela whispered to Vikram and Uma.

Uma paused. "I have left mata Shailputri's murti upstairs. I cannot leave without it," Uma rushed back upstairs to get the statue her mother gave to her on her wedding day. Leela watched as Charu drifted in and out of consciousness. Her fear intensified as Charu moved more.
"Vikramji you leave."
Leela was relieved to see Uma coming back. Uma whispered something and continued to run towards the exit. Uma crossed the threshold of the house and left it. Uma sneezed loudly. Leela stood frozen for a few seconds staring at Charu who was now wide awake. *O Guruvayur Swamy! She's awake!*
"What was that?" Charu asked groggily. Charu began look around to see where the noise had come from.
Ende Ammo she will see Uma. Leela did the only thing that occurred to her. She dropped some of the dinner on the floor. The sound of breaking china diverted Charu's attention. Leela saw that Uma tiptoed away. She faintly heard Amrita's car speed away.

A rush of adrenaline went through Leela. Even Charu shouting at her for smashing the plate could not dampen Leela's mood. *O Guruvayur Swamy thank you for your help.*

Chapter 78: Alice

Alice waited at the reception desk for Fatima to come back from the toilet. She crossed her legs desperate for the bathroom. She looked around and saw that no guest was around. *If I'm quick no one will notice anything.* She quickly ran to the guest toilets opposite the reception desk. She stumbled into Fatima who was stood opposite the mirror in the female toilet. Fatima was not wearing her scarf and jumped at the sudden intrusion.
"Sorry Alice maam, I was just readjusting my..."
For a second Alice stood rooted on the spot with her mouth open. She never realised that underneath the scarf Fatima had severe burn scars. The skin on her forehead was shinier then the rest of her skin, there were dark scars and light scars intertwined with each other. Fatima's hairline was light where there were scar tissues, but her hair at the back was beautiful. Alice momentarily forgot she needed to go to the toilet but remembered suddenly and ran into the cubicle.

Embarrassed and uncomfortable by her reaction to Fatima's scars she was unsure how to approach her again. She left the cubicle to speak to her. Fatima was no longer there, so she washed her hands and left the bathroom. When she returned to the hotel reception she saw Fatima looking normal once again. Her head was covered by her scarf. Alice gave a slight smile at Fatima when she looked over at her. *What do I say to her? She might not want to talk to me about it, she might feel self conscious.* Alice remembered her reaction. *She's probably already feeling self conscious. I need to bring it up somehow.*

Fatima began talking to Alice, it was as if Fatima read her mind.
"I was fortunate that most of my face was saved." Fatima said quietly. Alice was relieved that Fatima herself brought up the topic. She went and pulled up a chair and sat next to her. "I told you before; I got kicked out because I was accused of not being a virgin. I didn't tell you what happened after. Whenever I tell people what happened they ask me to remove the scarf so they can see my scars." Fatima gave a weak laugh.

"After I was kicked out my husband's brother, Farhan, began to follow me. He used to stand outside my house saying he wanted a go. He thought I was a whore so I would do things with everyone. I rejected his proposals all the time. I had no desire to be intimate with anyone other than my husband. He thought I gave it to everyone and wouldn't give it to him. He thought I was arrogant about my beauty. In a fit of rage he threw corrosive acid over me to strip me of my beauty. I screamed in agony and pain the moment the acid made contact with me. Allah was with me that day. Just as he went to throw it on me, I tripped over a rock on the floor and fell. He missed most of my face, but still destroyed me. I experienced pain worse than ever that day. The wounds have now healed but he stripped me of my confidence, my beauty. I was a disgraced woman."
Alice was moved to tears by Fatima's story. With her mouth open she was silent, unsure what to say.
"This is why I work so hard to make sure I can secure a good family for my sister. By paying a large dowry she might marry into a happier family than mine."

For a while both Fatima and Alice sat in silence. Unsure what to say, Alice felt she should break the silence.
"What happened to the guy who did this?"
"It took us two years to get justice. When we finally did he was sentenced to four years. He will be out of jail in six months."
"FOUR YEARS?" Alice shouted. "That's ABH, he should be in prison for longer. What bullshit."

Alice was about to vent her frustration more but saw a guest coming. She calmed down and controlled her anger. The guest smiled and approached Fatima. Fatima displayed her beautiful smile to the guest. Alice was about to break into tears again. She quickly went into her office before she cried in front of a guest. Alice admired Fatima for her courage. *She's lost so much but she's still fighting.*

Alice watched Fatima from the window of her office. Fatima engaged with the guest and made him feel welcome. *She's overcome everything and brought her life back on track. She says she's been stripped of her*

confidence but she still has a lot of courage. She stood in silence for a while thinking about Fatima. She felt her mobile phone vibrate and took it out of her pocket. *Vijay! Doesn't he fucking give up?*
"When will you get the damn message that I don't want to speak to you?" Alice fumed.
Alice was about to hang up when she heard Vijay's voice on the phone. *He's crying.* Alice felt a weird jolt that she could not explain at the thought of the man she once loved in distress. *Why is he crying?*
"I desperately need your help Alice."
"Why should I help a lying dickhead like you?"
"I made one mistake and she got pregnant. But I don't deserve what's happening to me now."
Alice felt a mixture of pity and anger, but predominantly anger. *You deserve everything you get.*
"What's happening that's so sad then?" Alice asked sarcastically.
"I told my wife I wanted a divorce. I told her I loved you and the one night we had sex was a drunken mistake. She wouldn't accept it and did everything to get me to change my mind. She even said she'll stay my wife just in name but won't expect anything. When she realised I didn't want anything she became crazy."
"Oh diddums."
"I don't deserve your sympathy after the mistake I did, but I do not deserve what she is doing to me."
"Is she going to parade you naked on the streets?"
"She told people that I raped her." Alice was stunned to silence. "She is telling people that my family abused her for a dowry. She's threatened me with court action, and is going to have us all imprisoned and take every penny I have."

Alice's anger against Vijay was overtaken by sympathy. *He is a dickhead, but I'm confident he would never rape someone. He deserves that stupid bunny boiler!*
"I don't understand how I can help you?"
"She claims I was abusing her in the months of April-October. I was with you in those months. If you give me an alibi you will stop me and my family from being ruined."
Alice was about to hang up when she spotted Fatima giving the guest a

key. She remembered what Fatima went through. *In this country some women climb mountains to get justice, and if they're lucky like Fatima their culprit will get a slap on the wrist. Then there's this bitch who abuses the system for her benefit. Vijay doesn't deserve to go to prison for crimes he hasn't committed. He was with me in those months. I should help him.*

Chapter 79: Amrita

Amrita walked around the living room not speaking much. She saw that Uma was rocking her daughter in Jaswinder's old cradle and Vikram sat down sipping tea. Amrita felt restless and eagerly awaited Leela's return from her morning shift at Rathod Haveli. She was eager to find out the aftermath of Uma's disappearance. Amrita heard the scraping noise the courtyard gate made each time it opened. She walked to her front door and saw Leela returning from work.

"Come in, come in. How was work?" Amrita asked Leela very quickly. Leela sat down and then looked at Uma, who was staring right back. "Everyone is tense," she said excitedly. "Purbai was at their house. Madhuji..."

Amrita hissed as Leela added Ji after Madhu's name. *Respect should only be given to those who deserve it.*

"Madhu," Leela corrected herself before resuming, "and Vijay were both crying the tears of fish and crocodiles. I think Madhu IS really worried about your whereabouts. But it is not out of concern for your safety. She is panicking that you will go to the police and they will get into trouble." Leela smiled and added "it seems to me that since the effects of the sleeping drugs ended, they have not slept for a single second. They are angry that you escaped them but are also terrified about what will happen next. They are all just pacing around their living rooms anxiously unsure what is going to happen."

That is exactly what I wanted to hear! Amrita thought delighted. *For now I am just depriving them of their sleep. They will lose a lot more once we are done with those scoundrels.*

"After Purbai left, I heard Jigar tell his family that his police friends are searching for you. They were talking of reporting you missing officially as well." Leela took a short breath. "I also heard Vijay sir tell Madhu what he told the white girl. Vijay told her that you have filed a police case against him and he needs a witness to say he is innocent. I think they are already plotting to cover their crimes in case you take the police to them."

Amrita felt rage rushing within her at the mention of the police. She exhaled and walked over to Uma who was still pulling the string to the cradle. She sat down where Uma was sat and faced her.
"Umaji," she said speaking directly to Uma. "I know this will be hard, but if you do not mind, I want you to tell me everything."
Uma continued to rock the cradle and did not say a word.
"I understand that it is very difficult, but if we want to help you we need to know everything from..."
"Maa told me to go into my in-law's home and become like the flame of a diva," Uma said quietly. "Like the flame of a diva, bring light, warmth and happiness into the lives of the family I became a part of. I failed."
Amrita took a deep breath mentally preparing herself as Uma recounted the story of what she went through with her in-laws. Amrita's emotions went up and down like a rollercoaster shifting with each sentence of Uma's story. She switched from anger to sympathy, sadness to fury, disgust to hatred. Even though she prepared herself for Uma's story, Amrita still felt severely distressed to hear Uma recall the story first hand. *Haai Rubba is this exactly what Nirmal went through? Did she feel the same as this woman feels? Isolation, depression, anger and subordination became a part of Uma's life. If this is what Nirmal's life became then she would have gone through many hardships in her final days.* There were times when Amrita came close to stopping Uma from telling more of the story, but she was unable to stop her. Amrita felt as though she was listening to a horror movie that she was unable to stop because she wanted to know what happened next despite being repulsed by the entire thing. Uma finally got to the pseudo burning and the plans Vijay had for using her to make money. At this point Vikram, Leela and Amrita all gasped with outrage.

Once Uma finished her story, Amrita felt abhorrence and severe hatred. *Nirmal, Leela, Uma and Raab jane how many other women go through their lives not knowing their rights. Perhaps if Nirmal had known there was something to help her she might be...* For a few moments Amrita felt totally helpless and was silent. She went back into her world where she thought "*what if this had happened, what if that had happened. Perhaps Nirmal would still be here.*" Amrita heard Vikram curse the Rathod family loudly which brought her mind back to the current situation. She pulled her thoughts together and remembered that they did not rescue Uma to simply save her and Sheela's life. There was another motive for saving her.

"Umaji, Leela tells me you are a religious person. I believe you will know Mahabharat?"
Uma had her face in her lap. Amrita assumed that Uma was still crying as the retelling of her story reopened the wounds inflicted by her family. Amrita saw that Uma made a slight nod, without lifting her head.
"Tell Me Umaji," Amrita persisted. "What happened when the Kauravs attempted to disrobe Draupadi and tried to molest her in front of Hastinapur's public?"
Uma looked up. She had a look of confusion on her face. Amrita knew it was because she was unsure about why Amrita was asking that question.
"Lord Krishna blessed Draupadi with a never ending sari," Uma said blandly. "They were unable to disrobe her."
Haanjee that happened, but that is not the answer I wanted. I will try again.
"Umaji can you tell me the story of Kaalratri?"

Amrita listened as Uma narrated the story of Durga's seventh form, Kaalratri. Shumbh and Nishumbh were two brothers. They travelled to Pushkar and underwent severe penance and purification rituals to please Brahma. Eventually, pleased by their dedication, Brahma told the brothers he would grant them a wish of their choice. Both brothers asked to be immortal. However, Brahma told them that immortality was against the rules of the universe and advised them they could instead choose how they die. The brothers pondered how they could cheat Brahma and make themselves immortal. The two demons eventually thought they found a loophole. They asked Brahma to be killed by the hands of a woman they were attracted to. Brahma granted the demons their wish thoroughly pleasing Shumbh and Nishumbh. The demons were delighted by the thought that they managed to trick the creator into making them immortal. The demons felt that a weak creature such as a woman could never kill someone as strong as them.

Under the illusion of immortality, they began to terrorise the world with their evil. They recruited other demons including Chand, Mund and Raktabeej who supported them. Anyone who disobeyed their orders was killed by the demons who worked for them. They especially targeted women just in case any of them turned out to be their killers. Once the result of their good karma ended, Durga incarnated as Ambika. Chand and Mund saw Ambika and were mesmerised by her beauty. They thought a beautiful woman like her should belong to Shumbh and Nishumbh. They immediately went over to the demon brothers to describe the beauty they had seen. The brothers demanded Chand and Mund bring her to them so they could marry her. Chand and Mund went back to Ambika and delivered Shumbh and Nishumbh's marriage proposal to her. Ambika declined, saying she took an oath that she would only marry a man who could beat her in battle. Chand and Mund were enraged by the woman's foolishness. Compelled by her beauty they decided to give her another chance to fall at their feet and accept their masters as her husbands. Once again Ambika declined and reminded them of her oath to only marry a man who could defeat her in battle. After being rejected a second time Chand and Mund decided to forcefully take Ambika to the brothers. When Chand and Mund attempted to fight her, both were killed giving Ambika a new name, Chamunda.

Enraged by the deaths of their two servants, Shumbh and Nishumbh sent an army of demons to bring Ambika to them. Ambika called upon the female energies of the gods to come and show the demons who thought women to be inferior to them how powerful women actually were. Vaishnavi, Maheshwari, Indrani, Brahmani and many more female energies joined the battle against the army of demons. The divine female powers killed the demon army one by one. Yet, there was one demon who astonished them all. Raktabeej was not only a powerful demon; he also possessed a special power making it almost impossible to kill him. Whenever one of the female powers killed Raktabeej, for every drop of his blood that fell to the ground a new Raktabeej grew in his place. Eventually the battlefield was filled with tens and thousands of Raktabeejs. No matter how hard the goddesses tried to kill him new demons arose from his blood. This was when Durga took her 7th form of Kaalratri. In her fierce and terrifying form of Kali she began to drink the blood of Raktabeej. Each time one was killed she drank his blood preventing any of their blood from falling to the ground. One by one she mowed down the army of Raktabeejs, and quenched her thirst with their blood, preventing more from growing in their place. Finally Shumbh and Nishumbh came to the battle enraged by the death of their demons and were killed by Ambika. Elated at the deaths of such evil, Kali began to dance in ecstasy. She was dancing with so much joy at the demon's defeat that she did not notice that her dance was causing cracks to appear on the earth. The people of the universe became worried she would dance through the core of the earth and release lava which would destroy the entire world. To save the world Shiva lay on the floor and allowed Kaalratri to dance on top of him, absorbing the shock of her feet. When the adrenaline of her victory wore off she realised that she was dancing on top of her husband. She stopped dancing. Ashamed of her behaviour she stuck her tongue out and finally calmed down. Once she calmed down, she transformed back into a more beautiful form of Durga.

Amrita listened patiently to the entire story Uma narrated. Once the story was over she began to speak again.
"So Kaalratri was a form of Durga who destroys evil. She was an inspiration to women. They should defend themselves and protect their rights." Amrita could tell that every eye in the room was on her. She continued saying what she wanted to say. "I believe that Mahishasur also met the same fate at the hands of Durga's sixth form Katyayini. He also thought women to be weak so asked Brahma for the same wish. He then began to kill all women to avoid any of them from rising up to him. But Durga killed him as well." Amrita looked at Uma's face. She knew she was going in the right direction.
"You were right before. When the Kaurav's tried to molest Draupadi, Krishna did bless her with a never ending sari. But let me reword my question. What were the consequences of the Kaurav's attempt to insult Draupadi and rape her in public?"
"Each and every person responsible for attempting to rape Draupadi was destroyed. The people who defended their actions also met the same

fate."
"Exactly! Your scriptures tell you many stories of men who dishonoured women. Ravan kidnapped Sita, his entire dynasty was destroyed. Our women like to follow examples of Savitri, Ansuya and other women who served their husbands and brought lots of good fortune on their family. They are told again and again to be like these women, so you idolise them and try your best to become them. What I fail to understand is why do you not idolise Kaalratri and Draupadi as well? Why are women not taught to be like those women who avenged themselves for the wrongs done to womankind?"

Amrita leaned in closer to Uma and looked directly into her eyes and she began to speak directly to her.

Chapter 80: Uma

Draupadi? Kaalratri? All of these women were divine. I have nothing in me like any of those powerful women.
Uma saw that Amrita was now kneeling down and looking directly at her. She saw a look of anger and hatred in her eyes. However, she knew that Amrita's anger was not directed towards her.
"It is time for you to show people that women like Kaalratri and Draupadi do not exist only in stories. A woman's role does not end at being a mother and wife. When she is provoked she can become a force of destruction," Amrita said with passion. As Uma listened to Amrita's speech she felt adrenaline rush through her. "The time has come for you to stop being Savitri. It is time for you to avenge every single tear that you shed because of those pehnchodo that you called your family. You will give a message to the filth who think women are weak and so they can do whatever they want them. You will show them that there are terrible consequences for playing with a woman's honour."
"Amritaji what can I do? I was always taught to forgive people. Obey my husband..."
"Forgiveness is a virtue but forgiving someone who does not deserve it, is a crime. Speak no evil, hear no evil, see no evil. If you ignore it and let it go you're just as bad."
"My maa..."
"... told you to become a diya, or diva as you Gujarati call it," Amrita interrupted.
"Bring light and happiness into people's lives."
"I am not telling you to stop being a diya. Remain a diya, but what your beeji did not tell you is that a diya does not just bring light and happiness. When people mess around with a diya, that single flame becomes a fire." As Amrita spoke, Uma felt warmth spread through her body. "This fire can become an inferno devouring and destroying everything in its path. Keep burning as the flame your beeji told you to be but not to bring them light and happiness; become the flame that will destroy and burn them. They shattered each and every single dream you had. You will burn their dreams to ashes. They took away your

happiness, your peace of mind and even the love of your life. The fire you light will take away their happiness and ability to sleep. They will burn day and night. Continue burning like a diya but not to bring them light, but to incinerate the kuttas."

An eye for an eye makes the whole world blind. That is what Gandhi bapu said? He did not free India from the British by revenge. He fought violence with peace. Maa also taught me that violence is bad. She told me those who find their happiness in the misery of others are never truly happy themselves. What would I gain from revenge? I have already lost my family, my happiness, my peace.

"Do your duty. Light a fire so intense that no matter how many tears they cry they will not be able to put the fire out," Amrita said before she stopped speaking.

The hairs behind Uma's neck stood on end as her heart beat rapidly. The intense heartbeats felt like the footsteps of Kali. Thinking of Kali caused Uma to sit up straight. She felt something move inside her. A vengeful Kaalratri had awoken within her. The anger she had contained within her finally erupted inside her and spread through her body like hot lava. Her body burnt with anger. Uma closed her eyes and saw the fearsome, bloodthirsty face of Kali. Her black skin colour, red tongue sticking out and deadly eyes wide open that could instil fear into anyone. Uma saw Kali dancing the tandav dance of destruction. As she danced she used her crescent moon shaped sword to cut off Madhu's head. Uma became delighted to see the woman she harboured so much hatred for meet a horrific end.

There is something I will gain from their destruction. Comfort! I will find my happiness in their misery because I am not happy but that is because those bastards made me that way. Uma felt as though Kaalratri would not end her dance of destruction until Uma avenged herself. *Maha Kali has awoken within me. The only sacrifice that will satisfy her is the annihilation of those demons. I attempted to fulfil my duty as a wife, mother and daughter but they took everything from me. I will now fulfil my duty as a woman to punish those demons.*

"I will show them. I will punish them," Uma whispered.

“What did you say?” Amrita said.
“I will show them.” Uma repeated.
“I cannot hear you.”
Amrita’s habit of making Uma repeat herself reminded her of Madhu. Thinking of Madhu added fuel to the blaze within her.
“I AM NOT WEAK!” Uma shouted. “I will show them. I will fight for my rights. I will make sure they regret taking me as their daughter-in-law. I will show them that women are not weak.”

Uma looked up to see Vikram, Leela and Amrita stood around her. All three of them had a smile on their faces. Uma’s determination evaporated quickly. *Jigar has the police’s support. They have so much money. How will I get justice? No one will listen to me.*
“Amrita, Vikram and I are here to help you every step of the way,” Leela told Uma.
Leela’s words fanned the fire inside her and it relit. *I have these three people to support me. I am a diva and, like the naked flame of the diva, I will burn them.*

Part IV: Kaalratri
(The Destroyer of Evil)

Chapter 81: Uma

Uma stood outside the police station and played with her fingers. Six weeks ago, she was rescued from Rathod Haveli by Leela and the Oberoi family. After weeks of planning their revenge everything had gone wrong. Amrita devised a new strategy for revenge, but before they could implement the new plan there was one thing Uma had to do. She stood at the threshold of the police station looking at the blue semi-circle sign above the entry gate. Uma took out her mobile phone and saw the time. *6.12, I still have thirteen minutes before my appointment with Inspector Lal.* Uma turned around and went to sit on the bench to wait until it was time.

As Uma sat in the shade waiting for the time to pass she saw Purbai walk past. Purbai looked at Uma who determinedly stared back at her. Without maintaining eye contact or greeting each other, Purbai quickly looked away and carried on walking. *At least you are too ashamed to look me in the eyes. You are a coward who is unworthy to look me in the eyes. One day you will need help and I hope they refuse to help you.* A few days after her escape from Rathod Haveli, Uma begged Purbai to be a witness for her so she could file a complaint. However, she had simply refused, saying she did not wish to get caught up in police proceedings and cases. Two weeks ago, Uma once again went to her home. She fell to her knees and begged Purbai to give a testimony. Her please fell on deaf ears once again. Uma looked away from Purbai and took a few breaths. *Purbai is not the real enemy here. She is just a weak woman who cannot stand up for justice. The real villains are-.* Uma stopped mid-thought. She saw Charu walking towards where she was sat. *What is it today? I keep seeing inauspicious faces. First Purbai and now this manhoos.* Charu was about to walk past Uma, without looking at her when Uma interrupted her.

"Have you come here to spy on me for your brothers?" Uma said.
Charu looked at her and seemed surprised to see her.
"Do not pretend that you didn't know I was here. You must know

everything."
She looked uncomfortable by what Uma was saying. She shifted a few times and began to walk off without saying a word.
Seeing Charu's cowardice made Uma's anger erupt once again.
"YOU DO NOT HAVE THE DECENCY TO FACE ME AFTER EVERYTHING YOU HAVE DONE," Uma screamed. "YOU KNOW YOU'RE WRONG AND STILL YOU DO NOT ADMIT TO YOUR CRIMES."
Charu began to walk quicker. Uma raised her voice.
"THE TEARS YOU AND YOUR FAMILY MADE ME CRY HAVE NOW DRIED UP BECAUSE THOSE TEARS WILL NOW LEAK FROM THE EYES OF YOU, YOUR BROTHERS AND YOUR MAA. YOUR TEARS WILL NEVER STOP. THAT IS MY CURSE TO YOU AND YOUR FAMILY. My curse to you."
Charu stopped for a second. Uma thought she would turn around to speak to her. However, she did not turn back around. Uma thought she saw Charu use her hands to wipe her eyes. She decided not to bother with Charu and sat back down to wait until it was time to meet Inspector Lal.

When there were less than two minutes left for her appointment, Uma stood up. She took a moment to gather her thoughts, her vision focused entirely on the building ahead of her. She forcefully took the first step towards the station. *I must do this now. This is the first step of our new plan to destroy the Rathod family.* Uma walked, what seemed like forever. Finally she reached the door of the police station. She closed her eyes and took a deep breath. She opened her eyes, pushed the door open and entered the police station.

Inspector Lal, the most senior policeman at the station, was already sat on his desk. His beige uniform highlighted every extra inch of fat that he had all over his body. When Uma saw his moving moustache she knew that he was eating. When he realised Uma was here, he stopped eating and licked each one of his fingers, before pushing the Pav Bhaji to the side.
"Umaji, welcome, welcome. We have been waiting just for you," he smiled and pushed his chair back. He put his right foot on top of his desk and then crossed his left on top. "What can I do for you today?"

How about the job that you're paid for?
"I am here to withdraw all the complaints I have made against my family." Uma told the inspector.
Inspector Lal smiled which infuriated Uma but she knew now was not the time to become angry.
"RAJPAL. COME HERE!" Inspector Lal shouted.
Uma saw a lower ranking officer walk over to the desk.
"Write down everything this lady has to say. Then get her to sign her statement," Lal said dully. Rajpal sat down with a pen and looked at Uma. Frustrated, she began to speak monotonously.
"I am here to withdraw the complaints I made against my in-laws and husband. They have apologised to me for their mistake. They have begged for my forgiveness. I want to give them a chance to give me the love and respect I deserve, which is what they want. I have accepted their apology for my daughter's happiness. So I am withdrawing my complaint. I want no action taken against my in-laws and husband."

Chapter 82: Purbai

Purbai walked into her home with tears in her eyes. *Swaminarayan Bhagwan will never forgive me for refusing to give a testimony in Uma's favour! But I was helpless I could not help her even if I wanted to.* She still remembered the day Uma came to her house seeking help.
"I need your help Purbai masi," Uma asked. "I know you are an eye witness. I need your help."
Purbai had been moved by Uma's plight. Uma told her that their maid was also a witness. *I should tell them everything I know and have seen. The right thing to do is to support them.*
"What happened to you is very sad," Kesar had interrupted. "But we have to think about whether we can help or not."
"What is there to think about?" the Sikh woman asked harshly.
"It's a very big ask," Kesar responded. "Now please leave our house and let us talk."

Once the Sikh man, his wife and Uma left their house, Kesar immediately spoke.
"You can't give the testimony."
"Why not?" Purbai asked confused.
"Jigar is a policeman. I don't want to lock horns with a policeman and his family. It could be dangerous for us."
"But Kesar, I know everything... I told you what I heard that day when Madhu and Uma were arguing in their house. You told me to ignore everything I have seen. Now we have to help..."
"Maaji," Kesar said firmly. "I told you that day why we can't help. The circumstances have not changed. What will we gain by making an enemy with the police? We will land ourselves into trouble. How will you give evidence against a policeman and his family? They will target us next if we speak out against them."

Purbai thought for a moment. *Kesar is right but how can I just ignore everything? If I ignore it then she will never get justice.*
"Also baa," Kesar continued. "I don't want to go through these

bureaucratic police procedures and court procedures. Why would we knowingly invite trouble and difficulties onto ourselves?"
"Kesar, I do not understand..."
"Jigar framed Samu's daughter. You have spent months telling me what a shameless girl my sister's beti is. You never thought to think about the reality behind it. My niece spoke out against the police for taking a bribe from a man who was teasing her. To silence her they maligned her character by spreading rumours that she sells her body to earn money."
"Your sister's beti is..."
"Don't finish the sentence," Kesar said dangerously. "My niece was framed because she spoke out against someone who paid the police. What will happen to you if you give a testimony against the family member's of a policeman?"
Purbai was silenced by Kesar.
"I have two daughters and another child on the way. I refuse to allow you to invite difficulties into our home. If you want to give a testimony, you will have to find somewhere else to live. I want no associations with you. I don't want to worry that my children are not safe in their own home."

Purbai fumed that Kesar was threatening to kick her out from her own home. *The money that I worked hard to earn built this house, and you dare threaten to kick me out?* Purbai calmed herself before she vocalised her thoughts. She remembered that she did not own the house. The house was now in her son, Khimji's name and Kesar had him wrapped around her finger. Purbai sat down after Kesar left. *Poor Uma needs my help! How can I not help her? Lord Swaminarayan has always taught us to stand by the truth and what is right. It is our dharma to defend justice and truth. But if what Kesar says about Samu's daughter is true then I might be endangering my own family. By helping Uma I might be doing the right thing. However, for me, my foremost dharma is to protect my grandchildren and family. I cannot put them at harm to help Uma. If I help Uma what if those demons turn on my family? If I help Uma, where will I go? Without anywhere to live I would end up in the old people's ashram or the widow's ashram. In these ashrams people are lonely, no one visits them and they will die all alone. I cannot spend the last days of my life alone and unwanted by my family. I want to be surrounded by the people*

I love. I am too young to go to an old people's ashram.

When the police came to take Purbai's statement the following day, she told them she did not know anything. She saw nothing and nor did she hear anything. Purbai, ashamed of herself, looked at the ground the entire time, making no eye contact with Jigar's colleague. Since the day Purbai lied to the police, she felt riddled with anxiety. A small part of her told her it was not too late to help Uma. Nevertheless, Purbai ignored her inner conscience each time. She lay awake at night some days unable to sleep as she thought about the lies she told to help her own family.

Whenever Purbai saw Uma she squirmed with shame and attempted to hide herself. There were times when they both walked past each other. Purbai felt too ashamed to look Uma in the eyes. She avoided gazing at the woman who she had betrayed. There were times when Purbai would look towards Uma to apologise to her and explain. However, during those times, Uma stubbornly looked away from her. *Even today when I saw her sat outside the police station Uma ignored me. I will go to jampuri for preventing a woman from getting justice, but what could I do? Her life has already been ruined. If I help her it won't make her life better and it could ruin the lives of my family, grandchildren and my own life. Hai Swaminarayan Bhagwan, only you can punish those demons and help that poor girl get justice. I pray that you find a way to help her.*

Chapter 83: Avantika

Avantika paced around her living room, walking back and forth. She was restless as she waited for Uma's phone call.
"Sit down maa," Gauri complained. "You're making me nervous."
Avantika ignored Gauri. *I can't sit down, if I sit down the clock takes forever to move. At least by walking the clock seems to move faster.*
Avantika looked at the time again. Three minutes passed since she last looked. *Come on Uma! Why have you not phoned yet?*
Avantika heard the landline ring, she immediately ran to pick it up.
"Hello Jay Shri Krishna?" Avantika nervously answered.
"Has Uma phoned yet?" Vinod asked.
"Na," Avantika said slightly disappointed that it was not Uma calling. "I am putting the phone down. What if Uma is phoning right now?"
She put the phone down and resumed her ritual of pacing around the living room. *Arjun has been in police lock up for a whole fortnight. Why hasn't Uma phoned yet to say he's coming home? What if she changed her mind?* A few minutes later the landline rang again. Avantika ran to pick up the phone again.
"Hello Jai Shri Krishna?"
"I have withdrawn the case. Arjun will be released tomorrow," Uma said.
Avantika felt a rush of adrenaline and gratitude towards her daughter
"U..." Avantika stopped. She heard that Uma had put the phone down.
Dejected Avantika too put the phone down.

Avantika walked over to the shrine in her home and stood in front of the idols unsure what to do. *I was in a lose-lose situation Mata Rani. If I supported Uma, Arjun would have suffered. If I supported Arjun, Uma would have suffered. I did the right thing but how do I make Uma see this? I had no selfishness in making her take the police case back this time. It was Arjun and Gauri I was worried about and not just our family honour.*

Avantika recalled the event, four weeks ago, which caused her world to crumble around her. It was 7.30pm and the Desai family had been about to start their dinner. Gauri was serving the food and Avantika was feeling proud of her daughter. It was the first time Gauri cooked a full meal on her own. As soon as they all sat down to eat the meal, the police came storming into the house. Shocked by the sudden intrusion, they all stood up. They were even more shocked when the police informed their family that they were there to arrest Arjun. Startled, Avantika asked the police what the charges against Arjun were. They informed the whole family a complaint had been lodged against him for eve teasing and he was being arrested for sexual harassment. Arjun denied all the charges and pleaded his innocence to the police. However, his pleas fell on deaf ears. The police handcuffed him and forcefully dragged him to the police van parked outside. Avantika begged the police to let her son go and bellowed her son's innocence. The whole family watched helplessly with tears in their eyes. Avantika argued with the police right until they put him into the back of their van and drove away. Once Avantika recomposed herself, she noticed some of her neighbours were sat outside their houses. They were the same neighbours who once admired the expensive cars parked outside their house. This time they were staring at her and gossiping about the events that had just unfolded. Avantika's biggest fears were coming true. *The Desai family name is turning to dust. By tomorrow these people will have told everything they've seen.*

After Arjun's arrest, Avantika thought her day could not get any worse. She found out she was wrong when she phoned Uma's in-laws to see if Jigar could help them. Avantika received more news which gave her a severe shock to the heart. Madhu explained how Uma ran away from the house with her daughter two weeks ago. Uma then lodged false allegations against her family for crimes none of them had committed. Madhu told Avantika to never phone her house again and put the phone down. Devastated, Avantika did not know what to do. Two of her children had brought shame on their family in one day. *Why did Uma not say anything about leaving her in-laws? She should have told us. We are her family.*

"Why would she tell you?" Gauri responded, when Avantika finally discussed her sorrow with the rest of the family. "You have both given

her away. You have no responsibility towards her."
"She is your sister Gauri," Vinod said angrily. "Do not say bad things about her."
"I'm not saying bad things about her. You and Maa both told her that your responsibility for her is over and she now belongs to the Rathod family. Why would she call you?"
"That is not what we said. What we said was for all of your benefits."
"You can only leave your in-laws on a funeral bier?" Gauri said. "If you said that to me I wouldn't say anything to you again. I would consider our relationship over."
Gauri's words hurt Avantika; there was an element of truth in what Gauri was saying. *We abandoned Uma because we were worried what people would say. We thought we were doing best for our children, but now everything is ruined. The respect I tried so hard to protect has turned to mud.*

The gossip got worse as the days went by. As the news of Arjun's imprisonment spread, the stories of his arrest got severe. People in Mandavi believed that Arjun was involved in a gang rape and was arrested on charges of rape. When people in the village saw Avantika approaching they went silent and ended their conversations abruptly. *This time last year these people would have licked the bottom of my sandals if I asked them to. Now they pretend they don't see me.* Eventually she stopped leaving the house, and only went out when she desperately needed to buy things. Even then she would go very early in the morning to ensure minimal people were around.

Eleven days after Arjun's arrest, Avantika finally managed to get hold of a mobile number she could use to contact Uma. Avantika initially raged at her daughter down the phone for everything that happened and the disrepute she brought on their family. However, she was stunned to silence when Uma revealed why she left the Rathods. She was forced to listen to the gruesome details Uma gave as she told her of the full extent of the torture her in-laws had inflicted onto her.
"Why didn't you tell me anything?" She bellowed. "We could have helped you."
"You were too busy keeping up appearances to help me," Uma quoted

what her parents had said back to them. "The house a bride's enters in a palanquin is the home she leaves on a funeral bier" Avantika had been silenced by her daughter. Uma's words stung her like a whip. There was no way she could justify what they said.

I am responsible for Uma's plight. That night as Avantika lay in bed her tears did not stop. The pain of Uma's words prickled her all night long. *Fearing the reaction of the society, I pushed my beti into a hell. I thought I was helping her; doing the right thing for her. What sort of life would she have without her husband? What sort of life would she have had as a single mother? I was too occupied with these stupid questions to realise that they were small matters. How will I ever heal the wounds those demons have given her? How will I ever help her overcome the ordeal they have put her through? How would I have got her back if they killed her? I prioritised my own image and my so called honour over Uma's happiness. Shame on you Avantika Desai you're unfit to call yourself a mother.*

The following day Avantika once again phoned Uma and promised to help her get justice. "Your battle is my battle. I'm with you every step of the way. People can point fingers all they want. Their opinion stopped affecting me weeks ago." Avantika's support for Uma was short lived. Three days later, Jigar came to their house in Mandavi. He was wearing his police uniform, which had a stain of blood on it. He sat down on the dinner table and began to eat the food being served.
"Get out of my house you benchod," Vinod fumed at Jigar. He stood up aggressively. Avantika assumed her husband would forcefully evict him from their house and was about to stop him; they could have got into more trouble with the police if they did anything to him.
"I'll leave if you want," Jigar said smugly. "But if I leave you'll never know how to get your son out of jail."
The entire Desai family looked at him. *This can't be good news. Whatever he is going to suggest won't be good.*
"We will do anything to get Arjun out of jail. Anything," Avantika told Jigar.
"I hoped you would say that," he said smugly. "If Uma withdraws the complaint against my family, I will let Arjun go."

"That's never going to happen," Vinod said aggressively.
"Arjun isn't enjoying prison much," Jigar said calmly. "He refuses to accept his crime. We have to beat him to get him to confess and he bleeds everywhere" Jigar touched the blood stain on his uniform and smiled.
"What have you done to Arjun?" Avantika shrieked with tears in her eyes. "If anything happens to him I'll..."
"Don't raise your blood pressure Avantika... aunty. Arjun can come home today if you withdraw all the complaints. Otherwise the poor boy will spend the rest of his life in prison for crimes he has not committed. I can arrange for him to never come out aunty." Jigar stood up. "Think about it. I'll wait for your decision." Jigar bent down and touched Avantika's feet. *May you and your family be eaten by ants you benchods.* Jigar got up and smiled. He looked at Gauri and looked her up and down and then winked at her before he left. Avantika felt Vinod lose control of his anger, but she held him back and restrained him. She did not want to give Jigar an excuse to lock up any more of her family members. Avantika's mind began to vision a bloody and beaten up Arjun. She knew what she had to do.

Avantika phoned Uma and went back on the promise she made. Initially Uma was reluctant to withdraw the case against the Rathod family. However, Avantika reminded Uma about everything her brother had done for her and how much Arjun loved her. She even reminded her of the promises they made every year to each other on the festival of Raksha Bandhan. Uma finally conceded. She told her mother she would take back the complaint the next day and would call them once she withdrew it.

Now Avantika was stood in front of the shrine. Uma had just called to tell her Arjun was coming home. The initial elation evaporated. *Was it right for me to ask Uma to make such a big sacrifice? I do not know what is right and what is wrong anymore. This is too much.*

Chapter 84: Madhu

Madhu gave a sigh of relief and hugged Jigar. She pulled back and looked at her son in his beige police uniform. Madhu felt immense pride as she looked at his brown belt and kissed him on the forehead. Jigar just informed her that Uma had withdrawn the police complaint against their family.
"Today you have saved our family from being ruined," she said proudly to her son. "You have repaid the debt of my milk by saving us all. Without you we could have been in serious trouble and I thank Bhagwan that I have a son like you."

Madhu had not faced such difficulties in her life since her father-in-law's death. After his death Madhu gained over everything, she felt nothing would ever ruin her happiness again. The past few weeks had proved her wrong. It started six weeks ago when she found out that Uma had disappeared from the house. The ox's wardrobe was empty and Sheela was gone. Flooded with fear, Madhu immediately realised that Uma had run away. Desperate to regain control she decided to find out Uma's whereabouts. She sent Jigar and Charu to the bus stands and various locations in Madhapar. Madhu sent Vijay to Mandavi to find out if she went to her parent's home and Madhu herself walked around to see if she could find anything. Despite her desperation to seek Uma's whereabouts, her attempts were futile. Worried about what Uma might do, Vijay phoned his girlfriend to tell her that his wife had lodged false complaints of abuse against him. Once he was off the phone, Vijay explained to the rest of his family that he was worried she was going to the police so he took Alice to his side as a witness. *Police? That stupid Ox would never take such a big step.* Yet, another part of Madhu told her; *I thought I broke the girl down. I thought she would never be brave enough to look me in the face, let alone run away. What if she has gone to the police?* Vijay's worries began to make Madhu feel uncomfortable. *Hai Bhagwan, if she has gone to the police she will ruin everything. She has gone with Sheela and... Sheela!* Madhu felt a lump in her throat as she realised that Uma also took away her granddaughter. *She has taken*

Sheela too. I have lost Indira again. Madhu sat down on the sofa to support herself with such grave news. Jigar assured Madhu that Uma would never go to the police because he would have his friends make sure her complaint fell on deaf ears. Madhu felt some reassurance by this, but not knowing where Uma was made Madhu feel uncomfortable. *What if she talks to people? People might come to my house with effigies and burn me. If she tells anyone she could ruin everything I strived so hard for.*

Within a week of Uma's disappearance, Madhu's worries materialised into reality. The police were on her door step. Initially Vijay thought they came to visit Jigar but Madhu's throat constricted when she saw them. She immediately knew they were at her house because of Uma. A group of police officers, men and women, came to arrest them. One of the male police officers informed them that they were all under arrest for dowry related crimes and domestic violence. Madhu fell to her knees to plead her innocence. Vijay swore to the police and made a number of threats. However, they were adamant that they would all need to accompany them for questioning. As Jigar was one of their colleagues he requested them that they let his family accompany them in a way that would retain their dignity. The police agreed and saved them from the disgrace of being handcuffed and escorted to the police car. Charu simply cried as the police took them all away. Madhu made sure that no tears came to her eyes. *If my neighbours see me I do not want them to see any weaknesses in me.* As she stepped outside the house she saw that a few of her neighbours were stood outside on the street gossiping. Most of them ignored the police car parked outside their house as Jigar worked for the police and his friends often visited their home. However, three of their neighbours did spot her family getting into the back of the police car. Madhu made eye contact with them and shifted uncomfortably with embarrassment. *Hai Bhagwan, Shanta, Dhanbai and Kesar have seen us. What will the rest of our neighbours say when this gets out? They will never trust us again.* She wanted somewhere to hide her face so that no one else would see her in the back of the police van. She covered her face with her sari until the car moved onto a busier road. When she removed the sari covering her face, she saw tears were still leaking out of Charu's eyes, and her face was drained of all colour. Madhu leaned

forward and put her hand over her daughter's hand. She squeezed it slightly and felt Charu jump up a bit.
"Don't worry beti. I will not allow anything happen to you," Madhu smiled weakly at her daughter. Charu did not smile back and continued to cry. The slight smile on Madhu's face dropped when she realised Charu's wedding was coming up. *What if Rajan's family find out about this and break all relations with us? Hai Bhagwan what will I do? Charu's life will be totally ruined. I need to do something to stop my children's lives from being ruined.*

By the time the police car reached the police station Madhu had formulated a plan. *I have been through so much pain and hardships for the happiness for my children. I am sure I could spend the rest of my life suffering for their happiness.* Madhu decided that she would confess to everything and take full responsibility for everything. The arresting police officer sat opposite them and produced Uma's statement. He handed over Uma's account to them and told them to read the complaint made by the girl. The more Madhu read of Uma's statement, the angrier she became. *The ox has this much courage that she would dare to file a complaint against me?* Madhu was ready to take the blame onto herself when she saw part of the Uma's statement in which she made allegations of rape against Vijay. *I can try and take the blame onto myself but how can I save Vijay?* That was when another idea came to Madhu's mind. *Cry Madhu Cry. Tears are not just a sign of weakness. As a woman you can use them to your strength too.* She began to cry and disputed the statement.
"My beta lived in Mumbai for the majority of their married life," she sobbed with crocodile tears. "He was not even around for most of the time she claims to have been subjected to abuse. She even says she was raped by Vijay but he is her husband. How can he rape her? This is just a plot by our bahu to malign us. I told you not to marry her Vijay," Madhu spat. "I told you these middle class people just want money and will do anything for it. Look at us now! She has completely ruined us by telling lies about us."
"Madhuji," the investigating police officer said. "Please calm down. I am not here to punish you."
Not here to punish us? Madhu stopped crying for a moment.

"I know Jigar," the policeman continued. "He is one of us. We cannot allow one of our police officers and his family get caught up in such a scandal. I brought you here to tell you about the girl's complaint. We also had to show people that we were doing our investigations by arresting you."
Madhu exhaled feeling relieved.
"I wanted to assure you and your family," the policeman told Madhu "that you have nothing to worry about. I will try and suppress this case. Jigar and Vijay have both helped me many times and now it is my duty to help you when you're in need."

Before morning all four of her family members were back home in their mansion. Madhu did not allow the luxuries of her home to distract her. She was seething with fury that the ox dared to make a complaint against her. She swore that she would make sure that the ox and her family paid for it. Over the next few weeks Jigar's police friends kept their family updated about Uma's complaint and how she was adamant to pursue it. They even discovered where Uma was living by having her followed. They knew they could intimidate Uma into withdrawing the case, but with Charu's wedding so close they decided to close the case without using any threats. The police tried to cite a lack of evidence amongst various other things in an attempt to drop the case. When Uma showed no signs of relenting, Madhu once again felt increasingly concerned and panicked at the thought of losing everything.

Three weeks after the arrest Jigar came home with a smile on his face.
"Why are you so happy?" Madhu asked her son. "Is the ox dead?"
"No but her complaint is about to fall flat in the mud," Jigar laughed.
Madhu sat up and paid full attention to her son.
"Today I arrested a maid for stealing. She stole some gold from the house of the people she worked for."
"Why are you telling us this?" Vijay snapped. "If the girl is hot you usually let her off the crime if she agrees to your conditions. Tell me how this bitch's complaint is going to end. You can tell me what she did to get off the crime later."
What sort of conditions does Jigar set to let people off crimes?
"It is related to that. Have patience, brother."

"OK, hurry up."
"As I was saying; she was arrested for stealing jewellery from the people she worked for. I arrested her and told her I would let her off the crime if she does something for me. I told her to file a complaint of eve teasing against Arjun and she would be free to go as long as she kept to her story. She agreed."
Madhu listened carefully, growing excited about the thought of avenging her insult by arresting Uma's brother.
"With her testimony we will arrest Arjun and my friends and I will make the evidence up. We'll tell Uma to drop the complaint against us in exchange for her brother."
"Make sure when you arrest him, you do it during the daytime and in front of all his neighbours," Madhu said bitterly.

Two days later, Jigar delivered the news that Arjun had been arrested. Jigar's colleague, much to Madhu's satisfaction, reported back how he handcuffed Arjun in the streets and made sure all of his neighbours saw. *I was fortunate. I told all my neighbours that I went to help the police with their inquiries as we were witnesses a crime. The ox's mother will die of shame. She will not even be able to justify her son being paraded in the streets with handcuffs on him.*

Sixteen days after Arjun's arrest, Jigar informed Madhu that the ox withdrew her complaint. Madhu's happiness knew no bounds. She felt like distributing sweets to people in celebration. *The ox has been forced into checkmate because of my Jigar's intelligence. Surely that animal must know she cannot win against me now.*
"We will let Arjun go tomorrow," Jigar informed his family.
"Make sure you beat him more before you let him go," Vijay said without any compassion.
Madhu laughed "This was the news I wanted to hear before Charu's wedding. Now this case is over I can rest with ease. I had nightmares about the police turning up to the wedding and arresting us all. Once Charu's wedding is over, I will make her pay. Now we know where she is with Sheela we can punish her."
"Mumma," Vijay interrupted her. "I forgot to tell you before but..." Vijay walked over to Madhu and stood in front of her. "Alice accepted the

wedding invite. She's coming."
Madhu took a deep breath. This news slightly dampened her happiness.
"I look forward to meeting her," Madhu said dully.

Madhu first heard Alice's voice when Vijay phoned her seeking her help. Madhu listened as he explained to her how his wife had filed a false complaint against him and begged her for help and her forgiveness. Eventually the white girl forgave him and agreed to help him. The white girl was still angry with Vijay but felt that he did not deserve to go to prison for crimes he was innocent of. Alice agreed to tell, what she thought was, the truth and give Vijay an alibi. Her usefulness did not just extend to an alibi. Vijay also worried that if Uma's case went to court, she would be able to take half of all of his wealth. Much to Madhu's frustration, Jigar highlighted the house and their money could also be taken by Uma. To prevent Uma from getting anything, Vijay signed over his hotel chains, his wealth and Rathod Haveli into Alice's name. Madhu was not keen on the fact that her son dated a white girl. She was even more mortified by the thought that Alice owned everything that was theirs. *At least she is not marrying my beta. Once this case is over, she will sign everything back to us and go back to where she came from.*

A few days after Jigar revealed his plan of fabricating a crime against Arjun, Vijay told Madhu about his desire to invite his girlfriend to Charu's wedding. Furious Madhu refused.
"What will people say if they find out you have a dhoiri... dhoiri rand?"
"Mumma, Alice is not a whore! I love her," Vijay told his mother in an aggressive manner.
Vijay told his mother he loved her more than he had loved Siya or Uma and was going to marry her. *Hai Bhagwan how can this love happen? My son and a dhoiri? This dhoiri will never understand our cultures and our traditions.* Madhu remembered how white people were treated like gods in India. *This dhori might overpower me. She might subjugate me and make me a servant in my own home. I will not allow it. I need to think of something. I refuse to become like Purbai.* Madhu and Vijay argued for a while and Madhu had to back down when Vijay threatened to leave the family if she did not accept Alice. Knowing how stubborn

her son was, Madhu relented and accepted his desire to marry her.

Madhu was unsure how she felt about meeting Alice for the first time. *I will need to step carefully. She is the malikin of our entire wealth. I overpowered Uma and Siya with force. I will have to use a different tactic on this Alice. I will drown her with love and make her feel overly safe here.*

"She's going to arrive a few days before Charu's wedding," Madhu heard Vijay say.

"Fine! I will prepare the guestroom for her," Madhu told her son.

"There's no need," Vijay said. "She's going to stay in my room."

"But people will..."

"She's going to stay in my room mumma. People can say whatever the fuck they want."

This is the very reason I don't want a dhoiri to be my bahu. White women are characterless and have no dignity. They're not married and already she is sharing his bed in public. They also have no respect for their elders. This girl has not even entered my home and already my son is arguing with me for her. What authority will I have in this place once the owner arrives? Now that Uma has lost, I will make sure the dhoiri signs everything back to my son. Vijay will own everything again, not her. Once I meet her I will find out exactly how to tame her.

Chapter 85: Amrita

"I told you at the very start that the police would be useless," Amrita said feeling vindicated. "We wasted two whole months, and we're back to where we were. All along I said we should serve them justice in our own way, but no one wanted to listen to me. Now you all know how corrupt the police are."
Amrita saw that Vikram, Leela and Uma were all sat around in the living room in silence. Amrita knew they were all feeling deflated after being forced into withdrawing the police case against the Rathod family.
I want them all to remember that I was right all along. They should have listened to me when I told them that the police would be in Jigar's pocket. They will do whatever Jigar tells them. I told them we should have adopted the brick in response to a pebble method. Eeth ka javab pathar se.

Amrita had felt increasingly frustrated the past few weeks. The news of the Rathod's arrest pleased everyone. Uma and Leela went to the police station everyday for two weeks. Each time they both came back they looked very pleased. Amrita knew the police were stringing them along. They did exactly the same thing to her and Gurpreet when they attempted to seek justice for Nirmal's murder. *In the end Veerji served them justice in his own way.* Two weeks after the complaint had been lodged, Uma returned to the house in tears. She informed everyone about Arjun's arrest and the conditions the police laid in front of her to secure her brother's release. At that time Amrita bit her tongue. *If they do not want to listen to my advice, I will not say anything.* Nonetheless, as time went on, it became harder for her to remain silent and stick to saying nothing. She contained her anger by devising detailed plans on how she will deal with the Rathod's in her own way. This planning kept Amrita from losing her temper every time Leela, Vikram or Uma wore looks of glee on their faces. However, now that they were all deflated, Amrita felt justified in telling them she was right all along. She decided to gloat before telling them about her plans of revenge.

"I said all along..."
"Yes OK we know you said all along," Vikram interrupted angrily.
"Taking the law into his own hands did not help Gurpreet. He became the criminal in everyone's eyes and ended up in prison."
"Gurpreet did nothing wrong," Amrita snapped back.
"I did not say he did anything wrong. I do not want Uma, or any of us to end up in the same situation he ended up in."
"Gurpreet's situation was different. He was hasty with his actions. If he had taken his time he could have made sure no one would have traced anything back to him, and this is why I disagreed with your argument about my veerji then. I knew the police will not do anything."

"Stop your gloating," Vikram said firmly. "How many more times will you say you knew all along? It would be more productive if you actually told us how you want to move forward."
"There is a Hindi saying everyone should be familiar with. Agar ghee sidhi ungli se na nikle to ungli tedhi karni parti hai. If the ghee does not come out with a straight finger you need to bend your fingers to get it out. If we cannot get our rights playing by the rules, we bend the rules. If they throw a pebble at you, we throw a brick back at them."
Amrita looked around and saw all three sets of eyes were focused on her.
"You all said you did not want to stoop to their level to get justice. I promise you that you will not go down to their level. Those benchods are not worthy of being called human beings. If we play dirty, we will still be higher than them." Amrita paused for a second and remembered examples she gave of Draupadi to Uma months ago. "Actually, I think even if we adopted their methods to punish them, we still will not be reducing ourselves to their levels. I watched Mahabharat on TV. The Kauravs were deceitful and evil. The Pandavs tried every way possible to seek justice. When no other route was left they went to war. Even in the great war of Kurukshetra they fought with deception. They killed Abhimanyu unethically. Krishna told the Pandavs to bend the rules if breaking them meant a triumph for good over evil. In the end the Pandavs broke many rules to vanquish evil. The Pandavs did not reduce themselves to the levels of the Kauravs, they ensured good did not lose at the hands of evil. By bending the rules you will not reduce yourself to

their level, it is your duty to punish evil. If you allow those bastards to get away with it today, what will they do to other innocent people tomorrow?"

Uma stood up and began to talk to Amrita.
"Amritaji, I knew the police would not work. You just told me about Mahabharat and how the great war of Kurukshetra was a final resort once everything else failed. In the same way I wanted to make sure every other path to punishing them was blocked before I broke the law to punish them. Now that every path IS blocked, I will do everything you tell me to do. Houn karis. I will do everything it takes to destroy them and bring them to their knees. By the time I am finished they will wish they had accepted being arrested by the police rather than the pitiful state I will leave them in."

Amrita felt excitement at Uma's words. Her arms were covered in goose bumps. *Do not let this fire inside her calm until she has her justice Waheguru.* Delighted, she gave the first genuine smile she had given since Uma arrived.
"If you have finished criticising us, tell us your idea. How will you help Uma?" Vikram said.
Amrita's initial resentment had vanished. She walked to the centre of the living room and unveiled her strategy to Leela, Uma and Vikram.
"When you were all busy going back and forth to the police, I began to devise a plan of revenge." *Mainu pata tha. Police would be useless.* Amrita did not vocalise those thoughts. She knew being smug would irritate the others. "Our first attack will take place in ten days from now. Leela tells me that is the day Charu is getting married." Amrita saw Leela nodding. "Charu is our first target."

Amrita began to tell Vikram, Uma and Leela how she will sabotage Charu. Once she finished telling them of her plan she saw a smile on everyone's faces. Amrita felt content at the fact everyone agreed to her strategy. *I have spent years devising this. It was meant to ruin Nirmal's in-laws, but I will use it to destroy Uma's instead. Finally I will get to put this plan into action. Finally I can turn my fantasies into reality. If Waheguru is merciful this will be a test run.*

Chapter 86: Alice

Alice groggily blinked her eyes; she took a few moments to gather enough strength to wake up. She saw her hands and realised it was the day of Charu's wedding. *Oh my God, it's already 10am, there must be so much to help with and I haven't even got out of bed.* Alice quickly ran to the en-suite bathroom in her and Vijay's bedroom to shower. She only recently made amends with Vijay after she discovered his wife accused him of rape and domestic violence because he confessed his love for her. She felt partially responsible for the condition he was in and decided to give him a second chance. She gave him an alibi to prove his innocence. Once they were together again, Vijay invited her to Charu's wedding. She had initially been apprehensive about attending Charu's wedding because Vijay always told her that his mother did not want a white daughter-in-law. That was the reason his family forced him to stay with his wife. Nevertheless, Vijay convinced Alice that his mother wanted to meet her and in the end she relented and agreed to come to the wedding. As Alice showered she thought about the few days she had already spent with Vijay's family.

Three days ago, she arrived at Rathod Haveli for Charu's mehndi night. The nervousness she felt in the lead up to meeting Vijay's family had been worse than the times she previously met any of her ex-boyfriend's parents. None of her ex-boyfriend's families thought the colour of her skin was an issue. When she arrived Alice put her hands together to greet Vijay's family. Vijay's siblings had both been welcoming but Vijay's mother made Alice feel uncomfortable. She exuded an icy attitude towards her.
Alice's first word to Vijay's family was "Namaste." Something she knew a lot of people in India said as a greeting. She hoped this would impress Vijay's mother. She was wrong. Vijay's mother looked Alice up and down.
"We say Jai Shri Krishna, not Namaste, and young people touch their elder's feet." Madhu said before walking away.
Alice felt speechless by Madhu's rudeness and if Vijay had not

convinced her to come to his sister's wedding she would have walked back out again. Everything became easier once Alice remembered an important fact. *I own this house. Why should I fear that narrow minded bitch? I will transfer everything back to Vijay once the divorce case is over but for now, I am going to enjoy owning everything and if she wants to speak to me like that I can put that bitch in her place.*

That night at Charu's mehndi night, her friend made beautiful peacock style henna patterns on Alice's hands. The girls even taught Alice how to do her own henna art. Alice was terrible at making henna patterns, but the five year old girl whose hands she decorated had loved her effort. Charu and her friends also taught Alice some Bollywood dancing. Since then Alice had been unable to get the song Ooh La La Ooh La La out of her head. Alice only knew a few of the words and made up the rest of it, but she had one of the best nights in India since she arrived to work. After the henna night, everyone was busy preparing for the wedding and Alice was left to herself. Even Vijay paid little attention to her.

Initially Alice understood there was a wedding coming up and they were very busy. Yet, slowly she started to feel like a spare part and bitter about the fact that no one was giving her any attention. *Without my alibi they would have all been fucked and they can't even make me feel welcome! If I hadn't been there for Vijay he'd be in prison, and now he can't even make time to explain things to me, or even just give me company.*

Alice showered quickly and walked out. Her bitterness vanished as quickly as it came. She was more excited about Charu's wedding. She had been to Indian weddings before because strangers used to invite her, because she was foreign. However, this was going to be the first Indian wedding she was going to attend where she actually knew the bride or groom. Vijay was in their bedroom adjusting the red scarf on his Indian outfit. *He looks so hot in that white Indian suit.*
"Mumma has given you a sari to wear for the wedding," Vijay pointed to a sari on the bed.
Alice picked up the blue and green sari with lots of white designs. Alice looked at the elaborate golden embroidery, beads and sequins. *Such a*

beautiful sari but I don't want to wear this. There's nothing worse than a white girl in a badly draped sari.
"I don't know how to wear one," Alice began to make excuses.
"Charu's friend is going to help you put it on."
"Uhhh OK," Alice still felt slightly uncomfortable but thought if someone put it on for her she might not look so bad. "When is she coming?"
"She is just helping Charu get dressed right now. Charu's getting ready for the Ganesh Pujan ceremony before the groom arrives."
"OK cool," Alice was unsure what to do. "Shall I wait here until I get ready? Or shall I do something else?"
"Just wait here. I'll tell her to come over to you when she is free." Vijay kissed her on the head. "Once you're dressed come down."
"OK." *Great! I'm going to be sat alone again for God knows how long.*

By the time Alice finished getting ready the Ganesh Puja was almost over. Alice felt slightly disgruntled because she wanted to see every aspect of the ceremony. However, she did not mind once people began to compliment how she looked. Charu's friend, Suneeti, did a very good job on her. The bindi, make up and jewellery Suneeti chose were simple, yet elegant. *I don't look like a Christmas tree at all.* Charu was sat with a man and woman Alice did not recognise.
"Who are those people Charu's sat with?"
"That's my mum's brother and his wife. Ravi mama and Vaishali mami will do the ceremony because our father's not here."
"What about your mum?"
"She can't do it. She's a widow. It's unlucky for a widow to perform wedding ceremonies."
Irritated by the draconian attitude, Alice began to complain but before she could Vijay walked away. Charu's puja was over and her family prepared for the groom's arrival.

Thirty minutes later, the room was abuzz with excited whispers. Alice looked around, not understanding what people were saying. She heard the Indian drums playing and a band from outside their house. The people in the room went towards the entrance of the house so Alice followed everyone, figuring the groom's party had arrived. Alice stood on tiptoes to see the welcoming of the groom. However, there were too many people in front of her to see properly. She saw there was some snatching and throwing things. Vijay's mother pinched the groom's nose, but it was all happening too quickly for Alice to see properly. By the time she got a clear view everything seemed to be over. The groom's party were entering the house and people were taking their seats again.

Vijay dashed around ordering the catering staff to ensure the groom's party were served properly and all of their needs were met. Alice pretended not to notice the stares she attracted as people entered the house. Some of the kids shouted "Hello Maam", whilst some men gawped at her. Alice ignored them all and just looked around absorbing the atmosphere. She spotted some other foreigners from the Groom's side and hastily went over to join them. Meeting Gregory and Cynthia made her feel more comfortable at the wedding. They too did not know what was happening, and Cynthia's sari was not draped properly. Before Alice realised it, the groom was already under the wedding dais and she heard the Indian drums, flutes and sitar play. Everyone's head turned to the entrance. Charu waited at the end of the aisle. She wore a red and gold wedding sari. The patterns and embroidery looked spectacular. There were eleven bindis on Charu's forehead and a tikka which glimmered in the light. *She looks so beautiful, like a twinkling star.* Vijay and Jigar both walked her down the aisle. When Charu was under the dais, the veil from the groom's face was removed and both bride and groom held hands. The priest began to talk and chant in Sanskrit. The wedding was just like other Indian weddings; no one remained silent and everyone spoke throughout the ceremony. Alice was sat next to Gregory and Cynthia closer to the front so they were able to see the ceremony a bit better. She watched as the bride and her husband garlanded each other.

Alice was distracted when she felt her mobile phone buzz. Someone sent her something by Bluetooth. *Who's sending me shit? I need turn my Bluetooth off or people might send me crap.* Alice opened the message and her mouth dropped at the image she had been sent. After a few moments, she finally managed to avert her gaze from the picture and looked around. It seemed the image had been sent to quite a few people as people were looking at their phones and showing it to other people.

Alice felt her mobile phone buzz again. A new image was sent by Bluetooth. Alice opened the new image and immediately shut it. There was a domino effect of more phones buzzing around the room. *Shit, the message is going viral.*

Alice felt her phone vibrate again, but she did not even open the message this time. *It can't be anything more respectful than the last message.* The next thing Alice saw was an older man running down the aisle. She was surprised a man could run so fast wearing a white sheet draped around his lower body. He shouted something in Gujarati that Alice did not understand. However, she knew he wanted to stop the wedding as result of the images.
Vijay stood up and shouted back at the old man in Gujarati. The old man took out his mobile phone and began to point to the people in the hall. She knew he was talking about the pictures she had received. Vijay took the mobile phone and looked at the pictures. Alice saw the colour drain from his face. He was speechless. Alice assumed the old man was shouting at Charu to get her to explain the photograph.
Alice saw Charu look confused at the phone. The groom also looked at the mobile and immediately stood up in anger.
Alice assumed Charu was denying that the photographs were of her as she was shaking her head.
Alice saw the groom argue with Charu as she sobbed.
"I'm innocent," Charu said amongst some Gujarati.
The groom returned to shouting in Gujarati. Alice heard the word "slut" spoken from his mouth and "lie."
The hall erupted in shouting and screaming in a language she did not understand. She could not even put the words together as there were too many people shouting. Charu was crying and pleading her innocence. Vijay and Jigar were shouting at the groom's family. Madhu was crying and begging the groom's family who were walking away.
"What is happening?" Cynthia asked.
"I have no idea," Alice said.
"I know Indian brides cry at the wedding, but I thought that happened at the end."

A few minutes later the groom threw his turban off and untied the knot between his scarf and Charu's sari. The groom's family stormed out of the room. A distraught Charu and Madhu stood under the dais. Vijay and Jigar chased the groom's family shouting profanities in a mixture of English and Gujarati. Alice opened the messages on her phone again. She looked at the pictures of a naked Charu kissing another man. *Who on earth wanted to ruin Charu's wedding so badly?*

Chapter 87: Uma

"The groom's party turned away. They left Charu waiting at the wedding dais. She cried her eyes out," Vikram reported back. Vikram's every word was like a melodious tune to Uma's ears.

As none of them were invited to the wedding, the only way to find out if their first attack had been successful was through the gossip amongst people in the village. Amrita sent her husband out onto the streets to find out what people were talking about. Vikram told them how the pictures his friend manipulated spread through the wedding hall and how the groom's uncle stopped the wedding.
"They thought they had checkmated you and your family. They made their demands when it was impossible for you to back out because backing out would have made it hard for you to find someone else. I'd love to see them try and find a new groom for Charu; she was abandoned on her wedding day and everyone thinks she is promiscuous," Amrita laughed. "Even a disabled man won't touch her now."
Uma laughed with the rest of them. Charu's plight filled her with bliss. She had never felt happier. *I think I am happier now than I was the day Vijay proposed to me.*

"What did Madhu say and do?" Leela asked eagerly.
"I didn't hear much about her," Vikram said. "I heard that Jigar tried to get violent with the groom for abandoning his sister. The groom's family didn't take kindly to his behaviour. The men from Rajan's family punched him and shoved him to the ground. Vijay ran forwards to help his brother. Kantaben was saying that Jigar looked filthy when Vijay dragged him back indoors."
"This story is like Krishna's flute to my ears," Uma said. "Are we going to phone them now or later?"
"We phone them today," Amrita said immediately.
"They can't know we are behind everything," Leela said worriedly.
"They won't. We're calling them to remind Charu of Uma's curse,"

Amrita said pitilessly. “And to rub salt into their wounds.”
“I bought this mobile SIM card off a tourist who was leaving the country.” Vikram handed a sim card to Uma. “They can’t trace our call. I’ll dispose of the SIM once we’ve used it. Give me Charu’s number.”
Uma recited Charu’s mobile number from the piece of paper Leela had with the phone numbers of the Rathod family.
“It’s ringing,” Leela quickly handed the phone over to Uma.
“Remember she can’t know that we’re behind everything,” Vikram whispered.
The phone stopped ringing. *She’s picked up!* Uma’s heart stopped for a second.
“Rajan?” Charu asked.
“You still think Rajan would want an impure slut like you?” Uma said scathingly.
“Who… who is this?”
“Everyone in Madhapar is talking about what happened at your wedding today. Everyone knows that you’re of loose character. I couldn’t believe it when I heard.”
“Who is this?” Charu screamed getting angry. “Did you make up those pictures?”
“No, no,” Uma laughed. “I wish I had. But I actually don’t need to do anything myself. I know that the curse I put on you and your family is working. The tears you and your family made me cry have dried up. Those tears will now leak from your eyes. Your tears will never stop.
“Uma? You…”
“Goodbye Charu. I’m going to enjoy watching you cry for the rest of your life.”
Uma cut the phone and looked around her. The satisfaction she felt was reflected on the faces of Amrita, Vikram and Leela. Uma returned the phone to Vikram and stood up.
I thought the phone call to Charu would satisfy the fire in me, but it’s only fanned the flames. Uma’s thirst for revenge increased. *I want the rest of her family to cry tears of blood!*

“I’m going to bed. I’m tired.” Uma was not sleepy. The adrenaline rushing through her would not let her sleep for hours. However, she wanted some time alone to convince herself that Vijay deserved the punishment they planned for him. Deep down she still felt something for Vijay. *I loved him with everything I had. He's the father of my beti! If I ruin her bapuji the way we plan to, what will happen to my beti? She will grow up without a father's shadow. Am I right to deprive Sheela of her father's love?*

"Hang on," Amrita stopped Uma. "This is our first attack. It's nothing. We have a long way to go. This is no time to sleep; we need to start on our next attack."
"This should wait till tomorrow," Uma said. Hoping she could buy more time for Vijay. "Let them reel over the events today."
"No," Amrita said firmly. "I don't want them to recover. Blow after blow, we'll bring them to their knees. But this time we will give them a bit of time to overcome the shock. Lull them into a false sense of security before our next attack." Amrita paused. "The people who wronged you don't just consist of the Rathod family. There are others that need to be taught a lesson too. Our next target will be Alice. She is going to learn what happens to whores who ruin other people's marriages. She's going to learn the consequences of giving false alibis. She is about to get trapped in a scandal which the British Government won't be able to help her out with. She is fond of false alibis. What will become of her if the Indian government believe she is using her hotel as a façade to traffic drugs."

I'd forgotten about that home wrecking bitch. That whore is the one who took Vijay away from me. She's the one who ruined my relationship and turned him into a demon. Before she came along everything was fine. She has to pay!

Chapter 88: Madhu

Madhu looked at the glittering decorations that adorned the room. She saw the six Ganesh statues that her daughter walked through when she made her way to the beautiful pavilion, specially designed by Charu for her own wedding. The blues, silvers and whites gave the room a cool Kashmiri feel. The room also contained three hundred chairs which Madhu ordered to ensure their guests were comfortable. They were decorated with white covers and a blue ribbon. Madhu sat on one of the chairs, speechless, as she looked around the room. However, she was not admiring the beauty of Charu's choice. She was haunted by the memories of the events that occurred a few hours ago. Her tears had dried by now but she was still reeling from the calamity of Rajan abandoning Charu at the mandap. When Madhu realised the groom's party was leaving without Charu she cried and sat down in one of the chairs she ordered for her guests. Madhu had not moved from the chair in over two hours. She simply looked around the room oblivious to what was going on around her and prayed that she was just dreaming.

Madhu's trance finally broke when she jumped in shock at the touch of her brother. She had not noticed him coming but, once her trance broke, Madhu felt severe disappointment again. *Hai Bhagwan, this actually happened. This was not a bad dream. This actually happened. What will I do? How will we show our faces to anyone?*
"Motaben," Ravi, Madhu's brother kneeled down to face her. "How are you feeling?"
"I am fine," Madhu said quietly. "Go home all of you. Why are you still here? The wedding finished hours ago."
Madhu felt her brother's hand grasp hers. "We are going to stay and help you. I..."
Madhu did not let her brother finish his sentence she abruptly pulled her hands away from his hands. *I already showed people that I am weak because I shed tears when Rajan's family turned back. I do not want to show anyone else anymore signs that I am weak.* Madhu was adamant that she would not cry in front of anyone. She stood up and began to

walk around attempting to find something she could do to occupy her mind. When she stood up she noticed some distant family members were still sitting around the living room. They were whispering quietly but stopped as soon as they saw Madhu approaching. She took a deep breath. *This is going to be my fate now, people whispering behind my back. Everything I built in thirty five years is ruined.* She could once again feel herself getting emotional but fought back her tears with all her strength. She focused her mind on the carpet covered with flowers, rice and other rubbish as she walked around trying to find her sons. She finally spotted Jigar and Vijay who were both sat together on a table in the corner of the room. They too were sat in total silence in a similar position to how she had sat. Jigar was looking down at both of his hands which were clasped together. Vijay was leaning on the table with his hands, looking forward with a blank expression on his face. Madhu noticed a bruise on Jigar's face and an open wound on his lip. Jigar's suit, which was pearly white at the start of the day, was now filthy and covered in mud. *Just like the Rathod family name. We have been tainted with so much mud that people will forever point fingers at us.* Madhu's anger began to rise once more. *That stupid girl has cut off our noses. Maybe this is why Harshad's mother never wanted girls. Where is this girl? She's destroyed our reputation and has then vanished herself.*

Madhu walked away from her sons attempting to find Charu. She could not find her daughter anywhere. *Perhaps she is in her bedroom.* Madhu took a few steps towards the stairs when she saw Charu coming down. The shameless girl was still in her bridal sari. The makeup, the jewellery, everything was still there. The only difference Madhu saw was Charu's eyes. They were red and puffy. *This is exactly what she should have looked like when she left this house to start her new life with Rajan. The only difference would have been is she would have had sindoor on her forehead.* As Charu came down the steps Madhu recalled the mixture of emotions she felt when Rajan's family abandoned her. Embarrassment due to the shame Charu had brought to the Rathod family. Anguish at the thought of Charu's abandonment and the pain her daughter must be feeling. Anger towards Charu, whose actions had ruined everything she and her sons worked hard to build. The closer Charu got towards her, the more Madhu's anger prevailed. When Charu stood in front of Madhu the anger that simmered inside her for the past couple of hours erupted.

Madhu slapped Charu with all her strength. Charu, who was not expecting the blow fell back a few steps. Madhu lost control of her emotions and began to cry as she stepped forward and began to use her fists to punch Charu who was now screaming.
"Sharam vagar ni. Did I bring you up for this day? So that you could repay me by bringing so much shame onto our family?"
Madhu continued to hit Charu and did not care where she delivered the blows as long as she was punishing her. Madhu was pulled away from Charu by Vijay and Ravi.
"Mumma what are you doing?" Jigar said shocked.
"I AM GOING TO KILL HER!" Madhu shouted. "SHE HAS CUT OFF OUR NOSES AND BECAUSE OF HER ACTIONS WE ARE NOT FIT TO FACE ANYONE."
"Motaben, she is an adult. You cannot hit her like a child," Ravi said.
Madhu looked at her daughter, livid with fury. Charu cowered on the stairs shielding herself from more blows.
"You filthy unchaste girl! Before you did such a shameless thing you should have jumped into a well and drowned yourself. Chi," Madhu managed to break free from Vijay and Ravi's grip and walked over to her daughter. "Why have you come back now? We do not have anything left after your shameful deeds. Have you come back to claim my life now?"
Madhu struggled as her son and Ravi got hold of her again and led her away from Charu. Ravi's wife held Charu and took her to another room.

"Motaben, what are you doing?" Ravi said. "That beechari has been punished enough for her actions. You need to support her."
For the third time that day, Madhu began to cry in front of other people. This time they were not tears of anger, but torment from feeling betrayed by her daughter.
"Everything I have ever done was to make my children happy," She said to her brother quietly. "My children were my pride, they were my life. They were my everything. I was going to make sure they had everything they could ever want in their lives to make sure they have no problems. Jigar and Vijay have never brought any shame on me, but where did I

go wrong with this girl? Not only did she indulge in vulgar activities, but she allowed photos to be taken of her." Madhu blew her nose in a tissue her brother gave her. "My sons have never been this stupid! They always used their brains to stay out of trouble. Now I know why my husband's mother did not want girls. They are all stupid, foolish and can ruin your family reputation in a moment."

"Beti where are you going?" Madhu heard Vaishali, Ravi's wife saying. "Come back here now."
"I need to talk to mumma," Madhu heard Charu's voice from a distance. *Vaishali better not let that rand come and see me.* However, Madhu saw Charu coming towards her, a struggling Vaishali failed to pull her back and both women were in front of her.
"Ravi tell her to go away before I lose my temper again. I do not wish to see her blackened face right now."
"Charu beti, your mummy needs some time. It is better to leave her alone right now," Ravi said.
"Ravi mama please let me speak to mumma. It's important," Charu begged her uncle.
"You should wait till tomorrow. Let her calm down. Speak to her tomorrow. Vaishali..." Ravi signalled to his wife to take Charu away.
"Don't touch me Vaishali mami," Charu screamed. "I came here to tell mumma something and I'm going to tell her. I don't care if she doesn't want to see my face, but I know she can hear me. Those pictures are not real. They are fake."

Madhu felt a jolt through her; *the pictures are fake?* She was not sure whether the jolt was of hope that everything was still salvageable, or a jolt because her daughter was still shamed, or a jolt because her daughter was lying. However, Charu now had Madhu's full attention.
"I don't know who the guy in the photographs is. I have never seen him before tamari kasam khau!" Madhu looked up. *My beti would never take a false kasam under my name. She is innocent?*
"Jigar bhai has already told me he will get his contacts to conduct tests to find out if the pictures are real or not. Once the pictures are proven to be fake, I will show the evidence to Rajan. He will have to marry me when he realises that I am innocent." Charu turned away from her

mother. “And you don’t want to see my face mumma? I promise you I won’t show you my face until I prove my innocence.”
Charu began to walk away when Jigar came to talk to his sister.
“My friend said he can do the tests on the photographs. I reminded him that he owed me a favour so he told me to bring the photographs over tomorrow.” Jigar walked over to his mother. “Mumma I don’t think Charu is guilty. I’ll have the evidence of her innocence soon.”

My beti is innocent? If she is innocent which nasty person played such a filthy game with her life? My Charu has never harmed anyone why would anyone do such a thing to her? Hai Bhagwan, please prove those pictures are not true. Please give us all evidence of my beti’s innocence otherwise this black mark against her name will ruin her life forever.

Chapter 89: Charu

Charu parked her scooter at the side of the road and got off. *She looked at her watch. I am very early. It is only 12.24. I will have to wait.* Charu was going to meet Rajan at 1pm. She had chosen the same place they visited on a regular basis. She was confident their marriage would be back on. She opened the storage box at the back of her scooter to find the evidence of her innocence. Earlier that morning Jigar took the photos to a friend of his who ran some tests to find out whether the photos were tampered with or not. Jigar's friend confirmed the photographs were modified. He then went home and gave Charu all the evidence she needed to win Rajan back. She did not even understand some of the discrepancies which the tests found. However, she immediately sent an SMS message to Rajan, telling him she had evidence to prove the photographs were fake and to meet her later that day. Charu was prepared to text him again and again, and even planned to turn up to his house in Kera. She was surprised when he promptly responded agreeing to meet her at 1pm. Charu reread the text a few times to make sure she was not imagining things. When she was sure the text was real she messaged back to suggest Khatri Lake and began to fantasise about her future again.

Charu grabbed the evidence from the storage box and held them close to her. After a few moments she felt tired of standing around and waiting. She checked her makeup in the wing mirror of her scooter one last time and then went and sat on a bench looking over the Khatri Lake. She was once again mesmerised by the different species of wildlife in the lake. A crane stood in shallow waters attempting to catch fish. The Lake was now home to a new species, pelicans, which were not there before. She watched as the pelicans swooped down and swallowed the fish in one bite. She could see the live fish moving in the Pelican's neck. She was so enchanted by the scene in front of her that she did not realise the time pass. She only realised it was 1pm when she spotted a man with sunglasses. Charu squinted her eyes to get a clearer view and saw it was Rajan. She nervously waved at him and he began to walk over to

where she was sitting. She felt her mouth go dry and her heart beat faster. Rajan sat down next to her, and put a large carrier bag at his feet. For a few moments they both sat in silence.
"Where are the crocodiles?" Rajan asked.
"There in the middle," Charu pointed to a bank on the opposite side. "There are two there."
Rajan stood up to look at the crocodiles for a few moments. He eventually sat back down. The icy silence took over again for a few minutes.
"So why did you want to meet me?" Rajan asked, breaking the silence once again.
Charu gave him the envelope containing the report from the digital forensics person.
"Read this," Charu told him.
"What is it?"
"Just read it," Charu demanded. "You'll know once you have read it."
Charu watched as Rajan flicked through the pictures. She began to panic at the indifference on his face. After looking through the pictures and report a few times he put the pictures back into the envelope and returned them to Charu. *Why is he not apologising to me? He should be hugging me by now, and telling me we should get married.*
"Did you look at everything properly?" Charu asked despairingly. She took out the report from the envelope and flicked to the final page of the report. "The final page tells you why..."
Charu stopped mid-sentence when she saw that Rajan was looking in another direction. *Why won't he look at the evidence I am showing him?*
"LOOK at this," she begged him. "I am not a whore. I didn't cheat on you."
"I know you are innocent," Rajan sighed. Charu felt a rush of adrenaline through her. *I knew it. I hope the auspicious date for the wedding is not months away.*
"I believed you when you text me. I do not need to see it again because it does not matter."
Charu stopped mid thought.
"What do you mean it does not matter?"
"Charu," Rajan said lowering his voice. "I can't marry you."
Charu felt as though she had been punched in the stomach and the air

had been knocked out of her. *Hai Bhagwan, what does he mean?*
"Before coming here, I told bai about your text," Rajan explained. "I told her you said the photos were manipulated. She told me if I want any respect from society I will need to marry a girl who is respected. She told me if I wanted to have any reputation in the future that I should not marry a shamed girl like you."
"What?"
"You're maligned. You're tarnished. Marrying you would reduce the prestige of my family. Bai said when she goes out of the house she does so with pride. Having a bahu with no respect for herself would cause her head to hang with shame. Bai said she would never be able to look into the eyes of respectable people again if she allowed her son to marry a whore."
Charu's eyes filled with tears.
"But I am innocent," she said desperately. "I have evidence. I am not a whore."
"It doesn't matter," Rajan burst out. Charu could not believe her ears. Rajan began to speak softly again. "I still love you Charu, but you have to understand."
"Understand what?"
"If people do not respect you, what respect will people have for me? If we associate ourselves with your... your sins then our family will be tainted. No one would want to associate with us anymore."
Charu listened to Rajan repeat the same point over and over again but he worded it differently each time. *I was everything he wanted, until he thought I wasn't chaste enough for his precious family. Why won't he understand it wasn't my fault.*
"WHY DID YOU AGREE TO MEET ME IF YOU DIDN'T WANT ANYTHING TO DO WITH ME?" Charu screamed and punched Rajan's arm a few times. "Why did you build up my hopes, just to break them like this? What part of I am innocent don't you understand?"
"How many people will we convince of your innocence? So many people saw those images, we won't be able to tell everyone. Most people won't even believe us, they'll believe what they saw with their eyes."
"Why do you care what people say? As long as we know the truth does it matter? Rajan..."
"Enough," Rajan picked up the bag he brought with him. "Bai wanted

me to give the shagun gifts back to you." Rajan handed the bag back to Charu. "Check it to make sure everything is there."
Charu held the bag for a second before throwing everything at him. "You men are all sister fuckers. You will fuck whoever you want, but the moment a woman shows a bit of flesh she is a slut and is worthless. Fuck you. Fuck your mum. Your mum looks like a slut, she is probably just quiet about it."
Rajan slapped Charu. She felt the burn on her cheek and went silent. "Don't you dare say anything about my mother," Rajan said through gritted teeth. "Do not contact me again. Goodbye Charu."
"Come back," Charu screamed. "You cannot just leave me like this. You promised to stand by me no matter what." Rajan did not listen to her. He continued walking without turning back. "BENCHOD," Charu screamed one last time, before she collapsed onto the bench and sobbed. Charu saw two cranes touching their beaks with each other. *I hope she breaks your heart you fucker.*

Charu sat on a bench near Khatri Lake for a while lost in her own thoughts. She wiped her tears when she remembered something Uma said to her a few weeks before her wedding.
The tears you and your family gave me have now dried up. Those tears will now leak from your eyes. The tears will never stop. Uma cursed me! My life will be full of these horrors because she cursed me! It's all because we wronged her. This is our punishment.

Chapter 90: Avantika

Avantika sat in the car with her husband looking at a large house from the car window. She had never been to the Oberoi's house before. She only discovered where Uma was living because a woman called Amrita took Arjun to her house to meet Uma after he was released. When Arjun returned home, Avantika and Vinod decided they wanted to bring Uma back home and asked Arjun where Amrita lived. Arjun described the location of Amrita's house in detail and told them what her mansion looked like. Vinod and Avantika resolved to bring Uma back by visiting the Oberoi House.

Avantika opened the door and stepped out of the car. *Is this definitely the right house? I don't want to just walk into someone else's house and make a fool of myself.* She looked around and saw three women standing outside, two dark skinned and one light skinned. She subconsciously decided that the light skinned woman looked most friendly and approachable and thus walked over to her.
"Benji, is this Amrita Oberoi's house?"
The woman nodded and carried on with her business. Avantika took a deep breath and walked towards the house. She stood outside the gate for a few seconds. Avantika had not seen Uma since she sent her back to Madhapar. She was looking forward to seeing her daughter after such a long time, but was equally apprehensive about the reception Uma would give her. *Uma never speaks harshly towards you Avantika. You taught her to respect her elders.* Avantika thought to herself. She paused for a moment and then turned the golden knob to open the gate to Amrita's courtyard. *I'm coming to take you back home beti. Everything's going to be alright, your maa is here.*

Avantika walked in and saw two children playing in the courtyard. They stopped when they saw her. Avantika paused for a second as she reminded herself how many years ago Arjun and Gauri played with their cousins exactly like these two children were playing. Avantika had flashbacks of Uma playing kabbadi with her cousins and brother. The

children used to make up their own rules to the game. Avantika remembered how once Uma pushed her way through Arjun and he fell over and bled everywhere. She had scolded Uma for being so physical with her brother before putting turmeric paste over her son's wound. Vinod then teased Arjun for being beaten by a girl. Avantika glowed at the fact her daughter had beaten her son. That was when she decided that her daughter would have the same rights as her son. Avantika's reminiscing was interrupted by a woman in a red Punjabi dress.
"Who are you looking for?" she said as she stood on the top of the stairs leading to the house.
The trip down memory lane caused Avantika to temporarily forget why she had come, but she recollected her thoughts. *I have come to take my beti back home.*
"Are you Amrita Oberoi?" Vinod asked. "Is Uma living here?"
"What if she is?" the woman asked harshly.
"Uma's our daughter... we're here to see her. We want to take her home."
The woman in the red dress sighed and walked straight into the house without saying a word.

Avantika turned to face Vinod who looked just as confused as she was by the woman's peculiar behaviour. *Are we in the right place? She didn't even say Uma lives here or if this is the Oberoi house. Where has this woman gone?* Moments later the questions Avantika was asking herself were answered. Uma stood at the threshold of the house. Avantika's heart leapt at the sight of her daughter. *Hai Mata Rani tara gana gana abhar.* Her eyes filled with tears as Uma walked to her. Avantika studied her daughter's figure and face the closer she got. She noticed that her daughter's ordeal had caused much of her beauty to fade and her previously perfect figure was gone. *She's lost so much weight. My beti was as beautiful as Aishwarya Rai. Why didn't I notice everything sooner? I thought her weight loss was to do with her dieting to fit in with her new status.*

When Uma stood five feet away, Avantika put her hands out to give her daughter a hug. She was desperate to hold her girl in her arms, to hug her and tell her everything would be alright. That was when Uma

stopped coming closer. It was too far to hug her so she took a few steps towards Uma. However, Uma put her hand out signalling Avantika to stay where she was.
"Stop," Uma said to Avantika. "There's no need for your displays of affection. Stop the drama and tell me why you came."
She felt an electric shock inside her at Uma's words. *Drama? How could Uma think my love for her is a drama?*
"Have you forgotten all decorum Uma?" Vinod said angrily. "Is that the way to speak to your mother?"
"If I had forgotten my decorum, I would have called her Avantika, but I still have some respect for the fact you raised me," Uma responded sombrely. Avantika saw Uma walk towards her father and she looked him in her eyes. "I think you are the one who has forgotten bapuji. You gave me away. My relationship with you ended the day you gave me away. Isn't that what you said?" Uma paused and then sarcastically added "bapuji."
"Uma beti..." Avantika began to say.
Uma looked directly into Avantika's eyes. Avantika saw her daughter's brown eyes looking directly into hers. They were full of hurt and anger. The way Uma looked at Avantika made her feel uncomfortable.
"Beti? I thought you ended that relationship when you gave me away?" Uma asked.
Avantika could not bear to see the pain she saw through Uma's eyes. She looked away from her daughter.
"I didn't say that Uma... we said...," Avantika said.
"Jee ghar ma beti ni palki jai, eej ghar ma thi eni aarthi oothe."Uma repeated their exact words back to them.
"Yes we didn't say you're not our beti anymore"
"YOU AS GOOD AS SAID YOU HAD NO MORE RESPONSIBILITIES TOWARDS ME!" Uma shouted. She then lowered the tone of her voice. "You left me to die with those people," she added her voice dripping with venom.

Uma's final words echoed in Avantika's mind and stunned her to silence, unable to say anything. *I left her to die with those people?* For a few moments, Avantika did not say anything then the impact of Uma's words hit her. *We should have allowed her back. I should have fought for her rights. I was too busy keeping up appearances, worrying about what the outside world would say about our family. I put fear of society over Uma's happiness. I have wronged the Lakshmi of our home. We both have.*

"My husband raped me maa," Uma said. Avantika once again felt a stab to her heart. Whenever she heard the truth about Uma's treatment by the Rathod family she mentally felt the pain herself. Whenever someone discussed what Uma went through she attempted to block out what the person was saying. However, this time there was no opportunity to block out what she was saying. "This happened because YOU sent me back. This happened because YOU wanted to keep your reputation and honour." Each word Uma uttered felt like a whip to Avantika's face. Her face burnt hot with shame. "You are one of the people responsible for what happened to me. You two are on the list of the people who wronged me. The people on that list are all my enemies."

Avantika felt as though a spear had been inserted into her heart and it had been pulled out. She never imagined a day when her daughter would describe her as her enemy. *Hai Mata Rani what is this?* Avantika thought desperately. *I thought Uma would be a little bit angry towards us but I thought she would be happy to see us. I never thought she would hate us. Na... Na... my beti can't hate us. Everything I did was for my children's happiness. I will make Uma understand this. How can she think I am her enemy? I never wanted any bad to happen to her.*

"Now you two should leave, before people see you associating yourself with a single mother. What will people say if you associate yourself with people like me?" Uma asked her parents.

Avantika desperately attempted to think of a way in which she could calm her daughter's anger.

"We came to take you back Uma. We..." Vinod began to say.

"I am not coming back. I have a child. If I come back what will happen to your honour and reputation?"

"To hell with all of that Uma," Avantika said shrilly. "I don't care about that! All I want is you to come back and be happy with us."

"I don't want to live with you. I've left your house in a palanquin," Uma said flatly. "Please leave. I'm not coming back home with you."

Avantika opened her mouth to respond to her daughter but was interrupted by the woman Avantika assumed was Amrita.
"If you don't leave now, I'm calling the police," Amrita said standing at the threshold of her house.
"But... but..."
Avantika felt Vinod grab her arm and he began to drag her away. "Come on Avanti we are leaving," He said.
"Vinod... we can't go... not without taking Uma home. She is our beti. We can't leave her here with strangers," Avantika said desperately.
"She is ungrateful for everything we have done for her. When your own child is ungrateful for everything, there is nothing we can do. Leave her here surrounded by strangers. When they get fed up of her, she'll come to her senses and return to us," Vinod spat.
"Let me talk to Uma for one minute. I want to apologise..."

Avantika released her arm from Vinod's grip and ran towards Uma. She intended on delicately putting her hands on Uma's face to wipe her tears, but Uma stepped back. Her husband grabbed her hand again and began to pull Avantika away.
"Come on Avanti. She's become a stone living with those rich people. There's no point talking to a stone."

She watched her daughter, helplessly attempting to speak to her as Vinod grabbed her and took her away. Vinod opened the car door for Avantika and made her sit in the car. He shut the door behind her and drove off. Avantika looked around to see Amrita's house vanish. Uma's words had made her numb.

The entire journey back to Mandavi, Avantika thought of no one but Uma. *The sweet little girl I raised with my own hands has turned against me. I cannot blame her. She is right. When she was a little girl and she fell over, I was really upset by the wound on her leg. I would feel the pain as much as she felt it, but when she went through all the torture I failed her, we both did. I was wrong to think our responsibility towards Uma ended once she got married. Our responsibility towards her should have been for life, not just until we gave her away. Hai Mata Rani I can't live the rest of my life thinking my Uma hates me. Please give her the strength to forgive my selfishness and my negligence.*

Avantika was so absorbed in thoughts of Uma, that she did not realise they were already back in Mandavi. Still dazed with what Uma said Avantika entered the house and saw the family photo that hung in their living room. The five of them were sat together smiling. *Dhiritashtra's ambition for the throne of Hastinapur lost him 100 sons. I tried to get the entire world to look up to me, but in the process I lost the respect of the people who really matter. Is there anything I can do to make things return to the way they used to be?* Avantika saw the picture of them looking so happy. She realised her emotional turmoil was about to be let out. She ran to her bedroom and bolted the door shut behind her. Uma's words had been like daggers to Avantika's heart. Avantika dropped to her knees and sobbed as she let the pain out.

Chapter 91: Charu

Rajan is engaged again! Suneeti came to break the bad news to Charu before going home. *Our relationship ended three days ago, and he is already engaged to someone else? How can he do this to me?* Charu walked into her bedroom and sat down on her bed. She rubbed her eyes and exhaled a few times absorbing the news. She stood up to let out a scream of frustration and sat down again. Despite their disastrous meeting, she was still hopeful that Rajan would change his mind and marry her. *He told me he still loved me; how can he go and marry some other bitch?* Charu wiped her tears. *This is all happening because of Uma's curse! We did so many bad things to her, and now her curse will haunt us forever!* Charu recalled the words Uma spoke to her when she last saw her: *The tears you and your family gave me have now dried up. Those tears will now leak from your eyes. The tears will never stop.*

Her curse will haunt me for the rest of my life. If Rajan marries someone else, then I will cry for the rest of my life. My entire life is ruined. What if her curse follows me to another life? Charu looked around her bedroom and saw the notebook she wrote in during her Sanskrit classes. She opened the book and saw an essay she wrote on the Mahabharat. She remembered Draupadi's insult and how it became a curse for the Kauravs. *Draupadi's curse annihilated the entire Kaurav dynasty.* She turned to a blank page in her notebook and tore it out. She began to write in Gujarati.

Charu was not sure how much time passed when she heard her bedroom door creek. She turned around and saw Vijay's white girlfriend walk in. *What does she want?*
"Hello Charu," Alice said awkwardly. "I came to check you were ok?"
"I am fine," Charu replied dismissively.
"Your friend... Suneeti, I think, told me about Rajan's engagement."
Charu felt another stab to her chest. *Everyone knows about his engagement. People are probably laughing at me everywhere. The tainted girl with a dirty reputation.*

"I just wanted to make sure you're alright," Alice continued.
"I'm fine... I don't-" Charu began angrily.
"There isn't anything I can do for you?"
"I'm fine... I,"
Charu stopped her outburst. She looked at the letter she had just finished writing. She picked up the letter and folded it into eighths. "Give this to Suneeti," Charu shoved the folded piece of paper into Alice's hand. She then began to push Alice out of her bedroom. "Now leave me alone. I need to do something. Leave. Leave."

Charu pushed Alice out of her room and locked the door to prevent anyone else coming in. She sat in silence. Darkness fell around her but Charu did not turn the light on. Darkness was all that surrounded her, as it was a moonless night. *My future is as dark as this night. Without Rajan what else is left?* Charu remembered the two dolls she had; Lado and Charu. She remembered the dreams she built around becoming a wife and her grand wedding. Now all of her dreams had crumbled. *I have everything except the perfect groom and, without the groom, how can I have a perfect wedding? I have spent eighteen years planning this day all for nothing.* Charu let out a silent sob. What do I have left now if my biggest dream is over? Charu recalled something Purbai and her mother told her. *"A woman is incomplete until she experiences two events in her life. The first is when she gets married, the second when she becomes a mother."* And then Charu once more recalled Uma's curse. *I am destined to have neither. No man will ever want me and without a husband how will I become a mother? Papa paid for me to study in Bangalore so that I could make something of myself and get the best husband possible. Everything has crumbled. I have nothing. Uma's curse will haunt me forever.*

Charu took out her mobile phone and logged onto Facebook. She immediately went onto Rajan's profile and felt another jolt. He had not only changed his relationship status to inform people of his new fiancé, but he also added new photographs of his engagement to a Shanti! *This girl won't keep him happy the same way I would have.* She looked through his albums to find the album which contained pictures of their engagement. She realised the album was missing. Angered by him she threw her mobile phone and smashed it. *My final hope of getting him back is over. Unless this Shanti dies of cancer or something.* Charu immediately reprimanded herself for a low thought. *You foolish girl! You do not learn from your mistakes. You cannot plant bitter neem and expect sweet mangoes. You reap what you sow. First you inflict terrors onto another woman and then you wish someone dies of cancer. Your thoughts are low. People like you deserve to be cursed. Curses like that are reserved for people who are an abomination on humankind. I have spread so much venom into other people's lives that there is now so much poison in my own life. There is only one way to nullify this poison.*

Charu walked out of her bedroom and went to the balcony on the top of their house. She looked at the view of Madhapar. She could hear the traffic of the city; thousands of cars, rickshaws and trucks beeping their horns every few seconds. *Life is continuing to move on whilst mine has come to a permanent standstill.* No tears came out of Charu's eyes, her ducts were dry from all the tears she had already shed. *I've failed as a woman. With no husband or children to look forward to, what is the purpose of my existence? There is one solution to free myself from Uma's sharap. I can start again and hope to be more successful in my next life.* Charu closed her eyes. *I have already written a letter apologising to Uma so Bhagwan, please let me get her forgiveness and let Uma's curse end now. I am going to punish myself for my sins.* Charu opened her eyes again and sat on the balcony railings. She took a deep breath and jumped, falling 35 feet.

Chapter 92: Alice

Alice tied her hair into a ponytail and looked at the new dress she bought. The joy she usually felt at buying a new dress was absent. She had to buy the dress because Vijay told her nothing in her wardrobe was suitable. Alice put on the Indian black dress that she assumed was appropriate.

Alice knew that there were lots of people sat downstairs in the lounge. However, she could only hear the voice of one man, who was preaching in, what she assumed was, Gujarati. Alice felt uncomfortable in her outfit. She was even more perturbed by the idea of walking into a room full of people she did not know. *She was his sister! I have to go and pay my respects.* Alice dragged herself down the stairs and immediately regretted it. *Shit! Everyone's wearing white. I thought people wear black to a mourning.* Alice saw the lounge full of people sat on the floor. The men sat in rows on the left side of the room and the women on the right. They both faced each other, leaving an aisle in the centre. At the end of the aisle there was a diva burning in front of a garlanded photograph of Charu. A priest sat next to the photograph reading from the Bhagvad Gita.

Alice spotted a place in the corner, behind all the other women and walked over to sit there. She noticed that a number of people did a double take to look at her attire. Alice spotted Madhu sat down with her face veiled by her sari. Alice felt extreme sympathy for Madhu. *Poor woman; no mother deserves to bury her own child. Cremate in her case, but still...* Alice felt a shiver run through her as she recalled the moment Charu had jumped from the balcony. Charu lay on the floor broken; her glassy eyes reflected the courtyard light that she could not see. There was blood splattered on the floor. Madhu's wounded howl at the sight of her daughter's body was a sound that Alice would never forget. The ambulance pronounced Charu dead on the scene. The news caused Madhu to fall unconscious. The distressing scene was etched into Alice's memory forever.

Unable to understand what the priest was saying, Alice felt that time was going slowly and she began to yawn. *Oh God how much longer do I have to sit here? I'm probably not allowed to stand up until he stops reading.* Alice bided her time by remembering Charu. She knew her for a short period. *The sweet girl who decorated my hands with henna sunk into depression after her wedding was ruined. The only time we spoke after her wedding was when she gave me that letter.* Alice became alert again. *The letter! She gave me a letter to give to... her friend Suneeti. What could be in that letter?* Alice became restless thinking about the contents of the letter. She decided that she was going to read the letter and find out exactly what was written in it. *I need to know what is in it.*

Once the priest finished reading she became excited but no one seemed to get up for a few minutes, which frustrated Alice. After what seemed like ages, one man stood up and began to walk to the exit. As soon as the first man stood up, others too started to leave collectively. When she saw some of the women leave, Alice took it as a sign she too was allowed to leave. Eager to satisfy her curiosity she quickly ran up to her bedroom to find the letter. Alice locked the door behind her. She picked up the trousers she was wearing when Charu gave her the letter and found the letter inside the side pocket. Alice was about to unfold the letter when she stopped. *This letter was written by a girl who died. She specifically directed me to give it to Suneeti. Is it right for me to pry?* Alice looked at the folded piece of paper. *I'll still be making sure she got the letter. It can't hurt to take a quick peek.* Alice's desire to find out what the letter contained prevailed. She quickly unfolded the letter. Alice felt disappointed when she saw the letter was written in Gujarati. *I will never find out what this letter says now.* Alice walked over to the bedroom window and watched the mourners leave. *I could perhaps get Suneeti to read it and tell me what's in it.*

Alice walked back downstairs with the resolve to find Suneeti. It was not simple to find her amongst people who were all dressed in white. She went out into the courtyard and saw Suneeti amongst a group of girls who were leaving. Alice ran after her and caught up with the group just outside Rathod Haveli.

"Suneeti, I need your help," Alice panted to her.
"What is it?"
"Not in front of everyone," Alice said as she looked at the other girls with Suneeti. "Can we talk in private?"
"Go on ahead," Suneeti told her friends. "I'll catch you up."
"Charu gave me this letter before she died," Alice informed Suneeti. "She wanted me to give it to you." Alice handed the letter to Suneeti who looked emotional.
Alice saw Suneeti's eyes fill with tears again. She knew that Suneeti must feel overwhelmed with emotion to receive a letter written by a friend who was dead.
Alice watched carefully as Suneeti unfolded the letter and read it. Her facial expression changed from sorrow to confusion as she completed the letter.
"What does it say?" Alice asked.
Suneeti handed the letter to Alice.
"I don't know how to read Gujarati, you need to translate it," she told Suneeti.
Suneeti took the letter back and began to recite one line at a time.

"Suneeti, please find Uma and give this letter to her whenever you find her."

Why does Charu want to write to a bitch that ruined her family's life?
Alice began to pay closer attention.

"This is the letter for Uma, it says:

Uma,

I am writing this letter to apologise for my actions. If you can forgive me, please forgive me. Me and my family made your life hell when you lived here, all because we wanted money. I was blinded by my desire to have a perfect wedding. Mumma tortured you every day and Vijay misbehaved with you. Jigar and his police friends falsely implicated your brother to prevent you from getting justice. I'm writing to tell you that you got your justice. Your curse ruined my life. Your curse came true. All I have left in my life is pain and emptiness. Tears are leaking from my eyes, and will leak for the rest of my life as you said they would. I am not strong enough to live with this pain for the rest of my life. I want to go quickly rather than suffer for the rest of my life. I don't want your curse to follow me into my next life so please forgive me for everything.

Charu"

With every sentence Alice felt a blow. *What the hell is Charu talking about? Vijay misbehaved with Uma? Madhu tortured her every day? I assume misbehave means...* Alice slowly came to the realisation what Charu meant. *Vijay raped her. All of these are the allegations that Vijay's wife put onto him.* Alice took the letter from Suneeti's hand and looked at it again. *Her allegations were all lies. Vijay told me they were lies.* Alice felt like she had been punched in the stomach. *That dickhead lied again. He fucking lied to me and I fell for it again. That fucking scumbag.*

"Are you sure that's what the letter says?" Alice asked Suneeti.
"Of course!" Suneeti told Alice. "I can't believe it. How could they have been involved in something so disgusting! Charu was helping me with the work I am doing around women's rights and her own family... chi."
Fuck my life! Alice blocked out Suneeti's rant. *I gave a witness statement to say that woman was a liar when in reality she was the victim in all this.* Alice felt weak at the knees. She ran her fingers through her hair and began to think. *What do I do now? How do I rectify my mistake?*

"Suneeti," Alice said hoping Suneeti could help. "Do you know where Uma is?"
"I know she lives with a woman called Amrita Oberoi. Charu told me they found out where..."
"Take me there."

Chapter 93: Amrita

Amrita pressed the red button on the remote control and turned off the television. She finished watching a Hollywood revenge horror movie, dubbed in Hindi, that she downloaded from the internet. Watching someone avenge themselves and torture their perpetrators had given Amrita comfort after Nirmal's death. These films allowed Amrita to fantasise about giving Nirmal's murderers a slow, painful and brutal death. Amrita became obsessed with the Hindi dubbed Saw film series. Many of her revenge fantasises involved her as Jigsaw and Nirmal's in-laws as the pieces of her game. Amrita even went as far as creating dangerous games that she would play with them. *One day I will enact one of these fantasies and revel in their pain.*

Amrita sat alone in silence. It was almost 2.30pm and everyone else was having a nap. She relived one of the games she often fantasised about. There were three pieces in this game; Nirmal's mother-in-law, Tejinder; Nirmal's husband, Navpreet and his younger brother, Jasdeep. Nirmal's mother-in-law would be tied to a chair so tightly she would be unable to escape. Sat directly opposite her were her two sons who were also tied up and unable to escape. This would be the start of her deadly game. When the three of them came into consciousness Amrita would enjoy watching their futile attempts to escape. She would take pleasure in them desperately begging to know who had tied them up and why, only to receive no answer. After a few moments a video featuring Amrita as Jigsaw would appear which would immediately grab the attention of her three hostages. The first thing she would say as Jigsaw would be "Kya tumhe ek khel khelna hai?" This would then be followed by Amrita describing the nature of the game. Amrita would explain to them that if the rules of her game are followed, the room would not blow up. If they break the rules of her game the explosives in the room would detonate, killing them all. Amrita would then speak directly to Tejinder and inform her that she alone has to complete the first phase of the game. She would have a minute to give her answer and if she fails to give an answer within the allotted time she would be the reason for her son's deaths. At this moment, Amrita would pause the video and give the Chadda hostages some time for the information to sink in, and see the explosives in the room.

Once the information sinks in she would ask Nirmal's mother-in-law the question she has to answer before the end of phase one.
"Listen carefully, Tejinder. There is a clock to your left. If you do not answer my question before the time in the clock runs out you will all be killed. You have a very difficult decision to make, Tejinder. You are in a sinking ship and both of your sons are drowning. You have one life jacket that you could throw to one of them and save him. Which son would you leave empty handed and leave to die?"
"What kind of question is this?" Tejinder would shriek. "A beeji treats all children equally. Both of my sons are equal to me and I would never be able to make a choice."
The digital clock would be counting backwards. As the clock began to make buzzing noises the lower the countdown got, Tejinder would have been forced into saying one name in order to save her son's lives.

Amrita always fantasised that Tejinder would choose Jasdeep as the son she would leave to die. Nirmal's husband, Navpreet, would be the one Tejinder would save.
"You have chosen to let Jasdeep die. Your love for Navpreet is greater," Amrita would say before leaving another gap for silence to draw out the torture. In this gap Tejinder would beg Jasdeep that she only responded so she could save them both. She would maintain that her sons were both equal to her.
Amrita would then speak again. "Jasdeep, I now speak directly to you. Your beeji loves your veerji more than you. The survival of your entire family now rests upon you. Listen closely, if you make a mistake, the explosives will be activated killing you all. You will have four minutes to complete the second phase of this game. Your time will start when you are released from the chair you are tied in. Once you are released, you will find a Kirpan in front of you. You will use the sword to release your brother. The only way out for him is to have his hands and feet cut off. If you are successful in releasing your brother, your beeji will automatically be released and you will all be allowed to leave. Your time

starts now." Jasdeep would be released and would immediately grab the saw. He will cut through his brother's limbs to save his own life and his mother's life. Navpreet's screams would feel like music to Amrita's ears. Once Navpreet is free Amrita would speak again. "Congratulations. Your beeji will be released just before the start of the final phase of the game. The exit will open the same time your mother is released. You will have a minute to find a safe way out before this entire building explodes. The moment the exit opens this place will be set on fire. Try and get out without being burnt."

Amrita would then release the mother and the exit would open. The fire would be set. In desperation to get out, it would be each man for him or herself. They would leave Nirmal's husband behind who would be unable to walk. Tejinder would be forced to leave her son to the flames they killed her sister with. The game would still not be over.

Amrita would have recorded the entire game, but only from a certain angle. The camera would have focused entirely on Navpreet, which would clearly show Jasdeep cutting off his brother's limbs. Amrita would send the tape to the police and other people in high places. Tejinder and her husband will lose all of their children. They will be left with a disfigured daughter, who Amrita's brother already punished. They will have a dead son and another son in prison for his murder.

Fantasising about various ways in which she could torture Nirmal's in-laws gave Amrita a lot of comfort and satisfaction. The games she devised acted as a mechanism for her to not go completely crazy with hatred. *The games I have fantasised for the past few years to stop myself being consumed by hatred will finally come in use. Perhaps the opportunity to finally enact one of these games for real will finally calm the storm I have contained inside me for the past six years. The only difference is the game I had devised for Tejinder, Navpreet and Jasdeep will involve Madhu, Jigar and Vijay instead. All I have to work out is how I will lure them into the secluded warehouse. Perhaps I can lure them there by telling them the person who sent the pictures of Charu is hiding there.*

Before targeting the Rathod family, they had unfinished business with Vijay's mistress. *She gave Vijay a false alibi. She is a part of their wrongdoings. She too must suffer and she will. Within seven days she will find herself...* Amrita's thoughts were interrupted when she heard a knock on her door. *Who has come at this time? And why are they not just walking in like everyone else?*
"Hello Jee, undar aa jao," Amrita shouted.
Despite Amrita inviting the person into her house, no one came in. She stood up to ensure the door was not bolted and saw it was unlocked. Agitated Amrita walked over to the door to open it herself. *Haai Rubba, better not be time wasters.*

Amrita pushed the door open and saw two women waiting at the threshold of her house. Amrita vaguely recognised the face of the Indian woman, but had no idea who the white woman was.
"Sat Sri Akal," Amrita said. "What can I do for you?"
"My name is Alice, Alice Henshaw," the white woman spoke.
Amrita did a double take in surprise at the name. She eyed the two women suspiciously. *What does this gori want? How dare this shameful woman come to my house and knock on my door. Who does she think she is?*

"Does Uma live here?" Vijay's mistress asked.
"No. Leave my house before I call the police."
Amrita gave Alice an empty threat. Under no circumstances would she call the police, but she did not want to engage in dialogue with an enemy.
"Please," the Indian woman said. "It's important we speak to Uma."
"I have something really important to show her. I'm... I'm so confused. I need to speak to her please," Alice whined and said really quickly.
Amrita surveyed the two women closely. *This must be some sort of trick on the Rathod's behalf. They have sent her to spy us. Perhaps they want to know if we were behind Charu's MMS scandal.* Amrita looked forward and narrowed her eyes.
"I am Suneeti," the Indian woman said. "I was Charu's friend. I know Uma lives here. We have important information for you. Don't turn us away."

Amrita turned her head and quickly scanned the living room to ensure nothing that could interest the enemy was out. *If I let them in, it could be my opportunity to find out more about the Rathod's weaknesses. Perhaps it isn't such a bad idea letting them in.* Amrita scanned her living room once more before stepping back and allowing the two women to enter her home. Amrita stared at Alice who willingly walked into her house. Her frustration with the characterless woman was vanishing. *The prey itself has walked into the hunter's trap.*

Chapter 94: Madhu

Charu! My beautiful surajmukhi. She is twenty two years old but still I have to do everything for her. Even now my Charu cannot do anything for herself. Madhu used a piece of string to tie both of Charu's big toes together. She covered her daughter's feet with a white cloth and then shifted herself to Charu's head. Madhu saw the cotton wool inside both of Charu's nostrils. *My Charu would hate it if people saw her with wool inside her nose.* Madhu picked up the white cloth covering Charu intending on lifting it to cover her face. Before she covered Charu's face she bent over to kiss her daughter's forehead. She felt Charu's stone cold forehead against her lips. Without moving her lips away from Charu's head Madhu began to sob again as she recalled the torture and torment she went through to have Charu. *I went through so much for you. I nurtured you with my hands day and night. I made sure you got everything you wanted. I even killed for you, and now you have left me like the rest of your sisters.*

Madhu recalled her marriage to Harshad, the son of a politician, one week after her eighteenth birthday. Madhu's father and Harshad's father arranged the marriage to strengthen the relationship shared between the two families. Madhu's father, a rich businessman, often financed Harshad's father's election campaigns. Harshad's father often supported Madhu's father's business by fast tracking planning permission requests and turning a blind eye to health and safety regulations. She had no choice in the matter but was assured by her mother that the marriage would improve her life forever. Her mother promised her that marrying into the family of an influential politician would increase her prestige in society. After her marriage, Madhu realised that life with the Rathod family was far from perfect. She possessed the lifestyle and glamour her mother promised, but she had become isolated. Her husband and father-in-law spent most of their time away from the home canvassing for votes or campaigning. Madhu feared her mother-in-law and made every effort to stay out of her way. As an only child, Harshad had no other siblings who Madhu could spend time with, and therefore she spent most of her time missing her own family or watching TV.

A year after her marriage to Harshad, Madhu discovered she was pregnant. *My child will drive away my solitude and give my life purpose. I will now have something to wake up for in the morning. People always say that a woman's life is not complete until she becomes a wife and a mother. I am going to become a maa and my life will become complete.* With the news of Madhu's pregnancy, Harshad worked from home whenever he could, so that he could look after his wife. Madhu's mother-in-law also began to interact with her. Madhu was surprised that her mother-in-law was actually very polite and enjoyed talking to her. Madhu's loneliness gradually vanished. The things her mother promised were finally materialising and for the first time since her marriage, Madhu began to enjoy her life with the Rathod family. Her love for Harshad began to grow as he took care of her during her pregnancy.

After months of counting down to when she would be a mother, September the thirteenth finally arrived. Madhu went through a long and painful labour. Thirty seven hours after the first cramp, she finally delivered a beautiful baby girl. Madhu forgot the pain she had been through the moment she laid eyes on her daughter. *Hai Bhagwan, you have given me Lakshmi. She is the most beautiful baby I have ever seen. It is almost as if Maha Lakshmi has incarnated herself.* An intense emotion swept through Madhu at that moment. She had never loved someone else as much as she loved the little girl in her hands. When she held the girl in her hands, the baby's little fingers grabbed hold of Madhu's finger. Madhu struggled to release her finger from her grip. *You are a strong little girl aren't you? My beti is going to show this world that a girl can do anything a boy can do. You will become a politician like your bapuji and dada but you will be better than them both.* The adrenaline rushing through Madhu's body prevented her from sleeping. All she wanted to do was show off her daughter to everyone. When her mother-in-law entered the room, Madhu attempted to introduce the girl to her grandmother. However, her mother-in-law was very dismissive of the baby. Madhu saw her face lacked the reflection of joy she felt herself.

Her mother-in-law brought Madhu a glass of warm milk, mixed with turmeric. She put the glass on the bedside table and left without a second glance at her child. Madhu felt slightly unnerved by her mother-in-law's behaviour but she heard the baby cry and she immediately attended to her daughter.

As each day passed, her love for her daughter increased. Traditionally a name was given to a child after it was sixteen days old, but Madhu knew she was going to name her child Indira, after Indira Gandhi, the world's first woman prime minister. Five days after her daughter's birth, Madhu put Indira back into her cot. Madhu lay on her side watching her daughter's chest rise and drop as she breathed in and out. She fell asleep watching her daughter. When she woke up in the morning she found her daughter's cradle was empty. *Where is Indira?* Madhu immediately jumped out of bed and went to look for her daughter. She ran around the house panicking unable to find her child anywhere. Madhu spotted her mother-in-law sitting in the courtyard. *Perhaps maaji has Indira, but you cannot take a child out of the house for forty two days.* She ran out of the house and saw that Indira was not with her.
"Maaji, where is my beti?" Madhu asked her mother-in-law.
Her mother-in-law's response shattered Madhu. She had not been prepared for the devastating blow she gave.
"Your beti died in the night. Harshad and Harshad's father have gone to bury her."
Na... na... Madhu fell to her knees and screamed like a wounded banshee at the news of her daughter's death. The dreams she saw for Indira were demolished. However, the agony that Madhu felt at her daughter's death was nothing compared to the pain she felt when she found out that Indira was murdered. Madhu overheard a conversation between her husband and his mother. She discovered that her in-laws wanted a grandson. Her mother and father-in-law had returned the girl to the gods, in the hope they would send a son next time. They sacrificed the girl by drowning her in a pool of milk and mother-in-law then ordered the two men to bury the girl in the middle of the forest before voters found out what happened. Hearing the way her daughter was brutally murdered caused Madhu to be physically sick.

Furious at the actions of her family, Madhu attempted to challenge her mother-in-law.
"How dare you kill my beti," Madhu shrieked at her mother-in-law. "Even animals love their own children. What kind of beasts are you? You killed your own pauti."
Madhu's tirade against her mother-in-law ended abruptly when her mother-in-law slapped her.
"This is another Rathod family tradition, bahu. We have no daughters," she coldly responded. "We did not gain this prestige by wasting our money investing in girls. Everything was invested in my son."
"How could you allow your own beti to be killed, Harshad? What kind of father are you?"
"Madhu beti," Madhu's father-in-law spoke without averting his eyes from the newspaper he was reading. "Harshad's mother is right. We did what we thought was best. A girl is expensive, we nurture her for years, and then we have to pay an extortionate dowry, then she goes and becomes a part of someone else's family. We cannot afford that. Girls are expensive."
"What is the use of all this money you have?" Madhu retaliated. "You have a mansion, but you cannot afford to pay for a little girl. Shame on you, chi."

This had been the one and only time Madhu spoke out against her in-laws. As a result of her impudence, Madhu was locked into a room for a few days. Her in-laws told her that she needed to learn to respect the decision of her elders. When she was finally let out of the room, her husband and father-in-law threatened Madhu.
"If you want to tell anyone what happened here, remember this," Harshad's father told her. "I have a far reach and wide network. Firstly, no one will believe you. Secondly, if you open your mouth, no one will ever hear from you again or know what happened to you."

From that moment, the house of her in-laws became a prison for Madhu. Three months after Indira's murder, Madhu was pregnant again. Once again, Madhu rebuilt the dreams she saw for her first child. She desperately prayed for a son, to avoid a repeat of what happened with her previous child. Nevertheless, Madhu also convinced herself that if another girl was born they would let her live. They might accept that god wants them to have a girl. They will accept their mistake and accept her. Madhu was wrong. Not only was her desire for a son smashed, but the hope that her in-laws would accept her second daughter was crushed. This time they did not even wait for Madhu to fall asleep when they snatched the girl from her hands. Her father-in-law took the girl away and Madhu never saw her again.

After the death of her second daughter and before the birth of Vijay, Madhu became pregnant two more times. The only thing Madhu was grateful for during those pregnancies was that her in-laws took her to the hospital to get her checked. They had tests conducted to determine the foetus' gender. Both times Madhu had been coerced into an abortion, as both times they were girls. Unable to give the Rathod family a male heir, Madhu's life with the Rathod family became torture. She was treated like vermin, a burden that was unable to fulfil her duty as a wife. Her in-laws took every opportunity to mock her and taunt her.

Finally, Madhu became pregnant a fifth time. The tests which determined the gender showed this time she was going to have a boy. The doctor advised her in-laws to have an abortion due to complications with the pregnancy. Having so many pregnancies so close to each other had left Madhu's body exhausted. However, her in-laws told Madhu to pursue the pregnancy. They signed forms at the hospital that stated that if a situation arose in which they had to save either the child or mother, the doctors would save the child.

After a difficult pregnancy, both Madhu and her son survived. The Rathod family rang bells at the temple to announce the birth of their son. They donated food to a thousand poor people and distributed sweets to all their friends and relatives. They showered gifts to priests at the temple to celebrate a son's birth with grandeur. Madhu did not partake in any of the celebrations. She was relieved that she finally had a child she could keep. She looked at her son who was opening and closing his toothless mouth. *You are as beautiful as your older sisters. I was not able to save any of them, but I will make sure I do everything I can to make you happy. I will make sure you have everything you ever dream of my rajkumar. If this world has it, you will have it.*

Before Madhu gave birth to Jigar, she was forced into another abortion. The eighth time Madhu fell pregnant, she was accompanied by her mother-in-law to the clinic where they pre-determined the sex of the baby. Her mother-in-law had waited outside whilst the doctor carried out the tests. Madhu's insides froze when the doctor told her she was going to have another daughter. Madhu sat up and put her hands together. With tears coming out of her eyes she begged the doctor to tell her in-laws that she was having a son. The desperation in Madhu's face convinced the doctor to lie to her mother-in-law. When the doctor told her mother-in-law that Madhu was going to have a son, she felt temporary relief but at the same time she felt uneasy. *How long can I hide the fact that I am going to have a girl?*

For days, Madhu nurtured her secret daughter with the fear that someone would discover her lie. One day Madhu woke from an afternoon slumber from the recurring nightmare of her daughter being killed. These nightmares haunted Madhu since she lied about being pregnant with a boy. She looked at her swollen red eyes in the mirror. *This is all you can do Madhu, show people your weakness through your tears. If you want to save your beti you need to do more than just cry. You showed everyone your weakness by shedding tears every single day. Now you need to stop shedding tears and start showing them your strength. You need to fight to save your beti, not cry.* Madhu took a deep breath. She placed her right hand on her stomach and looked down. *I will not be tortured or bullied into getting rid of you. I will die before I let any harm befall you.* Madhu paced around her room thinking about how she was going to secure her daughter's survival. *I have only one option left. I have to remove the people who would murder my daughter.*

Initially Madhu planned to simply use sugar to kill her father-in-law. He had diabetes, and she believed putting a lot of sugar in his food would give him a cardiac arrest. However, Madhu felt that method of murder would have been too quick for him. *I want that beast to suffer a long and painful death. I want him to have the opportunity to know why he is being killed. I want him to beg for the forgiveness I will never give him.* Desiring a more horrific fate for her in-laws, Madhu spent a few weeks meticulously planning ways to murder both of them without the murder being linked back to her. In the process of planning Madhu had a change of heart and decided to spare her mother-in-law's life. *Death is too easy for that bosrini. Living here has been worse than living in hell, and now I am going to give her a fate that is worse than death. Simply cutting that pikini's head off will not satisfy me. She will die, but she will die with severe humiliation.*

Madhu waited until Holi. As per tradition the Rathod family threw a grand Holi party in their home, and welcomed friends, neighbours and colleagues to celebrate with them. Traditionally on Holi people mixed drinks with marijuana and got thrills from the intoxication that came with it but, Madhu knew that it was also a hallucinogenic. She smuggled large amounts into her bedroom so she could put her plan into action. Madhu began to add marijuana to her mother-in-law's tea. When her mother-in-law's hallucinations started, Harshad and his father attempted to hide it from everyone else. They felt it may have a negative impact on their upcoming election campaign. Madhu thwarted their attempts by telling their maid everything about her mother-in-law's mental state. She even permitted the maid to tell people that her mother-in-law was going crazy. Once the news of her mother-in-law's insanity began to spread amongst their neighbours, Madhu knew that she was ready to cleanse her life from the people who would not allow her daughter to survive.

Madhu mixed sleeping pills into the evening tea she prepared. She administered the drugged tea to Harshad and his parents. Feeling drowsy they all went to bed earlier. When they all fell asleep, Madhu took some chloroform and made her father in law sniff it. When she was sure he was knocked out she dragged him to another room in the house and tied him to a bed as tightly as she could. She tested the ropes a few times to make sure there was no way he could get out. Once she knew he was securely tied up, she waited for him to wake up. After he woke, he groggily looked around, feeling confused. Madhu walked over to him and slapped him a few times to ensure he was alert. She then looked directly into his eyes and told him why he was there. As Madhu expected, her father-in-law cried and begged her to let him go. Madhu knew there was no going back. *If I let him go he will kill me. Hai Bhagwan, let him be eaten by ants in hell for what he did to my betis.* Madhu punched him in the groin and watched him scream. The look of agony on his face gave Madhu such a soothing feeling that she punched him a number of times. She then stabbed him in his arm and watched him bleed to death but before his life drained out she told him; "This is for all of my betis. Your bitch will join you too but, before she does, she has to go to prison for your murder." Madhu wiped the knife to remove her finger prints. She then wrapped her sleeping mother-in-laws hands around the knife before covering it up in a cloth. Madhu covered the knife with a cloth and then hid it in her mother-in-law's wardrobe. Madhu then drank the last of the drugged tea and fell asleep herself.

The murder of an influential politician caused high shockwaves in Ahmedabad. The fact that his own wife killed him caused even more ripples in society. Madhu's mother-in-law was arrested for the murder of her husband. Based on a number of witnesses, which included Madhu and Harshad's testimonies, her mother-in-law was institutionalised in a hospital for mentally ill patients. Harshad replaced his father in a by-election and Madhu gained control of the house. *I will never let myself be the servant of another in my own home. I will never allow someone to control me again.*

One month before Charu's birth, Madhu went to visit her mother-in-law at the psychiatric hospital. Madhu prepared a tiffin containing her mother-in-laws' favourite dishes. The bitch seemed happy to see all of her favourite food items in front of her. Madhu watched as she raised a spoon towards her mouth to taste the dhokla. After chewing for a few seconds, her mother-in-law immediately spat it out. Madhu had put too much salt in the dhokla. Another dish contained too much chilli powder, a third dish was bland and void of any spices. There was no sugar in the kheer Madhu made. Finally Madhu gave her mother-in-law mukhvaas.
"You are not that crazy that you cannot tell me what I have replaced the paan leaf with?" Madhu taunted her mother-in-law. "It is bhang. I have

been adding large quantities to your tea, to make you crazy."
Madhu's mother-in-law spluttered with anger. Madhu continued unperturbed.
"I killed your husband and then framed you for his murder," Madhu said casually.
She cackled in her mother-in-law's face when she screamed and cursed at Madhu.
"Eh pikini," Madhu bellowed, forcing her mother-in-law to stop cursing.
"Will you not ask me why I did this?" Madhu looked at the venom in her mother-in-law's eyes. "Na? Well I tell you anyway. I am pregnant... with a girl." Madhu's mother-in-law widened her eyes in surprise. "I told the doctor to lie to you and tell you I was having a boy. When I saved her from being aborted, I swore to myself I will not allow you or that benchod to kill her. I decided that if someone had to die, it would be your bastard husband. I am now going to spend your husband's hard earned money on my beti and fulfil every dream of hers," Madhu chuckled and stood up.
"You will never get away with this you rand. Karma..."
"Karma? You suffering in here is your Karma. And I have already escaped," Madhu turned her back and began to walk out of the room, but she paused before she left the room and turned back around to tell her mother-in-law one last thing. "I almost forgot to tell you. If you ever get out of this place, and come back to live in MY house; I will cut you into small pieces and drown your flesh in milk. My husband has a wide range of networks."
That was the last time Madhu ever saw her mother-in-law. She died in the same institution a few years later. Madhu went to her funeral and cried crocodile tears at her loss. By the time her mother-in-law died, Madhu knew what she had to do in order to survive and retain her position in society.

Madhu continued to sit at her daughter's body reliving her memories of Charu. When the priest announced it was time to take the body to the crematorium, Madhu had not heard and continued to recollect cherished memories. She remembered how Charu sat near her knees as she massaged coconut oil into her daughter's hair. The red ribbons I tied into your hair for your first day of school made you look so cute.

She snapped out of her trance when she saw Charu's body move. Madhu looked up and saw Vijay, Jigar, Ravi and other family members picking up Charu's funeral bier.
"What are you two doing?" she screamed at her sons. She attempted to grab Vijay's foot in an attempt to stop him walking out with Charu. "Whe - where are you taking her? I promised her I would die before I let any harm befall her. You cannot take her away."

Seeing their mother so helpless made Jigar and Vijay sob even more. Madhu felt two pairs of arms attempting to restrain her. Vijay managed to free his foot from Madhu's grip and began to walk towards the exit of their house. Madhu broke free from the people holding her back and chased after her son. She grabbed his white kurta in a final attempt to stop them leaving with her daughter. "I promised her," Madhu shrieked. "I promised her nothing would happen to her whilst I am alive. You cannot do anything to her."
Once again Madhu felt people restraining her, however, this time Vaishali and Purbai were accompanied by other women. As Charu's bier vanished out of Madhu's sight she realised that she would never see her daughter again. That was the moment Madhu let go of her pride. She tried her best to fight back her tears, but had already failed, but finally she did not care who saw her pain. All she cared about was the fact that Charu was gone and was not coming back. *My years of penance for you has all mixed up with the dust. The pain Madhu felt was worse than the pain she felt for Indira and her other daughters.* She fell to her knees and sobbed so hard that no noise came out.

Chapter 95: Leela

Leela went to Amrita's courtyard where Uma was sat on her own just looking at the sky. *She must be feeling the same things that I am feeling.* Leela began to walk over to Uma and recalled the events from two days ago when Alice finally came face to face with Uma.

Initially Uma declined to speak to Alice. She would not even face her and turned her back to Vijay's mistress. However, Alice forced a note into Uma's hand and made her read it. Leela saw the colour drain from Uma's face the moment she finished reading it.
"Charu is dead?" Uma whispered as soon as she finished reading the note.
Dead? Leela felt a jolt inside her. *I saw her three days ago, she was well. How can she be dead? Her death wasn't part of our plan. She was meant to live as a shamed woman.* Leela saw feelings of guilt and confusion reflected on the faces of Uma and Vikram. However, the look on Amrita's face told a different story. Leela felt that Amrita looked jubilant. Leela did not say anything in Alice's presence. She stood in silence and watched as Amrita, Vikram, Uma, Suneeti and Alice conversed in English. Leela had no idea what they were talking about but still stood with them to feel involved. Once Alice and Suneeti left, Leela was about to ask what they discussed when Amrita confirmed that she felt victorious about Charu's death.

"What does everyone want to eat tonight?" Amrita said happily. "I will cook us a feast."
"Amrita," Leela heard Vikram say. "Charu is dead..."
"One less evil person on this planet," Amrita spat at her husband. "It is a cause to celebrate."
"It is not right to celebrate someone's death. She was a young girl..."
"She was old enough to know the difference between right and wrong. If she was old enough to commit a crime, she was old enough to suffer the consequences."
"She was Uma's nanand, have some shame. We're not celebrating the

deaths of Nirmal's in-laws."
Vikram's words immediately doused Amrita's happiness, which turned into a bitter argument between the husband and wife.
"The day I hear that Nirmal's in-laws have suffered for their crimes I will feed a thousand homeless people. If they have excruciatingly painful deaths, I will feed two thousand. Charu was a blot on womankind. There are too many people living in poverty in this world. There are already limited resources for humankind, they were wasted on an evil person like her."
"Instead of showing remorse over our actions..."
"I didn't kill her. She reaped the fruits of her karma."

Vikramji feels the girl died because of our actions. Leela felt her stomach churn at his words. Vikram and Amrita's argument was the same conflict going through her own mind. A part of Leela agreed with Vikram. *Charu was wrong. She did deserve punishment for her actions. But did we take things too far? We ruined her life and made her become so helpless that self murder was the only path left for her.* The other part of Leela agreed with Amrita. *If she felt remorse over her actions she would have accepted her crime and accepted a jail sentence for the evil she did. If she accepted punishment willingly she would not have had such a brutal punishment. The girl paid the price for her greed, lies and evil.*

Charu never spoke much to me but she was never rude like her amma. The way Charu became is her amma's fault. She spoilt her. Charu knew how to get her own way. She would scream and cry until she got her own way. My amma would beat me if I ever disagreed with any decision they made for me. All that girl needed was a few beatings to instil morals into her.

Once the argument calmed down, Uma explained to Leela what Charu's letter contained. The feelings of guilt overpowered Leela's feelings of vindication. *She realised her error before she died. She could have changed; now she will never have that opportunity. O Guruvayur Swamy why do I feel so guilty? I was delighted when her wedding was ruined. I rejoiced at the news how Madhu cried. Hearing how Jigar fell to the floor and was beaten gave me such contentment then why am I feeling such guilt at this? Is it because I think Charu was not as evil as the rest of them? She was still involved with everything her family did to Uma. She supported them and those who support injustice are destroyed as well.* Leela remembered the excerpts from Mahabharat that Amrita recited to Uma to instigate her into taking revenge. *All those who insulted Draupadi were destroyed, all those who supported the perpetrators also met with the same fate.*

Leela, sat down next to Uma in silence to give her some support. *She looks as though she is going through the same turmoil that I went through two days ago.* Just as Leela was about to comfort Uma she heard the front gate screech. Leela saw Alice walk in.
"Amritaji," Leela called in Hindi. "That woman is here."
As soon as Leela called for Amrita she stood up and walked towards Alice. *She is looking very pleased with herself. She must have brought the evidence Amritaji sent her to find.*

Once Vikram and Amrita stopped arguing about whether it was appropriate to rejoice in Charu's death or not, Leela asked those present to translate what happened before Alice left. At this point Uma handed Leela Charu's suicide note and pointed out her apologies. Leela squirmed to see evidence of Charu's remorse. *The girl realised what she did was wrong, perhaps if we forced her into following the path of dharma instead of forcing her to live a shamed life she might still be alive.* However, before Leela could consider her regret further, Uma continued to translate the earlier conversation to Leela.

Uma told Leela that Alice wanted to know the truth of what really happened. She wanted to know why Charu was apologising for something her entire family were denying. Uma told Leela that Alice felt that Vijay's story no longer made sense to her and was desperate to find out the truth. Leela understood why both Uma and Alice were so upset when they talked to each other. Uma relived once again her ordeal, and Alice was discovering that she too was a pawn in Vijay's game.
"Alice said that Vijay told her that I was trying to trap him because he wanted to leave me," Uma told Leela. "She told me how she should have

left him tied naked to a chair. I don't understand what she meant by that but she apologised for giving Vijay a false alibi. She then asked if she could make amends for her mistake."
"She was about to give away the entire game," Amrita interjected. "At this point Uma was about to tell Alice about our plan to ruin them all. So I interrupted and told her to help us to find solid proof against the Rathod family. I told her to go home and find evidence for us that we could use against them."
"I don't understand why you did that," Uma told Amrita. "The police are useless they won't do anything."

"I know, but we did not know how much we can trust the woman. She might be a spy."
"I doubt she's a spy," Vikram said. "Her emotions seemed genuine to me."
"Anyway," Amrita dismissed her husband's comment. "I told her we could use Charu's suicide note as evidence, but we needed more proof. I told her to go back to Rathod Haveli and search for proof when people are busy. I have no intention of going to the police. I just need to be sure she's on our side."

Now two days later, Alice was back. Leela saw the front door to Amrita's house open. Amrita walked out towards where Leela and Alice were stood. Leela stood in silence again as Amrita and Alice conversed in English. She did not know enough to understand the full conversation. However, she concentrated very hard to try and decipher some elements.

Alice pointed towards the gate a few times. Leela assumed someone must be outside. Whilst pointing to the gate Alice also said the first word Leela understood. *She said help which means sahaiyko. She has brought someone to help us who is waiting outside maybe?*

Alice walked over to the gate to call someone else inside. She walked back inside with an Indian man.

Chapter 96: Alice

Alice brought in the man she bumped into on her way to Amrita's house.

During Charu's funeral ceremony, Alice rummaged through Vijay and Madhu's room for any evidence she could find. She was about to search Jigar's room when Suneeti informed her that everyone was back. Feeling she still had enough evidence, Alice told Suneeti to make excuses for her absence if Vijay asked where she was. She also informed Suneeti that she was going to Amrita's house to give them everything she found so far, just in case she lost everything. When she was a few streets away she was stopped by a man. Alice felt a jolt in her heart, which began to beat very fast. *Shit, I've been caught.* However, when she looked up at the person who stopped her she felt slightly confused. *What the hell is he doing here?* As her heart beat began to return to normal she remembered meeting the same reporter in Mumbai when she was shopping at a market with Fatima. Despite not asking the reporter any questions, he quickly began to tell Alice about his life.

Alice listened to Madhusudan inform her how he moved back home after completing his course. He thanked Alice for her involvement in his coursework documentary which got him a distinction, and as a result of the distinction he secured work experience with a Gujarati news channel. Alice smiled politely at the reporter but desperately wanted to get away. *Why do I care about all this? I did your documentary because you accosted me. I wanted to get away then, and I want to get away now. How should I get away without sounding rude?*

Alice was about to cut him off when he mentioned something which captured her attention.

"I am hoping to source a juicy, dramatic news story. If I get a very good one, I might secure a permanent job at the news channel."

Alice felt a light turn on inside her head. *There are so many reports in the papers about corruption. The media helps to bring justice to people. Madhusudan can help Uma along with the evidence I have.*

"Of course the local channel isn't my ultimate dream. One day I want to

work for ABP news and then maybe even BBC news but…"
"Madhusudan," Alice interrupted, appearing interested all of a sudden. Surprised by the change in Alice's demeanour, Madhusudan stopped talking.
"I have the perfect story for you. I can help you get that juicy headline if you follow me."
He got excited and started to prance around at the prospect of a news story. Alice walked him over to the Oberoi House and made him wait outside until she spoke to Uma.

As Amrita had approved of Madhusudan, Alice bought him in and introduced him.
"I'd like to introduce you all to Madhusudan," she said as she brought the man in with her. "He works for a Gujarati news channel. If the police won't help you to get justice, the media will. With his help we can expose the Rathods and the corrupt police."
"Police? Corruption?" Madhusudan's eyes lit up. "What corruption?"
"When I worked at the hotel we used to get newspapers in English for our guests. I used to read these and I read a number of news stories," Alice ignored Madhusudan's question. "A lot of these stories highlight the role the media played to help people get justice. The media create such a stir that closed cases have been reopened and investigated by other police teams."
"We do not want the police's help," Amrita snapped bitterly. "They're all the same! Bloody police."
"But in the public eye, the police cannot sabotage the investigation," Vikram's said excitedly. "They will be forced to conduct a proper investigation."
"We already tried the police. It turned out exactly as I said it would. What is wrong with what we have been doing so far? Everything has gone to plan."
"Not everything went to plan," Vikram interrupted. Amrita looked at him fiercely. "Let us not argue again about this and let Uma decide. This is her battle after all."

Everyone in the courtyard looked towards Uma. Uma looked towards Leela, who never spoke. Leela nodded her approval and Uma faced Alice.

"Charu's death opened my eyes. There are consequences to my actions," Uma paused. With her back to Amrita she spoke to Alice about her. "Amritaji has done so much for me and I am very grateful, without her help I wouldn't be where I am today, but I think we should try the media route."
"I was right when I said the police wouldn't do anything," Amrita snapped. "When this goes wrong, don't say I didn't warn you." Amrita stormed into her house leaving everyone else still standing in the courtyard.
"So I understand that I am helping you with something?" Madhusudan smiled breaking the awkward silence caused by Amrita's hasty exit. Uma looked at Vikram, who like Leela gave her a nod of support. Uma nodded at Madhusudan.
"Yes! If you can," Uma said.
"Tell me everything," he smiled. He opened his bag and took out a pen and a note book.

Uma started to tell Madhusudan her story. Alice had no desire to hear about Vijay's evil actions again. She distanced herself from the rest of the group as Uma narrated her story. She walked towards a wall and focused her thoughts on the artwork painted onto it. Once Alice realised that Uma had finished, she returned her attention to the situation in front of her. Uma had tears rolling down her eyes. Even Madhusudan looked very troubled, his eyes were slightly wet.
"What evidence do you have to support your story?" Madhusudan sniffed.
"I gathered a few things." Alice began to open her handbag and pulled the proof she stuffed inside. "Amrita told me to look for some things and these are the things that I found." Alice picked up the first bundle. "Bank statements," she told Madhusudan. "Uma told me about the payments her family made to Vijay's family. Whilst most of the money was cash payments, there were two payments that her mother made directly to Madhu's bank account. The bank statement supports this."
"If I ask my mother, we might be able to see the money she withdrew as well. My mother is also the type of woman to keep receipts. She will have kept everything."

One by one Alice presented the evidence she brought with her. Every now and then Madhusudan gasped dramatically. Uma and Vikram interrupted occasionally to add their thoughts onto the evidence Alice was presenting. Leela sat in silence. By the time Alice got to present her final piece of evidence, Amrita had rejoined the group outside. Despite hating Vijay, Alice felt her heart wrench as she held the final piece of proof she collected. She paused and looked at Uma. Alice knew that the document would shatter Uma again, just as it had left her feeling distraught. *Oh god there is no way to soften the blow.* She paused for a few moments.

"I found these two certificates," She handed over the marriage certificates to Madhusudan.

"Two marriage certificates?" he asked looking confused.

Alice closed her eyes. *I have to do it now.* Alice hoped that Uma would not hear what she was going to say. She looked at Uma and saw that her gaze was entirely focused onto what Alice was showing. She took a deep breath.

"One is Vijay's marriage certificate to Uma," Alice exhaled deeply before resuming. "The other is a certificate for his marriage to Siya."

Just as Alice imagined, Uma stood up looking confused.

"Siya? Siya is his wife? What are you talking about?"

"From this marriage certificate it seems as though Siya is his first wife."

"What?" everyone in the room said in unison. The maid looked confused and also stood up to see what was happening.

"Vijay's?" Uma asked flabbergasted. "Vijay doesn't have..."

Uma walked over to Madhusudan and grabbed the wedding certificates out of his hands. Alice could see the pain in Uma's eyes. *I felt exactly the same thing as you when I discovered his marriage certificates. He was married to someone else when I met him, and then he married you. We both know he's a lying dickhead but we both feel so distraught at the thought of another woman.*

"How come I didn't know about this woman?" Uma asked.

"I knew about her," Alice said. "Vijay convinced me you WERE Siya."

Alice looked at Uma who looked at her disbelievingly. Desperate to break the silence she continued to talk. "He obviously never got divorced and lied to remarry. Look at your marriage certificate. You are listed as a spinster and he is a bachelor. Not a divorcee or widower. He is a

bachelor on both certificates."
Alice saw Uma's eyes fill with tears once again.
I don't know why we both do this; why are we always shocked by his actions and then feel so much pain each time we discover more of his lies. We both know what a scumbag he is, why do we both still feel so much pain over it? Every time I think nothing he does will surprise me anymore I am proved wrong. I thought I'd stop caring but each time I discover more deception I feel pain worse than the last time. When will I get over this and stop being such a fool? When will WE get over this bastard and stop being so stupid? We're both idiots if we still get hurt by him. Alice recollected her thoughts and returned to the situation in front of her.
"The wedding certificate has Siya's home address on it. If we go to Ahmedabad, I'm sure we can find more evidence. I doubt you were the first woman they extorted for money." Eager to change the topic away from Vijay's other wife, Alice quickly presented the other piece of evidence they had. "And here is Charu's suicide note."
"Oooh once we've done a report on your story we can do another report on Siya's family. We can grip the nation with the story as we bring forward more elements to this heinous crime. We can unmask them one by one." Madhusudan paused. "There is one more thing we need to make this story sensational. We need a spectacle. I want you to ignite a bomb that will make the women of this village, state and country come out in arms to support you. The bigger the drama, the bigger the headline. If all of the women of Madhapar unite to punish them then we will have better scenes for the news."
"Which women will support you?" Amrita asked bitterly. "Did Purbai or anyone come forward to support you last time? No one even gave a testimony in your favour." Amrita stood up and walked over to where Uma was stood. "Umaji please think this through. Once you go to the media there will be no going back. Right now we have an advantage. The enemy thinks we have given up and they think we've lost. If we go to the media they might discover we haven't given up and might make things harder for us. I don't want you to spend weeks on this silly media stunt, only to return to where we were a few weeks ago. I've been there, I..." Amrita stopped. Her eyes were filled with tears. "That's all I want to say to you. Think about it. I'm going to see how the curry is brewing."
Alice looked at Vikram who immediately looked away from her. *Are you*

a dickhead as well; pretending to be decent?
"I help to drama," Alice heard Leela say in broken English making an explosion action with her hands.
This was the first time Alice heard Leela attempt to speak English. She knew that Leela was volunteering to help create the spectacle.

Chapter 97: Madhu

Madhu shut her bedroom door and turned the key locking it behind her. She was holding the sword which she grabbed from Vijay's room. She took out the sword, traditionally carried by the grooms on his wedding day, from its case. *I might need it for my safety. What if these people manage to get into my house?* She paced around her room for a bit and eventually sat down on her bed. Sweating heavily and panting for breath, she feared for her safety. Madhu spent the past fifteen minutes running around her house, as quickly as she could, locking all the doors and windows. Anything that could be used as an entrance into her home, she sealed shut. Now she sat on her bed listening to the chants coming from outside her house.
"Madhu Rathod Haai Haai. Jigar Rathod Haai Haai, Vijay Rathod Haai Haai, Rathod Kutumb mudrabad mudrabad"
Hai Bhagwan! Why are these jungali people outside my house? It has not even been a week since I cremated my Charu and these heartless demons are here to torture us. Madhu stood up and looked out of her window to see a bunch of protestors stood outside her house chanting. They were mostly women but there were also a number of men. Madhu noticed a person filming the protest. *This is nothing. The people of Ahmedabad knew how to protest. Whenever they had virodh rallies they were much more organised and powerful than this handful of peasants. Hai Bhagwan, please send Jigar home soon. A few beatings with a policeman's stick will sort them out.* Despite her confidence that the protests were minor; Madhu still sealed herself in her home for her own safety.

Madhu felt her mobile vibrate. She put the sword down on her bed and took out her phone. Her brother was ringing her. Relieved to have a loved one to talk to, she picked up the phone.
"Jai Shree Krishna Ravi, How are you?"
"Motaben, have you seen the news?" her brother asked quickly.
"No," Madhu said slightly worried. She instinctively reached for the television remote to turn on the television. "Is there a storm coming?" *I*

hope it's a storm, maybe it will blow the virodh rally away.
"No. Your family is on the news," he said.
Madhu remembered that a man was filming the handful of protestors outside her house. She froze in response to what her brother said, forgetting about the remote control in her hand.
"What? Why?"
"Just watch the news."
Madhu remembered she had the remote control in her hand and turned the television on and changed the channel over to ABP News.
"There is nothing on ABP News."
"Put it on the Gujarati news channel."

Madhu changed the channel a few times and found the channel her brother was talking about. She watched the news with her eyes wide open in shock. *This is why those jungalis are outside my house.* Madhu could hear her brother talking but her entire concentration was on the news story she was watching on TV. The news story was destroying her family name and ripping it into shreds. Madhu saw the reporter narrate how Uma had been extorted for a dowry by the family of influential politicians Subodh and Harshad Rathod. They highlighted the abuse inflicted onto her by reputed businessman Vijay Rathod and his mother. The news channel showed a reporter interviewing Uma. She described her ordeal in great detail implicating her entire family. Madhu felt her blood boil when the ox described the role Charu played in her abuse. *That witch won't even leave my beti's memory in peace? How dare she taint my Charu's name! My beti is innocent, she didn't do anything and yet this witch is maligning my Charu.* Madhu watched as Uma described how the police force was also involved. She told the reporter how the police falsely implicated her brother in a crime he had not committed. She was coerced into withdrawing her complaint in exchange for her brother's freedom.

"We have a witness here with us right now, who has witnessed, first hand, the atrocities Uma's in-laws inflicted onto her," The reporter with the high pitched voice broadcasted. "Purbai Rabadia is a witness to everything that happened."
That gossiping bitch! I always knew you were a liability, but I never

thought you would put a knife in my back. Just you wait. I will get Jigar to sort you... Hai Bhagwan, the police is implicated too. How will I sort everything out this time? Madhu watched the news report fluctuating between rage and worry. Purbai revealed how she saw Madhu verbally taunt Uma and on some occasions Madhu even locked Uma outside her home and made her sleep in the rain. Purbai even divulged how she overheard Uma yelling in pain describing her rape to her mother-in-law. "The protests in Madhapar are spreading," the high pitched reporter said. "I am informed that a women's rights NGO has started their own protest outside the police station. We will be showing you a report from there in a few moments."

Madhu became increasingly distressed at the report from outside the police station and turned the TV off. She began to pace around her bedroom panicking, thinking about how she could save her family from their impending doom. Madhu recalled the time the media discovered her husband and father-in-law's involvement in accepting bribes. They both used their charisma and PR people to resolve the matter. They claimed the false allegations were a ruse by the opposition to malign their name in a dirty attempt to win votes. *Hai Bhagwan, where can I get PR people to help me out of here? Maybe we can claim that Vijay's hotel rivals are trying to ruin our reputation.* Madhu picked up her mobile phone and attempted to contact her sons. She tried their numbers a few times but did not succeed in getting through. Madhu became extremely worried for her sons' safety. *Hai Bhagwan, what if something has happened to them? What if this news has instigated people into attacking my sons? My sons might be lying in hospital or in a ditch and no one would care, because this report has made them out to be demons.*

Horrible images of her injured sons began to flash through Madhu's mind, further fuelling her tension. *What if my sons are... Hai Bhagwan I will not think such inauspicious things. They will not have met the same fate as Charu.* However, as the images in her mind became more graphic and the lack of news from her son, Madhu convinced herself that something had happened to her sons. Once again she was sobbing. *I have not cried so much since the day I saved Charu from being aborted. Since the Lakshmi of our home has left my life, we've been plagued with difficulties.*

Madhu heard the crowd chanting louder and walked over to a window which faced the front of her house. She saw Jigar coming out of his car to disperse the crowd outside their home.
"That is Jigar Rathod everyone," Madhu realised the voice belonged to Charu's friend Suneeti. *Why would Suneeti do such a thing?* Before Madhu could contemplate Suneeti's actions further she saw the crowd turn on Jigar.
"You think you can abuse your power as a policeman and treat women like dirt?" one of the women shouted.
Madhu saw Jigar mouth something to the crowd as he looked terrified.
"BEAT HIM!" another protestor shouted.
Madhu witnessed the crowd pounce on Jigar. *Hai Bhagwan, I need to save my son. They might kill him.* She grabbed the sword on her bed and unlocked the door to her bedroom. Having witnessed her son's life in peril, Madhu no longer feared for her own safety. She ran as fast as she could to the front door and unbolted it before opening it.

Jigar was screaming with a high pitch, as a pack of women beat him with their sandals. Some of the men heartlessly kicked her son. *I have to save him.*
"EH," Madhu shouted at the top of her voice. Hearing Madhu's voice calmed down the crowd for a moment.
"It's Madhu Rathod, Uma's mother-in-law," Suneeti shouted.
The crowd began to move towards Madhu.
"TAKE ANOTHER STEP AND I WILL SLICE YOU UP," Madhu shouted at the protestors as she waved the sword. "Jigar beta, quick come inside."
"Stop him," a male protestor said.
Madhu stepped forward with the sword in her hand. Some of the protestors took a step back. "If anyone tries to stop me or my son from going inside I'll cut their hand off. Jigar, quickly."
Madhu watched as the protest rally stepped back and allowed Jigar to walk over. Jigar gasped in pain as he stood up. He slowly hobbled over to where Madhu was.
"Get inside beta." Madhu walked backwards into her house.
"We're not going to go away Madhu Aunty," Suneeti said.

Without responding she shut the door and locked her house again.

Out of breath, she turned around to see Jigar lying on the floor bloody and bruised. *What have these animals done to my son? Hai Bhagwan where is Vijay? What if they have done the same thing to him as they have done to my Jigar?* Madhu walked over to the part of the living room where they had their shrine. With shaking hands she put ghee into a diva holder and managed to light the lamp. She fell to her knees and began to pray for her son's safety. *Hai Bhagwan, Please bring Vijay back to me safely. Don't let me become the unfortunate mother who had eight children, but lost them all.*

Chapter 98: Uma

Eleven months ago, with the help of Madhusudan, Uma exposed the Rathods. As the family were relatives of famous politicians, the news report sent shockwaves all over India and her case was fast tracked in court to calm a nation screaming for justice. Madhu, Jigar and Vijay's trial started over a month ago and the day of the judge's verdict had finally arrived. Uma felt butterflies in her stomach as she stood outside facing the court. Amongst the many news teams, Uma spotted Madhusudan's team. She felt a rush of affection towards the reporter who had helped her to get to where she was. Without his help, her complaint would never have reached court. The corrupt police force would have suppressed the case making it almost impossible for her to find justice. Uma smiled as she watched Madhusudan briefing his team of reporters. The story he sourced meant that his position at the Gujarati news channel. He was promoted and became a permanent member of staff. *Hai Mata Rani, keep showering him with your blessings. He deserves all the happiness he gets.*

Before coming to court that morning, Uma had visited the Durga temple to pray. She wanted to go alone and thus all of her family and friends were already inside. *Today those demons will finally be punished for what they did to me.* Uma refocused her gaze on the court and took a step towards the building. With each step she took, she remembered the day she entered Rathod Haveli as a new bride. *I tipped a pot of rice with my toe to signify the entry of goddess Lakshmi into your home. You treated me like an ATM machine rather than a goddess. I left red footprints on your white marble floor to symbolise the entry of good fortune.* Uma looked back and saw the footprints her flip flops were leaving in the sand. *With each step I take towards the court I am taking a step closer to your destruction. The footprints I am leaving in the sand symbolises how your name will be mud after today.*

Uma made her way to courtroom one and saw the entire court already assembled. The defence and prosecution barristers, both women, were sat in the front. Jigar, Madhu and Vijay were stood in the dock. The family, friends and public were all sat in court. Everyone was waiting for the judge to come and deliver his verdict. As Uma entered the courtroom she noticed Madhu was looking towards her. They both made eye contact and Uma recalled Madhu's testimony in court.

With all the media coverage, Madhu had realised that Uma would get justice one way or another. Uma was shocked when Madhu pleaded guilty and accepted her crimes.
"In our society, a widow has nothing. The male relatives control everything. Before my husband died he transferred everything into the names of my two sons. I didn't want to end up in a widow's ashram. I used Uma and Siya as scapegoats to get money."
Listening to Madhu's testimony initially caused Uma to feel a strange emotion. She could not feel sympathy for the woman who tortured her, but she empathised with Madhu. However the understanding was short lived.
"My sons had no idea about anything," Madhu told the Judge. "I did everything without their knowledge."
Any understanding Uma felt vanished as she watched Madhu attempt to take full responsibility for everything, and acquit her sons of their crimes. Her blood boiled as she watched Vijay and Jigar deny having any involvement. All three of their testimonies matched and there were no flaws. It became quickly evident that the Rathod family planned on pinning everything onto Madhu.

Uma looked away from Madhu and saw that there was an empty space for her to sit next to Leela, Vikram and Amrita. As she walked towards them her eyes shifted towards the group of people sat on her left. It was her family. Her father, mother, Gauri, Arjun and Arjun's wife Priya looked at Uma as she walked in. She remembered her mother's court testimony.

Initially Uma was surprised to find her entire family come to support her. *Why do they want to support me now?* Her anger towards her family transformed into guilt as she shifted uncomfortably in her seat, listening to her mother's evidence. Uma's listened as her mother relived the struggle she went through to collect the dowry money. She told the court about her sleepless nights and the deterioration of her health. *Hai*

Mata Rani I said such nasty things to maa when she came to pick me up. I didn't mean any of those things I said. I just wanted her to feel the pain I felt when I was disowned by them. I wanted her feel the pain I felt when I thought they didn't care about me. The reality is maa never stopped caring, even after I was married she went through all those difficulties for me. They never abandoned me. Shame on you Uma! Sharam kar. I should fall at maa's feet and apologise for my shameful behaviour.

The evidence provided by Uma's mother was strong until the defence barrister cross examined her.

"I paid everything Madhu asked me to pay," her mother wept. "They had my beti. I did not want them to do anything to her."

"Avantikaji," the defence barrister said. "You paid everything Madhu asked you to pay?"

"Yes."

"So Mrs Madhu Rathod was the only one who made any requests to you?"

"Madhu asked, but Vijay..."

"Avantikaji I asked you a simple yes or no question," she snapped. "Was it only Madhuji who made demands from you?"

"Yes..." her mother responded quietly.

"My lord, Avantikaji accepts that my clients Jigar and Vijay never asked her for any money. Madhuji has already accepted her crimes. This case should be as clear as glass. Vijay and Jigar were not involved. They are being falsely trapped in a crime they did not commit because of the pressure caused by the media."

Uma sighed with disappointment when the defence barrister had found nothing from Avantika's testimony.

Uma looked away from her parents and looked at the family sat on her right. Siya's family had also come to hear the verdict.

There was now a national search for Siya. The Rathod family had denied having anything to do with Siya's disappearance and there was no solid evidence against them. Siya got lost at the Kumbh Mela and was never found again. When Siya's parents were first found they were hostile towards Uma. They felt Uma had taken their daughter's position and as a result the Rathod family did not care to find her. However, when they discovered that Vijay and Uma were dating months before Siya vanished, and that Uma had no idea about Siya until recently they directed their anger towards the Rathod family. Siya's family had also given testimonies, but the defence barrister had applied their testimonies to only Madhu as well. Siya's parents told the court that Madhu made all the demands and that Siya always spoke very highly of Vijay. Their daughter would never hear a bad word against her husband and as a result their evidence only incriminated Madhu. The prosecution barrister however, highlighted the fact that Vijay was already dating another two women whilst married to Siya. The defence barrister objected and said a man having extra marital affairs did not indicate he was abusing his wife. However the prosecution exclaimed that Indian law only allowed a man to remarry if his spouse had been absent for seven years. Siya has been missing for less than a year when he remarried. She also declared that Indian law stated if a man remarries after his spouse has been missing for seven years he is legally obliged to tell his new wife of the situation. Vijay has broken the law on both counts and is therefore could face imprisonment and a fine.

Uma began to walk towards Amrita, Leela and Vikram when she saw Purbai. Purbai was another person who testified in Uma's favour. Before the story hit the media, they visited Purbai's house once more. Kesar, Purbai's daughter-in-law refused to support them again. However Madhusudan emotionally blackmailed them.
"I think we could add an interesting slant to our report," Madhusudan said as he made a note. "When this hits the news channel and becomes a big story, we can highlight how the neighbours who knew so much didn't get involved because they wanted an easy life."
These words immediately changed Kesar's attitude. Once the Rabadia family knew that they had nothing to lose and everything to gain, they joined Uma's fight for justice. In the witness box, Purbai retold the judge everything she had witnessed and heard. She informed the judge how she heard Madhu verbally abused Uma and had witnessed her being forced to sleep outdoors.
"I know the other family members are involved as well," Purbai told the court.
"Did you ever see Jigar or Vijay misbehave with Uma?"
"No, but..."

"There you are my lord," the defence barrister interrupted. "Purbai never saw Jigar or Vijay assault Uma. She is basing her testimony on hearsay."
"I heard a few conversations between..."
"Conversations which could have been staged for Purbai's benefit. It is not solid proof my lord."
"When they locked Uma out of the house, Jigar and Charu were both there. They must have been involved..."
"Must have?" the defence barrister smiled. "Purbai this court believes in evidence. Eye witnesses and not assumptions. Unless you actually saw Vijay or Jigar physically torture Uma, please make it known now. If you did not see any of them torture her please leave the stand. I have no more questions."
Purbai failed to give examples of physical or mental torture inflicted onto Uma by Jigar or Vijay. However, she was able to recount many examples of Madhu's involvement.
Once Purbai left the stand the defence barrister exclaimed "Your Honour, no one has seen Vijay or Jigar torture Uma, no one has said they asked for any money from Uma. The fact is becoming clearer that Madhuji and only Madhuji was responsible for everything that happened to Siya and Uma."

Uma continued walking towards her seat when she spotted Alice, another witness. The defence barrister attempted to claim that Alice's testimony proved Vijay's innocence as he spent most of his time in Mumbai. However, the prosecution cleverly established that Alice's testimony matched Uma's. Uma said Vijay abused her after the exposure of his affair with Alice. Alice testified Vijay went home after the exposure. Consequentially, the defence's attempt to use Alice to prove Vijay's innocence failed.

In the early days Uma felt dejected by the way the trial was shaping. Many eye witnesses were able to prove that Madhu had been involved in abusing Uma. The only thing they seemed to be able to find on Vijay appeared to be unlawfully marrying Uma, whilst being married to Siya. Despite Uma's despair; Leela, Amrita and Vikram felt confident. The trial turned when Leela took the stand.

Leela was the first witness whose testimony implicated Jigar. She described Madhu's barbaric methods of starving Uma. She also reported witnessing Jigar, Charu and Madhu abusing Uma. Leela even informed the court about over hearing Jigar's boasts about bending the law. Once Leela gave her testimony, Arjun testified about his false imprisonment, and he was quickly followed by the maid Jigar bribed to lie about Arjun. The three testimonies back to back wiped the smile off Jigar and Madhu's face. Uma felt a flicker of hope again. She could see Jigar sweating like a dog trying to find ways to evade justice.

Uma looked at Jigar who was stood in the dock. Like his brother, he had lost his attractive looks caused by the stress of the trial. She smiled with joy as she recollected Jigar taking the witness stand. He maintained his flawless story to start with. Once the prosecution questioned him about the evidence presented about Arjun's false charges, Jigar cracked. He perspired and shook when he realised there was no escape for him. The prosecution told him he had violated his authority as a policeman. In a desperate attempt to avoid the blame, Jigar unintentionally implicated his colleagues.
"I filed a false complaint against Arjun because I did not want mumma to go to prison. If mumma went to prison, then Charu's wedding would have been called off. My colleagues suggested an idea to me. I went along with their plan because I was blinded by the desire to save my sister's honour."
"So you're admitting your police colleagues were involved in corrupt activities?"
Jigar stopped speaking when the prosecution asked this question. He realised in an attempt to save himself, he had implicated everyone he worked with. With a panic stricken face he looked at his mother and brother. Uma was satisfied to see that for the first time, Vijay expressed fear in his eyes. She knew he was worried that he may be implicated of more than just bigamy.

Vijay took the stand after his brother. With his elaborately planned story he detailed his desperate and futile search for Siya with crocodile tears in his eyes. He claimed he was unaware of the law that stated he was not allowed to marry within seven years. He denied Uma's rape and abuse claims. The prosecution barrister shrewdly tricked Vijay into confessing that he met Uma before Siya went missing. When Vijay realised his error he spluttered and attempted to back track but the prosecution barrister told him she had no more questions leaving Vijay standing in the dock with a red face.

After what seemed like a long walk, Uma sat down in the seat next to Leela.
"I thought you were going to be late," Amrita said to Uma.
"I went to mandir before coming here. There wasn't a rickshaw so I walked here." Uma smiled and looked at the empty judge's seat. *Soon I will know if I am going to get justice or if they will walk free.*

As Uma waited for the judge to come she recalled her own testimony. She relived her ordeal in court when she had taken the stand. The prosecution barrister asked her story and sympathetically got her to explain everything. The experience of telling her story in front of a court room was horrific for Uma. The months of hiding everything from everyone to save herself from shame was over. There was no escaping telling the world what happened to her. Uma did not know that the defence's cross examination would be worse than narrating the ordeal the first time. She had to justify her story to someone who did not believe her. Uma had to go through the embarrassment of going through each and every detail of Vijay raping her for the world to listen to. In front of a courtroom she was forced to show the judge where her husband touched her and how he touched her. She had to answer questions about how much she enjoyed sex with her husband before the affair. Once she went through the humiliation of answering all the private questions, the defence attempted to dismiss Uma by saying that's just how husband's show affection to their wives. At this point Uma felt Kaalratri awake inside her once more. She was ready for the final question.
"So your husband did everything to you when you were married and you enjoyed it. Why did it become rape?"
"When I loved him we made love. I enjoyed the... acts... SEX. I've talked so much about my personal life in this court, I shouldn't be ashamed to

say the word. So, Sex. Yes I enjoyed sex with my husband. I was allowed to enjoy sex with my husband. Why should I not be allowed to enjoy it? I was allowed to enjoy it just as much as he was allowed to enjoy it. Do you think women are just there to be enjoyed by men? We are allowed to enjoy it. At the same time if I don't want to do it, I am allowed to say no. When I say no, the act I may have enjoyed is not the same. It becomes an act to control someone and humiliate them. You have never been raped otherwise you would never ask me the difference between rape and sex. When I found out about his lies, I lost all respect for him. I didn't want to give my body to someone I had no respect for. He wanted to retain his power and control over me so he raped me. We were equals when we had sex. I was lower than low when he raped me. Another thing, you asked me if I dressed provocatively and behaved in a certain manner before I changed my mind. I thought at the time, was it the way I dressed? Was it the way I acted? Now I know that it doesn't matter if I was naked in front of my husband. If I didn't want to have sex it was my right to say no. It's not my fault. It's his fault. Instead of questioning me in this humiliating way, why don't you question what went through his mind? Question him if there was any difference in the circumstances. Question him why he couldn't control himself. Do you have any more questions for me, or are you done treating me like my husband's property?"
The defence barrister dismissed her and said she had no more questions, but Uma's testimony created a buzz amongst the spectators at court. She knew she had sealed the mouths of anyone who claimed a husband cannot rape his wife.

Uma heard the court attendant announce the judge was coming. Uma's heart began to pound. The man who was going to deliver the verdict was going to arrive. *Hai Mata Rani, will I get justice or will they escape?*

Chapter 99: Madhu

Madhu looked at herself using a mirror in the bathroom. The elaborately embroidered saris she usually wore had been ditched for a simple white sari with a blue border. The cheap sari felt rough on her skin as she was accustomed to wearing clothing of a higher standard. *These prisoner saris look exactly like widow saris but with some blue.* She was also stripped of the jewellery she adorned her body with. Madhu closed her eyes and exhaled deeply at the sight of her face in the mirror. She had never seen herself looking so tired and old. *I finally look how a widow should look. I tried so hard to avoid this but it finally caught up with me.*
"Eh Maharani are you going to make us wait all day?"
Madhu stopped looking at her reflection and turned to the pug faced prison guard who just taunted her. Madhu looked at her angrily. *Who does this kutri think she is? No one has spoken to me with such disrespect since I took control of my own life.*
The pug faced prison officer stormed towards Madhu and slapped her in the face. Madhu, shocked to have been slapped out of the blue, gasped and rubbed her cheek.
"What were you looking at?" The prison guard asked venomously. "If you ogle at me again with your big eyes I'll scratch them out. Now move." The prison guard shoved Madhu. "I don't have all day to deal with maharanis."

The prison guard grabbed Madhu's hand, causing her to gasp in pain again. She had grabbed her hand with such force that Madhu felt as though she was being dragged by the prison officer. She looked at the other prison officer to her left hand side. She was not as rough as the pug faced prison guard but Madhu thought she still looked scary. Together the prison guards escorted Madhu to her prison cell. She looked around the prison and saw nothing but walls that seemed to be grey. The walls were actually white but due to small windows and very little light, they looked grey. The prison was covered in cage like bars and many women stood at the sides watching Madhu, as she was escorted to her cell. *This is going to be my home for the near future. I am going to be living and dining with criminals and other low people. Murderers and thieves will be the only people I have for company. Hai Bhagwan where have you brought me?* Madhu looked around and saw the other female prisoners looking at her with interest. She felt discomfort at the way they looked at her.

Once they reached her cell, the nicer prison guard unlocked the door and moved to the side.

"Welcome to your mansion," the pug faced officer laughed. "If you want we can rename this cell Rathod Haveli?"

Both prison officers laughed at pug face's joke. Madhu stared at both prison officers, her blood boiling with anger at her mockery. The pug faced officer stopped laughing when she saw Madhu staring at her. She launched forwards and grabbed Madhu by the hair. She shrieked with pain.

"Eh Maharani! What did I tell you about staring at me? This isn't your mansion. I run this place and it will be in your benefit to understand that." Pug face let go of Madhu and shouted "SHAMLA... this maharani is too arrogant for this place. Starve her tonight. Maybe if she misses a meal we will see an improvement in her attitude." She turned to face Madhu "Now get inside before I ban you from eating all week." The pug faced officer pushed her into her cell. "I don't want any kech kech from you do you understand? If I hear a squeak from you, then you will miss out on tomorrow's dinner as well."

Madhu heard the door close on her. She could hear the two prison guards walk away laughing. As the sound of their laughter faded, she began to absorb her new surroundings. She was engulfed by darkness as there was almost no natural light coming into her cell. There were three beds in the room. One bed looked freshly made. *That must be my bed.* Madhu walked over to the bed and put her belongings on the bed. She felt her stomach rumble. Due to nerves, she had not eaten anything prior to her court hearing earlier that day. Madhu thought about her mother's paratha and which made her mouth water. Thinking of her mother reminded Madhu of something her mother used to always tell her. *What you shall sow, you shall reap. If you plant bitter neem then you won't harvest mangoes. I starved Uma whenever I wanted to. Now these people will starve me here. Hai Bhagwan! Are my sons going through the same thing? I will take the fruit of their bad karma on to my own head and suffer the consequences. Bhagwan protect my sons and make sure they do not go through what I am going through. It is not their fault! This is all my doing. They did nothing. This punishment is a result of the mistakes I made.*

When Vijay was born, I thanked god for finally blessing me with a son. My Vijay acted as a balm who helped me to forget the pain of the four betis I lost. From the moment I held him in my arms and he smiled at me, I fell in love with him. That moment I promised him that I will fulfil all of his desires. I told my Vijay that he will have everything handed to him on a golden plate. From that moment on Madhu fulfilled every single need and desire of all three of her children. Vijay was three years old, when Madhu went to great lengths to fulfil one of his unreasonable demands. Vijay demanded that Madhu bring him the shiny ball from the sky so he could play with it. Madhu tried explaining to her son that it was impossible to bring the moon down, which resulted in Vijay throwing a tantrum. Madhu, reluctant to fail her son's first desire, desperately attempted to seek a way to fulfil his desire. Eventually whilst watching Ramayan she saw Ram's parents show Ram a reflection of the moon in a plate of water. She filled a plate with water and allowed her son to splash around in it. *If I disciplined my son that day for his tantrum and curbed his desires then maybe I would not be here today.*

When Vijay was thirteen he wanted a pet dog. Madhu hated animals and refused to allow a dog into the house. Vijay's tantrums at not getting what he wanted got worse but Madhu still did not give in. Then Vijay locked himself into a room and threatened to kill himself. When Harshad managed to get the bedroom door open, Vijay was stood on his bed, with a scarf around his neck. The scarf was also tied around the ceiling fan. Terrified that her son had been about to kill himself, Madhu gave in and they got Monty for their son. *When I asked Vijay how he knew about hanging himself, he responded by telling me that he saw it on TV. I was terrified that my son knew how to do such things and would actually kill himself. Controlled by my fears, I never realised something from that day until now. He was stood on a bed and not on a chair. There is no way he could have killed himself. He knew how to play me and I*

was easily manipulated.
As Vijay got older, his desires also grew. Once he opened his hotels, he was constantly asking for money. It was too late when Madhu realised that her son had developed a gambling addiction and was spending all of his money on women, gambling and drinking. *If I asked him what the money was for then perhaps I could have helped him before his addiction got out of hand. Instead I gave him whatever he wanted, without asking questions.*
After Harshad's death, Vijay accumulated so much debt that the family was about to be declared bankrupt. They had no money to repay the people they owed money to. That was when Madhu started to request money from Siya's parents. The money they got from Siya's parents was used to resettle their affairs and prevent them from going bankrupt. Despite paying the debt collectors off and rescuing her son's businesses; Madhu continued to extract dowry money from Siya's parents. Vijay spent the money he earned through his hotels how he wanted. When Madhu had asked her son to control his expenditure and support his family, Vijay responded by telling her that he earns the money and he would spend his money how he wanted to. A lack of money to run her house and support Charu's education meant Madhu once again resorted to extracting money from Siya's parents. When this source of income dried up, Madhu once again told her son to support his family. However, her son had simply told her to get rid of Siya and find a new wife who would give him a child and her money. Madhu initially tried to convince her son to keep his wife but when he threatened to commit suicide if she did not get rid of Siya, Madhu picked her son's happiness over Siya. Once Siya was disposed of it was only too easy to trap another girl into fulfilling dowry demands.

Madhu fell onto the prison floor and lamented. *If I had realised my children manipulated me and if I curbed my children's unreasonable demands, and disciplined them, then perhaps my children would not have suffered the way they have. If I had instilled morals into my children instead of teaching them how to get what they wanted, perhaps they would not be rotting away in prison like me. Hai Bhagwan, please don't let Vijay and Jigar suffer due to my actions.*

Chapter 100: Alice

Alice sat on a bench inside the prison, waiting for Vijay. The prison smelt slightly musty, the walls built of dark stone. There was no natural light where they were. *It's a shame he's only in here for seven years. This place is built for rats like him.* Alice heard footsteps coming towards her. *He's coming!* She readjusted her hair to make sure she looked perfect and quickly rearranged her face to look bored. Vijay entered the room accompanied by two prison guards. He no longer looked handsome. He was unshaven and dressed in white prison clothes.

"Oh dear... not looking too pretty now are we?" Alice mocked Vijay with satisfaction. She was pleased that she looked glamorous and he looked like a vagabond.

Vijay sat next to Alice on the bench. They both sat in silence. She recalled the intense love she once experienced for the man, but all she felt now was hatred for him.

"Alice," he broke the silence. "I need to apologise..."

"I don't want your crap apologies," she spat. "I've seen enough of your crocodile tears and fake apologies to last me a lifetime."

Vijay turned his face and remained silent. Alice opened her handbag and rummaged through it. She found what she was looking for and took it out.

"I came to give you this," Alice handed over the leaflet to Vijay. She looked directly at his face; she could not wait to see his reaction. She had been waiting days to see the look on his face. Vijay looked confused. Alice felt triumphant. *Exactly how I thought you'd look. Start off confused... now ask me what this is about.*

"What... What is this?" Vijay asked. "This..."

"Is exactly what it says. I'm auctioning your house. I came to invite you," Alice paused. "If the prison guards allow you to come, please come and bid on it."

"You cannot sell my house."

"Of course I can," Alice patronised Vijay. "Do you not remember when you were worried? You thought you'd have to give Uma money in the divorce settlement. You signed everything over to me. I own everything,

matey. Your house, business empire, your money. I can sell everything."
Vijay's face turned from confusion to fear and desperation.
"You can't sell the house Alice. Please I worked hard for that."
"I believe I can sell the house. I own it. Look the invite I've given you. It proves that I can sell the house, silly."
"Where will we go?" Vijay asked desperately.
"Not my problem really. Perhaps you can go wherever Siya is?"
Vijay's desperation began to turn to anger. Alice could see the look of fury in his eyes. Everything was as she had imagined. *Go on swear at me next. Do it.*
"You fucking bitch. You don't know who I am."
"You're a spineless man without a penny... oh wait sorry rupee. You're a spineless man without a rupee to his name. You and your family are all criminals and are all rotting in prison. Is there anything else I need to know?" Vijay did not respond. Alice stood up. "I didn't think so. Vijay Rathod you thought you were clever escaping prison with just seven years after everything else you did. Just think, this prison could have been a home for you. Once you're out you'll have nowhere to live or sleep. You'll probably be desperate to come back here."
"I'll fucking kill you, and then I'll be happy to come back here."
"I'll be long gone by then sweetie. I'm selling everything and taking the money. Adios."
Alice waved at Vijay before she turned and began to walk home. Vijay then shouted obscenities at her. She paused and turned around.
"Oi dickhead, do you remember the last time you messed around with me? I took away your clothes. I thought that would teach you a lesson. But no, you still thought you'd mess around with me. This time I decided fuck your clothes so I took away EVERYTHING you owned. Think about this the next time you think you're a clever little genius. I will take more from you if you ever cross my path again."
Alice rolled her hand into a fist and moved to punch Vijay in his balls. Vijay flinched back knowing what was coming but Alice stopped centimetres away from making contact.
"Nah," she smiled. "You're not worth it, but just a warning. If you do want to cross me again, that's what I'm taking next."

Alice felt even more elated than she did when she tied him naked to the chair. She felt nothing for the weasel and walked out without turning back.

Chapter 101: Amrita

"Thank you so much for everything," Uma said with tears in her eyes. Uma bent over to touch Amrita's feet but Amrita took a step back reluctant to allow her to touch them.
"There's no need for that," Amrita said slightly embarrassed. "And by saying thank you, you have made me a stranger."
"I do not know where I would be if you, Vikramji, Leela, Alice and Madhusudan had not been there."
"I was doing my duty as a human being. If Leela had not said anything to me, we would never have known anything. She is your saviour, not me. I was just as passionate about making sure those vile beasts did not walk away with no punishment. I did it for me as much as I did it for you."

Amrita began to fill up with emotions. Tonight was Uma's final night with her family. The following day she was going to move back to live with her parents in Mandavi. Amrita became attached to Uma since she moved in over a year ago. Uma did not just become Amrita's friend; she became a part of her family. Amrita relied on Uma to help her with things; she enjoyed spending time with her, Leela and the other people who often visited Uma. *My home will become empty again when Uma leaves. She has just learnt to laugh again and my house will become vacant of her laughter.* Amrita told Uma she was welcome to stay as long as she wanted in an attempt to prevent her from leaving. However, Uma had decided that she would return home and live with her family. Before Amrita could become more emotional she decided to host a farewell meal for Uma.
"Dinner will get cold. I have made tip tap Punjabi food. Pure vegetarian of course," she added to Uma and Madhusudan.

Amrita made the most of the final meal with Uma. Alice and Madhusudan joined the rest of her household for dinner. Not wanting the night to end, most of them stayed up till the early hours talking and making the most of each other's company. *Once Uma leaves we will no longer have these late night talks.* It was 3am when they finally all went to bed. Amrita watched everyone leave the living room with a heavy heart. She stayed behind to quickly clean everything whilst the rest lof them went to sleep. *How will I let her leave my home tomorrow with a smile on my face? I do not want to cry and make her feel sad when she is starting a new life.*

Amrita dreaded the moment Uma would leave her home ever since she told them about her intention of moving back to Mandavi. Amrita almost felt as though Uma was her daughter who was getting married and moving to her in-laws house. *I am silly. Uma is no relative of mine. I should not be so sentimental. She is going back home to be with her family. Uma has promised me she will see me on a regular basis, and Mandavi is only an hour away. I can see her whenever I want.*

By the time Amrita went to her bedroom, Vikram was already asleep. So she did not interrupt his sleep, she left the light off. Once she bolted her bedroom door shut, she became engulfed by darkness. She realised the real reason Uma's departure was causing her so much grief. *This past year, she gave my life an objective. She went through the same thing Nirmal went through. I began to see Nirmal in her. I lived my ambition to destroy Nirmal's in-laws through Uma. My desire to destroy Nirmal's perpetrators left a vacuum in my life. I thought about avenging her day and night, and Uma gave me something to displace that anger. The real reason I am feeling so much sorrow over Uma leaving is because I am being stupid. Uma is not Nirmal no matter how much I think she's like Nirmal.*

Seeing the Rathod family fall to their knees allowed Amrita to fulfil her fantasies about the punishments she would mete out to Nirmal's in-laws. Since the Rathod family were imprisoned, Amrita's desire to ruin the Chadda family slowly got stronger again. Amrita was able to push away the urges by remembering the look on Vijay's face and by reminding herself that Uma won her battle.

Amrita stood in her bedroom. *Maybe Uma going is a good thing. With her around I forgot my true mission.* Amrita rolled up her sleeve and looked the N she once carved into her skin. Since Uma came to live with her she had stopped carving the N into her skin. *I let this wound heal before I avenged you Nirmal! I let you down. I should not have let this heal I still need to punish the Chadda family.* Amrita opened up her wardrobe and rummaged around the darkness. She eventually felt the package in which she kept her sentimental items. She pulled out the package and walked over to the foot of her bed. She sat on the floor and opened up the bundle. By this point her eyes had adjusted to the darkness and she could make out what she was holding.

Amrita knew she was holding the photograph of her family from when they were younger. She had tears in her eyes seeing the pictures of their mother with all three of her children in their lap. Amrita wiped away her tears. She picked up the blade which she used to carve the N into her skin. All the memories Amrita had displaced in the past twelve months rushed back to her consciousness when she saw the N and the blade.

Amrita held the razor blade in her hand. *All I am left with is the desire to punish Nirmal's in-laws again. Putting the Rathod family behind bars is not enough. The Chaddas still have to pay for every tear they made my sister cry. Waheguru it has been six years since Nirmal died, and I have not done a thing for her. My dreams of ruining them are getting nowhere. I cannot afford for Gurpreet to end up back in prison again. I was so engrossed in helping Uma, that I forgot what really mattered. Nirmal! I need to do something.* Amrita dropped the razor blade on the floor as she felt a light bulb turn on inside her head. She knew what she had to do.

She ran to her living room and turned the light on. She found the telephone directory and picked it up. She ran her finger down the index markers and found M. Amrita looked at the time. It was 4.35am. *He will be awake. He said he had to be up early today.* Amrita began to dial the number with her fingers shaking desperate that this was the solution she desperately sought for years. She heard the phone ringing. *Pick up, please pick up, pick up and say you can help me. Pick up and say you can help me, pick up and say you can help me. Pick up...*
"Hello?" Amrita heard the high pitched voice she recognised immediately.

"Hello Madhusudan," Amrita said. "I am very sorry to call you so early on but I need your help. You said I could call you whenever I needed your help."

Chapter 102: Uma

"This is the Shailputri murti maa gave me when I got married," Uma said as she handed the statue to Amrita. "It is a gift for you. Thank you for everything."
"Koi gal nahi. You are making me a stranger by saying thank you. You have already given us too many gifts Uma. You do not need to give us anything," Amrita said humbly.
"I wanted to give them. Please accept this Amritaben."
Amrita smiled. Without saying anything she accepted the murti. She walked over and put it in exactly the same place it had sat in when Uma lived with them. Amrita did not turn around for a while. Uma heard Amrita sniff and realised that she must be crying. Uma too began to fill up with emotions again at the thought of saying farewell. *Hai Mata Rani, please protect everyone from any evil. These people are good people. They deserve all the happiness you can give them.*

Uma wiped her tears away before they fell. She walked over to Vikram and folded her hands together to thank him. Uma then bent down and kissed both Jaswinder and Manpreet on their forehead.
"I will come and visit you both soon," Uma told them, crying once again. "If you ever want to go to the seaside come and see me in Mandavi. We will eat some chatpatti and pani puri on the beach."
Uma stood up and saw Leela stood next to the children. She went and embraced the woman who saved her life. They both hugged each other for a long time. Unspoken gratitude was exchanged by both women. Uma eventually pulled apart and saw that Amrita was facing them again. Her eyes were red.
"I feel like I am getting married again," she said laughing with tears in her eyes. Amrita, Leela, Vikram, Arjun and Priya all laughed.
"Make sure you take good care of your didi," Leela said to Priya and Arjun.
"We will," Priya said with a smile. "We all will."
Arjun had already put Uma's suitcases into the car. She took one last look at the place that was her home for over a year. *This is the place that*

gave me a roof over my head when there was nowhere for me to go. She remembered how she slowly came back to life living in this place. With Sharda, Leela, Amrita, Vikram and their children's help she returned to life. Uma was apprehensive about leaving the home to return to Mandavi but she knew that was the right thing to do. Madhapar had too many painful memories for Uma and she wanted to start rebuilding her life. Uma felt the constant reminders from seeing the same places and people were not helping her. Even though she was leaving Madhapar, Uma knew she could visit Amrita whenever she wanted. Uma knew she would visit, after all she had many happy memories associated with Oberoi House.

As they were about to leave, Priya picked up Uma's daughter, Sharda, and walked out of the house. When Uma got outside Amrita's home she saw that Purbai, Kesar, Suneeti and some of the other women who protested on her behalf came to say goodbye. She hugged each one of the women and thanked them for their love and support. She then put her hands together and sat into the car. Priya put Sharda onto Uma's lap before sitting in the front passenger seat. *Hai Bhagwan, this girl is getting so heavy* Uma thought lovingly. She took one last look at everyone who had gathered to say bye and waved at them.

As Arjun drove through Madhapar, memories began to flood back. The apprehensions, nervousness and dreams she came with when she first arrived in Madhapar; and how they all shattered. *I never thought this place would become home, but Amrita's home did become my home. Once again I am leaving one home behind to go back to another home.* Uma took a deep breath. This time she was moving with no dreams or ambitions for herself. She was returning with scars that would never heal. Uma tried her best to look towards the bright side of everything that had happened. *I made friends who were like family to me. I even got the most precious gift in this entire universe, she gave me Sharda. Mata Rani sent me there for a purpose.* Uma had always hated the name Sheela. The name was associated with the people she resented and so she renamed her with the name she had always wanted to call her; Sharda.

When Uma left Mandavi on the day she married she had not looked back to avoid bad luck. Even though Uma no longer believed in silly superstitions she looked ahead. Most of her memories from Madhapar were still very painful for her. Even though Arjun was careful to avoid driving past the place that was once known as Rathod Haveli, there were still many places Uma associated with bad memories. There were some places which sparked pleasant memories for Uma. Driving past the pani puri stall where Vikram treated everyone to celebrate the Rathod's arrest made Uma feel warm. Uma smiled as they drove past the school which Jaswinder and Manpreet attended. She remembered fondly how hard both children tried to cheer her up whenever her pain got too much.

Once the car left Madhapar and passed Bhuj, Uma began to feel some awkwardness about returning home. She spoke harsh words to her parents a long time ago. Both had now apologised to each other after the Rathod family's imprisonment and made amends. Nevertheless, an element of awkwardness remained. Uma was unsure whether the awkwardness rooted from the fact her parents were still angry at her, or whether it stemmed from the fact that she perceived it as a strained relationship.

I have a lifetime to rebuild these relationships. I will be living with maa and bapuji till I die now. I have a lifetime to make everything peaceful again. I will make sure things are like they were before I married. Maa will make me pauva and I will mix it with tamarind chutney. As the car pulled into Mandavi she saw the familiar roads again. She saw her home approaching on the horizon. Uma remembered the fond memories she had associated with the place she called home before marriage. *My Sharda will grow up playing in the same courtyard I played in many years ago.* Uma closed her eyes and prayed to Durga before she picked up her daughter and stepped out of the car to begin a new chapter in her life.

Part V: Siddhidatri (The Possessor of Powers)

TWENTY YEARS LATER

Chapter 103: Sharda

Sharda sat down on the floor with the residents of the women's home. It was the final day of Navratri and they were about to pray to Durga's ninth form; Siddhidatri. Sharda's mother told her how Siddhidatri was the possessor of eight powers: Anima, Mahima, Laghima, Garima, Ishitva, Vashitwam, Prapti and Prakamya. People who wished to possess these eight powers prayed to Siddhidatri. Sharda sat through the prayers. Once they ended she walked over to the photograph of Durga and her nine forms. She looked closely at the image and saw the main eight armed Durga sitting in the middle. She was surrounded by smaller pictures of her nine forms; Shailputri, Brahmacharini, Chandraghanta, Kushmanda, Skandmata, Katyayini, Kaalratri, Maha Gauri and Siddhidatri. Sharda focused on Siddhidatri and began to pray. *Hai mata Siddhidatri, in exactly twenty eight days I am going to become Mrs Yash Parbat. I'm worried I might not fit in with my in-laws and they might think mummy didn't teach me anything. Please grant me your eight powers to win over the love of Yash's family.*
"Sharda what are you doing here?" Jaya, one of the women's home resident said. She came over and held her hand. "Come and play Garba with us."
Sharda smiled and allowed Jaya to guide her to the circle of dancing women. As it was the final night of Navratri, Sharda danced until the early hours. She had such a good night doing various forms of Garba, Dandiya and Ramjaniyu. Once she became tired, she went and sat down to watch the other women dancing around the goddess.

Sharda smiled to see the residents of the women's home looking so happy today. She had never seen some of them smile before. The women who lived in the home came from abusive families. They were given shelter and support by her mother who transformed an old hotel into a safe house for abused women. Some of the women got better very quickly and rebuilt their lives; others took a very long time. Her mother and her friends did a lot for the women to help them. They provided counselling for women; they even inspired women to fight their cases in court. Many women in the home told Sharda how her mother had helped to transform their lives. Sharda closed her eyes and pictured Krishna in her mind. *They all look so happy today. Please keep them smiling forever and punish those who robbed them of their beautiful smiles.* She opened her eyes and started to feel sleepy. She bowed her head to the image of the goddess and began to walk home, which was just around the corner from the women's home.

The next morning Sharda woke up slightly later than she had hoped. *Oh my god I should have been up an hour ago.* She quickly jumped out of bed and began to rush around her room. *Yash's family will be here in an hour and I'm not even ready.* Yash's family were coming over to their house to finalise the wedding plans. They were going to meet her mother, uncle, aunt and grandfather to sort out the final preparations for the wedding. *We've planned everything, right down to the venue and catering. I don't know what else is left to organise but maybe there is something else that we forgot to do before.*

Once Sharda was ready she ran down to the kitchen to see if there was anything she needed to do to before Yash's family came. Her cousin Jaswinder was helping their aunt who was cooking her South Indian specialities; Idli and Vadah Sambhar.
"Why are you not ready yet?" her aunt asked her. "Go and get ready. Jaswinder and I will finish off all the preparations."
"What about the living room? Mummy will be annoyed if things are not crystal clean."
"Some of the women from the home volunteered to help us. They have already cleaned. Go and thank them they're in the living room."
"Where's mummy?"
"She had to go out and meet Subhadhra's solicitor. Subhadhra's case against her in-laws is coming up soon." Sharda paused to think for a second. Her aunt walked over to her and began to shuffle her out of the kitchen. "Go and get dressed. Yash will be here soon. We have everything under control."
She began to walk to her bedroom.
"Your mummy picked out the outfit she thought you should wear tonight. It is on her bed." Sharda heard her aunt shout from the

kitchen. Sharda walked into her mother's bedroom and found the yellow and purple chaniya choli on her bed.

By the time she was dressed she could hear her mother's voice coming from the kitchen. *Mummy's back*. Sharda quickly ran downstairs and saw her mother standing with her grandfather. Her mother was looking slightly frustrated.
"What is wrong mummy?"
"Nothing," her mother said with a smile on her face. "You look beautiful." Her mother touched her own eye and put a black mark behind Sharda's ear.
Sharda took a step back from her mother. "Mummy you don't need to do this kala tikka thing all the time. It ruins my hair."
"I'm just preventing the evil eye from affecting you."
"There is no such thing as the evil eye," Sharda told her mother. "People are just superstitious."
Sharda argued with her mother for a few moments when they heard the doorbell ring.
She looked to the front door and knew the Parbat family had arrived. Her mother started to look at herself in the mirror and quickly ran her fingers through her hair. Her aunt came into the hallway and saw her mother sorting her hair out.
"Uma, your daughter is getting married. Not you," her aunt, Leela, joked with Sharda's mother.
Sharda's mother pulled away from the mirror "Go and welcome them into our home," she said without laughing. "I will bring Sharda to the living room once they have sat down."

Chapter 104: Uma

Uma walked over and opened the door. She hugged Yash, his mother and grandmother. She put her hands together to greet the men of Yash's family.
"Please come in and sit down," Uma said as she showed them into the living room.
Uma began to gossip with Sharda's in-laws to be. A few minutes later Leela, Jaswinder and Sharda came into the living room carrying the snacks they prepared earlier that day. Uma was confident they would love the food cooked by Leela. *Leela is an expert at South Indian cooking.*

Yash's mother stood up when Sharda entered the room. "You look so beautiful beti. May no one's evil eye affect you."
Uma and Sharda both caught each other's eyes for a brief second. She was amused to see that Sharda was fighting back the urge to laugh. Half an hour after talking and laughing together, Uma thought it was wise to begin finalising the wedding plans Yash's family came to discuss.
"Vehvanji we should talk about the wedding plans that need to be finalised," Uma said. "I thought everything had been arranged?"
Uma saw Yash's father roll the tip of his handlebar moustache around his finger. "Samdhanji everything has been finalised apart from one thing," he paused. Uma saw that Yash's mother was nodding to encourage her husband. "You see as the groom's family we are entitled to some... gifts. We just wanted to discuss the gifts we would be getting."
The smile on Uma's face faltered. The room which had been lively with laughter moments ago was in total silence.
"Gifts?" Uma said confused.
"Yes it is traditional to give the groom's family presents."
Uma felt her insides go cold. She began to see flashbacks of Madhu's requests many years ago. *Surely they do not mean what I think they mean?* Uma could see her worries reflected on Leela's face.
"Vehvanji. You said you did not want a dowry," Uma said attempting to

contain her anger.
"I am not asking for a dowry Umaji. Just gifts."
"You see Vehvanji, it is traditional to give gifts to the groom's family," Yash's mother said, taking over from her husband. "We are not asking you to become paupers for us. Just a few token gifts to complete traditions."
I liked you until you opened your mouth. Uma progressively got angrier as the conversation continued. *You scheming bastard. That is exactly what Vijay's family did. Wait until after the wedding invites were sent out before making the demands. You know it would be very difficult for us to back out once it is public knowledge our daughter is getting married.* Uma looked at Yash's family. They all had a huge grin on their face. Uma looked at Sharda who looked slightly worried about the demands they made. *There is no way I will send my daughter into this family of greedy dowry grabbers.* Uma stood up to tell the entire Parbat family to leave her house immediately when she was interrupted.
"Can we meet you in a few days please," Sharda negotiated with Yash's family. "We just need a few days to discuss how much we can afford before we commit to anything."
Afford? Commit? Has this girl gone mad? I will not give them a single rupee.
The Parbat family agreed to wait a few days and decided to meet in four days time. Once they left their house, Uma demanded answers from her daughter.
"What are you doing Sharda?" Uma fumed. "We are not paying a dowry. A marriage is the union of two families, not a business deal."
"Mummy please! I love Yash. I want to marry him."
"I refuse to let you go into a house where..."
"Mummy let me deal with this," Sharda cut her mother off. "I know what I am doing. Trust me."

Uma could not believe what her daughter was saying. *Years ago maa must have thought the same thing when she accepted the dowry request.* She took a deep breath to try and calm herself down and sat down. *Maa I wish you were here today to talk sense into your granddaughter. I don't want to go through what you went through. I do not want Sharda to go through what I went through.*

"Sharda, you..."
"Four days mummy, give me four days. I'll sort everything out. Promise!" Sharda kissed her mother on the cheek and ran out of the room.
Uma was about to shout angrily after her daughter when Leela put a hand on her shoulder. She pacified herself and remembered the right she gave to her daughter to make the decisions that affected her life. *I thought she's too young to marry at twenty-two but she wanted to do it so I let her. How can I let her choose this path knowing where it will lead?*
"Sharda is intelligent," Leela said. "Give her the four days she is asking for. See what she does."
"It is not a question of trust. I trust her fully." Uma paused and spoke quietly. "I am only worried about how besotted she is with that Yash. When someone is so infatuated by someone they lose their ability to think straight. They try and find the good in everything they do, even if the person is vile. I did the same with V..." Uma paused. *I have no desire to talk about people who are worse than beasts on a day like Dusshera.*
"I just hope my beti does not make any wrong decisions that she will have to live with for the rest of her life."

Chapter 105: Sharda

I have full faith that I won't need to pay a dowry. Yash loves me. He will see his family are wrong and will convince them to see sense. Sharda sat on the wall near Kankariya Lake in Ahmedabad. It was in this place that Yash had proposed to her during the dancing fountain show.

Sharda saw her fiancé coming. She excitedly stood up and went to hug him. She held his hand and walked around the park to find a bench where they could sit and talk. For a while Sharda and Yash talked about their lives in general. Fifteen minutes later she steered the conversation into the direction she wanted to go in.
"Yash," she said confidentially. "Your family has requested a dowry from my family. What do you think of this?"
"Does it matter what I think?" Yash replied. "Everyone pays a dowry. It is tradition."
"No they don't. Dowries are illegal. They have been illegal since 1961. It's illegal to ask for one. It's even illegal for us to give you a dowry. My family would be breaking the law by fulfilling your family's request."
"My family asked for presents not dowry."
"Let us talk honestly Yash," Sharda snapped. "Your family disguised the fact they were asking for a dowry by using the words gift and present."

Yash sat in silence for a while. *He has nothing to say about my fact. He knows I am right.*
"My dadi bought a dowry to our house when she married. My mummy bought a dowry with her when she married. Bhavika will take a dowry with her when she marries. It is our family's tradition. My wife will have to bring a dowry to enter our home."
Now it was Sharda's turn to sit in silence. It was a few minutes before she spoke.
"So your family only join relationships through deals? A bit like merchants? Your family think the sanctity of marriage is like a market place where you can exchange commodities?"
"Do not pick faults with my family," Yash said starting to lose his

temper.
"I'm not," Sharda defended herself. "Honestly. I'm trying to understand how people can create a relationship between two families and fill this unity with love if the relationship started like a market place trade?"
Sharda saw Yash open his mouth to reply. She raised her voice to prevent him from speaking. "I fail to see why your family would only accept me and love me if I pay them enough money. Mummy always told me that money can buy me diamonds but not love. She always said money can buy me a house, but it can't turn a house of bricks and stone into a home. Money will buy me a car, but not friends or family to fill the car. I'm just confused because your parents are saying the total opposite. It seems that your parents would argue that money will buy me love, acceptance and a family to fill that big car." Sharda paused for a second. "So Yash, please tell me what is the cost of BUYING your family? How CHEAP are they?"
Sharda was pleased that Yash was silent once more. She waited for a few moments but he did not open his mouth.

"So I take it I'm going to have to buy your family's affection in order to marry you?" She said breaking the silence. "There is no way you would marry me unless my family agree to pay the dowry?"
"Mummy wouldn't..."
"I didn't ask you about Mummyji. I asked if you would marry me if my family didn't pay a dowry?"
Once again Yash was silent. Sharda felt severe disappointment in her stomach. She felt as though her heart would burst out of her chest. *Your silence tells me everything I need to know Yash Parbat.* She fought back any tears that could show weakness to Yash. Eventually Yash spoke.
"My parents wouldn't allow me to marry you unless you paid a dowry."
Despite being prepared for Yash's answer, Sharda's heart dropped. *I hoped the fact that we both love each other would count for something.*
Sharda got up. She paused for a second before she walked away. Without looking back at him she told him "I will see you at my house in three days time. We can finalise what your family want then."

Chapter 106: Uma

Uma was, severely disappointed in Sharda, who agreed to go ahead with everything the Parbat family wanted. She was sat in the women's home dining room with Leela. Together they both converted Vijay's hotel in Ahmedabad into a women's shelter.

"I was so proud of my daughter," Uma whispered to Leela. "The Sharda I know would have refused to pay a dowry and tonight when his family come she'll accept all of their demands. This whole dowry thing has reopened all of my old wounds."

"How will you stop the wedding?" Leela said worried. "Your beti is already engaged. The only choice she had left now is to get married or remain unmarried for the rest of her life."

"India has moved on a lot since..."

"HA!" Leela scoffed. "How many times will India claim they have moved on? Nothing has changed in twenty years. One crime happens the media makes a big deal about it, politicians blame women for instigating the crimes and then people forget about it. The world was up in arms about the bus rape in Delhi in 2012. We all thought there would be change, but things went back to the way they were, criminals just got cleverer. Dowries have been illegal since 1961. It is now 2033 but people like the Parbat family still cover it up. Testing your child's gender before birth is illegal to prevent female genocide. If India had really moved on, would Subhadhra have been forced into multiple abortions? Would she have had to escape from her in-laws and end up living here? You are now paying for the barrister fighting a case against them. If India had really moved on, would this home that you have created have so many women living here?"

Uma went silent. She knew Leela was right. *Eighteen years after we all opened this place, there are still as many women coming here as they were all those years ago. I will not let Sharda end up in one of these homes.* Uma's past flooded back. She did not know what became of Vijay or Jigar. She knew Vijay was released from prison many years ago and Jigar in the last few years. They both had nothing to their name,

and Uma possessed no desire to know what they were doing.
"My beti is walking down the same path I once walked down. I have to stop her Leela. Alice does not raise money for this women's home just so we can help support women. We also exist to prevent women from coming here to start with."

Many years ago Uma won her fight against the Rathod family. Her friend Alice, who lived in London, had cleaned the Rathod family of their entire wealth. As Vijay built his business empire on other people's money, Alice returned the wealth to the rightful owners. Alice gave one hotel to Uma. The police never found Siya so Alice gave one hotel to Siya's parents to allow them to rebuild their scattered lives. Siya's parents were able to plan for their other children's future through the hotel. Alice had kept the other two for herself. Uma ended up with a lot more money than her parents gave to the Rathod family. She returned her parent's money, but did not want anything to do with the excess money or the hotel. Uma was going to sell the property and put the money into a temple. However, Leela and Amrita both convinced her into using the property to help other women. Once Alice returned to England, she set up her own charity to help women in India. The money helped to fund shelter projects such as the home Uma set up with Leela and Amrita. The money also provided legal aid, lobbied the government to strengthen women's rights laws, produced merchandise to teach women their rights and campaigned to have women's rights as part of the national curriculum in schools across India. The charity hoped by teaching women their rights at school they would save lives.

Sharda knows her rights. I made sure she knew everything and yet she is agreeing to meet these people. What if everything I have worked hard for the past twenty years has been a waste? If they know everything but do not use it to their advantage, why have I wasted all these years of my life?
"Perhaps I should have been stricter with Sharda. I should have forced my own thoughts and beliefs onto her. Then she would not be so foolish. She has become so blind that she cannot see them for what they are."
"I think you should assert your power and reject the wedding," Leela said. "I think you should wait though. I trust Sharda. I think she has a

plan."
"You said that a few days ago."
"I am still saying the same thing. Have patience."
If this was happening to your own children you would not be so calm.
Uma was about to vocalise her anger but fortunately Uma stopped herself. She remembered that Leela had supported her through everything. She knew that Leela loved Sharda, probably as much as she loved her own children. Feeling slightly guilty about doubting her, Uma calmed down and agreed to wait.

Later that night the Parbat family, Uma's family and some of Sharda's friends sat around the table. Uma recognised the faces of Sharda's friends but did not know they were such good friends. Sharda had requested Leela to make dinner for Yash's family but Leela refused and so they got straight to the topic of the dowry payment.
"So what do you want?" Uma said flatly.
Yash's father took out the list and was about to read off the list. However, before he started he was interrupted.
"Sorry Sasurji," Sharda smiled at Yash's father. Uma's stomach churned at the sight of her daughter being sickeningly polite to the greedy bastards. "I have a request to make. Instead of you telling us what your family want, I'd love to hear it from their own mouth what they want. I love to give gifts. If each person said what they wanted for themselves it would please me more to fulfil their desires."
Yash's father gave Sharda a dirty look. Uma wanted to give her stupid daughter the same look.
"We are not asking for charity. We are asking for our right."
"I know. I know," Sharda said quickly. "But I only give gifts to people if they ask me for it. If you ask me for jewellery I won't give it, because I'll know it's not for you."
"Nautanki," Yash's father rolled his eyes. "Fine we'll ask for our own things if it means we can get this over with quicker."

And so the list began. Yash's father requested a TATA car and 10 lakh rupees in cash. Yash's mother requested new jewellery and a brand new fridge for the kitchen. Yash requested a latest Honda motorbike and a honeymoon in Australia. Uma listened to each of Yash's family make

their requests. Hearing their requests reminded Uma of her mother. She remembered all of the hardships her mother went through to meet the dowry payments. Once Uma returned to Mandavi everything returned to normal. However, the relationship with her parents seemed to take more effort than before. For many years Uma was unable to figure out why the relationship seemed superficial. Her mother fed her the same way, took care of her the same way and even spent as much time with her. She was unable to work out what was different. Uma got her answer the day before her mother died. Her mother's health was deteriorating, as a result of the diabetes. Out of the blue her mother apologised for prioritising what the community would say and turning Uma away all those years ago. "Even though many years have passed, I know I was responsible for everything. It eats away at me every single day. I thought making more effort with you now would relieve me of my guilt, but it hasn't. I don't have long left. I need to apologise before I leave this life."
"Don't be silly maa, if you apologise for everything then I will have to say thank you for everything you have ever done to me. You made one mistake, but you've done so much for me."
Avantika hugged her daughter and felt comfort at Uma's words. The next day Avantika had a stroke and died. *The guilt consumed maa every single day. If I stand by and don't interfere, I will live through the same guilt.*

Thinking about her mother reminded Uma of Amrita. *If Amrita was still here, she would slap some sense into Sharda and make her see sense.* Two years ago, Amrita died after a battle against breast cancer. Amrita successfully punished Nirmal's in-laws a year after Uma moved out from her home. After getting her justice, Uma saw a huge change in Amrita. She became happier, less angry and friendlier. Amrita helped a lot with setting up the women's home. Amrita's husband and children were like family for Uma, but none of them were as strong minded as Amrita. *Amrita would have made Sharda see sense.* Uma paused for a moment. *If Amrita was still alive today the first person she would slap is me for standing back and letting Sharda do this. I will never forgive myself if I let Sharda go through with this. What if she holds me responsible for this one day the same way I blamed maa?*

"I refuse to pay this dowry," said Uma, as she stood up rapidly.
The Parbat family all stared at Uma. Sharda looked at Uma too. Uma stared directly at her daughter. "How can you agree to this merchant's trade? This is not a marriage."
"Do you want us to call the wedding off?" Yash's father threatened. The silent room became noisy. Yash's family made noises of support. Sharda's side made noises of contempt. Uma looked at Yash's father with anger in her eyes. She hated everything about the man including his ugly handlebar moustache.
"Is this your final answer? You won't accept me without a dowry?" Sharda asked loudly to shadow all the voices around her.
"Yes. No gifts. No marriage," Yash's father said.
"Even though giving or receiving a dowry is illegal?"
"No GIFTS. No marriage."
"Fine," Sharda stood up and walked to her friends. Now that Uma paid closer attention to them; she realised who they were.
"These are my friends," Sharda announced. "This is Chandrakant Gupta, this is Lata Salwe and this is Gautam Rathod." Sharda paused for a second. "Go ahead guys."

The three friends Sharda introduced to Yash's family stood up. The friend Sharda introduced as Chandrakant Gupta took out a badge from his pocket and displayed it.
"I am Inspector Gupta. This is Inspector Salwe and Inspector Rathod. Mr Parbat, you and your family are under arrest for making demands for dowry. Inspectors, take them away and lock them up."
The entire room broke out in noise again. Yash's family attempted to make hasty movements to escape whereas Sharda's family let out gasps of shock. Uma was flabbergasted and confused at the same time. The entire Parbat family looked like lost puppies who had not quite comprehended what just happened.
"I tried to explain to you that dowry is illegal. I tried explaining that marriage wasn't a business deal. You didn't want to listen then. I hope you'll listen now though. Demanding a dowry is a prisonable offence. Enjoy your three years in prison. Perhaps you can rethink your traditions whilst you're breathing in jail air."
"You will regret this you kutri," Yash's father fumed. "You will never

prove anything. We will say it is a set up."
"Sasurji, oh wait, you won't be my Sasurji, I refuse to accept your family. Praveen..." Yash's father's eyes bulged when he was called by his first name. "Yes, I called you by your name. People like you aren't worthy of my respect. We filmed the whole thing too. Oh and we have this list that you so kindly wrote out for us. Thank you... Praveen."

The Parbat family were escorted out by uniformed police who had waited outside. Some of the Parbat family begged for Uma's forgiveness; others were escorted out cursing and swearing.
"You will rot as a single woman for the rest of your life. No one will accept you," Yash's mother cursed.
The fire Uma occasionally felt inside her erupted at the way Yash's mother spoke to Sharda. She stood right in front of her face.
"I would rather my beti remained single for the rest of her life than become a daughter-in-law for criminals like you," Uma shouted at her.
The word criminals had a drastic impact on Yash's mother and silenced her. "You criminals aren't good enough for my Sharda; now get out of my house."
Uma watched as the Parbat family were escorted out by the police. She then turned around looked at her daughter feeling immensely proud. *I have taught you well.*

TWO MONTHS LATER

Chapter 107: Sharda

Sharda looked around at all the happy faces smiling at her. Her mother had organised a surprise party for her at the women's shelter. Earlier that day, Yash and his family were formally charged with attempting to coerce a family into giving them a dowry. They were sentenced to three years in prison. The media had closely followed this trial as she was the daughter of Uma Rathod, who was once in the centre of a large dowry related trial. When Sharda arrived at the women's shelter, the residents, her aunt, uncles, cousins and grandfather had been waiting there to congratulate her. Sharda was taken aback by the reaction she received upon the success of her trial. *Why are they all celebrating? I don't feel like I have anything to celebrate.* To keep everyone happy she plastered a smile onto her face.

"Here is a card that Alice Aunty sent to you from London." Uma showed Sharda the e-card. Sharda looked at the card and smiled before putting it away. She walked around and talked to various women living in the home. Seeing these women celebrate her victory caused Sharda to forget the pain she felt when she realised that the man that she loved did not feel the same way. *These women are celebrating my victory as if they were celebrating their own victory.* She talked to the women, until she became overwhelmed by memories of Yash and she left the party to have some time alone. Sharda sat on the wall outside the women's home and looked at the sky. *I won against that bastard, but have I really won? Will I ever be as happy as I was when I was with him? Wasn't I better off being ignorant about the whole thing and getting married? At least we would still be together.* Another part of Sharda told her something different. *Your happiness was false. The guy you thought you loved wasn't Yash. He was pretending to be something else. But still I was in love! What if this feeling of emptiness never goes? People get one chance at love. I fell in love and made the wrong choice. Hai Krishna! What now?* She was so engrossed in her own thoughts that she did not notice her aunt sat on the wall next to her.
"I know what you are thinking."

Sharda jumped in shock and almost fell off the wall when she heard the voice. She was relieved to see it was just her aunt sat next to her.
"Leela masi!" Sharda said gasping for breath. "You scared me."
"Sorry," Leela masi apologised. "I just wanted to make sure you were ok."
"I'm fine," Sharda lied.
"Sharda beti, it is OK to not be happy all the time. If you're not happy it's alright. You can tell your loved ones about your fears and worries."
Sharda looked directly at her aunt's kind face.
"Talk to me," Leela masi said.
Her aunt's words felt like stinging antiseptic. They stung but she knew they were soothing her at the same time. Sharda broke down in tears and let out all of the feelings she had bottled up the past few weeks. She told her aunt all about how Yash left her broken hearted. She revealed her fears about never meeting someone else who she loved as much. She told her aunt about the emptiness she felt since she got the love of her life and his family arrested.
"Sharda beti, you are twenty-two years old. You're young. You will find someone. I was fifteen when I married. I was seventeen when I was kicked out by my family. I never thought I would trust another man again. I never thought I would find someone who loves me as much as I love them. When I was twenty six I found Shyam. Even though I never thought I would love someone again he won me over. I fell in love with him. We got married. Now fourteen years later, I am happier than I have ever been. We have two beautiful sons. There's nothing else for Lord Krishna to give me anymore. He has given me everything." Leela masi paused for a second. "He works in mysterious ways. If I hadn't been sold by my parents, I would never have arrived in Gujarat. If I hadn't become a victim of that horrible crime, I might still be married to that impotent man who thought the fault was in the women. What happened to me wasn't right. What happened to you was wrong as well, but everything that happened to me brought me to where I am today. If I hadn't gone through those tests I wouldn't be where I am today. I am happier than I have ever been. I never knew what true happiness was until I met Shyam. Sharda beti trust me! You will find someone who deserves you. Yash didn't."
"What if I don't?"

"Then you will be happier alone than you ever would have been with Yash," Sharda heard another familiar voice from behind her.
Sharda looked around and saw her mother was stood behind her.
"Leela was lucky to find the right man. She found her happiness. After your… the man who gave his sperm to create you… After I left him, I never found someone else. But I am happier now than I ever was living with that man. I loved him. I loved him with everything I had. When everything fell apart, I felt the same way you did. I wondered how I would live the rest of my life alone as a single mother." Sharda's mother sat down next to her. "Yash and Vijay are both made of the same rubbish. You do not need people like him. If you never find someone else then you escaped a bullet. The Parbat family would have brought nothing but misery to you. Believe me beti." Sharda felt her mother stroke her face. "I have been alone for twenty one years and I am happier than I was in that facade of a marriage. Yes I feel a void in my life at times. Sometimes I wish things had been different. But I hope you trust me when I say you will be happier alone than you ever would have been with Yash." Sharda smiled and nodded slightly at her mother's words. "You're a beautiful girl. I am confident you will find your rajkumar one day. When you're ready some lucky boy will come on a white horse for you. As for Yash and the pain you're feeling; time is a good healer. In one year, or two you'll have forgotten about him."

Sharda felt her mother wipe her tears from her face. "Beti you know that both I and your Leela masi are right. You might not see it now because the pain is too severe, but you will see it one day."
For a few moments the three women sat on the wall.
"Do you want to know why I arranged this party for you? I wanted you to inspire some of the women in our home. Some of them are still hesitant to go down the police route. I want your success to inspire them to seek justice. If you want you don't have to go back. We can both go home."
Sharda did not respond for a few moments. She wiped her tears and took a few deep breaths.
"I'll come in and celebrate," *When I'm alone Yash dominates my thoughts. At least with these women I can think of other things.*
Sharda stood up with her aunt and mother and walked back to the

house. *I hope the day I can wholeheartedly tell mummy and masi that they're right will come soon. Until then I need to find ways to keep my mind occupied.*

Chapter 108: Uma

The weather was unusually cool for a summer's day. A wedding hall located on the outskirts of Ahmedabad, was gradually emptying. Uma walked around with a huge smile on her face as she greeted the guests and thanked them for their presence at her daughter's wedding. Despite showing laughter and expressing warmth and gratitude to the guests, she secretly hid the inner turmoil raging within her.

Uma always knew that when Sharda married it would be extremely stressful. The reality however, had been a lot worse than she ever imagined. The women from the home, Alice, Leela, Arjun's family, Gauri's family, Uma's father and Amrita's family all contributed to help give Sharda her dream wedding. Uma recalled delivering the wedding invitations to her friends and relatives with a bounce in her footsteps. In fact everything was so similar to her own wedding. The only difference was Sharda's in laws had not forced their decisions onto the wedding. Sharda's in-laws actually contributed to the costs of the wedding by paying for the post wedding reception.

As the wedding hall continued to empty, Uma looked at the scrunched up and dirty serviettes on the floor. Some of the guests had not bothered to throw them into the bin. Fifteen minutes later she made up an excuse to get away from the wedding hall. She went into the room upstairs where they usually kept the bride's belongings. Uma entered the room which contained the belongings Sharda would take to her new home. She spotted a family photo they took when Sharda was thirteen. Uma walked over and picked up the photo. Her mother and Amrita were still alive and smiling when the photo had been taken. Even Alice was in the picture as she was on a visit. They persuaded her to join the picture because she was like family. Uma's gaze focused entirely on her daughter. Now that she stood in the room alone, the only person she could think of was Sharda. The memories of her daughter flashed through her mind. The first time Sharda called Uma Maa, the day she learnt to walk without holding my finger, the day she became Dr Sharda

Desai were some of the proudest moments in Uma's life. As time passed Uma recalled more moments that she had spent over the past twenty six years nurturing her beautiful girl. Sharda loved the stories of Goddess Durga, that her grandmother had told her. Uma used to tell her the stories as she massaged coconut oil into her hair. *I cried tears of happiness so many times, but today you will leave with tears of sadness.*

Uma recalled her own wedding day and remembered the fears she had when she married. She remembered how upset her mother was. Uma never imagined the pain would be as intense as it was. *I know Sharda's in-laws are very nice people, but what if Sharda fails to adjust the same way I failed? Hai Mata Rani make sure she has all the happiness in the world.* Uma's fears and worries added to the sadness she felt. She held back her tears as she sat alone in the room.

"The priest said you should be leaving soon," Uma heard Arjun's voice from next door. "Shall I let him know you are ready?"

"Yes," Uma heard Sharda say. "Tell him I'll be ready to leave in ten minutes."

Uma put the photo aside and sighed as she got up. She picked up a red box from the dressing table and began to walk towards the room where her daughter sat. The time came to say goodbye, but there were a few things Uma wanted to tell her daughter. *I taught Sharda to talk; I taught her the difference between right and wrong. It is time to give her a few last minute teachings.*

Uma opened the door of the room her daughter was sat in. She walked inside and saw that Sharda was no longer wearing her bridal outfit. She had changed into a green farewell sari. *Vehvanji has very good taste. My daughter looks beautiful.* The moment Sharda and Uma made eye contact, her vision began to blur.

"Can I have a few minutes alone with Sharda?" she asked Sharda's friends.

The girls in the room all murmured in agreement and shuffled out of the room. The moment the girls closed the door behind them Uma felt Sharda run into her arms. Uma felt a mixture of emotions; she felt warmth at her daughter's touch but also pined for her. For a few moments all both women just cried. She finally controlled herself and pulled herself away from her daughter.

"I have something I want to give you." Uma handed the red box that she was holding to her daughter. As Sharda opened the box, Uma explained to her, "I know how much you loved hearing the stories of Durga that nani and I always told you. So I bought you a statue of the first of Durga's nine forms, Shailputri. She was the daughter of the Himalayas." Uma watched as her daughter admired the idol and began to cry more. "You were my daughter for twenty six years. People say when you go to your in-laws you have to forget the norms and cultures you learnt from this family. My mother told me the same thing when I married. I do not want you to forget what I taught you. I want you to enrich your new home with the morals I taught you. Use everything I taught you to make everyone in your new home happy." Uma paused and then continued. "You need to become the daughter of a new family. Win over their love and find me inside your new mother." Uma watched as Sharda continued to cry. She used her fingers to wipe away her daughter's tears. "Your nani told me that the flame of a diva is tiny, but still the single flame is so beautiful that when people look at it they feel a sense of happiness and warmth inside them. The single flame drives away the darkness and lights up an entire room. My maa told me to burn like a diva in my marital home. Give people happiness and warmth. In times of sadness drive away the darkness in their lives and spread as much happiness as you can. I am now telling you the same thing Sharda, become like this diva. But always remember, being a diva does not mean accepting everything they tell you. Make sure you are happy as well. You will have to adjust to your new home, but do not kill your own desires and thoughts for them. I want you to become their daughter, earn their love and respect, but make sure they earn the right to have you as their daughter. Make sure they treat you the same way they treat Ganshyam's sister. I pray to Mata Shailputri and beseech that she helps you become the ideal daughter for the Joshi family." Sharda smiled as she held the Shailputri and said nothing. Uma put her hand on Sharda's cheek. "I have full faith in you Sharda, make me proud."

The two women had tears streaming down their face and continued to hug until Sharda's friends came back into the room.

"They're calling for her. The Groom's family is ready to leave." Uma prepared herself. *The moment I have dreaded for a long time is finally here.* She touched some of the eye liner from her eye and used the residue on her fingers to make a small mark behind Sharda's ear. This was something Uma did regularly to prevent evil spirits from harming Sharda. Now she had done it for the last time. Uma and Sharda's friends held Sharda and escorted her outside the wedding hall. Arjun was first to say goodbye to his niece. One by one all of Sharda's relatives came to say goodbye, all with tears in their eyes. Uma began to cry harder as she watched her daughter say goodbye to various family members. Ganshyam's mother Kokila came over and stood next to Uma. She held onto Uma's hand and said "Umaben, we're only going to be eleven kilometres away. It is not far from here, come to our house whenever you want. Come and see how happy Uma is in her new home whenever you want. Sharda is now my daughter. I will make sure she will be happy just like my own daughter. Sharda now has two mothers." Uma cried a bit more and hugged Kokila. Kokila comforted Uma for a bit and then pulled away.
"Thank you for everything vehvanji. I trust you will make Sharda very happy. If she makes any mistakes please..."
"Umaben please do not embarrass me. My own beti makes mistakes all the time. I will forgive her the same way I forgive my own. I told you already she will be my beti not bahu." Uma took a deep breath and said bye as Sharda left.
"And remember only eleven kilometres away, come whenever you want." Kokila smiled and put her hands together and got into the car.

Uma looked over at Sharda and Ganshyam and saw Ishita, Gauri's daughter and other female cousins teasing the groom. The girls successfully stole the groom's shoes earlier in the day and were now haggling for money to return the shoes before he left. After a few minutes of haggling Ganshyam gave each of the girls 500 rupees, and they then returned his shoes. Sharda and Ganshyam got into a white limousine decorated with flowers and ribbons. Ganshyam's uncle and his sister, Priti, joined them in the car. Sharda's cousins were still feeling mischievous and as per tradition stood in front of the car to prevent it from leaving. *I hope they never move.*

Uma heard Ishita saying "You are taking away our sister, we won't let you go unless you pay us more money." Ganshyam's uncle eventually got out of the car with a smile and gave each of the girls another 1000 rupees. Once the girls moved out of the way the car began to move.

Uma stood on tip toes and watched the car until it vanished out of sight. *May mother Durga bless you with more happiness than I had with my family.*

The Truth Behind Uma's Story

The Burning Bride is a work of fiction inspired by true stories of women living in India.

In 2013:

- 8,083 women were murdered for a dowry.
- 118,866 domestic violence cases were lodged, most of these cases were dowry related.
- 33,707 rapes were reported.
- 50 million fewer women than men were recorded as a result of female infanticide and sex selective abortions.
- An average of three women are attacked with acid a week

Get Involved:

I wrote this novel to help raise awareness about the harrowing reality faced by many women in India. If you found this novel a compelling read and you feel I achieved what I set out to achieve, please encourage at least two other people to read this book or help spread the message by sharing on Twitter and Facebook. By spreading the word, we could raise more awareness, and work towards ending dowry practises quicker.

I also wrote this novel to help raise money to fund projects in India.

Some of the money made from the sales of The Burning Bride will contribute towards projects in India, which aim to end domestic violence.

The Burning Bride will work with the Asian Circle to fund Oxfam projects in India. It will help implement systems to prevent cases of violence by working with government officials, communities and families. For more information about the project check out www.manojkerai.com/blog/asiancircle

If you would like to donate more money to fund the vital work please go to:

Website: www.justgiving.com/TheBurningBride

Or text to donate: BRID72 (£ Amount) to 70070

To keep up to date with developments on this project or to find out about my future projects you can:

Follow The Burning Bride on Twitter: @Burning_Bride

Like The Burning Bride on Facebook:
www.facebook.com/theburningbride

Or email The Burning Bride and request email updates:
theburningbride@gmail.com

I will also welcome any feedback so that I can improve my second book.

Thank you

Manoj Kerai

Acknowledgements:

The following people helped me in many ways to finish this book. These people helped in a number of ways which include proof reading, editing, giving me feedback to improve the content and keeping me motivated to complete the novel. Without their help and support I would never have published my work and so I am eternally grateful to you all. I want to say a massive thank you to:

Jashoda Kerai
Ramesh Lalji Kerai
Krushna Kerai

Elizabeth Appiah-Kusi
Sophia Bobdiwala
Hayley Chandler
Ruth Gibson
Jayshree Gorasia
Jasu Halai Momaya
Rochelle Haussman
Beena Hirani
Ramesh Valji Kerai
Jessica Kuehne
Kirsty MacDonald
Anjna Patel
Louise Pailin
Parbha Pindoria
Sharda Senghani

Once the book was completed a number of people helped me in various ways. Without their help and ideas I wouldn't have been able to get my story to my readers and therefore I also wanted to say thank you to:

Arfah Farooq
Nilima Bhat

Santosh Bhanot
Alys Hewer
Pat Loughrey
Ravi Patel
Suzanne Rodrigues
Eleonora Russo
Simon Scheeres
Daniel Villalobos
Louise Willers

Finally, I wanted to say thank you to all of those who have been helping to promote my work on social media. There are so many of you that I would need to write a whole book to name you all. To avoid missing out any names, I'm not going to list anyone here but I also wanted to thank all of those who have shared, retweeted and encouraged people to follow my social media channels. You've all been amazing.

Coming in 2016:

The Lost Sunrise

Keep in touch with Manoj Kerai's second project on:

Twitter: @Burning_Bride or @Manojiee

Facebook: www.facebook.com/theburningbride

Email: theburningbride@gmail.com to be put onto a mailing list.

Instagram: Manojie

Website: www.manojkerai.com